SCORNED BEAUTY

VICTORIA PAIGE

Scorned Beauty

ISBN: 979-8-9889501-5-8

Editor: Erica Russikoff, Erica Edits
Developmental Editor: Kara Merideth
(Kat's Literary Services)
Proofreader: Judy Zweifel, Judy's Proofreading
Cover Designer: Deranged Doctor Design

Author's Note

Part of the **Scorned Beauty** timeline runs in parallel to **Scorned Vows**. Although it can be read as a standalone, there will be spoilers of Scorned Vows mentioned here.

I've taken liberties in renaming the New York Five Families and the Chicago Outfit, creating my own world and rules. Check your triggers. It does contain profanity, explicit scenes, and sensitive content like mental health.

For a more complete list including a spoilery one, go to the book's page on my website or scan below.

Dream with no limits. Believe in yourself.

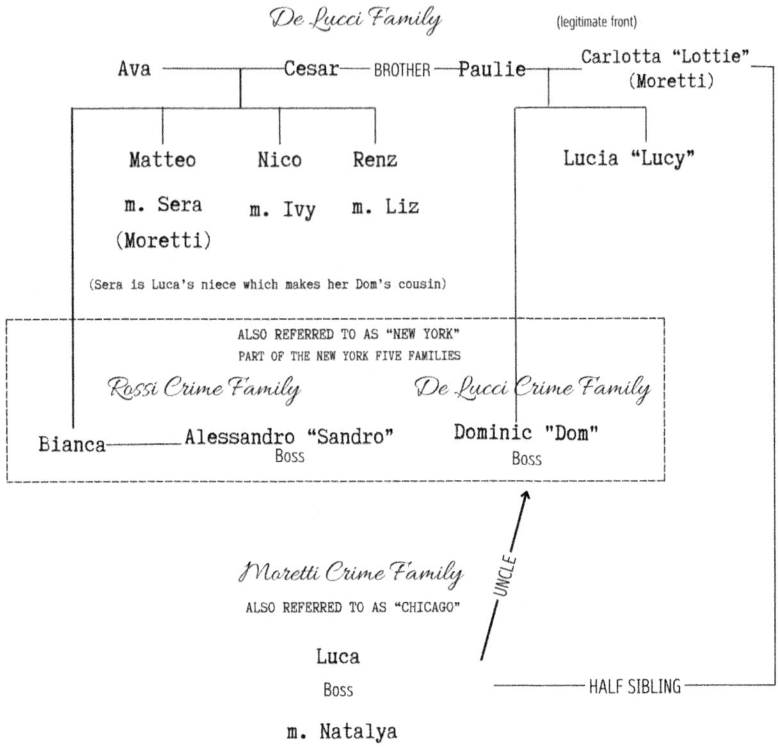
De Lucci Family
(legitimate front)
Ava
Cesar
BROTHER
Paulie
Carlotta "Lottie"
(Moretti)
Matteo
m. Sera
(Moretti)
Nico
m. Ivy
Renz
m. Liz
Lucia "Lucy"
(Sera is Luca's niece which makes her Dom's cousin)
ALSO REFERRED TO AS "NEW YORK"
PART OF THE NEW YORK FIVE FAMILIES
Rossi Crime Family
De Lucci Crime Family
Bianca
Alessandro "Sandro"
Boss
Dominic "Dom"
Boss
UNCLE
Moretti Crime Family
ALSO REFERRED TO AS "CHICAGO"
Luca
Boss
m. Natalya
HALF SIBLING

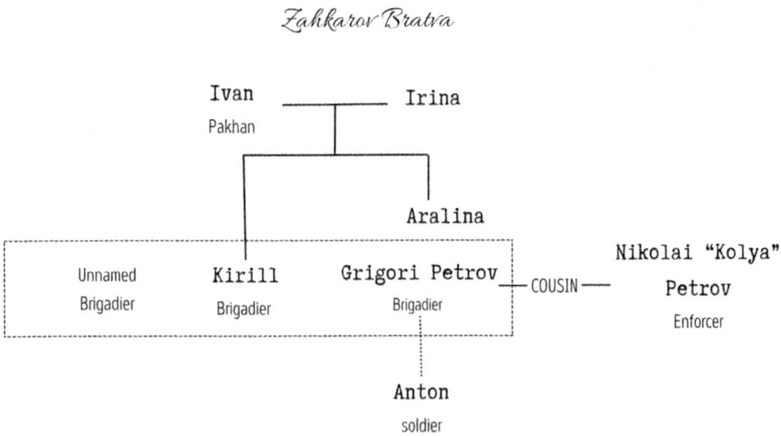
Zahkarov Bratva
Ivan
Pakhan
Irina
Aralina
Unnamed
Brigadier
Kirill
Brigadier
Grigori Petrov
Brigadier
COUSIN
Nikolai "Kolya"
Petrov
Enforcer
Anton
soldier

CHAPTER *One*

Sloane

An older brother was supposed to be a protector. He was supposed to shield his younger siblings from the world's evil. He wasn't supposed to be the one to put them in danger.

I must have been the unlucky one.

William "Billy" Scott was three years older than my twenty-seven years. He was the reason I was in Brooklyn, parking my van a street away from a building. A building that housed the bratva's many illegal gambling operations.

I made good money as a mob cleaner, but not when my clients were the Russians.

Billy liked to brag in underworld circles that he was a friend of the New York bratva. He couldn't brag to me because he frequently went into debt with them, and it was I who bailed him out. And how did I bail him out? By working for the Russians for free.

Last year, I had a windfall cleaning for the Italians, and that was why I could resume nursing school, which I had to put on hold several times. Since our deadbeat dad left us, Billy had been to rehab twice. I paid for his stays both times.

Every time I was catching up financially, the Russians came calling because Billy had fucked up again.

Like tonight.

Saying no wasn't an option because my brother was the whipping boy of Grigori Petrov—one of the brigadiers who made up the bratva's Triumvirate leadership under their pakhan. From what I gathered, he was the most ruthless and usually did the dirty work for their organization to give the other two plausible deniability.

I'd become so pissed that Grigori was the one contacting me directly now instead of going through Billy. I couldn't say no without repercussions to my brother. The last time I balked, Billy came home barely breathing.

In the van, I changed into coveralls and made sure I patted concealer on my lips to make it blend with the rest of my face. The problem when you were pretty and poor was that men like Grigori thought you were good for only one thing. He'd already asked me once if I could be a server in one of his clubs, but I knew if I said yes, it wouldn't stop at simply waiting tables. I turned him down with no backlash to Billy, but I sensed the clock ticking and my luck was about to run out.

I discussed leaving New York with Billy, but my brother was doubtful that Grigori wouldn't find and kill us. I'd debated asking for help from the Rossi crime family, but I didn't want them ending up owing Grigori favors.

I just wanted to graduate from nursing school, dammit.

After I'd put on my work face and uniform, I slid back into the driver's seat and headed to the building.

A soldier waved me through the cargo bay. I preferred it when a job didn't have a cargo bay like this. When I could park a street away, hauling my cleaning supplies in a cart, looking like a bag lady pushing her belongings down the street. I didn't care if it was more work. Because each time they shut the gate behind me, a claustrophobic itch crawled over my skin. But I didn't have a choice here. The Russians always wanted me to park inside their building.

Anton appeared at the driver's side. His hair was shaved close to his skull and his brawny tattooed arms strained against his muscle tee. As if I wasn't on guard enough. Because of his six-six frame, he had to duck his head a bit. "What took you so long?"

"Traffic." I returned his glare.

His scowl deepened before saying, "Hurry up." Anton was Grigori's top soldier who led the rest of his crew.

The desire to shove open the van door and hit this fucker's face was overwhelming, but self-preservation won out. The first time I had to work for free, I could barely contain my rage, and Billy took the brunt for my fury of words. Anton delivered that beating, and it set the tone for our mutual contempt.

I exited the van and headed to its rear, unfolded the utility cart, and loaded it up with what I needed.

Anton waited for me at the crisscross elevators, his mouth in a flat line. It was an awkward and painstaking ride to the top floor—the high-stakes floor. According to Billy, it wasn't unusual for oligarchs, businessmen, and kleptocrats to bet their properties or even companies.

When the elevators jarred open, the floor was relatively empty, save for a few people.

"Sis." Billy met me at the door. My brother was more pretty than handsome. He had an oval face with high cheekbones. Unlike my red hair, his was black. His eyes were more hazel than my green ones.

I glared at him. "What did you do this time?"

He had the gall to grin. "Explain later." Which meant never. My brother ran errands for the bratva. He usually did their collections and also managed a few of their poker games. It baffled me because Billy had a gambling problem, yet Grigori gave him those jobs. Although I wondered if they were toying with us because I always ended up paying for Billy's debts and it was a way to keep me on the hook.

"Gotta go." He waved at a distinguished gentleman sitting at one table shuffling cards. To his right sat another more sinister character I knew was the enforcer of the bratva.

Both men observed my approach with soulless eyes.

The first man who appeared to be playing solitaire was Grigori Petrov, a man in his fifties with salt-and-pepper hair. He had pale blue eyes and ashen-hued skin. The combination almost looked unnatural. Sickly. He was wearing a tailored gray suit and a white dress shirt with an open collar. Gold chains hung around his neck. He epitomized the Russian brigadier. I had not met the bratva's pakhan yet, nor the other brigadiers.

The dangerous man beside him was his cousin, Nikolai Petrov: "Kolya the killer." Jet-black hair, angular features. I could see the blue of his irises from where I stood, ten feet away. It didn't bode well that he was here. That meant someone was dead, and he had to take care of the mess.

See, I never did body disposal. Although I knew the mechanics on how to do it, I didn't have the stomach to dismember a human being and dispose of their remains expediently. When Grigori asked me one time if that was a service I provided, I unequivocally said no and I didn't care if he shot Billy or me right then and there. I would never open that door. When would it end? I definitely didn't want to end up like Kolya, who looked like the grim reaper with the way he was garbed in all black.

"You know, I could get rid of him for you," Grigori said, a smirk forming at the corner of his mouth.

"What?"

"Your worthless brother," he replied.

If he was worthless, why keep him? But I knew the answer to that. My stomach turned.

"What do I clean?" I asked.

"Changing the subject?" Grigori's amused tone held a hint of a Russian accent.

"There's no subject to change. I came here to sanitize the scene." With each of Billy's succeeding screw-ups, I wondered if they were hoping I had reached my breaking point and I'd say yes to having my brother whacked. But that would mean I would forever owe them. Well, fuck that.

I nodded to the spray of blood in the room. "Looks like someone was a sore loser."

Grigori gave a low chuckle and stood, walking over to meet me. "See, I like you, Sloane. You're smart." He reached out a hand and pulled a red curl from under my hat. "You keep hiding your looks under drab clothes, but we could make you real money with the bonus of getting rid of Billy."

His eyes roamed over my body, setting off a sensation of marching ants over my skin. Was he bluffing? I never doubted he knew I was downplaying my looks. But I'd been hoping every time I did a job, I'd become more like background clutter to him. I didn't know how long my value as a cleaner would outweigh my value to his nefarious plans for me. Billy had mentioned before how hard it was to find a natural redhead for one of Grigori's favorite clients and repeatedly told me to lie low. At least my brother wasn't thinking of pimping me out.

I was not a virgin. Hopefully, I was way above the ideal age requirement of their sex-trafficking business. Another rumor was the sex parties they organized in Europe.

I believed my defiance was what was fueling his interest in me, so I frequently reined in my feistiness. I lowered my eyes and stared at his shoes. "Please don't hurt Billy." The less I said, the better. My husky voice was another inconvenience in this job. I'd been propositioned more than once to work the sex hotlines. That was another reason I didn't do small talk when I was on the job with these guys.

"You deserve a better life." Grigori sighed. "Go on, then. Clean this shit up."

He and Kolya left me under the watchful eye of Anton. Depending on the job, I had to surrender the rags and vacuum bag to my minder for burning later. They didn't want any traceable DNA like hair follicles or particles of flesh and skin. My own special mix of cleaning agent was used to lift the stains left by blood. Its effectivity was thorough enough not to be revived by luminol. Most crime families had their own cleaners for mass casualty incidents where I didn't go in to do the initial cleanup. I was the in-between. For smaller jobs like this with only one or two bodies, I did both initial and main cleanup. Kolya, I was sure, was going to double-check my work later.

I worked briskly and efficiently. I wasn't an expert in blood spatter forensics, but I could tell this might have involved one or two people. Three at the most. The penthouse had wooden floors, and a carpet was already rolled up in one corner with a map of blood that could only have come from arterial bleeding. The wall near the table, which I figured was ground zero, had a blood spatter that might have come from a knife swipe.

It took me three hours to comb through the area and I had to use a UV light to make sure.

"Smells like bleach," Anton muttered when I turned over the trash bags for him to dispose of. It was a cocktail of sodium peroxide and other chemicals but I never elaborated.

"Remind Kolya to open the windows," I said.

"Tell him yourself."

My throat closed up, and it wasn't from the cleaning chemicals I inhaled but knowing I had to face the bratva's enforcer who had returned with Grigori.

They weren't looking at me but at the room.

I resisted the urge to fidget. The crawling-ants sensation returned and I silently cursed Billy for getting me into his fuckups. I was going to have a serious talk with him this weekend.

Grigori didn't seem concerned with my work and deferred to Kolya for final inspection. What took three minutes felt like ten, but Kolya muttered his findings in Russian to Grigori, who fixed his stare on me.

The corners of his mouth twitched. The asshole knew how uncomfortable I was, especially after he propositioned me earlier.

"Everything is satisfactory, I hope?" I asked, anxious to get this over with.

"Yes. You may go."

I gave them a brief nod and pushed my cart into the awaiting elevators. The pounding of my heart escalated and I realized I might be having a delayed panic attack. It always happened whenever I encountered Grigori. My reaction to the Russians differed immensely from the Italians. They seemed more brutal. Cold. I wondered if it was because of their harsh Gulag origins.

Shaking off the piercing dead stares of Grigori and Kolya, I packed my cart into the van, not bothering to disassemble it. I didn't want to spend another second on this property. Someone else lifted the garage gates, and I did my best not to screech out of the parking space.

The utility cart banged around in the back of the van, adding to my aggravation. I gripped the steering wheel until my knuckles turned white in an attempt to control the tremors shaking my body. Even when I was two blocks away from their building, I felt like I was still trapped in there. I needed fresh air and calm nerves before I ended up in a wreck.

I parked the van in front of a three-story building that had a butcher shop and coffee shop fronting the avenue. Streetlights illuminated the pavement. A drunk was singing near a twenty-four-hour bodega. I cut the engine and got out. I rounded to the side facing the sidewalk, slid the side door open, and climbed back into the van to unload the cleaning supplies from the cart and rerack the now bagless vacuum on the side rails. OCD had a lot of sway in my urge to get things back in order rather than quickly getting home. At least I could control that part of my life.

Remembering my empty fridge waiting for me in the apartment, I decided to grab food at the bodega.

When I jumped out of the van, a figure cast a long shadow over me.

My fight-or-flight was still engaged. I gripped the metal pipe that I always kept by the side door and swung, striking a man too close for comfort.

He fell back and growled, "Fuck!"

I blinked my eyes to make sure I wasn't imagining him.

No. Those dark eyes only belonged to one person.

"Dom?"

CHAPTER Two

SLOANE

"DO YOU ALWAYS ATTACK FIRST, ASK QUESTIONS LATER?" DOM staggered toward the van and sat on the step up.

"You surprised me," I said lamely, even when relief swooshed through me. The boss of the De Lucci crime family wasn't at the top of the list of people who wanted to do me harm despite the unfortunate incident when I accidentally shot him. Luckily he had on a bulletproof vest then, but every encounter with him since felt like a debt that needed to be paid.

It didn't help that he was ridiculously attractive, and his knowing appraisals always made me squirm. Although right now, I wasn't sure why he was in front of me.

"Same excuse last time." He glared at me from beneath his bleeding brow. "We need to work on your nerves. You're too jumpy."

Indignation ignited my temper. "My nerves are fine. You have the uncanny ability to startle me," I whisper-yelled my outrage. I peered closer. "Let me see."

Dom lowered his hand to inspect the blood on it. "You've put a scar on my brow."

I rolled my eyes. Dominic "Dom" De Lucci was the New York mob's fashion icon. Though no admission of belonging to the mafia was ever on record, it only increased public titillation, especially the women who loved a bad boy. To add to his infamy, a popular men's magazine awarded him New York's Most Eligible Villain title for a second year in a row.

Forget heroes, villains were in.

"It's not deep enough to require stitches."

Angling his body to the right, he exposed his white shirt underneath his dark suit. "It might not, but this might."

His white dress shirt's entire left side was steeped in dark red.

Realization dawned on me. "You were at Grigori's poker game!"

Instead of answering me, Dom muttered, "Come on."

"Come on, where?"

He opened the passenger side door of the van and got in. I was still reeling for a silence of two seconds before blurting out, "I'm not driving you anywhere!"

"Get in." Dom propped his head against the headrest and, without looking at me, said, "I'm about to lose consciousness."

"Dom!" He was so aggravating. And I wasn't sure what I was feeling. I didn't want the responsibility of driving a wounded mafia don around, but I was also worried for him. And what if he died while in my company?

"Hurry up, beautiful. You're the reason I'm bleeding out."

What did that even mean? And what was the deal with him calling me beautiful? I was always Sloane or Miss Scott to him. He must be delirious with blood loss. I slammed the van's side door and hurried to the driver's side. "I'll take you to the hospital."

"No."

"I don't want you dying in my van. You're bleeding all over it."

I felt Dom's gaze on me. Somehow, even in his weakened state, I could feel his humor drilling into me. "Are you worried about me messing up your van or me dying?"

"Don't get cute," I mumbled.

"Your home," he said. "In Jersey."

"I know you don't want to be questioned at the hospital, but Bianca's house is closer and I can stitch you up there." Bianca was his cousin who was married to Sandro, the current Rossi boss. The Rossi and De Lucci crime families used to have a cold war, but with the marriage between Bianca and Sandro, that had ended. I knew Sandro and Dom conferred with each other all the time, which made their house the most logical place to drop him off.

"I don't want the Rossis involved. Those who need to know have my whereabouts."

"That you're with me?"

"Yes." He raised his arm to point at the road that would take us to Jersey. "You better take this ramp on your next turn."

"You're so bossy, even if you're bleeding half to death," I retorted. "It will take me an hour to get to Hoboken. I need to look at your wound."

"I'll be fine. It stopped bleeding."

"You said you were bleeding out."

"I lied," he grunted. "Stop arguing and just drive." If he wasn't in any way injured, hot mafia boss or not, I would leave him on the side of the road. But an edge sharpened his voice, hinting that he was trying to keep the mood light. After another twenty minutes, we entered the tunnel on our way to New Jersey.

I shot him a quick glance. His head was thrown back and his

eyes were closed. The night had taken a weird turn, and I had a feeling I was in the middle of a power play. What did Dom mean by I was the reason he was bleeding out?

I met him last year when I helped Bianca escape to prevent further escalation of hostilities between the Rossis and the De Luccis. But that wasn't the end of it. As it turned out, someone in Sandro's past had come for revenge, which resulted in Bianca getting kidnapped. During her rescue, I accidentally shot Dom. He had a supernatural ability to make me jumpy. Yet when he appeared tonight, the jitteriness I had felt during and after I left Grigori's job faded. It was as if I was finally safe. Like Dom was my armor against the Russian bratva. Conflicting feelings seemed to be my default mode when it came to him. I tried to avoid him at De Lucci gatherings, but he always made his presence known. A secret smile would play on his lips. He would never approach me but watched me across the room. Like two months ago at Bianca and Sandro's wedding, his burning gaze willed me to look at him. And I wasn't imagining his attention because when I did glance at him, he raised his glass to me as if in a toast. I was a mouse, and he was the cat toying with me.

But this? "You okay?"

"I'm alive."

"Don't be dramatic."

A chuckle reverberated in his chest as he shifted in his seat. A pained groan escaped him. "Don't make me laugh."

"I'm not."

"Now is the time to get rid of me if you want to."

The drive through the tunnel was smooth. He wasn't wearing his seat belt, and I presumed it was so it wouldn't rub against his left side. I was glad that I'd disabled that aggravating sound that was a reminder to buckle up because I frequently put heavy loads on the passenger side.

"Tempting," I replied. "Anyone want you dead?"

"How much time do we have?"

"Wow, that many?" We had another thirty minutes to my apartment.

My peripheral vision caught him turning to me. "Bad idea to confess to you."

"The Russians?"

"No, my injuries are not because they want to kill me. At least, not Grigori." He muttered something under his breath that sounded like "I hope."

"Kolya?"

"What do you know about Kolya?"

"Nothing." That was the right answer, even when I knew something. You learned not to give direct answers that could come back to bite you in the ass when you were talking to anyone connected to the underworld. And Dom, despite his man-of-Wall-Street, trust-fund demeanor, was very much in the mob. "I probably don't want to know why you're bleeding out because of me."

"Oh, it's really because of you."

"You defended my honor?"

A quiet beat of tension descended and I could feel whatever scrap of humor get sucked out of the van. In its place, a pulse of raw fury hit me from the side.

"Is there a reason to defend your honor from the Russians?" His voice was gravelly, his breathing more ragged. I was tempted to pull over and check on him.

"Well, you said it was because of me."

He exhaled a hiss of air. "Later. We'll talk."

"How about we don't," I replied. We exited the tunnel and I made the turn toward Hoboken. "Look, I don't know why you think I'm involved with whatever shit you have going with the Russians."

"Stop talking."

"Excuse me?"

"Your voice," he muttered. "Your voice makes me hard."

"What the fuck?" My cheeks flamed. "You did not just say that to me."

"Shit." Dom gave a pained chuckle again. "Blame the blood loss."

"Shut up, then, so I will."

He grunted and shifted uncomfortably in his seat. I clamped my mouth shut, irritated he had to remind me again of my disadvantage. Usually, I could regulate the huskiness by staying hydrated, but nights like this when I was exhausted, there was no disguising the natural raspiness of my voice which an ex-boyfriend once described it like I'd screamed myself hoarse while he was giving me an orgasm.

As if. Fake orgasm maybe.

I concentrated on getting us quickly to my apartment and prayed that Dom was telling the truth and he wouldn't expire in my van. Also, I didn't think I could haul his…what? Six-four, two-hundred-plus-pound frame up to the fifth floor.

It was just luck a Ford sedan pulled out a block from my building. I lived in a busy neighborhood and it was a Friday night…well, Saturday morning already. There were folks coming home from one-night stands or a booty calls.

I gave myself a mental shake at my jadedness.

I cut off the engine. "You need help getting out?"

"No." He shoved his door open.

Still, I made it to his side before he fully cleared the van.

"I'm fine," he gritted. "Lead the way."

I held up my arms in surrender—for my own mental health and I'd practiced this enough with my brother. If a man said he was fine, he was fine. I never wanted to read between the lines, and I didn't know Dom well enough to waste a brain cell wondering if it was his

Italian machismo that made him resist my aid. I walked ahead of him toward my building. A rent-control ruling enabled me to afford it at a reasonable price. I was doing better financially, but I was by no means swimming in cash. Lost in my annoyance with my brother and the Russians, I failed to notice that Dom wasn't walking in a straight line. Just as I turned to him, his right foot snagged at the edge of a step. It wasn't a tall step, but Dom lost his balance and disappeared into the hedges.

My mouth fell open, blinking at the sight of one of the most feared mafia bosses in New York in an utterly undignified position.

Chest heaving, I tried to fight the laughter bubbling up my throat.

I failed.

Laughter erupted straight from my belly, the force of my amusement so huge, it was like the sight of Dom struggling to get up from the bushes sent a pin to a distended tension balloon that finally found release.

With tears in my eyes, I approached his flat-on-his-back form. He was cursing and grunting, but his struggles got him nowhere.

"Oh my God, are you all right?" I asked a coherent question in between fits of humorous exhalations.

His glare sliced me into ribbons. "I can't believe you're laughing. Help me up."

I extended my arms and braced my legs while sucking in my spine. An instinct honed from years of hauling heavy things around, including people. That was why when I did my clinical hours, especially in assisted living homes, I was a favorite.

Dom gripped my hands, and I gave him a heave out of the bushes. Our bodies collided. I lost my breath and became very aware of the heat of his body plastered to me like I was beside a furnace. We'd never been this close. I kept my eyes level with his chest. A sassy reply refused to form. Words dried up in my throat.

His arms swooped around me, his hands molding to my waist before sliding down my hips. I wasn't sure if it was to steady himself, or he was copping a feel. A pulse of excitement made itself known below my belly.

Dammit. No. No.

His gaze was intent. He was breathing as hard as I was, and this close, I caught a whiff of breath mint. I attempted to pry myself away, but he hauled me back against the hard length of him.

I couldn't do this.

I wasn't going to get mixed up with Dom. I would patch him up and call him a ride if I had to.

I swallowed and tried to speak, but no words would come. A connection short-circuited between us, and he was aware of it, too. I wasn't naïve. I was aware of my looks and he already said I made him hard in the van.

My amusement still hovered, making it hard to keep a straight face. It probably saved us from a point of no return. It was Dom who spoke first.

"Not a word," he breathed. "That was embarrassing."

I could only nod as a silent laugh shook my chest.

"I fell and could have had a concussion and you laughed at me," he said in an exaggerated, wounded voice.

Bianca once said that Dom was a drama queen, a trait he inherited from the Moretti side of the family.

"Do you need help to walk now?" I tried to inject compassion into my voice.

A man exiting the building saved him from answering. It was Phil Harding, my neighbor who looked like he lived in the gym. He'd asked me out on a date once, but I declined. I hadn't seen him in weeks. He said he was in sales.

"Everything all right?" he asked. "Saw you took a tumble into the bushes, man."

Oh my God, he had to point it out.

Dom tightened his arms around me. An air of possessiveness fuming from his side.

"He had a bit too much to drink," I put in hastily. "Can you hold the door open, Phil?"

"Sure, doll."

Dom grunted as we passed my neighbor. He was still plastered to my side, but he didn't say another word. I hoped he wasn't plotting Phil's demise. Working with the mob, I knew a few of them were on a trigger and the slightest provocation could mean death. But I also knew the De Luccis were of the more reasonable breed. I had no clue about the Moretti side of the family except Dom's uncle, who, according to Bianca, had the violent streak of a sociopath.

Although someone once said to be in the mafia, you had to be part sociopath.

"I'm on the fifth floor," I told Dom. "And I wouldn't trust the elevators."

Another grunt.

Okay, then.

We made our way up the staircase. I was on his right side. His uninjured side. He had one arm around me while the other was holding the banister. At around the third floor, his weight sagged in to me.

"Want to rest?"

A clipped "No" was his answer, so we soldiered on. As we neared my floor, I was wondering about my stupidity in taking Dom home with me. What if he coded in my apartment or died? I sure as hell wasn't calling an ambulance or the police. Kolya's face flashed through my head. Nope. I would have to call Sandro. Having a Rossi mediate between me and the De Luccis…that I was not responsible for Dom's death.

I tripped on one of the steps and nearly sent us careening backward.

"What the—" he muttered. "Are you trying to kill me?"

"Believe me, that's the last thing I want." We reached the fifth floor and thankfully my apartment was the second door. I had three other neighbors. All of us had one-bedroom apartments. It was a relief when I let us into my place. I turned on the hallway lights, took off my hat, and swiped the perspiration off my forehead. I was a tad out of breath.

"Okay, let me see."

Dom just stared at me. His hands by his sides.

"What?" I pointed at his side. "Let me see."

He quirked a brow. "No foreplay?"

"Dom," I growled. "I've had a trying night, all right? Having to take care of a prima donna don wasn't on my bingo card tonight."

"Are you saying I'm high maintenance, Miss Scott?"

There went my nipples with the seductive way he said *Miss Scott. What is wrong with me?*

Thankfully, he started stripping. Rather, he shrugged off his suit jacket, and, even injured, he made it look sexy. Mentally shaking off my attraction to him, I focused on the task at hand. His upper left arm was bleeding too, and he was slow in unbuttoning his shirt.

I stepped forward. "Let me do it."

He didn't argue, and I did my best to ignore the heat emanating from his body, the way his breath feathered my hair or how my heart rate accelerated because of it. When his white dress shirt came off to reveal an undershirt, I helped him out of it, too. I slid into clinical mode, even when it was hard to ignore all the tanned skin and glorious ridges of muscle.

"I'll throw this in the laundry for you. Your dress shirt is probably ruined. Come on."

I dragged him into the bathroom where the lights were brighter and left him standing there to retrieve my emergency kit from under the sink. I hadn't turned away from him two seconds before the sound of the shower turned on.

His fingers went to his trouser buttons.

"What are you doing?" I snapped.

"Getting clean."

"Let me check your cut first."

He rolled his eyes and waited for me to walk back to him. His arms hung loosely by his sides. I laid my kit on the counter and flipped the lid open to retrieve the mag light.

"You're a terrible patient, you know that?" I shined the light on the slash at his side and palpitated the surrounding area.

"Any pain?"

"Not really. It just stings."

The cut was still oozing blood, but it had slowed. It was deep, but not deep enough to do internal damage. Dom's ab muscles saved him.

"You're lucky."

I grabbed a single-use soap from the kit. "Use this to clean yourself. It's antibacterial."

All the while, I avoided looking at his expression, but it was getting too obvious that I was uncomfortable to be alone with a half-naked Dom. I lifted my gaze, deliberately bypassing his exposed chest—damn those corded muscles of his shoulders—and settled on his face.

"You need me to help you remove your pants?" I gritted.

His eyes were glassy, and for a moment, I sympathized with him, but the arrogant smirk forming at the corner of his mouth chased away all my goodwill.

"It'll help. Also, maybe you want to throw my boxers in the laundry too?"

I narrowed my eyes. "What exactly are you saying?"

"You're a nurse, right?"

"A nursing student."

"What would you say to a patient who has my injury?"

I grabbed a towel from under the cabinet and laid it on the vanity.

"Take off your clothes and put this on."

He raked his teeth over his bottom lip. Dom didn't move a muscle, but his gaze was veiled and his mouth twitched. "This should be interesting."

Why was I still staring? I pivoted and escaped the sudden suffocating confines of the bathroom, shockingly inadequate to contain Dom's overpowering presence.

I closed the door and leaned against it.

I let the devil into my domain and his name was Dominic De Lucci.

What have I done?

CHAPTER
Three

SLOANE

"WHERE DO YOU WANT ME?"

I didn't turn around when I heard the bathroom door open. I didn't turn around when steam saturated my tiny apartment with its warmth. I simply didn't turn around. I had drawn the curtains, so I wouldn't see his reflection in the window, hoping I'd imagined the whole night and I didn't have Dom inside my apartment, but hearing his voice made him real.

I debated having him lie on the couch, but it was too small for him. I had a keen misgiving about letting him lie on my bed, but it was the only way to treat him.

When I turned around to face him, and even when I was prepared to drool, nothing prepared me for the suck-in-your-breath gorgeousness that smacked me in the face.

Rivulets of water clinging to his thick raven-black hair, only accentuated the fascinating shape of his eyes that tilted up slightly at the corners. Dom had many sculpture-worthy features. His nose, which should have been too thin, complemented his full lips and chiseled, angular face. Strong and brutally beautiful was an apt description.

For his height, Dom's perfectly muscled frame defined a man in his prime. His shoulders, chest, and biceps were a product of being an all-around athlete. I knew he frequented his family's boxing gym and sometimes sparred in mixed martial arts.

"You're staring," he said. There was no teasing in his tone, but his voice took on the rough texture of gravel.

I decided I'd been on defense for too long; I was going on offense. "I am. I always wondered what you hid beneath your civilized suits."

As he approached, I had the oddest conflicting desire of either wanting the towel wrapped around his hips to unravel or remain plastered to his skin. The edge was already drenched in blood, reminding me I had to stitch him up.

He stopped inches from me and lowered his head. "Do I get to see what you're hiding beneath those awful coveralls?"

"If you're a good boy," I shot back and nodded to my bedroom. "In there. I've prepped my bed, but don't get any ideas."

"Yes, ma'am," Dom drawled. He turned and awarded me a view of his fine ass. No flat-butt male here. With everything going on in my life, I tried to be pragmatic. I wasn't a denier. I was an opportunist. If it were any person other than Dom, meaning not connected to the mafia, I'd be giving in to a hookup. My busy life and the people I was currently indebted to because of my brother didn't allow for serious relationships, which was why I avoided them. But this girl had needs. But my needs shouldn't be used as future blackmail.

When we entered the room, Dom paused when he saw the bed. I

had a plastic sheet covering the mattress and a folded bedsheet on top of it.

He cast me a brief glance. "Should I be worried?"

"What? That the Russians set a trap and I'm Doctor Death?"

"Not funny," he grumbled. He kept his eyes on me while whipping off the towel and handing it to me. I didn't break eye contact when I accepted it. His mouth lifted at the corner before he lay on the bed in all his naked glory.

I got an eyeful of an impressive semi-erect penis before I covered it with the towel. I put on my Sloane-means-business face.

"No anesthesia of any sort," he said in a quiet, lethal voice. After getting whiplash so many times with his attitude change from tonight alone—and I didn't mean mood swings—because Dom was in control of his moods, I became aware of the dangerous hypermasculinity he kept hidden under his drama queen persona.

"I was just kidding about the Russians."

"No anesthesia. I want to feel the pain of every stitch you give me."

"Why?"

His mouth curved into a teasing, evil smile. "So I'll remember what you owe me."

"You're speaking in riddles." And as much as I liked to spar with him, there was suturing that needed to get done. "Be right back."

"Where are you going?"

"To wash my hands."

I entered the bathroom that bore the remnants of Dom's quick shower. His trousers and briefs were neatly folded on the toilet seat. The man wasn't a slob at least.

After washing my hands with antibacterial soap, I returned to the bedroom. Dom was on his back. His left arm, unscathed from whatever encounter he had earlier, was crooked under his head, nonchalant as he pleased, like he was about to be serviced with a blowjob and not sewn up without anesthesia.

"Last chance. You don't need to prove your manhood by rejecting anesthesia."

"I'm fine, beautiful. It's not my first rodeo."

"Huh." I snorted and sat on the seat I already had in front of the bed and proceeded with his care.

I irrigated the wound with a sterile saline solution to flush out any debris, ignoring the hiss of Dom's breath. He asked for no anesthesia, so he could simply suck it up.

As a nurse, it was illegal for me to perform sutures. Only surgeons were licensed. But I had stitched countless gunshot and knife wounds, and injuries from impalements when the underworld came calling.

After I'd cleaned the cut, I picked up the hemostat with the threaded needle and forceps and proceeded to close Dom's four-inch uneven gash.

"So, care to explain what you meant when you said I'm the reason you got attacked with a knife?" I asked while I worked.

"I didn't say you're the reason I got knifed."

"You were lying?"

"No. I said you were the reason I was bleeding out."

I stopped after tightening a knot and stared at him. "I don't follow."

He peered down where I had paused and said, "Fuck. Remind me not to get into this position with you again."

This made me smile because it confirmed what I'd concluded about his tactics.

"Why, Dom, feeling vulnerable?"

"Whatever you say, sweetheart."

"You think I don't have the power right now? I have a pair of medical shears close to your jewels."

"You wouldn't waste a prime example of the male species without trying it out?"

The arrogance…but he was backing it up with the force of his personality. I even had the feeling he was reining it in. Saliva had deserted me. His cock was a hard line underneath the towel and it was growing bigger. Oh my God.

"Please," I taunted. "You're forgetting, I'm a nurse. I've seen every form of balls, penises, and assholes. You're nothing special."

"Ouch, beautiful. You know, you've just issued a challenge, right?"

My face heated and I squirmed in my chair as a pulsing wetness bloomed between my thighs. I swear I could hear it squelch. Dom's eyes glinted knowingly. I wasn't sure what his game was. Did he plan to sleep with me to get information on the Russians? I knew next to nothing. Or did he plan to torture me with orgasm denial?

Holy hell.

I concentrated on suturing, not trusting myself to speak. It was going to come out husky and then he'd get harder and then I'd get wetter. No. The sooner this was done, the better.

"In the interest of nondisclosure, since I'm sure we both signed an agreement before entering Grigori's den," he said. "Let's just say I can't talk about why or what transpired that caused the bloody mess you had to clean up. But since Bianca is my cousin, and she considers you family, I appointed myself your guardian angel after something I'd overheard."

Chills ran down my arms. I neatly finished the suture and carefully put the instruments away.

"Did Grigori proposition you?" he asked.

"I thought we had a nondisclosure agreement." I raised my gaze and held his.

His eyes narrowed. "We do, but we could speculate or hypothesize."

"Okay." I reached for his arm that had nicks from a knife. They appeared to have stopped bleeding, but there was one particular incision that was troublesome. I reached for the butterfly bandages. "Hypothetically, Grigori thinks he could get rid of my brother for me, but in return I do something for him, like entertain one of his friends."

Dom's face hardened. "You will say no. The whole reason you're doing the Russians' bidding is because you care for your brother and you wouldn't want him whacked."

"Grigori was just reaching." I applied a butterfly and stitched the deeper cut. "So hypothetically was that what you overheard?"

"Yeah, you can say that."

"And the reason you're bleeding out and why you say it's because of me is because you didn't take care of your injuries when you should have and instead lurked around Grigori's building waiting for me to show up because you knew they were calling me."

"You're doing good with your hypotheticals."

I laughed. "You didn't run after my van, though."

"I had a friend with me. I told him to drop me off."

"If I hadn't stopped, would you have followed me home?"

"Or cut you off."

"Seriously?"

"I wanted you to take care of me."

I rolled my eyes. "What are you up to?" I finished dressing the wounds on his right arm and stood back, my hands on my hips.

Dom slowly rolled out of the bed and stood in front of me, unmindful that he was completely naked and his cock was jutting out between us.

This was a man comfortable in his skin. He'd walk around naked like it was the most natural thing for him to do. Despite his complaints about me giving him a scar, he sported several jagged marks on his body and they only added to his brutal beauty.

"Thought I was doing my duty taking care of family," he said.

"I'm not your family."

"I know, but by association." He raised his arm. "Let me finish. Something got triggered tonight. We've been avoiding each other, but I'm not avoiding it anymore."

"What changed? Nothing from my end."

He stepped forward and touched my hair. "Liar. We have chemistry. Your fiery hair…I always wondered if you were a natural."

"Did Grigori say something to that effect?" I asked, outraged because even when my brother mentioned it to me, it pissed me off to be talked about like that, like meat to sell, which was what these Russians were doing.

"Hypothetically?" Dom rasped, dropping his arm to his side. "Yes. And I wanted to kill him and I didn't know why."

Heat flushed my skin, warring with the goose bumps that chased down my back at the intensity behind his words and sharp gaze. We were standing a foot apart, which was a blessing. "Probably chivalry," I said shakily. "Bianca…"

"Shut up." He closed the distance between us. "Spend the weekend with me."

An incredulous laugh escaped me. "What?"

"Please?"

Oh, he was trying to be cute.

"You're just thankful I took care of you."

A deep rumble of humor gusted past his mouth. "Beautiful, you shot me once. Conked me on the head tonight. I'm not attracted to you because I'm thankful."

"Are you a masochist?" I gulped. We kept veering into a sexually charged conversation and I was powerless to stop myself.

"No labels, but I can be a deviant." He put his hands on my

shoulders and lowered his head so his mouth was by my ear. "You make me fucking hard. And if you don't leave this room right now and continue talking to me in that fuck-me voice, I won't be liable for what I do next."

I was panting hard at this point, my feet glued to the orbit of Dom's magnetic pull, and I couldn't move.

"I'm going to throw you on that bed, bury my face between your gorgeous thighs, and lick your pussy until you scream my name and not care if I bleed all over you."

I gasped and stumbled back before I raced out of the room.

CHAPTER Four

Sloane

I was in deep trouble. The desire to rub one out in the shower was so tempting, but the lock on the bathroom was broken and I wouldn't put it past Dom to barge in here and finish the job for me. My imagination was running amok. But it was because he was unpredictable.

He was incorrigible.

Nothing fazed him.

At all.

Dom propositioning me was absurd. It was probably a side effect of blood loss or adrenaline and I was a convenient warm body. I shouldn't read too much into it. Besides, I couldn't afford to get entangled with him. We were not the same.

You are just trash who cleans my toilet.

A voice from my past reverberated inside my head.

I had to make him leave. It was too early to call Bianca to come and get her cousin. Of course I could just send him home in a ride service like I had planned to, but he had minions at his beck and call and he didn't need one. He could wear his trousers and jacket. His shirt and briefs were in the washing machine. I doubted he would miss them.

But he had to want to leave. I just had to be more decisive.

With renewed resolve, I exited the bathroom. Dom was lounging in the living room, flipping through channels.

He was still naked, thankfully, with a towel draped on his lap. I wasn't joking when I said I'd become acquainted with every part of the human anatomy, that it had become routine. Sometimes I didn't register that a patient was naked. I could attest that it was the reason my libido had been nonexistent. Nothing turned me on because I saw naked people frequently, so my attraction to Dom was troubling.

"I'll call you a ride."

His gaze flicked to me and he gave me a lazy head-to-toe appraisal. My hair was wet, and I'd twisted it up with a claw clip and all I had were scrubs in the bathroom.

"No need."

"Someone's coming to get you?"

"Your fridge is empty. I'm starving."

"Dom!"

"What?"

"You can't just bulldoze your way into my life and disrupt my plans."

He raised the remote and flipped through the channels. "What are your plans for later?"

"I have to pick up a cat and I've got errands to run." And I had no idea why I told him.

"Hmm…not too fond of cats. They shed."

"Well, luckily, it's not your problem." I crossed my arms. Exasperation with this man was zooming to a whole new level. It would be another three hours before I could whine to Bianca. Seven a.m. sounded reasonable enough, right? Except I had to remember I was the person who made shit happen.

Dom was a mere aberration.

"Look. I'm all out of juice. My clinical rotation lasted ten hours, and I had to do Grigori's job. Can you please have someone pick you up?"

His face changed, softening, and that sent a different kind of fluttering in my stomach. "I'm sorry. That was insensitive of me."

He was apologizing? I should be suspicious, but there was a thoughtful and sincere expression on his face. Up to this point in our interactions, Dom always put me on the defensive. Our first encounter was him waving a copy of my pitiful finances in front of my face. I held that grudge and still despised him for it.

"Go on and sleep," he said. "I got this."

"Dom…"

"I'll call someone."

Thank God.

"There's water in the fridge," I offered.

"Thank you."

And I considered that a win and retreated into my bedroom, closed the door, and locked it.

~

An alarm blasted me awake.

It wasn't my phone, but my smoke detector. An odor of something burnt invaded my nostrils. Panicked, I jumped out of bed and raced out of the room.

Smoke billowing out of the kitchen catapulted my heart into my throat, but when I stepped into the kitchen, confusion hit me.

A man in gray sweatpants and a white tee was fumbling through the drawers while a roaring fire burned in a pan. His broad back was to me and he was barefoot.

"Dom?" The events of the night came crashing back.

He turned and shot me a grin. "Hang on a sec, baby."

Hang on… What the hell is baby?

"You've got exactly two seconds to explain—"

He found a lid and, cool as you please, dropped it on the angry flame, effectively killing it.

"Make that smoke detector stop screaming." He handed me a kitchen towel.

Infuriated, I grabbed the towel and marched to the alarm that screeched me awake. I also opened a window before stomping back into the kitchen.

"You gotta have better pans," he muttered as he scraped what looked like charred bacon into the trash.

"I don't cook."

"Obviously."

"What are you still doing here?"

"Let me get breakfast ready."

He opened my fridge to get more bacon out. My mouth gaped. Eggs, yogurt, milk, and other groceries filled its depth. I was living in an alternate universe. My usually empty fridge was filled to the brim with food. When did he do this?

"Why don't you pour us coffee?" The only decent appliance in the kitchen was my coffeemaker. The microwave and toaster oven belonged to Mom. Like I told Dom, I rarely cooked. Since I lived alone, I didn't feel the need to mess up my kitchen since New Jersey had a fantastic street food scene.

"You don't have to cook me anything. I rarely eat breakfast." Coffee was needed for this conversation.

"Call it brunch, then."

I poured us each a mug of brew. "I don't think…"

He shot me a quick, pointed glance. "I would appreciate it if you threw on a robe or I might…" He cut himself off before adding, "Just…put something on."

Mortification crept up my neck as I was made aware of my state of undress. I'd just given Dom an eyeful of shadowed nipples.

"Fuck." I retreated to the bedroom, with the coffee sloshing all over my hand. I went to the dresser and pulled on clean panties and sweatpants. Exhaustion had caught up with me last night. I stripped off the scrubs I had on and threw on a negligee and fell into bed. I didn't even remember tossing and turning and fell promptly into a deep sleep. Somehow even with Dom in my apartment, I felt safe enough to relax after the night I'd had dealing with the Russians. But this morning, finding out he still hadn't left, I armored up with a bra and a thick sweatshirt. I took one look at the mirror and was satisfied I was back to my shapeless self.

Squaring my shoulders, I left the room. Dom had set up bacon and eggs and a whole plethora of breakfast breads.

"Not as good as Jabbin' Java's." He nodded to the croissants.

"Are we going to pretend that you being here is normal?"

"At least sit down and eat and we can talk."

"There's nothing to talk about, Dom. You filled my fridge with food and cooked me breakfast. You're thankful I stopped the bleeding and helped you out last night. We're even, okay?"

Dom narrowed an assessing gaze at me. I could see him contemplating tactics. "Please sit and enjoy breakfast. I'm sure you're hungry and not thinking clearly."

"Don't gaslight me."

"For fuck's sake." His veneer of calm cracked. "I'm losing patience with your denial. We don't have to be anything, but I acknowledge that I was overbearing yesterday and…" He stopped at my arched brow. "Right, I've been more than overbearing, bordering on rude arrogance and cockiness and it's not the way to…" He let out a deep breath of what sounded like surrender as he sagged into his chair. "Please sit."

I sat. It was a novelty to see him in full-blown frustration instead of me.

"I'm attracted to you. I admit it was more of a curiosity in the beginning for a woman who seemed to want to hide her looks beneath hideous outfits."

I was about to object but it was Dom's turn to raise a brow. There was no use denying it.

"And I get it," he continued. "We're a nefarious immoral bunch and not to be trusted, and the only reason no one has snatched you yet is because Sandro declared to us you are a friend of the family. You won't get trouble from the Italians, but the Russians are a concern."

"That's not your concern, is it?"

"It's my concern if I want to fuck you. In case you missed the part where I'm attracted to you."

"I can't afford to get mixed up with you."

Dom nodded. "I know. I can't afford it either."

"So, are you talking about simply hooking up?"

"Something like that."

His gaze lowered to the breakfast spread. "You're not eating. You want something else?"

"I'm not picky with food." I picked up a croissant and bit into it. "I eat when I can and I eat whatever."

"Say yes, Sloane."

"To be your fuck buddy?"

He paused, as if testing the words in his head. "That might be jumping ahead. How about we see how the weekend turns out first?"

I had to grin. Typical male with commitment issues.

"So, do we just get naked on this table and go for it?"

His eyes darkened. "If you want."

"I have standards."

"I don't date. I don't do romance."

"Wow, you really tell it like it is."

"I don't want there to be any misconception or expectations of what I'm capable of giving."

"Just orgasms, then?"

His eyes gleamed, and he shifted in his chair. "I'll give you all the orgasms you want," he said thickly.

I raised my mug and smiled into my coffee. This was proving to be fun.

"Like I said, I have standards." I cleared my throat.

"Like what?"

"I need to at least like a person I have sex with."

"I can be likable."

"And I'll need you to get along with Ginger."

"Who the fuck is Ginger?"

CHAPTER Five

Sloane

"Meow."

Ginger detested the cat carrier, and she made her displeasure known. After breakfast, Dom and I headed to the animal rescue center and picked up a former neighbor's cat.

We used Dom's Escalade because my van was being temperamental. Besides the groceries, Dom asked his minions to deliver him a car and clothes. Another glaring difference in our lifestyles. I didn't get to order people to do my bidding. I was the hired help.

If I had used Ginger to gauge Dom's likability, he'd have failed instantly. She hissed at Dom on sight, and Dom returned her reaction with equal distaste, as though Ginger was vermin.

A sadistic idea teased me about locking them in a room together. May the best asshole win.

You see, Ginger had a cattitude. She was independent, feisty, and had a problem with authority.

But I was looking forward to getting my first Dom-delivered orgasm. In fact, I questioned my sanity for delaying gratification, since it was obvious Dom was dying to bend me over the table and fuck me senseless. I questioned whether my little breakfast table could handle the promise of vigorous activity. I was no shrinking violet. I loved a hard fuck. I would be extremely disappointed if Dom didn't leave me with a few bruises.

And that was probably why I wanted to torture him. Dom seemed like a guy who thrived on challenges and the harder you denied him, the harder he'd punish you. And I was looking forward to the punishment.

But I also knew men could be touchy about their ride, so I didn't want Ginger distracting Dom by destroying his leather seats. This cat was vindictive enough to let me know that A) She despised being left in a shelter and B) She didn't trust Dom.

You and me both, girl, but he might be the salvation to my Sahara-dry vagina, which had certainly gotten its fair share of rainfall since Dom showed up yesterday.

And when you were parched, any kind of water would do, even when it was bad for you.

"Meow."

Dom glanced at me. "You can let her out."

"No, she's fine in there."

"So, why are we going to Delphine again? Your neighbor?"

"My visit with Harriet was cut short yesterday," I told him. I had been with her when Grigori summoned me. Ginger was her cat, but ever since my neighbor had to go into assisted living, Harriet's friend at the shelter tried to rehome the cat with no success. I was Ginger's last hope, although if I were to voice my opinion, Ginger didn't need an owner. She was perfectly fine roaming the catwalk in our building to visit different tenants. "Actually, you saved me a trip to the grocery store."

"Let me get this straight. You shop for other people, but not for yourself?" he asked. The Escalade reached a stoplight.

"Harriet's not other people, she's family."

"You're not related."

"Not all family is blood. You should know that better than anyone. She was there for us when Dad left and the first time Billy had to go to rehab."

"How long ago was that?"

I was uncomfortable with Dom's probing questions. I mean, I didn't ask him about the skeletons in his closet, and I was sure he had more than a few, probably even literal ones.

When the light turned green, I still hadn't answered him. He realized I wasn't planning to and remained quiet for the rest of the drive. But I felt like I needed to make things clear to Dom. I did not know what possessed me to have him tag along, although instinctively, I knew he would insist on coming along and I was saving myself the energy of arguing with him.

"I agreed to this weekend, but I think our private lives should remain off-limits."

This time, it was Dom who didn't answer me. Since it was Saturday, the tiny parking lot of the assisted living facility was at full capacity and he had to drive around to look for street parking. He slid into a spot a street over.

I waited until he cut off the engine before I brought it up again. "Tell me you're clear about that, or you can forget any chance of getting into my pants."

In answer, he shot me a dark, measured look. "I'm going to find out what made you put up such walls and I'm going to enjoy breaking them down."

"Are we clear?"

"You don't want me to meet your neighbor."

"Her name is Harriet."

"You're confusing me, woman. Do you want to keep our private lives separate or not? That's why I didn't use your neighbor's name, but you also insisted I meet your cat."

"Ginger will be coming home with me today. I need to make sure she's fine with a man she's never met in the confines of my apartment."

"So you're hinging your promised orgasms on a cat."

I laughed.

"Okay..." He raked his teeth over his bottom lip. "How are you going to bring in the groceries and the cat to visit Harriet without making two trips?"

He had a point.

"Don't let pride get in the way of common sense," Dom added. "I don't want any awkward introductions to Harriet about my presence. You can say I was simply a decent human being who found you struggling with the shopping bags and the cat carrier."

And with that zinger, Dom left me in the SUV, sitting in my embarrassment. Just a little. I was sure his ego could handle a bit of jostling. *This is self-preservation*, I told myself, although his threat of breaking down my walls rang little alarm bells in my head. He was getting presumptuous that I would give him my time past this weekend.

I grabbed Ginger's crate while Dom carried the groceries. I'd spent less than twenty-four hours with this man, but we were behaving like a domesticated couple. Unlike his suit yesterday, Dom had on a fatigue-colored henley tucked in dark blue jeans. He was wearing scuffed leather boots. He left his leather jacket in the SUV. His eyes were shaded by aviators. Despite his attire, he was still a far cry from pedestrian traffic on an early weekend morning. No, his entire vibe suited the night prowls.

"Not how you expected to spend your Saturday morning." I leaned in closer so only he could hear. "No criminal empire to run?"

His mouth twitched in amusement. "I'm taking a break. The empire is in good hands."

"I hear you have an office at the De Lucci Transnational offices. Do you go in?"

"I attend board meetings just like any executive." He walked in relaxed, confident strides I tried to match by walking twice as fast.

"Executive, huh? So what's your title?"

"Director of Operations."

"Really?" I laughed lightly. "That has a broad meaning."

"In short, I get shit done."

We made the trek to the Delphine building with small talk, coming to a mutual truce of sorts, and stayed away from touchier subjects. As I'd discovered, Dom had an uncanny way of turning innocent conversation into pure sexual innuendo that rattled me. I chanced a glance at him. I wished I had on shades to disguise my eyes because I couldn't see his and discern his mood. Poker face must be second nature to him with his position as don of the De Lucci crime family, and I had trouble reconciling that man with the man beside me, even from that man last night.

"How's your side?"

"It's fine," he said shortly. "I hardly feel it."

"I'll look at it later."

"I have plans for you later," he promised.

When we arrived at Harriet's room, I pushed open the door. "Look who's here?"

I meant Ginger. My octogenarian former neighbor was on the sofa reading, but when she looked up, her eyes bypassed the cat carrier and zeroed in on Dom.

"Where do you want these?" he asked.

"You can drop them just inside the door—thanks for your help."

I lowered the cat carrier so abruptly that Ginger complained.

But I had to get Dom out of the room before Harriet asked him questions.

Dom had an amused tilt to his mouth as I hurriedly shoved him out. "Thanks again." And slammed the door behind him.

Harriet, though, didn't get to the age of eighty without wading through bullshit. She got up slowly and hobbled over. She usually had a cane for longer distances, but shuffled around just fine in smaller spaces. The past year, she'd moved to the Delphine Assisted Living Home because her mobility had deteriorated. That, coupled with her emphysema from a lifetime of smoking, prevented her from independent living. "Was he your emergency appointment yesterday?"

"Don't be silly." I let Ginger out and she immediately wrapped around Harriet and started purring. "Oh, she missed you."

"Don't change the subject."

"He saw me juggling the bags and Ginger's crate and offered to help."

"You're full of nonsense, missy."

My phone chimed. I ignored it.

"Aren't you going to check your message?"

"I have no pressing matters to attend to, so it can't be important. If it's Billy, he's on his own."

"You shouldn't judge your brother that harshly."

Billy was a sore subject between us. I felt resentful for how Harriet had such compassion for my brother when he screwed up over and over. He was the reason why I nearly missed a payment for Harriet's stay at Delphine, because Billy somehow overspent his cut of the deal he made between the Russians and the Albanians. If it weren't for Sandro and Bianca and the jobs they threw my way with a generous tip that was more than what the job cost, I wouldn't have been able to resume nursing school and keep up with the Delphine payments. "He's the reason why I'm still at nursing school, eight years later."

"The cleaning job pays, though."

I caught myself from lashing out. Harriet never asked for my help. I offered it. I loved helping people who had no expectations. That was probably why every scrape that Billy found himself in was like nails on a chalkboard because he expected me to bail him out.

"So going back to that young man," Harriet said while carefully sitting in the armchair. Ginger immediately hopped on her lap and started kneading her thighs.

"Not talking about him. Nothing there." I started putting the groceries away.

"How about the one who took over my apartment?"

"Phil Harding? I hardly see him. He travels."

"You said he asked you out."

"And I said no." Although I didn't want to explain that I had a grueling series of awful clinical rotations where I'd seen enough penises, balls, slits, boobs, and asses that seeing someone in clothes was a novelty. The desire to get naked with someone was nil until Dom propositioned me.

Ginger, thankfully, had commanded Harriet's attention, and it gave me an opportunity to check my phone. Dom sent me a message.

DOM

Just text me when you're done.

ME

Leave me. Do boss things. I'll find my way home.

I didn't wait for him to reply and gave my full attention to Harriet. She was a true crime aficionado and took part in several message boards. A hot topic right now because it was local to the tristate area was the reemergence of the Mistress Strangler. I kept asking her questions about the case so she wouldn't remember to press me about Dom. And I succeeded. Ninety minutes later, I was on my way out with Ginger when I spotted the facility administrator.

"Hi, Miss Sheila!" I called out.

She was a tall Black woman with locs and spectacles. She smiled when she saw me, but there was a trace of sadness in her eyes.

Oh no.

"Sloane, I've been meaning to call you about your Capstone proposal."

As part of a nursing student's last semester, I had to present a case study with a practical application. My project was assisted living facility improvement. Capstone wasn't merely a thesis. It was based on real-world issues more than theory.

I braced myself.

"The board is not keen on a nursing student studying our operations. There is no money to spend on improvement."

"It's a proposal. They can take it or leave it," I said.

"They're also concerned you're going to take too much of the staff's time, and I can't push your agenda right now if I want to hire more people."

What she wasn't telling me was they didn't want anyone poking in their business. It was the wrong time for me to be invested in something like this because nursing homes had come under scrutiny for neglect, staffing issues, and lack of training in senior care.

I blew out a breath, deflated. "Thanks for trying."

"I'm sorry, Sloane."

I shrugged. "It didn't hurt to ask."

Dammit. It did hurt. I was feeling dejected when I exited the establishment, but experienced an odd lift in my spirits when Dom was waiting in front of Delphine.

He was on the phone, but quickly ended the call when he saw me.

Unnerved at the sudden spike of my heart rate, I flushed. I had to remind myself that he wanted sex. I didn't need wooing. Wooing led to feelings. However, I also told him I had to at least like someone I had sex with.

And I liked this very much, judging from how I couldn't help the smile that stretched my mouth. And given the Capstone rejection, this was a boost to the self-esteem I needed. I didn't want to wallow in self-pity, but I welcomed getting lost in the promised orgasms. *Please don't disappoint.*

"How long have you waited out here?"

"I drove around and got us more food since you gave what I got for you away. So, around fifteen minutes."

He reached for the cat carrier.

"You actually did the shopping?"

"What?" he drawled. "Like it's hard?"

This man. He was equally charming and aggravating. I felt sorry for anyone who had to go up against him. Dom possessed overwhelming self-assurance, and I was sure it was on its lowest setting when dealing with me. And there was nothing more that turned me on than a confident man, which partly explained my attraction to him.

I got into the vehicle, and after he deposited Ginger in the seat behind me, I watched him saunter around the front of the SUV.

"Looks like I'm in deep trouble, Ginger."

"Meow."

Dom slid into the driver's seat and glanced at me. "Any more errands to run?"

"No, it seems you've taken care of it. I'm not going to starve. How sure were you I hadn't left?"

"The receptionist had my number. She was going to tell me if you had left since you refused to answer my text."

When I remained quiet, he asked, "No comeback?"

I looked out my side of the vehicle and answered as nonchalantly as I could. "There's nothing to discuss yet. Especially if we don't know if our hookups will last past this weekend."

Dom gave a deep rumbling chuckle before making a turn toward my neighborhood. The assisted living home was around fifteen minutes from my apartment.

"Bianca mentioned this about you."

"Oh, what about?"

"You don't like to waste time repeating yourself."

"It saves us from confusion later," I said. "In my business, the less said, the better. Too many details can muddle the main points."

"So assuming we continue to hook up…"

"We'll need defined boundaries."

"I'm intrigued. I should be the one with boundaries."

I snorted. *Typical*, but I expected nothing less. "I have more to lose here because I could lose my business and my reputation as a nurse before I even graduate. Your organization is built on the illegal and morally gray. No one expects you to be a saint. They would say you're sowing your wild oats. You may even get a pat on the back. Meanwhile, a woman who enjoys sexual freedom is called a whore."

"Hey—" Dom cut in so sharply, it pulled my gaze from the window and I looked at him. "Never call yourself a whore. I don't know what kind of men you've been associated with, but I admire a woman who is sexually in tune with what she wants."

"Really? Don't they have a virginal bride lined up for you in an arranged marriage?"

"Probably. However, a virgin is not on the list of my requirements."

Though this was not news to me, especially with the more progressive crime families, I couldn't help being a little more curious. "Why aren't you married, Dom?"

His jaw hardened, and I thought he wasn't going to answer me until he said, "I thought we were not letting our personal life get mixed up."

"Wait, if you're engaged—" My heart clenched painfully at the thought.

"I'm not," he snapped. "I'm not with anyone. Otherwise, I wouldn't have propositioned you."

Hmm, he was sensitive to my question. Maybe he was recently jilted. That would explain using me as a rebound. Not that I minded. He could totally use me as a rebound as long as he gave me all the orgasms I wanted.

"Good," I said as the Escalade found parking near my apartment. "Let's see if your ego is writing checks your cock can't cash."

Dom's chest shook with silent laughter before a suppressed chuckle escaped past his mouth. "Sweetheart, you know I've been hard all day and each word out of your mouth has me imagining ways to make you beg."

I clenched my thighs. *Here we go*. This man was fun to rile up.

He glanced behind us. "What are we going to do about that pussy?"

CHAPTER *Six*

SLOANE

GINGER SOLVED OUR PROBLEM. SHE TOOK HERSELF OUT OF THE equation. Dom had bought several trays of the premium canned tuna. Now I wasn't sure if it was a bribe, but it certainly sounded like it. He personally opened the can and dumped it in Ginger's bowl, stood back, and crossed his arms.

He wasn't sold on cats yet and made no attempt to pet her.

In return, Ginger eyed him suspiciously, but the aroma of the gourmet feline food was too much to resist. She snuck to her food bowl and started gobbling.

Dom shot me a triumphant look.

I rolled my eyes. "You must have had help. Ginger is very picky."

"My uncle loves cats. I called him when I was at the pet store and he told me what to buy."

"Wait…your uncle…the Chicago boss."

"Yep."

"That sounds oddly domesticated." And oddly disconcerting.

"Luca likes cats more than people."

"I like him already," I murmured, then remembered something from past conversations with Bianca. In the early days of her captivity when she was forced into a marriage with the Rossis, she was cursing Dom's uncle, Luca Moretti, for facilitating Sandro's acceptance into the made man sanctum. "He's your uncle who's still looking for his wife, right?"

Dom shifted uncomfortably and moved away from me to go through the grocery bags to put the items away. My pantry and fridge were sparse of contents to begin with, so he had free rein on how to arrange them.

I didn't push him to answer, and Ginger distracted me. She finished eating and jumped on the window ledge and proceeded to groom herself. I knew her well enough that she was going to demand to be let out. She enjoyed traversing the fire escape ladder to the rooftop after she ate.

I opened the window. Since it was November, a chilly breeze swept through. It was two weeks before Thanksgiving, which reminded me I hadn't checked on Delphine's holiday schedule yet. Harriet moved in this year, but if I remembered right, next weekend would be the residents' Thanksgiving dinner. Nursing school didn't assign us a rotation on Thanksgiving Day itself, so I was looking forward to a break. Our supervisor said we could expect plenty of missed holidays when we became licensed nurses.

After a while, Ginger was done, and without another meow or purr, she left my apartment.

"So, she just left you with a stranger after you went through the trouble of rescuing her from a shelter."

Dom leaned nonchalantly against the counter and was watching me. The cold draft sent goose bumps racing across my skin, but a furnace heated somewhere below my belly.

"In case you haven't noticed, cats do as they please," I told him and crossed my legs.

"They have no sense of loyalty, unlike dogs."

"So I'm taking you do at least like dogs, but they shed too."

Dom straightened from his lean and approached me. "I grew up with dogs, but it makes little sense to have one if I don't have time to walk him since I live in Manhattan."

"That's why there are dog walkers."

"I'm rarely at my penthouse, even in the evenings."

"Then maybe you need a cat. They're self-sufficient."

Dom's gaze drifted to the window. "I can see that. But so far, I'm not convinced to get a pussy…cat." The way the word pussy rolled over his tongue made me swallow.

He leaned closer, bracing his arms on either side of me, but kept our bodies from touching.

"You seem determined to get to mine."

Dom chuckled. "Are we still talking about Ginger?" His mouth was by my ear. "Or redheads in general."

My body seemed to sway toward his and my breath hitched. "You know what I'm talking about."

"I have a different menu in mind." He leaned back and shot me a heated look that made my toes curl. Damn this man and the potent sexual cloud that surrounded him.

Before I got caught in the tailspin of his seduction, I blurted out, "So what are our rules for the weekend?"

"I always fuck with a condom," he said.

"I don't have any right now."

"I've got that covered. I always use my own."

I quirked a brow. "Paranoid much?"

"Just careful."

"What about—"

"Enough." He nipped my bottom lip, and before I could react, he crushed my mouth in a bruising kiss. His hands went under my ass and lifted me. No foreplay, no teasing. Outright domination. His tongue forced its way between my lips and dueled with mine. Actually, there was not much forcing, but my pussy spasmed against his torso and I had the urge to ride his belt buckle. Cold metal against hot pussy. Oh, God. I was a hair trigger away from coming.

Our mouths continued clashing before I heard my bedroom door slam.

He broke the kiss and snarled, "I swear, woman, I have a lotta patience, but you've pushed my limits more than once."

"Your stitches," I screeched.

"I'll survive." Then I went flying across the room and landed on the bed. Dom pulled off his henley, and sure enough, he was already bleeding.

"You're going to ruin the mattress," I breathed. But did I care? No.

"I'll buy you a new one," he growled. "Now shut up and let me have you before I lose my damn mind."

He tossed my sneakers and he was yanking my joggers off. "I wanted to do this with more finesse…" he continued to mutter. "But you've been driving me crazy since last night."

I braced on my elbows, utterly fascinated to see Dom fumbling with my clothes. "What? No foreplay?" I managed to tease before he peeled my panties away.

"Foreplay?"

The sinister gleam in his eyes subdued my teasing. It looked a lot like retribution and I was anxiously anticipating, achingly aroused, and all out of fucks. I was getting filled with a Dom-sized cock and it better be worth it.

He positioned himself between my thighs, his expression

hungry. "This is all the foreplay you're getting." He dove in and tongued my clit before letting the rest of his mouth wrap around the sensitive flesh, swollen with all the blood rushing to it. Dom wasn't even gentle. He ate and bit. Swiping, sucking, and nibbling. He was everywhere, all at once. My orgasm came fast and furious, and the pulses surged and kept on going. I inhaled sharply, not able to exhale. He seemed to know how to pace my orgasm and relented a fraction to let me catch my breath.

He inserted his fingers. I had no clue how many, but a delicious stretch had me aching for the real thing.

"Fuck, you're so wet for me, Firecat." They glided in and out so easily. I was embarrassingly slippery. "Give me more, baby."

I realized I was gasping at the ceiling, but when I looked back between my legs, it was to see Dom watching me intently, devouring me with his gaze while my juices glistened on his lips. And it was the most erotic sight. Like he was salivating and couldn't get enough. There was nothing more arousing than a man who liked to eat pussy. With his eyes on me, he withdrew his fingers and casually slipped them into his mouth and slowly dragged them out. "Delicious," he murmured before he resumed his attack between my legs. I lost count of how many times I'd come. My voice was hoarse, but Dom seemed to relish making me scream.

And scream I did, over and over.

I wondered if I should worry about a neighbor hearing me, but with Dom, my inhibitions seemed to have taken a vacation. He rose above me, scorching me with the hunger in his eyes, and that hunger made me powerful.

He removed my top and unhooked my bra, carefully exposing my breasts. He visibly shuddered and his Adam's apple bobbed. From my face, his silently assessing gaze traveled down my body, now bare for his scrutiny.

I was blessed with fifties-pinup-girl proportions, and this was a rare moment when I embraced my body with pride. I lifted my chin with defiance, waiting for Dom to say something.

"Good God," he rasped. "You *are* perfection." His belt buckle clinked. The lowering of the zipper was loud in the room. It signaled our point of no return. Then he was on top of me, shoving my thighs apart and surging inside me. Out of control, he rocked into me. Filling me with cock, shocking me with its girth and length. The harsh thrust stealing my breath.

"Dom!" He withdrew and thrust hard. It was only on the third pump that a warning told me why it felt so good, and on the fourth, I registered that I didn't hear the rip of the wrapper of a "condom."

He froze, his eyes sharpening in horror.

"Fuck," he muttered.

"Put one on," I urged.

"Are you on birth control?"

"Yes! But…"

He withdrew instantly, and a hollowed feeling replaced the loss. I heard the ripping packet, and he slid right back inside me.

He cupped my face. "Sorry…too excited."

I laughed. "Me too."

He resumed pumping, but his face grew troubled. "Never happened before."

I cupped his cheek. "That's okay."

He gripped my wrist by his face before letting it go to clamp his fingers around my neck and squeezed. His pounding intensified, speeding up his thrusts and ramming inside me over and over. Yes!

"Come for me," he grunted. His hand around my neck loosened, and an orgasm ricocheted through me, blinding me behind my eyelids like a supernova. I was still coming when Dom folded me over, pushing my knees almost up to my ears. His face was right beside me, panting with his efforts, and his glorious grunts of exertion sent another shockwave rippling through me.

He thrust in one more time and stilled before giving me his weight. His chin was over my shoulder and he was breathing like he'd just crossed the finish line in a sprint. A film of sweat covered our bodies, and the familiar scent of sex shrouded us. We were quiet for a while and I wondered if Dom had come to the same conclusion I had.

I wanted to do this again and not just for the weekend. I wanted mind-blowing sex that would leave me satiated and boneless and thoroughly fucked.

Dom lifted off me and rolled onto his back.

Random deep exhales were the only rough sounds in the room. I didn't want to look at him. I was suddenly very self-conscious.

"That felt more like a main course than a taste," I teased, trying to lighten the mood. I'd never been devoured to within an inch of my life and I wasn't referring to Dom eating me out. Just the way he fucked me. It was wild and cathartic. Animalistic. He seemed angry about forgetting to put on a condom, not that I didn't welcome his savagery in pounding me into the mattress. That was delicious. I sensed he didn't lose control like that and it freaked him out, but I didn't want to gloat or analyze his lack of control earlier. He did, after all, suffer blood loss—

Oh shit.

I shot up in bed. Sure enough, drips of blood seeped through the bedsheet. The comforter would have helped, but I neglected to fix my bed this morning.

"All right," I said, patting Dom. "Get up before you ruin the mattress."

He winced as he shifted to a sitting position. "I'll replace it."

"We can avoid that if you get off the bed now."

He emitted a disgruntled sound and rolled up. He peered at his side. "The stitches are fine."

"Good. Still, vigorous activity should be off the table for now."

A ghost of a smile touched his mouth. "Does that mean we're more than just a weekend thing?"

"Maybe," I said, tapping my mouth as if I was considering it. I didn't misread him. He wanted more of me and that gave me confidence to set the rules. "I'm a fan of spelling things out, but right now, I'm hungry for something else."

"I'm all for refueling." Dom opened the bedroom door and paused. "What the…your cat is a pervert."

"What?" I went around him and dissolved into laughter when I saw Ginger sitting primly at the entrance, looking curious.

"I guess you're used to her eavesdropping or voyeurism?"

"Let's just say it was a good idea you shut the door." I didn't have to tell Dom that one time Ginger scared one of my regular hookups into not coming back when she positioned herself in close proximity to his hairy balls.

I needed Dom to fuck me again.

~

"No gifts?" Dom raised a brow at my second rule below the "no dating" one.

We had both showered and I rechecked Dom's stitches. We were currently in the kitchen eating shrimp fried rice, lo mien, and beef broccoli from the Chinese restaurant next door.

"Is it because it's the holidays?"

"Not really. But seriously. No gifts. No demands on time and I'm sure you'll appreciate that, too."

He made a humming sound while chewing on a bite of noodles. He chased it down with beer, appearing contemplative. "Look, I said that I don't like the expectations that come with the term *girlfriend* or *mistress*, but it doesn't mean I'm a scrooge. I enjoy giving jewelry after I have a good time with a woman."

"Or when you end things?"

"Well, there's nothing to end, remember?" He exhaled an exasperated breath.

"True, this isn't a relationship."

"You have a very negative perspective about relationships. Worse than mine. Who hurt you?"

"That's not important, but we're shaped by our pasts, right?"

"But we're not allowed to talk about anything personal. How would I know not to trigger you?"

"I'm more Teflon than you think."

Dom grumbled something unintelligible, attacking his plate with chopsticks. "I don't have a problem with that, Sloane, but I have to go to events and I might have to take a woman as a *date*. Can you handle that?" He shoved a mouthful of noodles into his mouth.

"As long as you're not sleeping with her."

"I can't claim you in public. It'll be disastrous for you when we end our…whatever this is."

His remark should hurt, but I was weirdly relieved. I wasn't kidding when I said I had to at least like the person I had sex with and not simply bang random strangers I met at a bar. So this monogamous, no-strings-attached-sex arrangement was the perfect solution for me. Now that I'd proven that Dom could deliver on orgasms, it was a plus that he wanted a no-commitment commitment like I did.

Keeping it under the radar would prevent other crime families from getting ideas about using me against him. Being out in public with him was a disaster for my independence. That was probably another reason he didn't do girlfriends, especially if it was an ordinary person like me whose family couldn't afford a legion of bodyguards.

He finished chewing before he answered, "There might be tabloid speculations about anyone I'm seen in public with." At least he wasn't one of those annoying men who talked with their mouths full.

"I promise not to cause drama as long as you're honest with me. Besides, that might be advantageous so people won't be suspicious about us." I rose from my chair because I was craving wine for this discussion. I never expected the "no gifts" rule to open so many avenues of discourse. I grabbed one of my $10.99 bottles and twisted the corkscrew into it. "You don't always have to tell me when you have an event because you only call me when you want to hook up." I wiggled the cork out and dropped it onto a tray where I'd been collecting them. "I might not always be available because I'm in the last year of nursing school, but I'm not down with you having sex with someone else while you're fucking me."

He narrowed his eyes. "Same."

"You don't want any drama. You won't get any from me. But I'd appreciate a call or a text to tell me we're done."

Dom spooned over a mountain of fried rice on his plate and resumed eating. "You know this sounds like a guy's dream relationship but—"

"We're not calling this a relationship."

"If this is about money—"

"Maybe it is." It totally was. After Dad left us penniless, my mother always reminded me to have my own money. To never surrender financial power to a man or be dependent on him for survival. Dom and I were worlds apart, both financially and in social status. But if what he gave me was just sex and after receiving a prelude to what was to come—no pun intended—I wanted more. What I didn't want was the complication that came when money was involved, because what he would give me would be more than I could ever afford. It wasn't the same as a cleaning job where I charged exorbitant prices. In my twisted mind, because of our wealth imbalance and because we couldn't be seen in public, it was like he would be paying me for sex. Fuck that. In the bedroom, we were equally matched.

"I'm still replacing your bed. No arguments."

His blood had ruined the mattress. I wasn't attached to it since it was lumpy as hell.

"I said 'no gifting.'" I paused and took a dramatic sip of my wine. "I didn't say I wasn't practical."

CHAPTER
Seven

Dom

I STARED INTO NARROWED GREEN EYES. "WHAT THE FUCK!" I yelled, coming fully awake as I flung the orange blob of fur across the bed. The shriek of an animal reached my ears while Sloane rushed into the room and gaped at us.

Crouching sideways, Ginger's ears flattened. She was howling and hissing threateningly like a creature needing an exorcism. This was no scaredy-cat and she wasn't one who backed down.

"That thing was on top of me." I refused to move because I was completely naked under the blanket. What if she came after my balls?

Sloane, meanwhile, erupted in laughter and walked into the room and gently patted Ginger. "What's got you caterwauling, Ginger? Was the big man mean to you?"

"Cater-what?" I asked. "And I wasn't mean to her. I just woke up."

"It's a special language of cats when they're in heat or fighting."

"If that's your way of discouraging us from having sex, it's not going to work," I warned, only half kidding. As much as the cat almost gave me a heart attack, my cock gave a hearty nod to Sloane's attire of nurse scrubs. We spent two days fucking, eating, and drinking, but I was getting more drunk on her.

At Sloane's husky laugh, my cock rose.

Her eyes fell on its outline and she shook her head. "I'm late."

Her body was a work of art. I considered myself an ass man, but there was so much of Sloane to explore. Sucking on her tits got me hard, but the thought of burying my mouth in her sweet cunt got me harder than a tire iron. And thrusting into her? I wished I hadn't felt her bare because I could weep every time I had to use a condom, but I couldn't risk getting her pregnant.

Her heart-shaped face and her thick-lashed emerald-green eyes enthralled me. I always thought her lips were unusually pale, but it was one of her disguises. She deliberately covered her freckles and her defined cheekbones with makeup so she would appear flat. Even at Bianca's wedding, she was in the most shapeless dress with barely any makeup probably because many of the guests were in the mob.

In her nurse's uniform, Sloane's face was once again a pale canvas. I knew what her face looked like when framed with her glorious red hair, but at the moment, it was twisted into a severe bun away from her features. To say I was intrigued with Sloane Scott was putting it mildly. She said we should keep our personal lives out of the arrangement, but it didn't mean I wasn't going to have a report on her by the end of the day.

"How about breakfast?" I waggled my brows.

"No. My pussy is still sore from the weekend." She nudged the cat off the bed. "No snuggling today, kitty. You'll get fur all over my scrubs." She glanced at me again and bit her bottom lip.

Fuck. I was imagining them wrapped around my cock.

"I have to go. There's coffee. I always leave the window open a crack so Ginger can come and go as she pleases. All you have to do is turn the flat lock on the knob when you leave."

"That's not very secure."

"It'll do for now."

"Or you can give me a key."

"We're not at that stage yet." She checked her phone and cursed. "Okay gotta go…I guess I'll see you when I see you."

I jumped out of the bed to at least cop a feel of her ass, but Ginger ran in front of me and I nearly tripped over her.

Damn cat.

The door slammed.

I'll see you when I see you.

That was my line. No-strings-attached arrangements were my forte but for some reason I didn't like it when I wasn't in control. Sloane's aversion to relationships was equal to mine. I might even say it was even more. I should consider myself lucky and roll with it.

I glared at Ginger. The cat appeared extremely pleased that she thwarted my attempt to catch Sloane. "You and I need to come to an understanding," I told her while returning to the bedroom and stabbing my legs into a pair of athletic shorts. "You don't get between me and Sloane. Got it?"

The cat's answer was to whip her tail up and down before giving me a view of her rump while walking away.

"I'm talking to you, dammit."

Was I arguing with a cat? Me? Dominic De Lucci. The boss of the De Lucci crime family had been reduced to feline ridicule.

When I made sure there was a barrier between my testicles and her claws, I headed to the coffee machine in the kitchen to pour myself a mug of brew. Ginger had positioned herself along the back of the couch, lying down with her paws folded in front of her.

"Why don't you go chase rats somewhere?" Never had I paid attention to anyone's house animals. They served their purpose of sitting pretty, being appropriately groomed, and looking like part of the decor. Obviously, outside the pampered pets of Fifth Avenue and Manhattan's elites, there existed a feral variety with obnoxious behavior.

"I paid for that premium tuna, just so you know."

No response. No meows or hisses. Just silent, judgy eyes.

So far, she hadn't cockblocked me from Sloane and was surprisingly absent during our energetic bouts of sex. My phone buzzed on top of the kitchen counter and I winced. I had set a do-not-disturb feature and it finally expired at nine a.m. Monday morning.

Back to reality.

I WALKED INTO THE GRAND FOYER OF MY HUDSON YARDS penthouse. Soaring ceilings and arched windows, the vastness of its interior and blinding light, were a far cry from the cozy two days I spent holed up at Sloane's. The main dining area and eat-in kitchen alone were bigger than her apartment. While my residence comprised of five bedrooms, a den, five full baths, two half baths, and an elegant sweeping staircase to the second floor and third-level roof landing, I also had an abundance of outdoor space across three floors.

Yet I lived alone. De Lucci Transnational was a big player in the real estate market both in the US and abroad, and when this penthouse came on the market, Matteo told me it was a steal at twenty-five million.

I never, not once in the four years that I'd owned this place, brought a woman here. It was my sacred place. I hadn't had a girlfriend since college. For a few years after I became boss, I enjoyed hookups with mafia groupies and socialites who loved living dangerously, but it only took one failed paternity suit to reevaluate my approach to sex. I became more cautious, and more selective, and always used my own condoms. My sex life became secretive and the tabloid that followed the mafia exploded into speculations. One time they even wondered if I switched teams and was gay. It took one date with a popular socialite to dispel that rumor.

I showered and changed into sweatpants and headed to my den to join a web meeting with De Lucci Transnational. Matteo and Nico usually tag-teamed on that. I was merely a figurehead because the things I did for the company were best discussed face to face.

As the meeting droned on, my mind drifted to how I managed to avoid the overzealous *Manhattan Tattler* from discovering who I was sleeping with. Recently it was because I was test-driving a dating app for the rich. Developed by a friend from college, the app ran on the dark web. Several luxury apartment buildings were scattered around Manhattan and were used as a rendezvous for sex-only hookups between the rich and rich. Individuals who prefer not to use an escort service and risk exposure. A carefully curated membership included an intense background check with a minimum net worth of thirty million dollars. There was even an anonymous rating system to keep egos in check and ensure continued membership. No money was exchanged beyond the membership fees and use of the opulent suite for the tryst.

A message came over my phone from the concierge of the building. "Sir, your mother and cousin are on their way up."

Fuck.

I texted Matteo who was leading the video call.

ME

Is your wife on her way to ambush me along with my mother?

MATTEO

Serves you right. Where were you this weekend?

I left him on read and signed out of the meeting, leaving him to explain. I was crossing the foyer when Ma walked in with Sera. I should revoke their access to my penthouse.

Annoyance was written all over my mother's face. Meanwhile, Sera struggled to keep the humor off hers. Gio, her son, was with her.

I gave the boy my attention. "What do you feed this boy?" I picked up the toddler and held him in my arms like a shield against the storm my mother was about to unleash. It confused people when I tried to explain that Sera and Matteo were my cousins, but they were married to each other. They were not blood related. Sera was my cousin through my Moretti side, while Matteo was my cousin on the De Lucci side. It was too early to tell who their son would take after.

"He eats a lot," Sera said.

"How old is he now?"

"Nine months."

"Is he walking yet?"

"Well—"

"Dominic, seriously?" my mother snapped. "What's with the small talk?"

I grinned at her and walked over to give her a kiss on the cheek. "Morning, Ma."

"It's afternoon," she shot back.

"I was on my way to the kitchen for a shot of espresso. Anyone want one?"

"*Si*, might as well," my mother muttered. I handed Gio back to Sera.

"Can we wait for you in the living room?" Sera asked. "Gio is starting to pull himself up to stand and likes to grab things."

Ma gave Gio a fond look and then looked pointedly at me. This was going to be an uncomfortable conversation. Giving her grandchildren was not in my five-year plan.

I put a plate of butter biscuits and their espressos on the tray and headed for the living room. I used to have fancier pastries in the fridge. My longtime housekeeper quit and moved back to the Midwest, saying she'd had enough of city life and wanted to be closer to her grandchildren.

Poor Ma. My sister and I were not keen on domestic life anytime soon.

"So, what's with the visit?"

Ma took a sip of her espresso. "You're still playing coy. I told you to be at the dinner party last Saturday."

"I was out of town."

"That's what Sonny said. Also, you were not responding to calls or texts." I needed to touch base with my underboss, Sonny. He was in charge of our street business of smuggled goods and construction schemes while I kept our public face clean.

"I was in Cape Cod, in the middle of the ocean. No signal."

"Didn't I tell you it was an important dinner? Margo Winthrop was there."

Margo Winthrop was the matchmaker of the mafia, billionaires, and politicians. She ran the company called Marriage Ink. She had contacts from powerful politicians to the powerful players in the underworld. Her expertise was to secure alliances.

I relaxed against the sofa. "I'm not ready to consider marrying into the Russian bratva to solve your problem."

"My problem?" Her voice rose. "It's a Moretti legacy."

"If it was considered a legacy, Nonno shouldn't have promised it to the Russians when you were not committed to the arranged marriage."

"Let me remind you, *caro mio*, that you and your sister wouldn't exist if I didn't marry your papa."

"Then why are they so important?" The properties in question were five luxury villas scattered along the Amalfi coast that were used as a dowry for Ma's arranged marriage into the bratva, which she called off to marry Pop. The Morettis gave up those villas to avoid conflict with the bratva. The Russians accepted them to avoid embarrassment on both sides.

"Your nonno was heartbroken to let them go." Ma pounded on her chest. "Before he died, I promised Papa I would get them back."

"By offering me on a silver platter?"

"You're not in a relationship with anyone. You're a don. You need a wife, and it's time for you to get married and give me grandchildren."

I exhaled a heavy breath and glanced at Sera. "Now would be a good time to chime in."

"Oh, I don't know. I'm not the one promised to a bratva princess, and it would be nice to get the properties back."

"Thanks, cuz," I grumbled. Unknown to my mother, Sera and I had discussed the villas owned by the Russians, but I was hoping Grigori Petrov would be my solution. My mother didn't know that the Russians were using it for their sex parties. According to my contacts, those properties were under scrutiny from the feds for sex trafficking. That was why Grigori had put that business on ice under orders from his pakhan.

So Grigori was a problem and a solution.

He could convince his boss to let the problematic villas go in exchange for business with the De Luccis. That was my reason for being at his poker game last Friday with one of my entrepreneur friends. Unfortunately, hotheads prevailed during the game and a guest of his had a problem with mine. I intervened, but I ended up getting knifed. However, it was Kolya who took care of their problematic guest.

According to Sonny, Grigori had been inquiring about my welfare, worried the bloody poker game would turn me off from continuing to bring him high-profile players.

Sloane hadn't been part of the plan. Admittedly, it was stupid of me to follow her and proposition her, but I always had a hard-on for the enigmatic mob cleaner. I simply never acted on the attraction until last Friday. In my blood-deprived head, I thought if I had her once, I could move on and tell Sandro Rossi that going after Grigori Petrov was a bad idea.

You see, Sandro came to me and floated the idea about getting rid of Grigori, so Billy, Sloane's lowlife brother, would get free of the Russians, and therefore free Sloane from the bratva's clutches.

And therein lay my dilemma. I needed Grigori's support so I could avoid marrying into their organization. It was not in my best interest to have him whacked.

Sleeping with Sloane was a complication I didn't need.

"I hope you'll think about family since the holidays are near." Ma excelled in sensing my guilt and had a way of piling on top of it. "Find a way to bring Lucy home for Thanksgiving, but especially Christmas."

"She's busy playing fixer in DC," I said dryly. "Besides, she'll respond more to Pop than to you or me."

Ma huffed. "Then convince your zio Luca to come visit with Elias."

"Sera is more convincing with him than I am. Besides, she can use Gio to entice Luca as a playmate for Elias."

"I'm visiting him for the New Year," Sera told my mother. "I want to be around the De Luccis this time for Christmas, but I'll see if I can convince him."

Ma's face crumpled. I grabbed the tissue dispenser and passed it to her. She sniffled and dabbed her eyes. Even though Luca was thirty-seven years old, he would always be Ma's baby brother. We'd flown to Chicago the past two Christmases to show him support. Luca had been a wreck after Natalya disappeared, and if it wasn't for his son, Elias, he would have gone down a dark, destructive path to seek retribution. Two years had passed. Life had moved on, yet for Luca, it hadn't. He was still looking for Natalya, which reminded me, I needed to get with Trevor, my intel guy, with information he'd gleaned from an asset that maybe, just maybe, Luca was not crazy and Natalya was alive.

A chill ran down my spine.

I sat beside my mother and put an arm around her. "If Sera won't be able to convince him, then I'll give it a shot and let him know he has a second family with us."

"*Grazie, figlio mio*," Ma whispered. "I just worry about him."

"You worry too much about everyone," I told her gently. I continued to comfort my mother as my eyes met Sera's across the room.

She nodded at me.

She would call Luca, and if she failed to convince my uncle to come to New York for Christmas, then I would step in. If I had to, I would fly to Chicago and physically put Luca on a plane.

It was Christmas.

The bonds of family clamped around my chest and I waited for the usual suffocating tightness, but it didn't come.

I wondered if my weekend with Sloane was simply that. A relief from the power of my position, but I didn't have time to dwell on that thought.

Duty called.

CHAPTER *Eight*

SLOANE

THANKSGIVING HAD COME AND GONE WITH NO WORD FROM DOM. Oh, wait. There was. Kind of. Two days after he'd successfully rearranged my insides with his massive cock, I received a call from a furniture company for the delivery of a new mattress.

What was a girl to expect? A booty call that weekend, right? I shaved, I pussy-landscaped, and I endured a hair and hand mask. My hair and hands suffered the most from my job as a cleaner and now as a nursing student. Constant handwashing was a killer on the skin, especially when it was thirty degrees with low humidity.

But it was now the first week of December and still no word from Dom. There was no response to the message I sent informing him of the mattress arrival. Maybe I had come on too strong and was too expectant.

I brought up the message.

ME

Mattress was delivered and signed for. Are you ready to wreck it?

I winced. Maybe that was too forward. I never angsted over my regular hookups. How was it so different with Dom? Maybe because on Thanksgiving when I'd been hanging out with Harriet, she shoved her tablet under my nose to show me an article of Dom escorting a gorgeous brunette to a holiday gala.

"Hey, isn't this the guy who brought in my groceries last week?"

I glanced nonchalantly at it. "Could be." It didn't really bother me then. Our boundaries were clear and he wasn't just anyone. He had responsibilities, including attending events with women who could never be me. But we agreed to be honest. I decided a month was the max I'd wait to hear from him before I followed up my text to tell him I was moving on. In no way was I giving him an ultimatum. That was never my style. In my opinion, if a man really wanted to be with me, he'd make time. I was giving him the courtesy of that time because he was the head of an organization and also knew the De Luccis were family oriented, most especially around the holidays. In retrospect, we should have set a time limit for how long we would wait with no contact.

Dammit. *In* retrospect, I shouldn't have started anything with Dom. The last thing I needed was to obsess over a single text message. I despised how I put myself in this position.

If I hadn't, I wouldn't be in this funk, feeling so alone during what was supposed to be a festive time of the year. I was glad Harriet had her mahjong buddies. She was actually having a game tonight. As for Billy, I hadn't heard or seen a peep out of him since that night Grigori called me.

I didn't want to flunk this semester. Next semester would be my last. Since my Capstone proposal failed, I was looking for a preceptorship in the ER, which was why I needed to ace these tests. Grueling clinical rotations would start on Monday as part of my final exams. Maybe I should have fun this weekend.

Mind made up, I shot off a text to Bianca and asked if she wanted to go clubbing or to a bar. She became the point of contact for the girls' night after Sera had given birth. She immediately responded that they were having a family dinner. Bianca even invited me over to the De Lucci mansion to join them.

Hell no.

And it really sucked. Because if I didn't worry that Dom would be there and think I was stalking him, I would jump at the chance. Bianca and her mom were fantastic cooks.

And as if that weren't enough of a bummer, I'd also started my period. The cramps were creeping in, but I was determined nothing was going to stop me from enjoying myself tonight. After my shower, I piled up my hair and dragged out my train case with my rarely used makeup. Setting it on top of my tiny bathroom counter, I flipped it open. Four identical photographs spilled out.

I stiffened. I forgot about those. They were in a compartment behind the mirror of the train case. Someone sent them to me. A reminder that I was trash. A reminder that my dad leaving us wasn't the worst thing that nearly left my mother and me living on the streets.

No. It was my sixteen-year-old self who thought my pretty green eyes and my beautiful face had the right to dream big.

It was that woman with the emerald necklace who taunted me to try it on, saying I'd look like a princess wearing it, only to turn around and accuse me of theft.

Even to this day, I scorned my eyes and their reflection in the mirror because it reminded me of that necklace.

Well, fuck her. She had no control over me anymore. I should have thrown those pictures away, but now and then, I used them to remind myself not to get too complacent. To know my place in society. That I could be successful as long as I was realistic about the limitations of my position.

Tonight, I was going out for me, and I was going full-out glam. It took a while to give myself a blowout. I wore a flowy black dress that hit mid-thigh and pulled on my thigh-high boots which were too pricy to use but once or twice every season. Another reason to put them on.

Ginger appeared behind me.

"Oh, you're back?" I sassed her. She'd been gone for two days to God knew where, probably bugging another neighbor since the premium cat food Dom bought ran out. "Well, I'm going out. You're on your own tonight."

She made a tiny chirping sound. "Oh, is that approval?"

Another tiny meow.

I breathed in a laugh. "You're pushing me out the door? Was I looking so pathetic and that's why you abandoned me?"

"Meow."

"I wasn't," I said. "I was busy, too. You know he's the boss of a big organization and he's probably swamped."

Ginger turned away and walked into the living room.

"I'm not making excuses for him!" I yelled at my cat. Grr…

Before I lost the will to leave, I grabbed a bolero jacket from the closet and marched out the door. I furiously descended the steps as if the hounds of hell were nipping at my heels, ready to drag me back to my apartment. There was nothing more I wanted than to curl up on a comfy couch and stream a new season of *True Detective*, but there was also that defiance burning inside me, telling me I was an independent woman who needed no one to be happy.

My eyes blurred staring at the blinking lights decorating one of the residents' doors at the bottom landing of the first floor. The landlord should ban that. It looked tacky.

I was behaving like a scrooge. Christmas lights were supposed to be tacky. That was why there were tacky light tours.

I was still glaring at the lights when I rounded the staircase and slammed into a wall.

Or rather, the bulky chest of my neighbor.

"Whoa there, doll, where's the fire?" Strong fingers gripped my elbows, and I stared up into concerned brown eyes.

I usually saw Phil in suits or in gym attire, but his tie was off, and his dress shirt was partially unbuttoned like he was unwinding from a long day at work.

"I need a drink," I muttered.

"You have a date?" His brow shot up.

"No. I don't need one to go to a pub."

I realized he hadn't let go of my elbows and I was still plastered to him. Embarrassed and a little sad that I had zero lusty reactions to him, I stepped back. Besides, I wasn't ready to get over one hookup by getting under another one.

"I'm sorry for not looking where I was going."

"No problem." His eyes gave me an appreciative once-over. Heat crept up my cheeks. It was not the kind of leering that made my skin crawl. It was even respectful and oddly ego-boosting, especially with my pity-party-of-one earlier.

"Meeting friends, then?"

His probing questions were making the air between us awkward, so I gave him a small smile and said, "I need to go."

I was on my way out of the vestibule when Phil called out, "Want company?"

Phil was good company. We ordered a ride and headed to the waterfront. We ditched the first pub we went to because it was crowded with holiday revelers and hopped to another, where we managed to grab a table and actually got our drinks within twenty minutes. Beer for him, and a fancy crème brûlée martini for me.

With booze loosening my tongue, the tightness across my shoulders also relaxed.

"So that guy a few weeks ago…he's your boyfriend?" Phil asked.

"No, just a friend," I said.

Phil took a sip of his beer. I couldn't tell if he believed me. Not that I cared. "So, going anywhere for the holidays? You're not from these parts, right?"

"Actually, I am," he said. "Rochester. Dad was an accountant; Mom was a schoolteacher."

Oh, we were sharing that now? "Was?"

"They died in a car accident."

"I'm sorry."

He shrugged. "That was twelve years ago. My sister and I got by. An aunt took us in and I was already in college."

I tried to do a mental calculation, but Phil smiled. "I'm thirty-two."

"Well, I'm twenty-seven."

"I thought you were younger."

"You know, I'm at an age where I'm not sure if I should take that as a compliment or an insult."

Phil shook his head and grinned into his beer. "Sorry."

"You're forgiven," I deadpanned. "Where's your sister now?"

"California…soooo, I might not see her and her family this Christmas since it's time to hit quota for my job…"

"You said you were a sales agent…"

"Software."

"Oh, ha…" I laughed. "I was thinking something more tangible."

"Network security software." He noted my wide-eyed expression, and it was his turn to laugh. "No, not the one that almost brought down the planet."

"Geez, it's so scary nowadays that our lives are dependent on computers."

"How about you? Any siblings?" He probably knew by now I had no parents.

"Well, you've met Billy." My brother at least helped me clean out Harriet's apartment in time for Phil to move in.

"I haven't seen him around."

"Oh, he's around." I drained my martini. And I prayed Billy left me alone until Christmas. I was sure he was going to show up and ask for money. At Phil's inquisitive eyes, I gave him more information just so I could get it off my chest. "Our dad left when I was fourteen. Billy took it hard. Mom took it harder. One could say she died of a broken heart."

"Oh, wow, I'm so sorry."

"I just want to put it out there since we're in a sharing mood, but that's as far as I'm willing to share."

"I got it," Phil said. "We can just gossip about our neighbors."

I grinned at him. "Now you're talking."

My phone buzzed. It was Bianca.

BIANCA

I'm feeling so guilty. Did you find someone to hang out with? I can come over later with wine I stole from Dad's cellar.

Bianca…so sweet. I smiled and typed back.

ME

I'm fine. I have a hot guy with me.

You're just trying to make me feel better.

ME

I'm really fine.

BIANCA

I wish you had come over for Thanksgiving.

I told you I had to be with Harriet. Now hush, I'm being rude to Phil.

Phil? There really is a guy?

😱You really think I'm that pathetic to make one up?

Proof or I don't believe you.

I burst out laughing.

"What's going on?" Phil asked, his mouth twitching in amusement.

I swiped the tears from my eyes. The evening was going better than I expected. Phil provided surprisingly fun, no-pressure company, and I had good friends who worried that I was alone for the holidays. I guess I was the type of person who wanted to be invited, even when I knew there wouldn't be any chance I'd accept. Bianca had a lot of love surrounding her, but she was so empathetic, she wanted to share her family with me. Admittedly, I was reluctant to depend on anyone, especially with the way I grew up, asking for favors came with a price. Being around Bianca and her family had shown me what unconditional love looked like. I just wasn't sure it was meant for someone like me.

I showed Phil Bianca's text because I was still laughing.

"So I'm a hot guy, huh?"

"You know you are." I gave him a wink. "But this is still not a date."

"Lady, I wouldn't take you to a bar for our first date."

I stared at the text message. "Should I send her our picture?"

"Sure," he chuckled. "Don't want to make you a liar."

I raised my phone to take a selfie.

"Here, let me do it." He took my phone and held it up. *Click.*

We actually looked good together. For some reason, I was pleased.

I sent it off to Bianca.

ME

There, happy now? Can you relax so I can relax with my guy?

BIANCA

Wow. Okay, let me show the girls.

"Hey, can you send that to me?" Phil asked, whipping out his phone. "I'll send it to my sister so she can quit bugging me to fly to California for Christmas."

I had him from my contact list because of Harriet's move and dropped it to him.

Before I set my phone down, I saw a notification of a message from Dom.

This pissed me off. The timing probably meant that he was at the De Lucci dinner and he saw the picture I sent Bianca. Nothing I did broke the rules. If I had an inkling of attraction to Phil, I would have sent Dom a text ending our arrangement.

Dom could fuck off.

CHAPTER
Nine

Dom

"He's six-six and two hundred forty pounds, but he's dumb as a rock," Matteo told Sandro.

We were having drinks before dinner and the men were talking about the Game of Bosses, a tournament sponsored by the Moscow mob that was held every five years. The next one was coming up in May. Many crime bosses waited until the games to settle their differences. If you asked me, it was simply a lot of testosterone posturing. Being boss was more than brawn.

Sandro was being challenged inside the Rossi crime family. Apparently there were lurkers still wanting to usurp the position, especially since Sandro had turned the family around and sent their profits soaring.

"I'm not worried." Sandro glanced at me. "Didn't Luca win one a long time ago?"

"Yes." I took a sip of scotch. "He beat Vasily Orlov nine years ago, and the Russian wants a rematch."

This time it was Nico who snorted. "Is he considering it?"

In our huddle were Matteo and Nico, Bianca's brothers and my cousins who were as heavily involved as I was in the Archer Syndicate, an organization that kept the underworld in check. And the only reason we were ahead of Luca's hackers in finding out what had happened to Natalya was because an online vigilante we worked with had access to clandestine databases and surveillance.

"Hell no, especially not now." Besides keeping tabs on Grigori Petrov, I had my hands full unraveling the mystery of Natalya's disappearance. There were more public cam sightings of her, but we were selective of what information we fed Luca's team looking for Natalya. I didn't want to get my uncle's hopes up and then disappoint him when our leads led to nowhere.

"You need to spar with Ivy," Nico told Sandro, while shooting his glance over to where the women were chatting.

"Are they still talking about the serial killer on the loose?" I asked.

The Mistress Strangler had seen a resurgence in headlines in the past three months after the unsolved murder cases four years ago. One of my contacts in the feds said that the killer might have gone to jail on a different charge and was recently released. Or it could be a copycat.

"Well, the wives are happy," Sandro chuckled. "No one wants to be their husband's mistress right now."

"Yeah, Sonny said the same thing," I replied. "Fewer complaints from the wives. You wonder if the killer was a woman."

"So your underboss is handling the wives?" Sandro asked.

I shrugged, but I was on guard with his question because historically, being single was a disadvantage to becoming boss and I couldn't use Luca as an example anymore. Ma was constantly fielding arranged marriage proposals from other organizations, but she had her heart set on a union with the Zahkarov bratva.

The women erupted in oohs and aahs.

"That doesn't sound like serial killer talk," Sandro mused. As usual, the husbands were attuned to their wives' interests and collectively moved toward them.

I followed more leisurely, internally rolling my eyes about how pussy-whipped they were, when Sandro said, "I didn't know Sloane was dating."

"He's hot," Ivy gushed.

"Hey," Nico growled.

I found myself shoving Sandro aside to look over Bianca's shoulder and a vein popped in my temple.

I nearly blurted out, "that's her neighbor," but caught myself. I turned around and walked away, whipped out my phone and texted her.

ME

We had a deal.

AND WHEN THERE WAS NO RESPONSE.

I'm not done with you.

"Dinner is ready!" Ma announced from the mouth of the living room. Her eyes fell on me. "What are you doing there, Dom, ignoring your cousins?"

"I had to settle a situation."

"What situation?" Sandro asked. His eyes were studying me intently. If I left now, there would be more questions.

"Nothing that concerns you," I shot back in a tone so unlike one

I'd ever used. Terse. Irritated. I was always the annoyingly cool one.

His brow lifted.

"Hey, don't be mean to my husband." Bianca planted herself between us. Normally I would find it hilarious for my dear cousin to think that anyone could be mean to Sandro without consequences. He used to be a deadly contract killer before he became the boss.

I put on my signature charming smile. "I wouldn't dream of it. Come on, cuz. Let's see what our moms cooked."

Sandro, Bianca, and I followed the others to the dining room. "I invited Sloane to this dinner." Bianca was talking to Sandro. "But she turned me down. She likes Mom's cooking and usually doesn't say no."

Probably because she was avoiding me. Admittedly, I'd been an ass to her. I checked my phone. No response.

So I typed:

ME

Don't ignore me.

"She probably didn't want to make the trip, baby," Sandro replied. "Traffic has been a nightmare."

"True. The subway is no picnic either," Ivy said. "Several lines are under maintenance."

"It's just she's so alone during the holidays," Bianca mourned.

The guilt burrowed itself deeper into my chest.

"She's been busy with school, right?" Sandro said. "Maybe she just wants to chill."

"Well, she wanted to go out tonight. I think her finals are next week, so she's trying to blow off steam before then."

Fuck, it better not be with Phil Harding. Yes, I had a file on him already.

I sat away from my mother, Sandro, and my cousins. I ended up sitting beside Cesar, who was at the head of the table. My dad sat beside him, so we were face to face. Ivy was on my left, but she was busy chatting with Nico and Sera.

My father, Paulo De Lucci, or Paulie, was Ava's best friend before she even started a relationship with Uncle Cesar. Pop and Ma were already married, and I was four years old by then. That was why I was closer to Luca's age than I was to my cousins, despite Pop being younger than Cesar.

Both Uncle Cesar and Pop stayed out of the made man business, so they rarely bugged me about my shit.

"Dom," Cesar greeted. "All's well?"

"All's good," I lied. I was itching to get out of this dinner and go to New Jersey to confront Sloane. For weeks, I was able to pack her into a corner of my mind, which I took out to play with when I wanted to jack off in the shower or when I woke up dreaming about her. Fuck, those dreams were getting worse and worse and I was getting flashes in the middle of the day of our writhing bodies. I was hoping to squeeze in a weekend with her before Christmas, but the longer I didn't text her, the harder it became to do so. I knew I was behaving like a dick and at the same time I was trying to excise her from my mind after Ma reminded me of my family obligations. Not that I was considering the arranged marriage, but while working on Grigori to get the properties back, it was hard to be around Sloane.

We made the rules to this affair. We were just hookups. But I was possessive. Probably a trait I inherited from the De Luccis. No one was going to fuck her until I was ready to let her go. But what did I do at the first sign of her moving on? I was in danger of losing my shit.

Hypocrite much?

Pop gave me that concerned-dad look when he handed me the appetizer plate they were passing around. I shrugged and gave him a tight smile. Good thing Cesar pulled him into a conversation about the latest real estate deal Matteo and Nico were negotiating.

The seconds passed excruciatingly slow. Sloane wasn't answering my texts, but I was tracking her phone. She moved to another pub on the waterfront. At least she hadn't gone home with that fucker yet. I couldn't help myself from typing another text.

ME

I'm coming over. You won't be able to sit for a week.

I was looking forward to spanking her. I wasn't sure if she was into that shit, but I was feeling very aggressive right now in showing her she was mine…

Fuck…I caught myself.

She was mine…until I declared we were over. I controlled whatever the fuck we were.

"You're not eating, Dom?" Ma asked.

Fucking Ma. Then I apologized to the Lord for cursing my mother. Everyone's attention swung to my sparse plate.

My eyes met Pop's again. I could feel Cesar's stare burn the side of my face.

"Uh, I had a late snack at the club." Then I leaned over to look at Ava at the other end of the table. "But you know I love your cooking."

"I can pack you a box in case you get hungry later," Ava said.

"Hey, I thought I was getting all the leftovers," Nico grumbled.

Ivy laughed. "They might think I don't feed you enough. Although, come to think of it, you do most of the cooking."

"No need, Aunt Ava." I tapped my wineglass. "Just need to drink some more." Maybe an entire bottle.

"So it seems Luca and Lucy are spending Christmas with us," Pop piped in, distracting everyone from my uncharacteristic silence.

Excited chatter exploded about their impending visit. We called Lucy Luca Junior. I didn't know how that started, whether it was because their names appeared similar on paper or it was my sister's rebellious attitude, which Luca seemed to approve of.

After getting a reprieve with the help of Pop's diversion, I forced myself to get a grip and eat a decent serving of the roast lamb and cheesy Brussels sprouts I'd normally wolf down and have second servings of.

Dinner lasted an agonizing two hours before I could leave with a valid excuse that I was needed at Cardo—a De Lucci-owned dance club. Our special rooms were fully booked months in advance, more so for the holidays. I jumped into my Ferrari, debating now whether I should switch vehicles, knowing I'd be parking on the street, but the desire to get to New Jersey as soon as possible won out.

When I arrived in Hoboken, it took me another half an hour to find parking. I was gritting my molars so hard because Sloane's location showed she was on her way back to the apartment. When I finally squeezed my sports car between a Dodge sedan and a pickup, I hustled over to her street and watched her dot move, thankful for the traffic slowing her down.

It was a chilly night, but I was steaming in my suit and overcoat. I loosened my tie and blended into the shadows in front of Sloane's building. I glared at my phone, specifically at her location dot approaching.

A white sedan pulled up beside the space by the fire hydrant in my line of sight. I could tell there were two people in the back of the vehicle.

The fucker stepped out to the traffic side first. He tried to round the vehicle quickly to help Sloane out, but she didn't wait for him. When he put his hand on the small of her back, the muscle beneath my left eye started twitching.

I was done watching.

I emerged from my stakeout position and crossed the street, my eyes still glaring at the hand on her back. They must have seen my rapidly advancing figure reflected on the glass door because they stopped and turned my way.

My eyes narrowed at the coat over Sloane's shoulders. It was a man's coat. His coat.

"Dom, what are you doing here?"

"I texted you, baby," I replied.

The fucker had the sense to drop his hand from Sloane's back, but was an idiot not to move aside. "I thought you didn't have a boyfriend."

"I don't," Sloane replied instantly. "Dom is the cousin of one of my best friends."

I raised my brow at Sloane. I derived fleeting amusement from the awkward way she tried to explain who I was to her. She could hardly say friends with benefits now, could she? Although at this moment, I was more frenemy with benefits. I was definitely more than a hookup or a fuck buddy.

But Phil's next words sent my already simmering temper skyrocketing. "Is he harassing you?"

I erased the space between us and snarled into his face. "Fucker—"

Sloane grabbed my arm to yank me away, practically shoving me inside the building as she muttered breathlessly, "I'm sorry, Phil. No, he's not harassing me, but I got this."

"You sure?" He followed us inside.

"Yes."

He was lucky my need to pound into Sloane was stronger than my need to pound him into the wall. Searing possessiveness entangled itself inside me, locking muscle and sinew. Possessiveness wanted to explode out of my skin. And with the way Sloane was clinging to my arm, she was sensing it too.

I frequently diffused tense situations, not caused them. I watched over people who I considered family. Sloane was an outlier, an undefined entity, because the urge to say "fuck it" was overwhelming.

Instead of giving in to planting my fist in Phil's face, I whipped his coat off her shoulders and shoved it at him. "I believe this is yours."

He shot me a glare, and I returned it with a smug smile. I even felt a little sorry for the prick. He must have paid for the ride and the drinks, but I was the one going up to Sloane's apartment. I fell back behind her, just because I didn't like how short her skirt was, and Phil was still at the bottom of the staircase.

I didn't want him seeing up her skirt.

She dressed up for him?

Wait. Did he already put his hand up her skirt?

"You have some nerve," Sloane muttered when he was out of earshot. "Showing up here just because you think I reneged on our agreement."

"You were ignoring my texts."

Sloane laughed without a measure of mirth. "And you? I didn't hear from you for weeks."

There were two more floors before I stripped her naked, or maybe I was gonna spank her first.

"And you sent that picture to get my attention?"

"That colossal ego of yours is like the size of an overgrown tumor." She muttered the words under her breath and stomped up the steps ahead of me. *Just a little more defiance, Firecat. You're getting me so hard.*

Sloane unlocked the door and walked in. With the way she

disappeared into the bathroom and slammed its door, she was as furious as I was.

The water started running.

"Sloane."

"Would you give me a minute, you fucking jackass."

The edge and irritation in her voice sent warning bells through me that the evening wasn't gonna end in cathartic angry sex. I sensed these things. There was zero sexual tension coming from Sloane. In fact, it was like she was done with me.

In retrospect, and if I was thinking like a sane person, she had more reason to be pissed at me because I kinda ghosted her. Kinda…because we had no expectations of each other. And from what I'd learned about Sloane so far, she was a practical girl. No nonsense. This woman wasn't pining for any man.

I waited patiently for the water to stop running. Was she showering in there?

When she finally came out, I was leaning against the wall.

"You could have waited for me in the living room." She made a feeble gesture with her arm.

"I'm fine right here." My eyes studied her. Why didn't I notice her pinched expression earlier? *Because you were all about your outrage, asshole.* "Did you get sick?"

"No," she groaned. She was still wearing her tall boots and shuffled to the couch and plopped on top of it, falling sideways, burying her face in a pillow. Ginger immediately jumped up, but Sloane pushed the cat away. "At least not from the alcohol."

"What is it, Sloane?"

"I'm feeling nauseous," she whimpered, drawing her legs into herself in a semi-fetal position.

A chill crawled up my spine, and I walked toward her like I was approaching a coiled cobra. "Are you pregnant?"

Might as well get that question out of the way, no matter how the thought made my erection deflate and my balls retract.

She laughed into the pillow. "No, jerk, I got my period. The cramps are killing me."

"Oh." Relief swept through me and the weakening in my limbs made sitting down a good idea. As I sank into the couch, I thought of a sympathetic response to say. Somehow, saying *I don't mind period sex* would come off as insensitive, even as a joke. I had a partner before tell me sex helped with cramps. I didn't mind messy. I didn't mind blood. But I did mind when a woman was uncomfortable with it, and judging by how pale Sloane's lips were, she would feel better sleeping it off. There was an overwhelming need to make her feel better. I wasn't down about leaving her alone, especially when I'd decided to spend the night with her.

"You're not getting sex tonight."

"I'm getting that," I clipped. How dare she think I would be so selfish with my needs when clearly she was in pain? I wanted a woman to enjoy sex. I might not be husband or boyfriend material, but if we were talking about ego, I prided myself on giving a lady pleasure first.

She snorted. "I should have ended it with you right outside if I didn't think doing it in front of Phil would bruise your outsized ego."

She was ending it? Whatever *it* was?

"We're not talking about this right now."

"I don't care," she said and shifted with difficulty on the couch.

My mind was contemplating on what to do next, and since I was still wearing my overcoat, I walked back to the pegs right beside the entrance to figure out my next moves.

After she realized I wasn't leaving, she croaked, "What are you doing?"

"It looks like you need help." I folded my suit jacket over the couch.

"I'm fine. Just go," she groaned. "Let's just end this now. It's a sign."

"Fuck your sign," I snapped. "I'm not leaving you here while you're in pain."

"It's not the first time. This will pass overnight. I just need to sleep it off."

"Well, you don't look comfortable. Should you transfer to the bed?"

"It's a new mattress. I don't want to ruin it."

"I'll buy you another one."

"Dom!"

"You can't kick me out," I said with determination. "I'm staying and taking care of you."

CHAPTER
Ten

Sloane

"Ugh, you don't have to do this." I didn't have the energy or temerity to argue, but Dom was already on his knees removing my boots, and when he liberated my feet from them, I could've wept in relief. I couldn't even bend down in the bathroom to unzip them, because the second I folded over, I would collapse on the bathroom floor. The only thing I managed was to change my underwear, put in a fresh tampon, and splash water on my face. Not necessarily in that order. "This is not part of the arrangement."

"Quiet," he ordered, spearing me with a censuring gaze. "As a friend, I would have had the decency to do this at least."

He scooped me up in his arms and headed to the bedroom. "Would a warm bath help?"

"Yes." When he was about to lay me on the bed, I said, "Lay a towel on top of the sheet. They're in the bathroom closet."

The way he set me gently on my feet made my heart squeeze. It was as if I was an injured kitten. The sound of the bathtub faucet running made me smile. For a hookup who wasn't getting any sex, Dom was going above and beyond. He returned with a towel and set it on the bed.

I sank into the high-end mattress that Dom bought to replace the one he ruined.

"Where are your pajamas?"

"They're in the corner." My closet space was probably five percent of his, maybe even less. I usually had to swap out my clothes for the seasons. He came back with a set and went directly to the dresser to open the top drawer. He'd seen me get underwear from there, so I wasn't surprised that he had my change of clothes ready.

"Do you want tea?"

"Dom, you've done enough."

"Well, since I'm here, I want to offer you my services."

"That's quite a one-eighty from your rude texts earlier."

He winced and sat on the bed and stroked my leg. "I'm sorry. I was being an ass."

I waited for him to elaborate.

He huffed. "I should have responded to your last text about the bed."

"Why didn't you?" I challenged. "I don't like games and the only reason I didn't respond to your texts earlier was because you were like a dog with a bone." When his eyes flared, I added, "Don't deny it."

A muscle worked in his jaw, as if still debating whether to deny my accusation or admit to it. "I wanted to see you, but family business required my full attention."

"I'm not asking for a lot. The reason this was supposed to work was because we were both too busy for a relationship." A faint smile quirked my lips. "The sex is great, Dom, but show me respect.

My time is as valuable as yours. If you can't see me as an equal in that regard, then this ends now."

My body was struggling with the pain in my pelvis, but I held his eyes. I thought he was going to scoff at my words, use his position as boss to belittle what I did, but by now I'd concede that one reason I was attracted to Dom was because he was one of the good-guy mobsters. I'd met a lot of assholes where misogyny and entitlement were embedded in their DNA, a birthright, but the De Luccis were more evolved, judging by how Bianca, Sera, and Ivy were thriving. Bianca's mom Ava headed a successful Irish pub franchise, and I heard how her husband, Cesar, empowered her.

My information was sparse regarding Dom's parents, other than his mother was the sister of Luca, the Chicago crime boss who Bianca wasn't too fond of.

So Dom was still a wild card to me, but if he'd been a doctor, I would've commended him on his excellent bedside manner.

"Do you have a heating pad?"

That question caught me unaware, and at the furrowing of my brow, he said, "What? I have a sister."

"Her name is Lucy, right?"

"Yeah."

The only time I'd seen her was at Bianca's wedding. She was one of the bridesmaids.

"So, were you a doting older brother or the type who dismembered her Barbies?"

"That last bit was oddly specific. But I was both." He winked and rose to his feet. "I'll check on the water."

I hugged my knees to my chest as another cramp hit me, but my thoughts drifted to Dom's sister. From what I'd gleaned from my chats with the girls, Lucy was the rebellious child of the De Luccis. She didn't get along with her mother, but I didn't remember why. She seemed to get along with Bianca and Sera at the wedding, although I wouldn't describe their interaction as spontaneous. It was more typical of a relative who you see during the holidays and not the daily-text-exchange type.

Dom returned. "Ready, Firecat? I'll undress you in the bathroom."

"I can walk," I protested, but he'd already lifted me.

"Why deny yourself a full-service spa experience?" he drawled.

"I don't want to get used to this," I argued, but I burrowed deeper into Dom's chest. This was surreal. I'd seen flashes of his caring side, his ideal-boyfriend material side, and at times it made me wonder why he wasn't in a relationship. Then these past two weeks of silence reminded me why. But he followed it with this. I had to remind myself that the reason I didn't want to ask for help from other people or depend on other people was because then I wouldn't get hurt when they abandoned me. If Dom hadn't texted me for another week, I would have moved on and excised him from memory and never given him a chance again.

What if I hadn't sent that picture to Bianca? Would he be here?

When we entered the bathroom, the tight space was already filled with steam. Dom set me down, and helped me out of my dress, and slid off my panties.

He kissed my forehead before turning me around and kept my back warm in my nakedness while we waited for the tub to fill up.

"I wish I could have rinsed first before getting in there," I said. Dom's chin was resting on my shoulder.

"And I wish I could get in there with you."

Despite my wooziness, I laughed a little. "Your long limbs would make it hard. I can barely fit in there."

My tub was tiny. I was lucky this unit had one at all. But it was a combo tub and shower. Dom must have found my lavender bath bombs because the scent reached my nose and it was soothing.

"Come on, baby." Dom edged me closer, bent past me, and shut off the water.

"I need to remove my tampon." My cheeks burned. "Can you..."

I was about to ask him to leave the bathroom when I felt his fingers between my legs.

I gasped, "Dom!" and squeezed my thighs together, trapping his wayward hand, my mind spinning on what he was about to do.

He lowered his head by my ear, "Open, baby."

"What are you doing?"

"Removing your tampon."

"I can do it myself," I hissed, but he continued to wedge his hand higher.

He nipped my ear, temporarily weakening my resolve and releasing the press of my thighs, and allowing him to touch my pussy. He inserted his fingers.

My cheeks were on fire. No, scratch that, my entire body was on fire.

"Dom," I said his name weakly.

"See," he murmured by my ear. "Was that so hard?"

"You're impossible."

"Blood doesn't deter me. Haven't you figured that out yet?" He wrapped it in tissue and discarded it in the wastebasket. He rinsed his hands before coming back to help me into the tub.

"I'll get you all wet."

"You worry too much," he said. "Now, just relax."

When I settled in, Dom stood and stripped down to his boxers. Then he grabbed the sponge hanging by the shower handle and lowered to a crouch. "How's the water temperature?"

"Perfect." I closed my eyes. The hot water gradually penetrated my muscles. I felt the sponge glide on my back in circles. I leaned forward and let Dom massage my lower back. He circled round and round in soothing therapy. The pain in my belly dulled.

"Better?" Dom asked huskily.

I popped one eye open. "I don't want to leave the tub."

"Let go, baby. I got you."

I WAS SUBMERGED IN A COZY HAZE. SOMETIMES I EMERGED FROM the cocoon of warmth, and at times I retreated. My limbs were lethargic, yet my whole body was alive. A pleasant sensation low below my belly stole my sleep.

Dom was palming my pelvis and alternately rubbing the top of my mound. I was familiar with those sensations. It was the buildup to an orgasm.

"What are you doing?" I asked, voice scratchy.

He was curled behind me, and I could feel his erection pressing against my ass. I didn't know how we got from the tub to the bed.

"Did you know orgasms alleviate period cramps?" he murmured.

I had to smile. I was surprised he didn't propose this earlier instead of going through the trouble of running me a bath. But then again, I got the feeling Dom enjoyed taking care of people.

"Yes, the uterine muscles contract during orgasm and relieve cramps. Not everyone, though."

Dom chuckled. "I was thinking along the lines of endorphins." He started rubbing my clit. "Do you wanna?"

I was usually horny during my period anyway if the cramps didn't get to me first. I woke up with an orgasm pulsing between my legs the other night, but attributed it to Dom playing a starring role in my dreams.

Wetness pooled between my legs. I hoped we weren't making a

mess again, but I was greedy enough to take advantage of this new experience.

"Yes."

Dom groaned and circled my sensitive bud harder. He inserted his fingers. The slide of them was different. There was something so raw about it, so elemental, that my orgasm took me by surprise.

I cried out.

Dom withdrew his fingers and climbed over me so we were face to face. This time, he used the heel of his hand to prolong the pressure. Wave after wave, my orgasm pulsed through me.

"That's it…ride my hand," he rasped before silencing my scream with his ravaging mouth, so out of control, like my orgasms were fueling his desire.

I needed something else, though. I broke away from him and moaned, "I need you inside me."

Forget out of control, my request turned him feral. Pushing my knees up to my ears, Dom rammed inside me.

He pounded me fast and hard until I was coming again.

"Fuck, Sloane, fuck," he growled. "You feel so good, baby."

His cock turned rock hard. His agonized eyes met mine before he squeezed them shut and groaned deep. He grunted. He continued to pump, but his hooded eyes assessed my face as if searching for discomfort.

When a lazy smile stretched my mouth, his expression softened, then he withdrew and looked between us.

"There's a theme of blood each time we have sex," I laughed lightly.

"We should do a blood exchange next." Dom rolled on his back.

"I need to get cleaned up again."

"In a minute." Dom flung an arm and a leg over my body, effectively trapping me. "I'm enjoying this post-coitus."

"Post-coitus. How romantic."

He nuzzled my neck. “I really am sorry for being an ass.”

“Let me get this straight. You’re sorry for today. For simply showing up here after I didn’t answer your texts.”

“That…and…” He exhaled heavily and let me go to sit up. “I know it’s not fair to you. I don’t want to stop sleeping with you, but this month is going to be hectic as fuck.”

“I’m busy too,” I retorted.

“Finals, right?”

“Yep, and then it’s winter break.”

“Have the Russians been bothering you?”

“Nope, they’ve been quiet. I haven’t heard from Billy.” Which was a good thing.

Dom merely nodded and muttered what sounded like, “That’s good. That’s good.”

“Is there anything else? Because I really want to hit the shower, wear jammies, and sleep the entire weekend.”

“Sloane, I’m going to have to take other women to holiday events. This was scheduled before—”

I held up my hand. “We’ve already talked about this. As long as you don’t have sex with them—”

“If it becomes too hard for you…”

“Stop, okay?” I rolled out the other side of the bed and padded around it to get to the door. “You’re making it complicated.”

“No, I’m not.” He jumped out of bed and clasped my arm. “Knowing that you were out with Phil—”

“You thought I was going to sleep with him?”

I shook my arm free and crossed my arms. “Wait a minute, you’re not suggesting while you take beautiful ladies to these galas, I’m not allowed to go out with guy buddies.”

He scrubbed a hand down his face in frustration. “You can’t deny that Phil wants to get into your pants.”

When I didn’t say anything, he put his hands on his hips as if saying *I rest my case*, but I couldn't help admiring his toned abs and his semi-erect cock which hadn't fully gone down.

"Baby, if you continue looking at me like that…"

"And I'm sure the women you take to these events want to sleep with you."

"But I'm not remotely attracted to them."

"Neither am I with Phil and if you say he's a man and he could take advantage of me, see yourself out."

His jaw clenched. "I'm worried about you…what if I assign you a bodyguard?"

"Hell no."

His phone went off. Taking advantage of his distraction, I slipped out of the room and into the bathroom. Physically, I was feeling much better, but my brain was fuming at Dom's double standards and it was giving me a migraine.

I was already in the shower when Dom came in.

He yanked the shower curtain aside. He was dressed.

"You're letting out the heat."

His answer was to grab the back of my skull and plant a forceful kiss on my lips.

"That was the club. I'm going to call or text you tomorrow. I'm not disappearing for weeks again." He released a fractured breath. "We'll figure this out."

He followed that with a lighter kiss and closed the curtain.

There was something in Dom's voice that sounded like surrender. I wasn't sure how I felt about it because that would mean I needed to give in a little, too. But what he didn't understand was I had more to lose.

Right now, I needed rest and to prepare for a week of tests.

CHAPTER
Eleven

Dom

"Thirty minutes to ball drop, Zio. What are you doing out here?"

Luca was standing on the balcony of a private room at Cardo. It was New Year's Eve and the party was getting too loud and too festive for my uncle. Since he arrived last week for Christmas, it had been gut-wrenching to witness his struggle. He smiled only for his son, and at times, sadness would cloud his features. It didn't take a genius to guess he was thinking of Natalya and wishing she was at his side. The second Elias was out of sight, Luca's face transformed into a remote, chilly mask.

I debated whether it was wise to secretly feed that cam sighting of Natalya to his hacker team back in November. It might not even be Natalya, just someone who looked like her. Now, weeks later, and without further leads, I worried about Luca's sanity.

He turned to face me. "I checked on Elias."

Luca had brought his longtime housekeeper, Martha, and his soldier, Tony, to help look after Elias. For this visit, they stayed over at Sera and Matteo's Fifth Avenue penthouse so Elias and Gio could hang out together. "He should be asleep by now, right?"

"No, Samantha insisted on a pillow fort. They are watching the ball drop, too."

Second to Luca, my cousin Renz and his wife, Liz, took some convincing to leave their seven-year-old, Samantha, on New Year's Eve to celebrate with adults.

"I shouldn't have left Elias at all," Luca grumbled. He checked his watch.

"He'll be fine. Even Matteo and Sera were relieved to have an evening out."

Luca's mouth twitched as he glanced past my shoulder. "Sure about that?"

I turned around to see Matteo, Sera, and Liz already wearing their coats.

"Ready, Zio?" Sera asked. "Renz is waiting with the Expedition."

"Why are you guys leaving before the ball drops?" I glanced at Matteo. "Didn't you say you were looking forward to adult time?"

Luca clapped my shoulder. "When you have a kid, you'll understand." Then, addressing the trio, he said, "Give me a few minutes. I have something to say to Dom."

I stiffened, wondering if he found out about who was behind the cam sightings. Matteo's eyes briefly shifted to mine, and I figured he was thinking the same. Matteo was the head of the Archer Syndicate, so it was *his* head on the platter if Luca found out we'd been manipulating the information.

"Don't take too long," Sera said. "The penthouse is five minutes away, but traffic—"

"I know," Luca said. "Go on…"

When they disappeared, Luca faced me. "So, I was meaning to ask you, have you considered any of the arranged marriage contracts yet?"

"Did Ma get to you?" And why was he bringing it up now?

"She's mentioned it, and I told her you will look into it when you're ready." His gaze bored into me. "But now I wonder if it's because of that redhead you've been eye-fucking all evening."

Goddammit.

I thought I'd been careful by not singling out Sloane for attention and I was sure I would have succeeded if Ma hadn't planted the idea in Luca's head. Presented with a problem, he became a truth-seeking missile with a nose for bullshit. He'd also become shrewder and more ruthless with each passing year. All my efforts were concentrated on avoiding detection that I was helping him find Natalya.

Our goals were different.

His end goal was Natalya. Full stop.

The Syndicate's goal was to thwart human trafficking but it so happened that our goals intersected. Our latest intel indicated that the head of the most powerful mafia in Italy was connected to Natalya's disappearance.

"I hear she cleans for the Zahkarov bratva," he said.

Not to mention, I was also working on Grigori.

I nodded, my chest screwing tight. If Luca had suspicions, who else did?

"I'm the last person to lecture you about conflict of interest, especially with those villas involved that Lottie wants you to get back."

"And do you want them back?" I challenged.

His phone buzzed and he looked at the message. "I got to go." His eyes were somber when they met mine. "Do you love her?"

His question shocked me, and I was a little disconcerted. Luca was the last person I expected to ask me this. "Sloane and I are not like that." Did I just admit to Luca that there was something going on between me and Sloane?

"She's your mistress, then?"

If it were anyone but Luca, I would tell him to fuck off.

"No. She's too independent to be anyone's mistress. Look, I'm not comfortable discussing her."

"Fair," he replied and made a move to leave, but paused and turned back to me. "But let me be your cautionary tale, Dom. You're my nephew. I don't want you to end up stuck in purgatory like I am. In our world, you make a choice. You protect that choice with your life, *capisce*?"

For the first time, I saw the glistening regret in his eyes and it communicated the raw anguish he was experiencing tonight, the devastation Natalya's disappearance had inflicted on him that he couldn't move past, two years on. "Zio."

"I gotta go." His voice was gruff with emotion and I watched him go, shoulders drooped and defeated. A far cry from the proud Chicago boss I had known him to be. Luca would need a minute or two to collect himself before he faced the rest of the family.

I returned to the festivities. At least some of the De Luccis were still here. Cesar and Ava were standing beside Pop and Ma. Beside them stood my sister Lucy, who seemed bored. She arrived for Christmas and was staying until the New Year.

Nico and Ivy were in a huddle with Bianca, Sloane, and Divina, the wife of Sandro's underboss, Tommy. I was glad Sloane could join us tonight. I'd been dropping hints to Bianca to invite her to the family gatherings.

This past Christmas, the De Luccis and McGraths went on a Christmas lights tour of Manhattan. Sera organized the event and rented limousines, mainly to cheer up Luca and Elias, but Sloane was invited, too. The tour ended up at the De Lucci mansion where

Sloane and I snuck a hookup in the second-floor powder room. We nearly got caught by my mother, but that was the thrill.

We'd been better about communicating. I texted her daily. She'd been busy with her nursing exams and I'd been fine with her one-word replies.

I wasn't a texting guy. I lurked mostly in the family group chats. Sloane would send me a random meme. The queens of memes were Ivy and Bianca and they would send it to our family chat. Sometimes I'd forward one to Sloane, too.

Sloane caught my eyes across the room. I grinned. I hadn't been planning on kissing her at midnight because I wanted to keep an eye on Luca. But now I was free.

ME

Want to watch the ball drop in the Lava room?

She glanced at her phone and texted back.

FIRECAT

You're free now?

Yeah, Luca went home to be with Elias.

Aww...

My eyes scanned the room, making sure Ma wasn't looking for me. Sloane excused herself. Bianca said something to her, but Sloane yelled something back and walked away. It was seven minutes to midnight. We walked parallel to each other. God, she was breathtaking. I couldn't wait to wrap all that red hair around my fist. She was wearing that black dress the night I behaved like a jealous boyfriend. I didn't dwell too much on my reaction. I was possessive of her. End of. I wasn't sure where our affair was heading. I'd take the mind-blowing sex for now. Plus, that husky voice of hers got me hard in an instant and it also had the power to lull me into a deep, dreamless sleep. I slept better when I was with her and woke up refreshed.

I didn't see myself giving up Sloane anytime soon.

"Dom," a low voice spoke in front of me while I was busy looking to my left, fantasizing about the ways I would bend Sloane like a pretzel.

Shit. Sandro. Tommy was standing right beside him.

"Where are you going?" he asked. "It's almost midnight."

Instead of answering him, I stopped a server handing out champagne. "Where are your drinks, man?" I handed them each a flute. I didn't need one for myself because I had a bottle chilling in the Lava room.

"Go." I pushed them toward Bianca and Divina. "Enjoy the evening with your wives."

"I saw Luca…" Sandro started.

"Later, man. Gotta check and make sure everything goes off without a hitch."

Confetti, balloons, and streamers were set to fall at the stroke of midnight, but I didn't really give a shit other than their release camouflaged our escape. As I reached the corridors that led to different rooms, the sound from the party receded. Most of the guests had already taken their places. I'd already done my host speech. The DJ and emcee were entertaining the crowd with a banging playlist. My job was done.

I caught a flash of black. I crossed the carpeted path connecting to the parallel hallway and slipped up to Sloane.

A vision of shapely legs and a short skirt made me salivate. I'd been semi-hard all night thinking about starting the new year buried inside her tight, warm pussy. Fuck me. I wanted to do filthy things to her.

She paused at the end of the hall beside a bank of elevators and peeked to where she was expecting me. I crept up behind her, snatched her around the waist, and clapped a palm over her mouth.

She squeaked.

I moved my other hand from her waist to grab a tit and squeezed. "Gotcha, baby."

I hauled her towards the elevators. If anyone were viewing the CCTV, they would see me kidnapping Sloane and dragging her away, and maybe I'd earn my title as most eligible villain.

Once inside, I spun her around and pressed her against the wall.

"What are you doing?" she whispered into my mouth.

"I've been dying to be inside you all evening." I punched the number for the floor above us. My hand snaked under her dress, straight for her hot soaked center, and plunged in. "You're dripping all over my fingers, Firecat."

The short ride interrupted my exploration, but the caveman in me wanted to dominate. When the doors slid open, I tossed her over my shoulder.

"Dom, what the…" She pounded my back.

My hand caressed her round ass.

Mine.

Sloane once complained about her curvy ass, but I debunked her of that notion by leaving possessive marks on it with my teeth and fingers. After sex, it was one of my favorite activities to do while I recharged and then fucked her all over again.

The Lava room was two doors from the elevator. A floor-to-ceiling window overlooked the celebration below. With the change of plans, I was restrategizing the many ways I was going to worship her body. I entered the room, kicked the door closed, and lowered her.

I checked my watch.

Five minutes until midnight. I sauntered to the ice bucket of chilled champagne. "Take off your underwear and face the window with your legs apart."

Sloane crossed her arms. "Make me."

Electricity pinged between us. *Oh, baby, wanna play? I'm game*. Amusement curved my lips as my gaze shifted to hers. "You want it rough?"

"I got all wet when you surprised me from behind and covered my mouth."

My movements froze while the predatory instincts I'd been harboring toward her all evening heated my veins. I lowered the champagne and prowled toward her. Her throat bobbed.

"Do we need a safe word?"

"Or I can just kick you in the balls."

That sass. I would take pleasure in choking her with my cock, but I was desperate to have the walls of her cunt strangling the life out of it instead. Tense need stiffened my posture.

"Just so we're clear, you want me to force you?"

"Yes. It's called consensual nonconsent."

I occasionally went to sex clubs and became familiar with this kink. I chuckled and her mouth was forming a smile when I surprised her and spun her around. Pushing her toward the couch, I shoved her to her knees and bent her at the waist so her upper body was splayed across the couch. Capturing her wrists in one hand, I unbuckled my belt and whipped it off. She tried to buck me off, but having people in this position was second nature to me and it wasn't always a sexual scenario. I leaned over her. "If I'd known you had the rape kink, I would have prepared better."

"Fuck you."

She continued to struggle, and I lined my erection between her shapely ass, letting her feel how much she aroused me. "Soon, baby."

I looped her wrists together behind her back. I was so hard for her, I could rub myself and come right there, but why deny her a fantasy?

I got up to get the champagne.

Sloane knee-walked a turn so she could glare at me.

"What?" I smirked. "I was getting the champagne."

Three minutes to midnight. "You look so pretty on your knees."

"Go to hell."

"Tsk, tsk, such language."

I tipped the bottle and drizzled it all over her.

"Ahhh…shit, Dom, that's cold!"

"It's not. Stop being a wimp and you're supposed to be scared or pissed."

She glared up at me. I lowered my hand and thumbed her fat bottom lip.

"Baby, how I want to shove my cock in your mouth right now and have you gagging, but that'll have to wait. I'm going to lick every inch of you, starting with your cunt." Then I yanked her up. "Now, let's welcome the new year while you scream my name."

I positioned her against the window. It had a reflective coating that wouldn't allow anyone from the outside to look in, so anyone in the celebratory room who looked up wouldn't see Sloane spread-eagled with me feasting on her from behind. But with her hands bound behind her back, it presented me with a problem.

"Now, how do I get the dress off?"

Her eyes widened and her mouth parted. "Don't you dare."

"Shh…this is your fantasy, remember?" I was going by instinct now. The instinct to give her what she needed. The instinct to deliver on her kink. I reached for the knife in my ankle sheath. Fear momentarily passed over her features before her eyes flashed with rebellion.

That's my girl.

My fingers grasped the neckline of her dress and, making sure I shot her a villain-worthy smile, I sliced the fabric in two, exposing her tits and those pouty nipples.

"No bra."

"You asshole."

"Ah…ah…don't move." I traced the tip of the knife down her neck. Her pulse fluttering madly sent a gaping hunger inside me; I was drooling for a taste of her defiant fear. I tossed the knife away. There was more of this game to explore, but making her bleed wasn't on the agenda tonight. I sucked on a nipple.

"Get off me!" She fought and I bit her on the side of her breast. Leaving marks was my kink, but only with Sloane. I was self-aware enough to admit that I wanted to remind her she was mine because I didn't see her as often as I'd like. Her knee came up and I knocked it away.

The crowd below us roared. Less than two minutes to make her come.

I spun her away from me and flattened her chest against the glass.

"Are you sure they can't see us?"

"What do you think?" I rasped by her ear.

"Dom."

"You're at my mercy, got it?" I stabbed two fingers into her pussy. "Fuck, baby, you're soaked. Really, really soaked."

"Get off me!" She punched her hips back, then she immediately went slack. "Shit, did I scream too loud?"

I chuckled. "One of these days, I'm going to get you to a cabin in the woods and live out whatever fantasy you want."

As much as she was enjoying this, she hadn't completely surrendered her inhibitions yet. "Let go." The scent of her excitement hit my nose, and I forgot our game. Dropping to my knees, I dragged my nose up her thigh, letting my tongue lick up the traces of her arousal. I nipped the fat lips of her pussy.

"Ahhh, please..."

"Please what?" I murmured, inhaling her deeply. God, I'd been dreaming of this all night long. "Please let you go? Please make you come?"

"Make me come…"

"You've been a brat, haven't you?" I tongued her one last time before I discarded that flimsy fabric she called underwear. Without wasting another second, I buried my face between her legs and got lost in the pleasure of her taste.

My God, she was delicious.

Tongue plunging inside her, I unleashed my hunger and ate and ate, licking every drop she gave up. The revelry below us grew louder, and I wished I could hear Sloane's cries as I made her come. Her clit was swollen and she gushed all over my tongue. I licked every drop before realizing the countdown had begun.

I rose to my full height and freed her wrists, then I gently turned her around.

We stared at each other. She was panting. Her mascara had smeared, but she was still the most gorgeous woman I'd ever seen.

Tenderness and an unnamed emotion tugged at my chest.

The count hit one, and cheers erupted. "Happy New Year!"

"Happy New Year, baby," I murmured against her lips.

"Happy New Year," she whispered back.

Then we kissed, gentle, and then deep. I unzipped my trousers and freed my cock, then lifted Sloane against the window and fucked her.

CHAPTER *Twelve*

Sloane

Spring

Today was not a day when I was thrilled about landing my preceptorship in the emergency department at New Jersey Medical. In lieu of a Capstone project, I'd been offered a stint in the ER. Making friends during my last semester of clinical rotation was at the bottom of my list because my life was an oxymoron, if not hypocritical.

I went to school to save lives, but I worked for the mob to erase evidence that they had taken one.

It was not enough that I had to downplay my looks, but I had to dumb down my skills, too. But the instructors had noticed my deftness in drawing blood, my aptitude in making patient assessments, and my calm when dealing with surly relatives and had suggested I would be a good fit for the ER.

I couldn't tell them I had a lot of practice with the mafia.

Nurses weren't allowed to do sutures. They were considered minor surgeries only doctors should do. Nursing students weren't allowed to run IV lines on patients without close supervision. Procedures I had vast experiences with and were second nature to me. That was one reason I didn't make friends with nursing students. I didn't want them to be comfortable enough to ask me why I was so skilled with techniques which even a newly registered nurse would struggle with.

I made connections with the instructors and charge nurse who mattered to my goals. I didn't care if that didn't make me well-liked among my student peers. Because no one liked someone who was a know-it-all and made them look bad. And even when I dampened my skills, I wasn't one to wait around like my classmates who stood idle and complained of boredom because of nothing to do. There was plenty to do. The nurses were just swamped. So instead of wasting time, I hustled and asked the nurses who looked like they needed help. I was proactive in reading the patients' charts, so I'd already figured out what had to be done and all I needed was their approval. And I carried my clinical handbook at all times and memorized what I could. I drew blood, changed bedpans, fixed the beds, and familiarized myself with vitals. Grunt work, but a vital step to become a nurse.

But being in the ER surrounded by the aftermath of violence, the conflict of my two worlds was colliding.

"GSW to the chest," the EMT yelled as a gurney was wheeled in. "Suspected hemothorax." Unlike most of the GSWs coming through here, the man was dressed in an expensive suit and I spotted the equally pricy watch on his wrist. Dom had a similar one, and I was guessing it was the same brand that cost three times as much as a nurse's annual salary.

ER personnel swarmed. Nurse Addy was one of them, and she was my preceptorship mentor. Her shift was my shift. Instead of my six to eight hours, I'd been going eight to twelve.

I was still confined to patient intake and drawing blood. But just to be exposed to the rush of the ER and the variety of cases that came in made the grueling hours worth it.

But tonight was different because I spotted Anton walking in. When our eyes clashed across the room, he spun around and exited.

"Did you hear me, Sloane?" Nurse Addy asked.

I dazedly looked at my mentor. All the blood had drained to my toes. "Uhm…I'm sorry."

She frowned at me. "Here, finish taking the patient's information."

We burst into an ER exam room where X-rays were quickly taken.

But there was extensive damage. The patient coded, and after a few minutes of trying to revive him, the nurse called the time of death at ten twenty-four p.m.

This wasn't the first death I'd seen during my shifts, but somehow this one hit me the hardest because there was a part of me that felt responsible. That I was part of the problem.

Later I would find out that the patient was a lawyer. He'd been shot outside his office building and the police who'd come in considered it a mugging. So many questions. The people responsible had taken his wallet but left his expensive watch?

I was a zombie for the last few hours of my shift. Finally, in the locker room, Addy and I were preparing to go home.

"You did good today, Sloane," Addy said.

"Thanks."

"I noticed this last GSW hit you hard," she said. "We see all kinds of injuries in the ER and some deaths hit us harder than others. But there was nothing we could have done for him. His heart had too much damage."

"I know," I whispered, closing my locker.

"Take a break this weekend and recharge, all right?"

"Thank you, Addy."

I had taken the bus to the hospital. Now I wished I had driven the van tonight, but it'd become temperamental lately and I didn't have time to take it to the shop. I debated whether I should call for a ride, but I didn't want to waste money. Besides, I could never hide from the bratva if they wanted to find me.

A shadow detached from the dark corner of the building. I hated it when I was proven right.

Anton stood in front of me.

"Is that your work in there?" I asked.

"Is he dead?" he asked.

All my disgust and guilt about the situation shot through my head.

Fury erupted, and I slammed my hands on Anton's chest.

"Fuck you," I snarled. "Who do you think you are?"

I must have shocked him with my defiance.

"My brother may have sold his soul to the bratva, but don't think for a minute you can ask me for more. This hospital," I hissed, "is my life. My sacred space. You do not ask me to sacrifice whatever decency I have left."

Fingers grabbed my neck, and my head bounced off the wall. I started choking. Oxygen became a scarce commodity as my body fought for survival. Should I have kept my mouth shut? Should I have given Anton what he wanted? It wasn't just a fight to live, but it was a fight for my dignity. My soul.

I couldn't scream. My eyeballs bulged, so I couldn't glare. But my mind screamed.

Fuck you!

"*Suka*," he growled. "We own your brother. We own you. Just because we haven't bothered you in months doesn't mean you're free."

Black dots danced along the edges of my vision.

A rush of oxygen sent relief crashing through my limbs. He'd let me go. I hated that I sank to the ground, and I was close to tears.

He kicked my thigh. "Grigori likes you, but you're nothing special. If you cease to be useful, then you can start digging your own grave because that's how it's going to end."

He walked away. I didn't know how long I sat there, seized by an involuntary shuddering. I wanted to hide in some small town or another big city and be done with this bullshit.

Another nurse coming off shift found me and I made an excuse that I had a blood sugar crash. I didn't know how I got home.

I spent a long time in the shower as if the hot water would scald away my guilt. Finally, I crawled into bed. Ginger hadn't fussed when I came home. Dom still bought the expensive tuna for her, but I knew I was going to be late today, so I left her enough kibble.

My cat jumped on the bed. I was on my side, and she burrowed into my arms.

Exhaustion drained me, but my sleep was fractured. I kept seeing Anton shoot the lawyer. I kept seeing the lawyer being wheeled in, leaving a trail of blood.

Of blood erupting from his chest cavity like a fountain.

Then the patient sat up on the exam table and pointed a finger at me.

Anton's fingers tightened around my throat.

I started screaming.

"Sloane!"

But how could I scream when I was choking?

"Sloane, baby."

My eyes opened to see Dom's worried face.

"It's you," I rasped, and I winced at the pain needling my larynx.

The concern in Dom's eyes slowly morphed into rage.

Wait, was he mad at me? But no, he was glaring at my throat.

"What the fuck?" His fingers traced my neck. "Who did this?"

Dom

Some fucker strangled Sloane. She had fingermarks around her neck. Someone was going to die.

"What piece of shit did this?"

She grabbed the covers and pulled them over her head. "I can't right now."

I dropped to my knees, trying to rein in my anger because if Sloane was a victim of violence, my fury was the last thing she needed to see. "Talk to me, baby, please?"

I gently drew back the blanket to expose her eyes. "What happened?"

"Why are you here, anyway?"

"You haven't been responding to my texts tonight, and I got worried."

"Didn't you have a gala this evening?"

"Yes." And my date was pissed because she thought she was going home with me. It was the third event in a row that I'd asked her to be my date. The evenings always ended up with me taking her home.

"How did it go?"

Frustration at my inability to protect her clawed at me. "You're seriously asking me about an event when you're lying here hurt?"

"I can't talk about it."

And there it was. Suspicions scrambled my brain. It wasn't a mugging. It couldn't be the Italians, so it could only be the Russians. But why? I made sure Billy got sent away to Florida, involving him in a high-stakes gambling operation I'd partnered with Grigori. That way I had more control and cover for Billy in case he fucked up and keep the heat off Sloane. Meanwhile, Grigori had kept me dangling on the properties. He was saying he'd been in talks with their pakhan to sell them back to me.

But the properties weren't my priority right now. Luca had issued a lockdown last night. He wasn't forthcoming with information, but everyone I contacted in the Moretti crime family denied or blocked my calls. We were on edge not knowing what was going on, and that was why I panicked when Sloane wasn't responding to my texts.

And I found her strangled?

"Was it the Russians?"

Her lips trembled. "You can't do anything about it."

"The fuck I can't."

"You and Grigori have business together," she whispered. "Don't think I don't know that. Billy…you had Billy sent to Florida." At the narrowing of my eyes, she added, "He sent money for Harriet and called me. We had a chat. But this has nothing to do with Billy. It's just…my life associated with the mob is catching up with me."

Did that include me? No. I was projecting my own guilt because I was a part of the world responsible for the marks on her neck. We kept our relationship a secret. It worked fine until the inability to protect her started eating at me, especially now that Luca was up to something. He was in a tit-for-tat war with the Russians in Chicago, which made my association with the New York bratva treacherous. One wrong move and we could end up in a bloody war.

"I don't want to leave you here."

She pushed up on her elbow and then slowly rolled to a sitting position, swinging her legs off the bed so we were face to face. "I think we shouldn't see each other for a while."

"What? No," I growled. "I'm moving you to The Grindhouse." The Grindhouse was our building in Hell's Kitchen. The Syndicate and De Lucci crime family met in the basement we called The Underground. The first level housed the family's boxing gym and Jabbin' Java, Renz and Liz's café bakery. Above it were apartments and the third-floor unit was frequently used by the De Luccis for safe houses or simply a place to crash in.

"And what? Just advertise to the entire underworld that we're together?" She shot up to her feet and scampered out of the room, mumbling about needing water. I stalked after her. She filled an electric kettle and plugged it in.

"I need you to tell me what happened." Frustration gnawed at me.

"And what, Dom? What will happen, exactly? There will be questions. We are nothing more than an affair and it's becoming more complicated."

I wanted to grab her shoulders and shake her, but I settled for lightly clasping them instead. I was glad she didn't flinch, so whatever fucker strangled her didn't leave lasting trauma, although it might be too soon to tell.

"We've been good together. It's been working."

"Has it? Or has it been working more for you? You bring women of your social standing and class to all—"

"Don't you dare accuse me—"

"I'm not. It's not working anymore because it's hurting."

An unexpected nausea pushed up from my gut. It must have shown on my face, because Sloane's expression cracked with a misery that made me want to roar.

"I can't see a beautiful woman on your arm one night and then have you fuck me the next evening. This last time you came straight to me and her perfume was all over you."

"You made me shower it off, so it wasn't like I fucked you with her smell all over me." She flinched at my words, but I didn't regret them. The reason Sloane and I worked was because we were honest about what this was and now she was changing the rules? I normally would have had more decency than to go straight to her from the arms of another woman even if it was just for show, but our affair, plus my responsibilities as the head of the De Lucci crime family, were weighing down on me. Sloane was my escape.

I wasn't willing to give her up yet, and I certainly wasn't down with her being in danger from the Russians.

"I'll move.you to Venezia Tower. It's in Manhattan and I could get to see you more often and not have to make the hour and a half trip it takes to get to you."

Fury replaced the misery in her eyes.

"You asshole," she whispered.

"What? I'm the asshole?" I pointed at her neck. "This is what your desire for independence cost you."

"I happen to go to school in New Jersey."

"And look what happened!" I roared. "I have enough people I have to worry about and I don't have room to worry about you too!"

That inexcusable statement escaped my mouth before I had the control to stop it.

Her throat snagged, and tears filled her eyes. "Then don't."

But what did I do? I doubled down. "We agreed this needs to be drama-free and—"

The electric kettle shrieked.

"And I'm causing drama?" she shot back, ignoring the annoying screech of the appliance.

I walked over to shut it off and went to the cabinet to get her a cup. "What tea do you want?"

"Stop it, Dom! Stop trying to take care of me. I don't need your help. Get out."

I slammed the cabinet and faced her. "Are you ending it with me?"

"You said if one of us wanted to end this affair, there would be no questions asked."

"You think I'm going to abandon you after you got attacked?"

"There's nothing you could have done. It's not what you think, so don't go stirring up shit with Grigori because then it'll only make it worse."

"Just tell me what happened!"

She crossed her arms. "No. I don't owe you that. This ends now, Dom."

"This isn't over." I slipped out my phone and texted her the address of the Venezia Tower. "When you come to your senses, I want you to give the apartment a look."

"And become your mistress?"

"No." I closed the distance between us. "More."

"Mistress and more come with expectations, remember?"

I stroked the side of her cheek and gave her a firm kiss on her mouth. Anything more and I wouldn't be able to leave, but I had an emergency meeting at The Underground in an hour. I wasn't supposed to be in New Jersey. "Just give me time to sort my shit together."

"I'm serious, Dom. We're over."

I didn't answer her because I had none. I didn't make promises I couldn't keep. It killed me to leave her, but making sure she had protection wasn't up for discussion. I didn't have time to argue with her. I called in a favor to an associate in the executive protection business. This had to be covert. Knowing Sloane, she wasn't going to appreciate someone shadowing her. The De Lucci side of my family, including the Archers, had their hands full with whatever was going down with Luca.

CHAPTER
Thirteen

DOM

IT WAS SIX A.M. WHEN I PULLED INTO THE PENTHOUSE. FUCKING hell. Luca found Natalya. She had amnesia, so she couldn't tell him who was behind her kidnapping yet. Our minds were reeling with this turn of events. After more than two years of obsessively searching for her, he'd finally brought her home. Emotions of grief mixed with hope were a palpable ache in my chest. Grief for the lost years, not only for Luca but for their son, Elias. Hope because I would finally see my uncle happy instead of barely existing for the sake of his son.

But the challenges were only beginning.

And it seemed I had another challenge awaiting me at the penthouse.

She texted me earlier.

Only close family had access to my residence.

Lucy was one of them.

She was waiting in the living room, watching Manhattan wake up.

She spun around when I walked into the foyer.

"Is it true?" she asked. "Zio Luca found Natalya?"

"Yes. Who told you?"

The Archers and De Luccis agreed to keep this information on a tight leash, and I was glad I went to Sloane before we all met at The Underground. And I lucked out that Sloane needed space from me. It would give me more breathing room to deal with the family.

"Mamma." Lucy never outgrew the way my mother insisted on being called, and despite how my sister despised my mother's dream of marrying us off to suitable families with noble bloodlines, the Italian word for *mother* stuck for my sister.

"You can't share this with anyone, Lucy." I shrugged out of my suit jacket and sprawled on the couch, drained.

"Don't you think I know that?" she snapped and sat in the armchair across from me. I quirked a brow at her. She was in an oversized Georgetown sweatshirt over jeans. Her hair was in a ponytail, not the fancy twisted knot I usually saw her sporting.

"Are you staying?" I asked.

"Depends."

I vented an irritated breath. "Out with it. I'm fucking tired."

"I think I'm in trouble."

"What trouble?" Lucy reminded me of Sloane. Aggravatingly independent. She finished law school but never took the bar exams. Instead, she mingled with the DC crowd and had her own friends in high places. Being a De Lucci opened many doors, but her friends were the fucking elitists I steered clear of. Lucy hated the violence that was associated with the mafia. She was on Pop's side when I announced I was joining the crime family. She blamed our mother's method of guilt-tripping for my choices. What my sister didn't understand was I wouldn't thrive like Matteo and

Nico in the world of real estate and finance. I preferred backroom deals and blood oaths…okay, maybe not blood oaths. I liked making money. And I preferred if the government stayed the fuck out of it.

"A friend of mine, a lawyer, got killed last night."

I leaned forward, my annoyance at my sister swiftly changing to concern. I trusted my instincts and Lucy's. She handled her problems with her "I know a guy" routine. She knew that I knew that she was the go-to for the power players in DC for her ability to get information and dirt on people. A fixer's fixer. We just didn't talk about it. I had security on her and Lucy was aware of this. She just didn't want them tailing her like the Secret Service.

"When you say got killed…"

"He was shot as he was coming out of his law office and the cops already classified it as a mugging and it's not."

"Okay, why do you think it's not?"

"I just know."

"Lucy, I need more than 'I just know.' Jesus, you're a lawyer—"

"Technically, I'm not."

I jumped to my feet and sighed. "Come on. I think I'll need caffeine for this."

As we settled in the kitchen with our espressos, I asked her to continue.

"Wade was working on gathering evidence against Congressman Tomlin."

"Lucy," I groaned. "Of all the problems you bring to me—"

"He's corrupt, Dom."

"Most politicians are, especially the powerful ones. We have a couple of them who work for us too. And weren't you supposed to be a fixer, not the one to start a scandal?"

"Sometimes you fight fire with fire. My client wants to discredit Tomlin because of a bill they wanted to pass in congress, but it led me to Wade. He gave an interesting seminar about corporate corruption at Georgetown and we'd been friends ever since."

Fascinating that my sister was interested in corporate corruption when that was the lifeblood of the modern mafia. Sometimes I wondered if she was actively trying to put me out of business. I should pay attention to what she was doing. I'd always considered her crusade against the "mafia way" harmless, but she wasn't an idealistic college student anymore.

We were eyeing each other like a game of chicken. She was trying to get a confession out of me whether Tomlin was one of ours and I was just bluffing. He might not be one of ours, but he was definitely Grigori's guy and the Zahkarov bratva had bankrolled the congressman's campaign through one of their shell companies.

"So, are you worried that whoever killed Wade is coming after you? Is it because you're simply associated with Wade?"

"I have the evidence."

"Jesus fucking hell." I slid off my perch on the barstool before I gave in to the urge to throttle my sister, which reminded me of Sloane. I received a text that her bodyguard was in place. Just a temporary guy. She would need to be watched twenty-four seven.

"Where is it?"

"It's a who." She rounded the counter and stood before me with pleading eyes I hadn't seen since she was a child. "His witness has the evidence. I need you to keep her safe."

~

Sloane

Billy was back.

It had been two weeks since I ended it with Dom. Following our confrontation, the De Luccis had closed ranks, and the Rossis had closed ranks with them. I wasn't self-absorbed enough to think it was about me because I'd heard chatter about something big going down. I'd never felt more alone in my life and I was depressed enough that I welcomed my brother's company.

It seemed Anton had informed Grigori about my defiance at the hospital and found new ways to torture me. I was exhausted enough after my ER shifts, but Grigori seemed to have me back on his on-call rotation. And it was not only cleaning. A few jobs were assisting their mob doctor in surgery. I couldn't say I hated the work, but I was wary of what they had in store for me.

Especially since Grigori actually handed me money. It happened after one of those surgeries. Billy was helping me clean up all the blood in the basement when Grigori entered. Anton was with him.

"How's school?" he asked.

I stopped mopping and looked at him, startled by his question. He raised a brow.

"It's going well."

"You've been an asset to the organization, Sloane, and I think it's time we talk about your future in it." At this, Anton scowled, but quickly straightened his face. It appeared he wasn't on board with Grigori's plan.

"What exactly are we talking about?"

Grigori nodded. "We have connections in the New Jersey hospital system. Be a nurse practitioner? A nurse anesthesiologist. Be involved in bespoke healthcare with select membership?"

He looked around him. "You don't have to clean anymore."

My body went cold. I wanted to get out of here. I wanted to leave. I forced myself to keep my face neutral.

"You get to enjoy what you want to do." Grigori looked paler than normal. He had dark circles under his eyes. Stress? But I always wondered if he had a blood disorder. He certainly showed the signs of anemia. "Save lives." He glanced over at Anton. "Yes, he told me what you said. It was admirable really, and I think I've found the right person to be on my team."

Team. He meant criminal organization. One of his crew. Billy continued scrubbing as if he already knew about it.

I laughed nervously. "I have graduation to think about. And the NCLEX."

"Yes, yes." He waved his hand in an offhand manner. "You don't have to worry about that."

"I want to pass it legally and on my own merits."

"Ah, Sloane. Just think about it." He tossed an envelope on the table, motioned to Anton, and they left the room.

Billy approached the envelope.

"Don't you dare touch that!"

"What?" He smirked. "Afraid of blood money?" He gave a low whistle. "This looks like twenty grand." If there was one thing he was good at, it was flipping through cash to check denominations and then weigh it in his hand to tell how much it was. He was like a human money counter. Probably why Grigori liked using him in his casinos.

"What do you say, sis? Where are we going for dinner?"

Two thousand miles away from here. I snatched the envelope out of his hand. "Let's finish cleaning." It took us another hour before we could pack up and leave. We were on a side street when my stomach heaved. Seeing an alley, I yanked the van over, causing Billy to curse and hold on to the handle.

"What the fuck?"

I didn't even shut off the engine. I jumped out of the van and ran over to the side and retched, narrowly missing my work boots.

Billy's shoes appeared in my peripheral vision. "Are you pregnant?"

I laughed at the absurdity of the question. Dom always used a condom, and I was vigilant about taking my pills, but because of how hungry we were for each other, we always ended up having frenzied sex. Dom would remember gloving up after already thrusting inside me. There were several bouts of shower sex where the condom safety was in question. Shit. Shit. The last thing I needed was to bring a child into the fucked-up world I was trying to escape.

"No, I'm not."

Billy popped a can of Coke and handed it to me. I straightened from bending over, but I was still feeling queasy. "Do you mind driving?"

"Not at all."

When we were back on the road, I asked, "Would you come with me if I wanted to start over somewhere else?"

He hesitated before answering. "That's gonna be hard."

"You have to stop owing Grigori money. Do you still?"

"Nope. I was doing well in Florida, so I'm surprised he called me back. So yeah, I'm getting tired of this fuckery. It's like damned if I do, damned if I don't."

My stomach roiled again but for a different reason. It was looking more and more that Grigori was using Billy, deliberately making him fuck up so I would owe them. I was the target.

"Are you still using?"

He cast me an annoyed glance. "I've been sleeping on your couch for over a week. Have you seen me using or needing to use?"

"I'm sorry."

"What's up with you anyway, sis?" He was staring straight ahead. "You seem…subdued."

"I'm about to become a nurse, yet I work for the mob."

"Feeling like a hypocrite?"

"It's just a weight inside me." But the weight wasn't only my moral compass. I missed Dom with an ache hollowing my rib cage and I wondered if my stubborn independence finally made him see the light that I wasn't worth the trouble. Would it be so bad to be kept safe while he needed to do what he needed to do for his family? I went over this in my head with the time-out we'd given each other. It wasn't just my independence. If I were honest with myself, I was starting to want more. I was starting to resent him when he took other women to events. Events I had no desire to be at.

Resentment was a poisonous thing, so I pushed him away instead. The thing was, it was the same as cutting my nose off to spite my face. Maybe I should give in a bit more. Total silence from him after five months of daily texting and regular, fiery hookups was like cutting out an essential organ to live. Our stolen moments were frequently cathartic. A respite from my busy and tension-filled life. He was a bad habit. He wasn't good for me because I was using him as a crutch.

But the sex-only affair was a lie. Feelings for him slithered under my skin and it was too late to expunge them.

I missed Dom in two weeks more than I missed my brother in four months.

I gripped Billy's arm and pointed to the turn. "Make a right here."

"That leads to Manhattan."

"There's something I need to check out."

"You're the boss."

After another twenty minutes, I told Billy to slow down in front of the Venezia Tower. My eyes bugged out. It wasn't a new building but had the charm of the New Georgian architecture, typical of the 1940s. I couldn't imagine parking my clunker of a van inside that building. I couldn't imagine walking through the entrance that had a doorman in my coveralls or scrubs.

Okay, maybe scrubs wouldn't be so bad. The residents might think I was a doctor.

"Is that Dominic De Lucci?"

Startled by my brother's question and as though my imagination had conjured him up, Dom suddenly appeared at the side of the building. He was stalking after a tall, drop-dead-gorgeous woman with voluminous blonde hair wearing a hot-pink spring coat that probably cost ten times the rent of my apartment.

"I think so," I croaked.

"Looks like he's in the doghouse," Billy commented, idly amused and unaware that my heart had iced over before shattering inside my chest. Shards that shredded my vocal cords, making it difficult to respond.

I could only watch the incoming train wreck in agonizing slow motion.

Dom caught up with the mystery woman and gripped her shoulders, gritting words into her face. I found myself raising my phone and taking several pictures of the fighting couple. Then the woman freed herself from his hold and ran into the building, leaving him standing there frustrated.

I was so familiar with the set of his shoulders when he was out of patience.

I was more familiar with the way he raked his hand over his face.

The familiar deep exhale that followed.

Then he pursued her into the building.

"What are you doing?" Billy asked.

"Taking pictures for Bianca. She said Dom's been secretive about a woman." Not exactly a lie, although Bianca was too wrapped up in Sandro's problems to worry.

"You're done? Should we go home?"

Home. What a joke. I lived with my brother and a cat.

"Hey, how about we pick up dinner and pay Harriet a visit?" Billy suggested.

That lifted my spirits a little. "Shawarma?"

"Sounds good."

After placing the order, I couldn't leave well enough alone. I had to know where I stood with Dom, so I texted him.

ME

Can we talk?

I waited for a couple of minutes. When there was no response, I pocketed the phone in my coveralls' thigh pocket.

Later, Billy and I were in the assisted living home, having a comfortable dinner with Harriet. It reminded me of old times after Mom died and she was the one who looked out for us. Still, I couldn't help feeling edgy with Dom's lack of response.

He finally texted me two hours later.

DOM

Now is not a good time.

I waited for him to elaborate. He did not.

"What's wrong?" Harriet asked with her probing eyes.

Billy was oblivious, his attention on a game Harriet and I had no interest in watching.

"Shift change," I lied.

She smiled and patted my hand. "You're almost done."

Somehow, the sympathy on her face only made me want to dissolve into tears.

I exhaled a shuddering breath.

I should move on, because clearly, Dom had.

CHAPTER
Fourteen

Sloane

Another two weeks went by before Bianca revealed what the secrecy was all about.

Sandro was in an underground tournament called the Game of Bosses. But the biggest shock of all was Dom's uncle Luca found his wife alive and had his own fight against the Russians in Chicago.

My loyalties were to the Rossis. My affair with Dom didn't make me loyal to him. We kept it a secret for a reason. But a month of being shut out by everyone except Grigori of all people had taken its toll on my mental health. I woke up this morning hollowed out of purpose, and I struggled to get out of bed.

With politics between the Russians and Italians shoved to the forefront, those who didn't pick a side were left floundering. That was why Grigori was trying to lock me down to work for him. A cleaner like me couldn't play both sides. No matter how each job with the Russians felt like blackmail, I had a feeling choosing a side was imminent.

Grigori needed unquestionable loyalty. I didn't blame the Italians for keeping information from me. I was a weak link.

It made the address of the cleaning job worrisome. It was at the Venezia Tower unit 504.

"Did you know something that was going down tonight?" Billy's voice was suspicious. "Isn't that the building you had me do a drive-by weeks ago?"

Queasiness rocked my gut. I'd missed my period, but it could be from all the stress. I was oddly numb about the idea of pregnancy.

"I told you it was for Bianca. She gave me the address," I lied. "It's probably a love nest of sorts for mobsters."

"You could be right. Maybe Grigori whacked one of his girls."

I glanced at Billy sharply. "If you've been helping that asshole—"

"What the..." My brother's eyes widened, staring straight ahead and shouted, "Watch out."

My head whipped forward, my heart lurching in my chest with the most feeling it had in weeks. A blacked-out SUV screeched to a stop in front of us.

"Oh my God." My foot slammed on the brakes, but instincts had me reversing only to be blocked in by a police cruiser.

"Shit," Billy muttered in a way that told me he screwed up.

Dread slithered up my spine. "What's going on?"

"Stay here," my brother said. He got out of the van and jogged over to the driver's side of the black Chevy Tahoe.

He was arguing with the driver. My gaze shifted to the rearview mirror to see cops redirecting traffic.

Billy returned and said, "Follow the Chevy."

"What the hell is happening?"

"Sis, for fuck's sake, listen to me. Follow that Chevy and don't call any more attention to yourself. This wasn't supposed to go down this way."

I followed the SUV and crossed the intersection. "Are you a snitch?" Because that SUV had *feds* written all over it.

He didn't answer. He didn't have to. Five minutes later, the Chevy pulled into an alley and I parked right behind it.

Three men emerged, but betrayal smacked me hard when I recognized one of them. I couldn't trust anyone anymore.

My neighbor Phil stood right in front of the van. But he wasn't looking like the software salesman. He was in black tactical gear.

I glared at him and got out of the car. "I take it you're not a network security vendor."

"Sorry for this, Sloane."

"Who the fuck are you? Fed?" My gaze swept to his other companions. One was in a suit. The other was dressed similarly to Phil.

"Phil is fine."

"Fuck you."

"Listen, Sloane, you're on limited time. Grigori is expecting you at the Venezia Tower."

"You bugged my phone?" How? "What else did you do?" Oh my God. He would know about Dom. The familiar turmoil in my stomach started. I clapped a hand over my mouth, barely keeping down the tacos I'd eaten for dinner.

"I'm sorry." And he really looked apologetic, but it could all be an act. After all, he fooled me. "I cloned it. But I was under orders from my superiors."

His words went in and out of my ears like a faulty radio because I was drowning in the sea of repercussions of Phil being a fed. The outing at the pub. That was in December. That was the only time he would be close enough to clone my phone. Oh. My. God. I didn't care about Grigori, but the catastrophic consequences to Dom terrified me.

I could only manage more than a whisper. "If you want me to ghost Grigori, you better have new identities for me. My brother. And…and Harriet!"

"No. We want you to go through with it."

"Then I don't understand. If you want me to hand over evidence, you must know I never leave a job with it."

"We know that."

I glared at Billy, who had gotten out of the van and was standing motionless, letting Phil do all the talking. There was time to interrogate my brother later.

"And you're very thorough about it. You don't even leave traces of it in your vehicle."

I narrowed my eyes. His meaning clear. He'd broken into my van.

"We lost contact with our informant and we have a feeling the Russians got to her, so it was a break when they called you."

"Then what?"

"We're going to outfit you with a camera."

"Oh, hell no!" I snapped. "You're going to get me killed. Anton is going to be there, and he scrutinizes every inch of me, waiting for me to fuck up."

"Put it on me," Billy offered. "They tend to bypass me, thinking I'm dumb as fuck and wouldn't try anything like this." My brother winked at me.

"We're not sure what we're looking for, but our informant hinted about a thumb drive that could win the case for us." Phil looked at my brother. "He'll fill you in on the rest. You gotta go."

It took all of ten minutes to give us instructions. It wasn't hard to follow. They wanted me to be less than thorough with my cleanup. Plus, the primary objective was to know who was there, and that all important thumb drive.

When we were back on the road, and when I'd calmed down some and gotten oxygen back into my lungs, I asked Billy, "Fill me in."

"I didn't want to involve you, but you know you have that picture of De Lucci and their informant on your phone."

"The woman is a fed informant?"

"Or would-be whistleblower. They're trying to build a corruption case against a politician. I'm not clear about the details. But they want me to feed them information about Grigori's sex-trafficking ring, but it was leading nowhere because I got sent to Florida."

"So all these fuckups…" I whispered.

Billy exhaled heavily. "Some of them were my stupidity, but I found out Grigori became less guarded around me when he thinks I'm just a dumb henchman who did as he commanded, no questions asked. Phil approached me early last year after he'd moved to Harriet's apartment. The feds had been looking for the weakest link in the bratva." He gave a brief self-deprecating laugh. "Apparently that's me."

"So you're okay getting out?"

"Yeah."

I wasn't touchy-feely with Billy, but at that moment, I wanted to hug my brother. I settled for reaching for his hand and giving it a squeeze instead.

"I wish you'd kept me in the loop! We could have made plans."

"No, Sloane. You had enough to think about with school, with keeping Harriet in that nursing home…listen. Let's get through tonight…all right? Then see if we can get Phil and his boss what they want."

"They're just after Grigori?"

"The New York Russian bratva is too big to take down. They'll settle for the brigadier running the sex-trafficking operation, so yes, just Grigori."

"What did they promise you?"

"New identities for you, me, and Harriet. A fresh start somewhere."

I chewed on the chain of events. I thought back to the man who died in the ER, Wade Stephenson. His name was etched in my heart. I wondered if he was connected to all this, but if the feds were involved, then it would be a district attorney issue, not a corporate lawyer from New Jersey.

When we arrived at the Venezia Tower, we were directed to the rear entrance where we took the service elevator to the fifth floor. Anton admitted us into the apartment. He had scratches across his face and arms. He was wearing a shower cap same as I was because the cleanup job location wasn't owned by the Russians.

My eyes drifted to the room. The place was completely ransacked.

"Scope?" I asked because if they expected me to put the stuffing back into the throw pillows, they were dreaming.

"Blood and hair."

"Where's Kolya?" I asked. *Please say he isn't here because I don't want him double-checking my work.*

"He's out of town."

"The package?"

"Grigori has someone else taking care of it."

"Okay."

"Don't worry, Sloane." Anton laughed. "You're not dismembering anyone else yet."

And I never would because after this I was gone.

"Vacuum and mop the entire place. Wipe every surface clean," he continued. "I'm bagging the pillows and taking them with me, so don't touch them."

He was probably looking for the evidence.

"On it," Billy said and looked at me. "Why don't you take care of the blood?"

I unpacked my tools and cleaning chemicals. Crouching by the concentration of blood saturating the floorboard, I analyzed the scene. It appeared the subject hit her head and she was dragged across the parquet flooring. If there was any doubt about the identity of the victim, the strands of blonde hair mixed with the blood were very damning.

An hour had passed when Anton came back to me. "Sloane?"

He didn't tell me what he needed, but expected me to follow him into the bedroom. The nightstand lights were lit, illuminating a custom-built bed with luxurious bedding. My gaze numbly transfixed on that bed and wondered if Dom and the woman ever spent time on it. Although given the feds and Russians' interest in her, a large part of me still believed Dom's association with her wasn't sexual but a power play.

Still, I couldn't help fretting that he wanted to set me up in a luxurious place like this.

"Sloane! What the fuck?"

Jolted out of my torturous thoughts, I turned to Anton. "What do you need?"

"Go through the pockets. Any storage device, give it to me."

So she had evidence against the Russians. Was Dom making moves on the Russians and they found out because this building belonged to him?

Forty-five minutes passed, but we found nothing. The hot-pink coat I'd seen the woman wearing was hanging in the closet.

I was sick to my stomach how this life had spiraled so far into the dark side, every fiber inside me was screaming to pack Harriet and Ginger in the van and get the hell out of Dodge. Because if my only choice was working for the bratva, I would be left without a soul.

I didn't know Grigori's plans and endgame, but it only made sense he was making his moves tonight because the entire underworld was focused on the Game of Bosses. There was no other brilliant night to execute whatever plot he had in mind.

Anton left me to finish up and exited the room. He appeared agitated, and it didn't take two guesses why. He killed the only person who had the evidence that could incriminate them. But if the evidence was a thumb drive, then it would be floating out there. Anton was more brute than brains. He probably intended to knock the woman around. She slipped, hit her head, and died.

When I left the room, he was on his phone. "Done?"

I nodded.

Anton returned to the caller. "Okay, send them up. Make sure the cameras are on a loop. This needs to be quick and clean."

"Can Billy and I go now?"

"We'll all leave through the service elevator."

Billy and I exchanged a look. That sounded ominous.

Men in ski masks came in and hauled out the garbage bags. Anton was still on the phone inspecting my work. I held my breath. He didn't have Kolya's cold, meticulous eyes, but he had the malicious eyes of a bully.

"Let's go," he muttered. We rode the elevator in silence. Billy usually made conversation, but I guessed he was nervous because he was wearing the wire. Meanwhile I had a death grip on my cleaning caddy. We emerged from the building into the alley where I parked my van. Regardless of what the feds planned to do with us after, I was going to try to run.

Fuck this life.

I had enough money saved under Harriet's name. I could buy a new identity, except hauling an octogenarian with me could be tricky. It was up to Billy if he wanted to come with us, but I was done with Manhattan.

I was walking steadily to my van when Anton grabbed my elbow. “Grigori wants a word with you.”

“He can call me and set an appointment.”

Billy came between us. “Let my sister go, man.”

Anton whipped out his gun and pointed it at Billy. “You wanna say that to me again?”

“Why does he want to talk to me?” If Phil was seeing this, I hoped to cause enough delay for them to spring into action.

“Listen.” Anton lowered his head and snarled, “If Grigori says jump, you ask how high?” Another thing I despised with this Russian was his tough-guy clichés. I would have rolled my eyes, but the precariousness of our situation was trilling alarm bells in my head. He yanked at my elbow again causing me to drop the caddy. My brother intervened and shoved Anton with surprising strength that made the big guy stagger, loosening his grip enough for me to break free.

Billy grabbed my arm and we started running. We left all our shit behind.

I spotted Phil and his feds at the mouth of the alley.

“Come on!” Phil yelled.

Just when we dashed past our van, a shot rang out and a gunfight erupted.

Billy fell and dragged me down. I banged my knee. I was still gritting at the pain when I closed my hands on his shirt, attempting to yank him up.

“Go,” he roared.

“I’m not leaving you!”

“Get her out of here,” Billy growled just as hands closed around my biceps.

My body left the ground, swung up bridal-style and I was spirited away from the chaos.

Muzzle flashes flew past us and sparked against the dark alley walls.

I heard a grunt, and then my body was free-falling.

The pavement rushed up to greet me.

Blackness.

CHAPTER
Fifteen

Sloane

"Are you sure about this?" Phil asked while we waited in his parked SUV outside the Hummingbird Room.

"I'm sure."

Five days had passed since the shootout at the Venezia Tower. Phil was the fed who carried me out of there, but he was struck in the back. Fortunately, he'd been wearing a vest. I suffered a concussion.

One of their agents wasn't so lucky. A round struck his neck and he bled out instantly.

No word about Billy. Anton took him.

Phil kept me in a safe house. Without the thumb drive, they didn't have enough to prosecute the politician and incriminate the Russians other than breaking and entering the Venezia Tower. To make matters worse, their higher-ups considered the operation a bust and shuttered it.

Phil said it was to avoid blowback, and politics above his pay grade were at play.

The New York bratva and the De Lucci crime family had formed an alliance to insulate themselves from whatever Grigori had done. Apparently he'd been going against the wishes of his boss —the pakhan. Also probably why Grigori had gone to ground. His own bratva was hunting him down.

As for me, I was feeling like a stalker. Phil had only this week to watch over me before a new assignment would leave me on my own.

Dom's limo pulled in front of the Hummingbird Room.

Ambushing him in this manner was the last thing I wanted to do, but all my attempts to contact him failed. He might have blocked my number. I didn't want to involve Bianca, because I still didn't trust the feds. The ripple effect of this new alliance was unknown, and until I had more insight into it, I blocked the girls' numbers, too. It hurt to let go of my girl gang. Come to think of it, our closeness hadn't been the same since the New Year when the situationship between Dom and I heated up. In my attempts to hide the affair from them, I effectively alienated the girls into thinking I was too busy with nursing school to hang out with them.

Anyway, I was getting rid of my number after this. Getting rid of it and disappearing.

I braced myself when the limo door swung open. The last time I saw Dom, he had his hands on another woman. A woman who was most likely dead.

Seeing him emerge from the limo, dressed in an expensive tuxedo and looking every inch a man who bled power and money, I was reminded that my time with him was nothing but a pipe dream.

He fixed the cuff of his sleek jacket, but it was as if I'd willed him to look in my direction.

His body stilled. His eyes darkened, which sent a chill of unease racing down my spine. This was not the man who I'd indulged a fun clandestine affair with. Well, it was fun in the beginning until I caught feelings.

"Dom," I whispered and did a lame wave. There were security personnel scattered around. It wasn't a crowded celebrity gala, but there was no question it was a rich-people event.

For a second, I thought he was going to ignore me. A man suited up like the Secret Service was already asking me to move aside. Me. Who was dressed in an oversized touristy sweatshirt with the words "I love New York" emblazoned across it. Ill-fitting sweatpants and canvas sneakers finished my pathetic look. I hadn't been back to my apartment yet, but that was on my to-do. I wasn't leaving town without Ginger.

"That's okay," Dom told the guy. "I need a word with her."

Dom clasped my elbow and led me to a quiet corner. "What are you doing here? Do you have a death wish?"

"Grigori—"

"You fucked up," he gritted. "I figured you for everything else, but not a rat."

I flinched at the last word. In the mafia, to be called a rat was a death sentence.

"I'm not."

"Oh, no?" He raised a brow and slid out his phone. "I saved these photos so I could shove them down your deceitful throat."

He held the screen to my face. I didn't have to look too closely at the first one, but I recognized it. My heart plummeted to my cheap white sneakers. It was the picture I took of him and the woman in front of the Venezia Tower.

"How—" I was still processing how he was in possession of those pictures.

He cut me off. "Look at this." He swiped to another one. A picture of me and Phil. What the hell? "You and your neighbor together. You've planned this all along."

"This was the night of Grigori's job," I whispered, mind reeling from the damning evidence that proved my duplicity without a way to defend myself. *That would only mean*…a queasiness roiled in my gut. The feds got to Dom.

"At the Venezia Tower," he stressed. "I expected you to warn me since I'd sent you that address, but you couldn't, could you?"

He returned the phone to his pocket. His gaze shifted to an arriving limo before falling back on me. "The feds were waiting for me when I returned from Chicago."

"When was this?" I whispered.

He shook his head. "It doesn't matter anymore. We're over, remember? You ended it. I should have known better than to go slumming and sleep with someone beneath my league."

Talons of anguish incapacitated my throat, worse than the time Anton had strangled me. I feared if I opened my mouth, I was going to cry and wouldn't be able to stop.

Dom gave me one last scathing look before he made a disgusted sound and walked away.

"Dom," I cried, stumbling to follow him. I forgot about my pride. I forgot about my dignity. I forgot about the walls I'd erected so I wouldn't end up in a position of being ridiculed for daring to want more. But who was I kidding? I was on the streets begging a man who was way above my station to listen to me. Because this was more than about me. I needed Dom to help me find Billy. If he had formed an alliance with the Russians… "Dom, Billy is missing!"

He paused and turned to me, but the condemnation in his eyes slayed me. "Not my problem." His mouth twisted cruelly. "He's trash. And I don't deal with trash."

"Are you saying I'm trash?" *You're nothing but trash.*

I needed him to say it. I needed him to hurt me enough that I could delete the feelings I have for him. I needed him to validate why people like me could never be with people like him.

He raised a brow. "You said it, not me."

He couldn't have stated more clearly what exactly he thought of me.

You're nothing but trash.

Those hated words echoed in my head. The ringing in my ears blocked out the sounds of my surroundings. My gut heaved. My chest grew tight. My emotions blurred my vision.

You're nothing but trash.

I will not cry. I will not cry.

Cruelty I'd never seen before carved itself on Dom's face.

"Make sure she leaves," he spoke to the suited security who stopped me earlier.

The man blocked me from getting near Dom. "I'm sorry, lady. Leave or I'll have to call the cops."

"I got her," Phil said behind me.

Dom glanced over his shoulder and saw the fed. He emitted another disgusted scoff and returned his attention to the arriving limo.

"That was hard to watch," Phil muttered.

But Dom wasn't done shredding my heart. He opened the door to the luxury vehicle. Even with Phil dragging me away, a compunction to stay became an overwhelming defense mechanism to torture myself to the point of obliterating my feelings for this man.

Like a horror movie unreeling, I watched a tiny woman gowned in an exquisite blue satin dress, plant her golden-heeled dainty feet on the ground. Her hair fell in glorious blonde waves around her.

A suppressed cry hitched in my throat.

"Let's go, Sloane." Sympathy dripped from Phil's words.

The carnage decimating my heart was too enormous to contain, and I emitted a wounded sob.

Dom smiled charmingly at the blonde. He helped her out of the limo, not once looking my way as if I'd already been forgotten.

I didn't know how I made it back to Phil's SUV. It was as if my brain had ceased processing information, simply locked in the scene's agony. I only became aware of my surroundings when we reached the tunnel.

"You can't stay around here while things are hot," Phil told me.

"My brother is missing," I said, drained and listless.

He didn't say anything. The hole in my chest expanded, threatening to become a swirling abyss that was going to pull me under. If I wasn't already seated, I would have crumpled to the ground.

"Dom has pictures of you and me," I said woodenly.

"He has men following you."

"What?" This jolted me out of my zombie-like trance.

Phil glanced at the rearview mirror.

"Are they following us right now?"

"Yes. They're tracking your phone, and that's why I confiscated it when we went to the safe house."

"What the actual fuck? And you didn't think it was a good idea to inform me?"

"Leave town, Sloane. If anything, Dom still cares for your safety."

"I don't need him to care for my safety. I need him to help me find Billy!"

When we cleared the Holland Tunnel, I had Phil pull into a public transit parking garage.

I narrowed my eyes at the vehicle that discreetly parked behind another car.

"When did you know I had a tail?"

"The night Billy was taken. My men were clearing the area, and they acted suspicious."

"Well, you know what? This stops now." I dialed 911.

HALF AN HOUR LATER, A POLICE CRUISER CAME BY. I LET PHIL BE the go-between with the cops and the men Dom hired to tail me. One of the officers interviewed me first while the other one detained Dom's men. I gave a convincing account of emotional distress from the unauthorized bodyguard detail, saying an old boyfriend had trouble letting me go.

I stayed in the car and almost fist-pumped with glee when Dom had apparently unblocked my number.

DOM

That was stupid. They're for your protection.

ME

Stop playing mind games. Either you care or you don't.

I don't want your death on my conscience.

Fuck you, Dom. I blocked his number, turned off my phone, and took out the SIM. I exited the car and stomped the sliver of circuitry under my shoe with so much satisfaction and vigor, it gave me momentary respite from my tattered heart and pride. I plopped back into the passenger seat and dug into my backpack to extract my burner.

Phil had a wide grin on his face when he slid into the driver's seat.

"That was petty as fuck, but entertaining," he said. "Remind me not to get on your bad side. The officers gave them a warning. Stalking is illegal and carries a fine and jail time. If they come anywhere within your visual or physical proximity, they'll be arrested."

And that took care of that. I was still seething. Typical Dom. There was comfort that he cared, but I wasn't a toy he could stick in the corner shelf until he decided he wanted to throw me away permanently after he'd settled on a newer model.

Phil found parking near our apartment building. Logistically, I couldn't leave with Harriet, but Phil promised to look out for her and I'd set her residency payment to auto deduct from the bank account.

Wherever I landed, I needed to settle in first. I rented a storage unit on the outskirts of New Jersey where I had a trunkful of things, including emergency cash. All I needed was Ginger, important documents, and my laptop. Clothes maybe, but I could always buy more.

Phil accompanied me to the fifth floor, but when we reached my unit, the door was ajar.

"Fuck," he whispered.

Our eyes locked.

He drew his weapon. "What do you wanna do?"

My shoulders slumped. I was so fucking tired. "You can leave."

His eyes flashed. "The fuck I am. I got you into this."

"If they're in there, then I'll know what happened to Billy."

Before we could come to a decision, the door opened and Anton stood there already pointing a gun at us, or specifically, at my head. "Are you guys coming in?"

I stalked past him. "Where's my brother?"

"Well, that's why we came to get you. He needs a doctor."

"I'm not a doctor." I blew out a breath. "Are you saying he's still alive?"

"Barely."

I squeezed my eyes shut for a second. Maybe I said a prayer

even when I wasn't the praying kind. I looked around the apartment. "Where's my cat?"

"If you're talking about that she-devil, she better not show up." I noticed the scratches on Anton's arms.

She was alive, then.

"Kindly let Phil go."

Anton had two henchmen with him who brought up the rear, forcing Phil to give up his weapon.

"Fuck, no," Anton said. "This man is a pain in the ass."

"You can't have a dead fed—"

"What's another one? There's already a manhunt for us, not to mention our own bratva is turning on us…fucking rats."

"You know, apparently I'm a rat too, so I can commiserate."

Phil was looking at me like I was crazy. A lethal calm had settled over me in the last few seconds since I realized Grigori's men had come for me. I was tired of the anxiety I'd been living with. I wanted to know what my fate was. Or hope had died in me, and I wanted Anton to end my misery.

"And this man here"—Anton got close to Phil—"is a pig."

He wheeled his arm and sunk his fist into Phil's gut. Phil folded over with a groan, then Anton grabbed the collar of his shirt and tossed him on the couch.

"Stop it," I yelled.

"Hold her back," Anton snarled.

Phil staggered to his feet, cocked his elbows, and issued a cocky gesture. "Come on."

The two men clashed in the center of my small apartment, sending my furniture scraping across the floor. Both of them landed heavily with a thud.

"My neighbors are going to call the cops, you dumbasses," I shouted. We were not going to get arrested and miss the opportunity to find my brother. I knew what Phil was doing.

Well, he wasn't dying on my watch.

"Stop it now!"

Anton might have a little brain, but he was a bruiser of a fighter and turned Phil's face into a bloody pulp in a flash. Then he dragged him across the room and unlatched the door leading to the fire escape.

I tried to wrench myself free from the goon holding me, but he gripped my upper arms painfully. I jerked my elbow to his chin and stomped on his feet.

He spun me around and punched me in the stomach. "Bitch!"

I fell to the floor and tried to get up, but a wrenching pain low in my pelvis had me crying out.

"Boris, dammit, what did you do?" Anton roared. "Grigori said unscathed."

"I hit her in the stomach. He can't see it." The man hovered over me, nudging me with his boot. "Stop pretending. I didn't hit you that hard."

An orange missile jumped on his back, and he started screaming.

"Fucking cat!" Boris yelled.

"Don't hurt her." I strained to get on my knees, fighting against the nausea building inside me.

I whimpered when I heard the breaking of glass and Ginger's yowl. Tears streamed down my cheeks. "Ginger…Phil…"

I glared tearfully as Anton returned. "You're so much trouble, *suka*."

"What did you do to Phil and my cat?" I gritted through the wrenching pain in my belly. I couldn't stand up straight. Rioting fear replaced my earlier calm. Instinctively, I knew the worst was yet to come.

"They took a tumble down the fire escape."

A horrified gasp escaped me. That was five floors.

"Don't worry, the bastard hit the landing midway down the building. I'm not too sure about your cat."

"Monsters. You're all monsters."

"Yeah…luckily Grigori doesn't want any bruises on your face." He gripped my chin. "He has plans for you, so ketamine it is."

A needle pricked my neck.

CHAPTER Sixteen

Dom

The phone vibrated in the inside pocket of my tux jacket. I tried to concentrate on the words of the former pakhan of the New York Russian bratva, Ivan Zahkarov. Tonight was the formal turnover to his son, Kirill, the cold-as-ice fucker sitting across from me. I bristled at the way he was eyeing Lucy, who was forced to make nice at this event because, after all, it was in trying to help her I landed in the FBI interrogation room.

"The caviar on that oyster is the best Russia has to offer. It just arrived this morning," Ivan told me. "It's Aralina's favorite." He gave a pointed look at the beautiful blonde beside me.

In their eyes, I was considering the arranged marriage. We were in a gathering of fifty guests. Seated around our table were Ivan, his wife, Irina, their son Kirill; and daughter, Aralina; and Kolya. Kolya Petrov took over the reins of brigadier from his cousin Grigori.

From my side were Pop and Ma, my sister, Lucy; and my underboss Sonny.

The good news: Grigori had fallen from power and I didn't have to deal with him anymore. After Lucy had brought his dealings with the congressman to my attention, the goal to bring that fucker down became the priority and the properties had fallen from favor. I made this clear to my mother. It also served its purpose of freeing Sloane and her brother from Grigori's dominion.

The bad news? Nobody knew where he was, and Sloane was already in the middle of this clusterfuck. She chose to work for the feds and screwed me over with those damning photographs. Now the feds' lead witness went missing, was probably dead, and I was the last person who was seen having an altercation with her, courtesy of Sloane's photographs. Betrayed was too tame a word when they shoved those photos under my nose. They told me Sloane and her brother had been snitches for the feds for a long time. My mind had a hard time wrapping itself around what they were telling me. The person who interrogated me in that room smirked as if he'd been hanging on to further evidence that could bring me down.

The bratva was also doing damage control. Grigori made a move behind their backs and landed them in hot water. Through our mediators, we came up with this bullshit united front because our combined political clout was potent and influential.

My phone buzzed again, and it was burning a hole in my pocket. "Osetra is indeed the best caviar." I shot Ivan a tight grin before smiling apologetically to Aralina. "Excuse me." I stood up. "I'm expecting an important call."

Ignoring my mother's disapproving stare, I slid my chair back and fished out my phone.

Two texts from Sandro.

SANDRO

Call me.

Dom, call me right fucking now! I don't care if you're having dinner with the fucking king of england!

If one knew Sandro, he rarely used an exclamation point. He was typically concise in his messages because the fucker hated texting. That he used my name sent foreboding rippling through me. You see, when Sloane called the police on the security I hired for her, I couldn't leave well enough alone. I told myself she was dead to me. One rule after we ended the affair was we weren't obliged to check on each other. But did I abide by that rule? No. I put security on her and continued to receive reports on her activities because it gave me peace of mind and I could do my job as the head of my family.

I was pleased she showed up at Venezia Tower and I was assuming the text she sent me was to consider living there. But the timing couldn't be worse. I had been dealing with Lucy's witness. And as if that wasn't fucked enough, Luca's troubles with the Russian mob in Chicago heated up. In my defense, the entire underworld was riveted by the unfolding drama of my uncle's life. Amnesiac wife who was a hacker and had stolen millions from Russian organized crime. That kind of shit was made for Hollywood, but how did I ever doubt that Luca's life wouldn't be that colorful? Luca kept the "stealing" part on the down-low under threat of death because he didn't want Natalya to be further targeted.

I searched for a private corner, nodding briefly to the security standing around guarding the lobby of the event facility.

I called Sandro. He answered on the first ring and I heard mayhem around him.

"What the fuck, De Lucci?" he growled.

"What's going on?" I asked carefully. I found a deserted corridor and headed further in.

"You told me to check on Sloane." He was having trouble regulating his voice like he was jogging. "I was wondering why you would ask me that. Then I find police cruisers and cops crawling all over the place."

"Sloane?"

"I don't know. They wouldn't let anyone in. All I know is one of the residents fell from the fifth floor."

A vise screwed my chest tight and I grew lightheaded. "Male or female?"

Sandro paused. "Was she with someone else? Start talking, De Lucci. We need someone who has access to Hoboken PD if we want to get in there. I sure as fuck don't."

We were in a cold war with the Italians running New Jersey, but I knew someone who did. Grigori. I could probably navigate through my associate list for favors, but it wouldn't get us in there as fast as I wanted to. As in, as soon as it would take me to get to Hoboken. Hell, my underboss would know more than I did. I'd been playing politics at the higher level, so I had lost touch with the street game.

"I'll make some calls," I told him. Though Sandro cemented his place as the head of the Rossi crime family by defeating his challenger in the Game of Bosses, his people skills needed work. "Find out information, but don't piss anyone off."

He grunted, "I swear to God, if you got Sloane into trouble."

"Talk later." I ended the call.

Dangerous static clotted the air behind me. I stiffened, and even without turning around, I knew who I would find.

"Don't you know it's impolite to eavesdrop on people's conversations?" I faced Kirill.

Indeed, he was leaning indolently against the wall. "I needed a smoke."

"You're not allowed to smoke in here."

"As if that would stop you." He extracted a cigarette and offered me one.

I shook my head. "I need to make more calls."

I started to walk away from him, but he wasn't done.

"For someone trying to protect his sister, you seem to have other priorities tonight."

Aggravation and fury shot through my veins and clenched my fists. This unity between the Zahkarovs and the De Luccis was to show Congressman Tomlin he had nothing to worry from us. In our clandestine meeting, Kirill expressed disdain for the congressman, but the politician was greasing some business for them. Lucy and her dead lawyer friend's digging had triggered a backlash to one of the Russians' investment firms, putting it on the radar of the SEC. Not that I didn't applaud Lucy, except the corruption and moral charges against Congressman Tomlin disappeared with our witness and the death of that lawyer.

To the public, Ivan stepped down as CEO of Zahkarov Holdings. Behind the scenes, he stepped down as the pakhan of the bratva.

Lucy's involvement in their troubles had put a bull's-eye on my sister and Kirill had put a contract out on her while the feds had been interrogating me.

Dinner was tense as fuck, but it was a temporary Band-Aid hatched up by my mother and the matchmaker Margo Winthrop that enabled this truce.

Kirill canceled the contract but required my family to appear at this dinner to honor his father as an apology.

It was a quick fix, and it was hard to swallow. Ma was all for it,

Lucy was still defiant, and Pop wanted to put a contract out on Kirill in retaliation.

Fuck me.

So this was the initial remedy. Neither of us could break the truce without our scandalous secrets being spilled, and Margo definitely had more than a few.

I invaded Kirill's personal space. He was the same height as me. The same build. Same dark hair. But that was where the similarities ended. I doubted if there was an emotional bone in his body. Like he showed emotions because it was required of him. Though he seemed to genuinely care for his mute sister.

Sonny laughingly suggested that Aralina Zahkarov would make the ideal wife who didn't talk back. But she was only twenty-one for fuck's sake.

"Who do you know in Hoboken?"

He raised a brow. "Are you asking for a favor, De Lucci? Who called you?"

"You're looking for Grigori, then I might have a lead."

He returned the cigarette back into the case. "You're going to Hoboken right now?"

Nothing would stop me. I nodded. "Are you going to hurt my sister?"

He chuckled. "And risk Margo's wrath?"

My mouth twitched at this. I didn't know what dirt she had on either family, but there were enough stories to back up the claim that once you entered a covenant with Margo Winthrop, you never broke it.

What I knew of her was that she had connections in high places. Old money. And the matchmaker role she currently held was passed down from generations. Marriage Ink, her luxury full-service wedding business, was just a front for a secret society that went back centuries.

They'd been trying to bring in new money in the last hundred years. Merge old and new families. The Zahkarovs were descendants of Russian nobility. De Luccis and Morettis were Sicilians. Our ancestors worked the land. Although I heard Margo was already eyeing Luca's son, Elias. She might not have arranged the marriage between Natalya and Luca, but it was no secret that Luca's mother was an Italian contessa.

"Come on, De Lucci, I think it would piss off our mothers more if we leave now," Kirill said. "You're not escaping this circus without me."

Neither Kirill nor I wanted to ride in the other's car. We ended up going to Hoboken in separate vehicles. Thankfully, Trevor was assigned security during our event and I commandeered his Patrol.

Kirill came through though. Sandro was able to get into Sloane's apartment. But the traffic backup grated on my nerves as Sandro gave me a play-by-play of what was going on.

"The man who was thrown off the fifth floor is Phil Harding. He lives on the ground level. He's FBI. Did you know Sloane was talking to a fed?"

"Not until four days ago."

"Fuck, man, was that why you were hauled in?"

Close family knew the FBI picked me up, but I kept the details to myself. Instead of answering him, I asked, "What else?"

"Signs of a struggle. Broken window. The fire escape gate was unlocked." He paused. "There's blood."

I gripped the steering wheel. "And…"

"CSI tech said not enough to bleed out and die."

"Where did they take Harding?"

"New Jersey Medical. He's in surgery. I have one of my guys circling the hospital. It's crawling with cops."

"Do we know how badly he's hurt?"

"No."

My phone pinged with a message from Bianca.

BIANCA

What the fuck, Dom? You and Sloane?

IVY

That explains why she's been hiding from us.

SERA

I was telling Matteo I suspected she had blocked us.

BIANCA

I was feeling terrible because we had to keep this secret about Luca and Natalya from her and I thought that was why she blocked us. But it was you, my prick of a cousin. So what did you do?

I growled at Sandro, "You told the women?"

"Of course. I'm fucked up with guilt, and so is Bianca. But this is Sloane. We knew she understood mob business, so this whole shit was because of you."

"You don't have to bury the guilt any deeper."

Sandro scoffed. "Just so you know, I want to bury my fist in your face."

"Might I remind you that Sloane is working with a fed? She played me."

"I haven't mentioned that part to the women yet."

I snorted. "So I'm painted as the bad guy."

"Well, you're certainly not a victim here. My hunch? Sloane

didn't have a choice. Especially with her brother who kept screwing up."

"And she couldn't have told us?"

"Yeah, well, she's not around to defend herself, is she?"

Sloane's betrayal stung deep, but Sandro giving her the benefit of the doubt while I refused to listen to her, while I wanted her to suffer for her betrayal, stung deeper and pierced an uncomfortable shard of disgust in my chest.

"I told you Grigori needed to go. I should have acted on my own and not looped you into it," Sandro said.

Sloane and I agreed to nothing personal. But I let my pride get in the way. I hid behind my responsibility to family. Sandro considered Sloane a friend. Did my five months with her, fucking her in every position, spending time with her mean nothing? It did. Otherwise, I wouldn't have put security on her and that was why I was panicking when I lost control over Sloane's movements.

"I have no time for this blame game," I warned. "Kirill Zahkarov is with me."

"And you're all about appearances, aren't you?"

I ignored his jibe. "Talk to you later."

Sandro wasn't kidding when he said the place was crawling with cops. He met me and Kirill on the ground floor. He and the Russian exchanged brief nods. I wondered if Sandro had ever taken a contract from them. They had Kolya, but he usually only did things for the bratva and didn't contract out his services.

I wasn't prepared for the feeling that hit me when I entered Sloane's apartment. The place looked like an all-out brawl had taken place. Coffee table smashed, barstools overturned, and the couch where Sloane and I had fucked countless times was at an odd angle. Parallel chaos was roiling my insides.

Something nagged at me. I was hyper-aware. Glasses were being dusted off by the tech, and evidence markers planted.

I walked into the bedroom. The closet door was open, and the mattress was tossed. Did the Russians think Sloane was hiding something, or were they setting this up as a burglary?

I kept nothing here, not even a toothbrush. Once or twice I checked us into a hotel, but Sloane preferred I didn't spend a dime on us, which irritated the fuck out of me. She started pushing back on groceries. Interestingly enough, she never said no to Ginger's prissy food…

Ginger.

I rushed out of the bedroom and spotted the cat's empty bowl. "Did you guys see a cat?"

Everyone narrowed their gazes at me as if I'd lost my damn mind.

"It's an orange cat," I persisted.

I got a few headshakes, mostly shrugs, and then one of the CSIs said "no" before returning to his task.

Sandro's gaze burned a hole through me while I stalked around the overturned furniture and headed to the fire ladder door.

"Don't touch anything!" the CSI tech yelled.

I grunted, not used to people treating me like I was dumb as a rock when it came to situations like this. Of course I wasn't going to touch anything unless I wanted to get rid of evidence. I shouldered the ajar door that led to the fire escape. I wondered whether one of the residents had Ginger or she was on the roof.

I glanced up to see if she was peering down and observing the activities like a curious cat would, but I didn't see her. My eyes traveled down the catwalk and immediately spotted an orange blob beside the dumpster in the alley.

No.

Fuck, no.

I barged back into the apartment, out its door, and raced down the stairs. I would have looked like a fleeing suspect if I hadn't been wearing a tux.

Once outside, the brisk air failed to displace the foreboding festering inside my chest. It only expanded and tightened its band around my lungs, making it difficult to breathe.

I ran into Bianca.

"Dom, what are—"

I ignored her and sprinted round the building into the alley. Conflicting emotions grappled inside me…of wanting the orange blob to be there, and wishing it had disappeared because that would mean Ginger was alive.

But it was still there. I stopped two feet away from it.

"Dom…what are you doing?" Bianca asked. Then she must have seen the form I was too chickenshit to approach.

"Oh, is that Sloane's cat?"

A lump lodged itself in my throat and roughened the single word gusting past my mouth. "Yes."

I took one step, and then another, until I sank to my knees and, for the first time since I'd met the feisty feline, touched its fur willingly, desperately.

Ginger moved and tried to raise her head to look at me. Then she laid it down again and ignored me.

"You're alive."

"She's hurt?" Bianca's voice trembled. "You think they threw her from the fifth floor too, like that guy?"

"Ginger," I whispered gently. "Can I move you, girl?" I stroked her fur. She was able to move her head and gave me hope she hadn't broken her back. There were no signs of blood on her coat or around her, and the biggest concern was if she was bleeding internally. "I'll give you all the tuna you want."

The word *tuna* did it.

Ginger pushed up on her forelegs, struggling to lift her

hindquarters, but she managed it. Her tail didn't flick in sass, and she appeared to be hunched like an old cat rather than a feisty three-year-old. She also appeared thinner than last I saw her, and she was shivering.

Overcome with relief, I shrugged out of my tux jacket and wrapped it around Ginger. She didn't protest and appeared to welcome the warmth of my clothes.

Cradling the bundle of fur in my arms, Bianca and I walked out of the alley where Sandro met us.

"That's the cat?" he asked.

"Yes," I said. "The fuckers must have thrown her out the window."

"Well, they say a cat has nine lives," Sandro said.

I stared at Ginger who seemed to be content and wondered how many of those lives remained.

"Do we have any leads on Sloane?" Bianca asked.

"I'm going to ask Trevor to review surveillance footage around the area, but I need a favor from you."

"Anything," she said.

"Take Ginger to the emergency vet and do a full workup." Sloane would have wanted me to take care of her cat. Then I immediately did a mental headshake. I was talking about Sloane like she was already dead. I refused to believe it. Self-recrimination battled against the logical steps I had to take to make sense of what happened here.

Eventually, there'd be time to wallow in regrets, to figure out how I fucked things up so badly, but not right now. Sloane was out there and she needed me.

CHAPTER Seventeen

DOM

IT HAD BEEN A WEEK SINCE THE RUSSIANS HAD TAKEN SLOANE. From the surveillance footage, the fucker who'd captured her appeared to be Anton. Trevor was busy dropping hints to the feds on where to search for her, but so far, they'd been hitting dead ends. Kirill hadn't been helpful in providing the name of the properties where Anton or Grigori could have taken her.

Phil Harding had been in a medically induced coma to ease the swelling in his brain caused by the fall. He was lucky all he suffered besides brain trauma was a broken leg and collarbone considering the height he'd fallen from. His spine remained intact, and he wasn't paralyzed. The second they removed his breathing tube, the detectives took his statement.

When he finally saw me, the disgust on his face spoke volumes and managed to make me feel an inch tall. He witnessed the cruelty I'd inflicted on Sloane.

"Find her…"

I wasn't sure if it was a statement or a question.

"I was hoping you could help me find her," I said.

He didn't say anything but breathed heavily. "Don't deserve her."

"If there's anything…"

"She didn't betray you." His heart monitor ticked up.

That was neither here nor there. Though Sloane and I avoided sharing personal stuff, we did spend five months together, and when I was able to think clearly, it left me with a certainty that she was coerced to work for the FBI. That she was cornered and didn't have a choice. I lied to myself when I said she was dead to me, but I wasn't prepared for Phil's next words.

"I cloned her phone."

The words didn't register at first. My mind rejected them. It rejected them because that would mean Sloane was innocent. That there was no gray area to bargain with and make me feel better even when her shattered look haunted me.

The look as I spewed those venomous words and rejected her.

Ridiculed her.

Degraded her.

Called her a rat.

Trash.

No. No. No.

The unfairness of it all. My misplaced outrage and pride. I fucking destroyed her.

A faint smile curved Phil's mouth. He was delighted to watch the slideshow of horror playing on my face.

"You framed her?" I choked.

And if the nurse hadn't rushed in, I would have grabbed him, post-comatose or not, and strangled the life out of him.

Dazed, I didn't even fight the nurse when she shoved me out of the room. I staggered a few steps into the hallway with no direction. I paced in circles.

I fought through the roaring in my ears, the pounding of my heart, and the inability to breathe without snagging on what suspiciously sounded like a sob. Sloane never betrayed me. Sandro was right. The FBI framed her. I scrambled through our text messages and cross-checked them to the messages from the bodyguards I assigned to her.

I battened down the nausea of self-disgust rising inside me when my brain came to the undeniable conclusion of Sloane's innocence.

Since that night she disappeared, my days were spent on the streets talking to informants or riding Trevor's ass on dark web chatter. Any clue that would lead us to Sloane or even Billy.

Kirill issued a warning that Grigori was his to deal with, but fuck that.

I also had Harriet watched. Trevor, at first, thought I'd lost my mind to consider stalking an octogenarian, but after we'd discovered the auto-monthly debit of her stay in Delphine had been cancelled only to be paid up for a year from an untraceable shell company, he agreed. I didn't know whether Harriet knew what happened to Sloane and I wasn't about to give her a heart attack with bad news.

I would return to my penthouse in the early hours of the morning, but today, after finding out that I'd misjudged Sloane, I didn't have the energy to haunt the streets or hound Trevor, so I returned to my penthouse early.

Six p.m. to be exact.

Here, Ginger was my constant companion. Surprisingly, she'd acclimated to being confined to an indoor space, noting said indoor space was ten times the size of Sloane's apartment. Apparently, she had a taste for fine living and expensive furniture. I kept her fed in style and she'd been gaining weight, her coat getting healthier than it'd ever been.

I would sit in front of the television, and her acceptance was the only thing keeping me on the edge of sanity. Because it was the nights when the regrets came and tonight the enormity of the injustice I'd inflicted on Sloane was magnified a thousand times worse. Sloane and I had embarked on a physical affair, but we were in denial that emotions weren't involved. I was used to playing boss, concentrating on keeping the gears working smoothly in my organization, so I didn't notice how she'd crept under my skin and burrowed into my heart. I was such a fucking asshole. Phil was right. I didn't deserve her. I kept her boxed in a corner because I figured she would never survive the scrutiny of my position and leave me. Even now, I didn't want to present her to my mother, not because I was ashamed of her, but because Ma's disdain at my choice of partner would drive Sloane away and make her end things between us.

But I didn't have to worry. It was I who ruined us.

I was selfish.

She'd hinted, hadn't she? That she was feeling more and seeing me go out with other women was wearing her down. I was a coward and hid behind my responsibilities, but in doing so, I'd forsaken who was turning out to be the most important person in my life.

Luca once said when I made a choice, I should protect that choice with my life.

I didn't.

I didn't fucking deserve her. And I might be too late. I didn't know whether Sloane was dead or alive. My thoughts went to Luca. Were the Moretti men cursed to suffer the same consequences because of our quest for power?

The sound of the key turning made me sigh. It was the women.

They'd been trying to corner me for a week, but I'd been one step ahead of them.

I typed a message to Trevor and Sandro.

ME

Fuck you, guys.

TREVOR

Take it like a man, bro.

SANDRO

Fix this.

Fix what? I didn't owe them an apology. The only woman who was getting an apology from me was Sloane. I would grovel and crawl over broken glass if only I could find her.

Ginger jumped off my lap to greet the women. I had a suspicion they'd been coming into my residence to play with her.

"Ooh, he's here," Sera snipped. If there was a silver lining that came out of Sloane's disappearance, it was that it seemed to have united my female cousins and my sister against me. Sera picked up the remote and turned off the television.

"Didn't Matteo ever teach you not to touch a man's remote?" I grumbled.

"Trust me, cousin, Matteo lets me touch everything."

"Gag." Lucy made the vomiting gesture. Of course, Bianca would be here. She was leading the charge to castrate me for what I'd done to Sloane. And that was without knowing what went down between us.

"I don't know why you girls are here. I'm no closer to finding Sloane than a couple of days ago."

"We went to visit Harriet," Bianca said.

"Why?"

"The question is why haven't you?" Sera asked.

"She doesn't know me. Sloane never introduced me to her. But I know Harriet's got a heart condition. I don't want to shock her with the news that Sloane is missing."

Bianca rolled her eyes and looked at the girls. "Know what? I have my answers. Sloane and Dom were nothing but hookups and obviously she didn't share her personal life with him."

"And how much did Sloane share with you?" I challenged.

"Did you know the reason she tries to be so independent and didn't want to depend on any man was because that's what her mother told her when her father left?"

I frowned. "That's not bad advice. Talking about her family is off-limits. That was our deal. Any attempts of mine to pry were shut down. But we don't need to look too far. Billy…"

"That's what I don't get," Bianca said. "Harriet has a soft spot for Billy no matter how many times he's fucked up."

"How did she react when you were all looking for Sloane?"

"She knows," Bianca said.

"What?"

"She doesn't know where Sloane went, but apparently Sloane had been planning it for a while."

"Sloane had planned to leave?"

"Yes. But the day after everything went down, the administrator of the facility told Harriet that her stay was paid up for a year." Bianca exhaled a sigh. "She's sad, Dom. Harriet thinks Sloane found out about Billy and was mad at her and left."

Confused, I said, "I'm not following."

"Duh, you think we do? Use your sneaky boss connections and dig."

Lucy whipped out her phone. "I know a guy…"

"No," I snapped. "You've done enough."

My sister was on thin ice with the way she skated into shit without covering her tracks. She needed to stay far away from the political crap right now or risk another contract on her head she expected me to fix.

My phone rang, flashing *Trevor.*

"You have something?"

"Yeah."

THE OLD COLONIAL HOUSE WAS ON THE OUTSKIRTS OF MANHATTAN, so it was to our advantage that agents from the New York field office and local cops were able to piece together the journey of a truck used by one of Grigori's men. The plates turned up as one of the pay-here-buy-here lots that required GPS tracking to be installed and it led to this house before it was eventually ditched in the Bronx and ended up in one of our chop shops.

The house was in poor condition and clearly hadn't been maintained well. Fresh tire tracks indicated recent use, but hope deflated when the property appeared abandoned.

When the lead agent declared it clear, he approached me with a somber expression. "There's something you need to see."

"Is she dead?" The words scraped my throat like sandpaper.

"No, but there's a basement," he said. His eyes grew shifty before they fixed on the K-9 vehicle. "We're going to let the scent hounds do their job. We can call you—"

"No," I said firmly. "Show me now."

The agent led me into the house. I forgot that Trevor was beside me until he said in my ear, "The owner of this property is a dead end. I think Grigori's been using shell companies to hide the movement of his trafficking rings from his boss."

His boss meaning Ivan. If anything, the former pakhan accepted the blame for letting someone like Grigori loose, and that was why he stepped down to let Kirill take over. Sandro didn't have to remind me he once offered to take out Grigori because he was concerned for Sloane, but I had my own agenda then. I'd assigned Sloane to a corner designating her as the woman I had sex with. She didn't influence my policies as a boss. Except Sloane refused to remain in the corner and she forced me to choose before I was ready.

I chose wrong, and I fucked up.

It was late spring in New York, and the basement was cool and humid. When we reached the bottom of the steps, a single light bulb illuminated the area.

A ragged inhale blew past my mouth and I couldn't prevent the burning in my eyes.

Bile, like churning acid, backed up my throat as the stench of copper assailed my nostrils. People had died in this basement. They were tortured first. And I tortured myself with thoughts of Sloane as a captive. Was she locked up? Chained? Did they starve her? Was she cold?

There were cages, but also a chain attached to the wall. They treated people like animals in this space. Impotent rage engulfed me when I spotted the dried blood on the floor, smeared almost two feet wide. Whoever was hooked to that wall couldn't have survived.

A darker, more concentrated patch of blood was a few feet away.

I shuddered another exhale as my mind filled in the blanks of what happened here. I wondered what nightmare Sloane endured, all because I fucking refused to help her find Billy.

I was still processing the horror unspooling in my head when someone hollered at the top of the stairs. "The dogs found something!"

I raced up the stairs despite the lightheadedness threatening me with collapse. Despite Trevor yelling my name. Despite the scream that wanted to tear out of my chest.

Across the parking lot, I spotted the K-9 and ran toward it. What did it find? A body? A grave? Clothing?

I reached the fresh grave and what followed was a blur. The rush of the ocean in my ears. My chaotic breathing. The odor of lime and earth. Someone hauled me up. Got in front of me, yelling at me to get a grip. I stood dazed and stared at my hands, at the dirt under my fingernails. I'd been digging with my bare hands.

My fault.

I did this.

I fucking did this.

Sloane's suffering was because of me.

This wasn't happening. I wasn't about to find Sloane in a grave. Never to see her vivid green eyes again or hear her husky voice that lulled me to a peaceful sleep.

Barking around twenty feet away jolted me out of my trance.

"We have another one!"

I closed my eyes, drained and resigned. "Sloane and her brother." My voice cracked.

Trevor stood silently beside me and put a hand on my shoulder as we waited.

It would take another forty-five minutes for the forensic archeologists to arrive. The feds set up a command center under a tent. I didn't leave the site as they worked. It was a shallow grave and perpetuators had used lime to mask the smell and speed up body decay. If this was what an out-of-body experience felt like, then I was living it. It was as if I'd become two beings. One in my physical form: stoic and emotionless in watching the proceedings. While my soul stood beside it: screaming, roaring, and raging.

They unearthed a black-tarp-wrapped form.

An exhale loosened my chest as my consciousness fused together. The body was too big to be Sloane, but my relief was short-lived when the technician revealed the face of the person who was buried.

Billy.

I squeezed my eyes shut. Sloane had asked for my help to find Billy and I viciously turned her down. But like that night of her disappearance, I willed my mind not to think of regrets. I forced my limbs to take me to the second burial site.

The techs who were dressed in biological hazard suits were carefully laying the body on the ground beside the hole. The shape could pass for Sloane's build.

God no. I mumbled a prayer despite the desolation drowning me.

"Let me do it," I said. I wasn't running from my guilt. If Sloane was beneath this plastic, I wanted her face to haunt me for the rest of my life.

It was nothing less than I deserved.

After donning gloves, I gripped the blade in one hand and sliced the tarp. Exhaling, I dropped the blade and opened the slit.

Oxygen deserted me for a split second and I rocked and fell on my ass, crab-walking backward from the body.

"It's not her," I gasped, turning over on all fours as an overwhelming relief washed over me. "It's not her."

Hope came flooding back.

Trevor peered at the corpse on the ground. "Wait, is that…?"

"The missing witness."

THE FEDS TOLD ME IT WOULD TAKE THEM SIX DAYS TO GET BACK the results from the blood in the basement and longer for their coroners to do autopsies on the bodies. Kirill wasn't happy that I went behind his back, but he was the fucker who was obstructing the progress of the investigation.

But money buys everything including a rushed DNA analysis, and I could have the results within twenty-four hours.

I was telling myself that if the bigger map of blood was Sloane's, then her body would be in one of the graves. My bet was it was Billy's. He had a longer time to bleed out. *Cold, I know.*

I was pacing the living room of the penthouse. I was promised the results before midnight.

Ginger was sitting like a sphinx on the leather ottoman as if she was waiting with me for the results.

I banned everyone from coming into my penthouse. I wanted to be alone in my misery. I wanted to suffer alone in my guilt and self-loathing.

I took a swig of whiskey when my phone rang with the number from the private DNA lab.

"Mr. De Lucci?"

"Yes."

"This is Carter. Lucy's friend."

"Yeah, I know who you are." What could I say? My sister offered her help, and I pounced on it even when I had other companies lined up who could do the work, but I discovered this Carter guy was the best in his field. I didn't know how my sister found these people, but maybe she should work for me.

"I'm sending you the results on a secure link you can download, but I want to confirm that the set of DNA coming from subject A—"

"That's the one closest to the wall?"

"Correct. I can confirm is William Scott."

"And the second set?"

"This is where it could get tricky."

"What do you mean?"

"There's fetal tissue mixed in it."

"Fetal…" The implications of what this meant ripped a hole inside me so agonizingly visceral, I could barely speak through the crippling pain squeezing my rib cage.

"Subject two was pregnant."

"Was?" I could only manage one-word responses now.

"The maternal DNA was confirmed to be Sloane Scott's."

"Pregnant…"

"So, in the interest of saving time, I asked for permission from Lucy to use her existing data in our database."

"You could have called me…" I finally strung a few words together. I was reeling. Spinning. Thrashing in a sea of unexpected loss and stew of emotions I couldn't identify.

"This was faster and I can retest…"

"Just tell me!" I roared, the thread of control finally snapping. I had to know. But I already knew the truth, didn't I? Because karma had a way of doubling down on my guilt and shame. "Am I the father?"

"Lucy and the fetal tissue share a match, so you are potentially the father."

"What happened?"

"I'm not in forensics, but it appeared it was a miscarriage."

"The baby did not survive?" I whispered brokenly.

"I'm sorry, Mr. De Lucci."

My hand lost its grip on the phone.

Sloane had been pregnant.

The news slowly registered in my head, but my body was already processing the sweeping devastation liquefying my insides, draining the blood from my head, and threatening to suck me in its undertow.

My knees crashed on the wooden floors, and even then, I

couldn't keep the rest of me upright. Piercing pain in my gut and chest hunched me over and I crawled on all fours. Crawled across the floor to a dark corner and wept. Wept for the baby—*our baby*—who never had a chance to live.

CHAPTER Eighteen

Seven weeks later

Sloane

Breathe in. Breathe out.

That was the mantra I repeated every morning. I'd wake up from troubled sleep and struggle to leave the bed. Almost two months ago, I grabbed a chance for a new life. I left Harriet behind, knowing I couldn't take her with me in my fragile condition. My mind and body were in a state of numbness; even taking care of myself was a chore. The woman who cut me a deal assured me that Harriet would be cared for. I didn't feel guilt. I was too numb to feel anything. Her deal seemed the easiest, and that was to stay away from the upper East Coast for two months. Specifically, no contact with the De Luccis and, by extension, the Rossis. I was never to step foot in Manhattan again.

I didn't even ask her why.

Get up, sis, Billy said.

"Easy for you to say. You're dead."

I wasn't actually hearing Billy's voice, nor did I see him. The isolation in this beach town at the Outer Banks fueled imaginary conversations. I remembered little about the time I was taken, but I remembered in vivid detail my brother's dying moments in that dungeon.

"Wake up."

My brother's voice was like an annoying mosquito in my ear. It was like I was eight again, and Billy was eleven. He and Harriet took turns getting me ready for school and feeding me breakfast, especially when Mom had been working late, exhausted, and fast asleep. As usual, Dad was drunk on the couch or hadn't come home from a night of gambling.

But it was the painful cramping in my stomach that finally roused me to my dark and dank surroundings. I had difficulty opening my eyes, as if someone glued my lids shut. I pulled my knees against my chest and wished I was eight again. When nothing mattered but sleep and school and playing and eating the buttered biscuits Harriet used to make. "Ahh...that hurts."

"She's bleeding between her legs." Grigori's voice. "What did you guys do?"

"We didn't do anything!" That was Anton.

Their arguing sounded far away, sometimes muffled, my comprehension of their words going in and out of my hearing like a poorly tuned radio.

"Sis, wake up," Billy said again.

This time I pried my eyelids open with whatever willpower I had and stared at him. He was sitting against the wall. Hands tied behind his back, but he was looking pale, his mouth almost bloodless. Eyes sunken.

"Am I dreaming?"

He chuckled painfully. "'Fraid not." He scanned my body. "You're pregnant, aren't you?"

That was when I realized I was on the floor and the ice-cold concrete against my cheek felt soothing. I tried to push up, but the stabbing in my belly restricted my movements. Warm blobs of blood gushed out of me like the heaviest of menstrual flow.

"Maybe I am." Dom's baby. My heart clenched. I was losing his baby, and he didn't know. But my mind focused on my brother.

"You're dying," I croaked.

"It's okay, sis," he said.

"What?" I tried to push up again but failed.

"I'm tired," he said.

"That's because you're losing so much blood." Somewhere I found the strength to power through the cramp twisting my lower abdomen into a constricting knot. I got on my knees.

"You can't save me, so listen." His breath rattled.

I could have saved him. For the first time I asked for someone's help—Dom's—and he turned me down, ridiculed me even, and shattered my heart.

I scrutinized Billy's face. Without even looking, I knew his wound was infected. He was probably septic, not to mention his blood loss. He looked gaunt and feverish, almost like a person in a zombie movie before they turned.

"It's okay," he said when my face must have shown my morbid assessment of his condition. The ketamine Anton injected in me muted my emotions. Otherwise, I would be bawling my eyes out right now.

"Billy, I'm sorry," I whispered.

You couldn't have saved me. Billy in my head said, *I have to go. I've had a death wish for a while and you can't keep saving me.*

"So your answer was to take yourself out?"

If you don't get up, then I'll have wasted my life.

"Fuck you." And that was usually when I'd ignore the aches in my muscles and roll to my side, sit up, swing my legs over, and plant my feet on the floor to get up. I'd started going to a therapist three weeks ago, and I'd been taking medication. I had done enough clinical rotations in the psych ward to know that I was falling into depression over Billy's death and losing the baby. The catastrophic combination of the events and the imbalance of my hormones had consigned me to this state. Still, the idea of asking for help after Dom rejected me almost prevented me from seeking therapy for my mental state. Because to reject help meant that I was strong. And I wasn't fooling myself into thinking I was strong enough to survive this without assistance. So I forced myself to talk to someone. A stranger without preconceived notions of who I was, where I was from, and what I had done.

I stared at the ocean, convincing myself once again that I was not weak for seeking help. Grim thoughts languished in my mind. Was it a coincidence that I woke up in a pretty cottage on an isolated beach? Had the woman who paid for me to leave hoped that I would end my life on my own?

It would be so easy.

The ocean was right there.

In my drugged-out state after Grigori surrendered me to that woman, I remembered being taken to a hospital or a clinic. After that, my mind was blank. I woke up in this house with a note and specific instructions, along with bottles of pain medication and sleeping pills. I could stay in this beach house until the end of summer to recover—or join my brother.

The ocean was right there.

But after witnessing Bianca almost drowning, I shuddered to entertain that idea. Plus, I intended to check on Harriet eventually after I'd forgiven her for the secret she shared with Billy.

Phil Harding lived. I found an obscure news clip about a man falling from my apartment building and surfing the fire escape. There was an odd reference about an orange cat being taken in and adopted by a Good Samaritan. I was keeping my fingers crossed it was Ginger, and she was okay.

My van was parked in front of the cottage. I didn't know how it got here. It needed maintenance, but I used it to go into town for groceries. It was the middle of summer in the Outer Banks. The enthusiasm and carefree life of college kids slowly rubbed off on me, giving me a shot of levity during my darkest days. Normally, I'd be resentful that they got to do their vacations in between semesters while I slaved away as a cleaner, but now I was paid to take a break. Little by little, with the sun on my skin giving me a shot of serotonin and with the meds, it took the edge off the feeling of drowning.

Fifty thousand in cold hard unmarked bills didn't do it.

But talking to someone who didn't judge me for my past did.

Grief and loss were irrevocably intertwined.

All I had to do was continue breathing.

In. Out.

After coffee, I walked along the beach. The sound of the waves calmed my senses and infused my system with a rush of energy that seemed to desert me each time I woke up from a restless sleep.

The vastness of the ocean made me feel small and big at the same time.

My heart rate sped up. Yesterday, I finally swam in the sea, trusting myself not to let myself drown.

Taking a dip in the ocean and breaking to the surface was cathartic. It made me feel alive.

I peeled away the sarong around my waist and dropped it on the beach and waded in.

The surf rushed around me.

I laughed. For the first time in weeks, I laughed. And that made me cry.

Face it, Sloane, you're still a wreck.

Against the backdrop of a clear blue sky, I focused on the sailboat a few hundred yards out. I thought I heard my name. A rough echo in the wind.

The feeling of sand sinking around my toes. The heft of the water as I moved against it. I soaked up every sensation, reminding me I could feel. That I wasn't numb. Enjoying life's simple pleasures was a start. It was a matter of coaxing one foot in front of me and forcing the other to follow.

Then I stepped into nothing.

The ocean swallowed me up. After my initial panic, I calmed enough to let buoyancy do its job. But then I wanted to experience the deep again and dove back in. A glimmer of sunlight illuminated the sandy and rocky terrain, beckoning me to swim toward it.

Can you hear me down here, Billy?

I stayed suspended in the ocean's depths.

You need to head back, he replied.

Back where? I have nowhere to go.

I'm sorry, Sloane. Forgive me.

Powerful bands clamped around my body and hauled me upwards. I struggled against the tentacles gripping me tight. I choked on salt water.

My eyes watered.

Panic seized me.

Lungs. Heart. They jump-started my survival mode.

I kicked.

I broke the surface, spitting water. My nostrils burned.

And then I realized what was happening.

Some idiot thought I was drowning. Infuriated, I let my body go limp and let him perform his heroic duty for the day.

"Goddammit, Sloane! Goddammit!"

Wait. Dom?

"Let me go!" I only managed a croak.

"Fuck that!"

My feet dragged along the surface of the sand, letting me know we were back in shallow water.

Before I renewed my fight to be free of him, he swept me into his arms and I was staring into his furious eyes.

"I wasn't trying to kill myself," I informed him.

His eyes were too dark for the morning. He was angry.

Well, I was angrier. *How dare he infiltrate my newly found peace?*

"Could have fooled me," he gritted.

We were back on dry land, and he set me flat on the warm sand. And before I could jackknife into position, he flung his body on top of me, trapping me on the shore.

His chest flattened my breasts while his hands cradled my face.

I glared at him. "I was just taking a swim."

A muscle pulsed at his jaw, and his gaze studied me. I discerned a softening in his eyes and the shuddering of his body before his forehead dropped to mine. "Thank God."

"Get off me," I snapped.

He raised his head to look at me, regret etched on his face. "I'm sorry, Sloane."

I wasn't even going to pretend not to know what he was sorry about. He obviously found out I never betrayed him. "If I give you blanket forgiveness for all the nasty shit you said to me, will you leave me alone?"

He sighed and rolled off me to stand up. He extended his arm to give me a hand up, but I ignored it and pushed to my feet on my own. I grabbed the sarong and tied it around my waist as I started for the house.

"That right there says you're lying," he said, following me.

"What the fuck are you doing here?" I worried about the deal with that woman. It wasn't any written contract, but the fact that Grigori gave me up to her meant she could return me to Grigori any time. And the efficiency at how she got me medical help, took care of Harriet, and transported me while unconscious told me everything I needed to know. She was a pro at relocating people. Maybe she was a branch of witness protection.

Did I break our unwritten contract if it was Dom who followed me here? I didn't even question how he found me.

"What do you think?" he responded as if him being here was the most natural thing in the world.

I walked briskly to put distance between us, but his long easy gait kept pace with me.

When we reached the white picket fence of the house, I spun on him. "You're not coming inside."

His gaze shot to the beach cottage behind me and then shifted to rest on my face with a longing that made me squirm with the first hint that this was once a man I was strongly attracted to.

But he cut me off so ruthlessly when I asked for his help.

My eyes swept him from head to toe. His shirt and shorts were plastered to his body as if he hadn't been expecting to take a dip in the ocean. They also revealed how he seemed to have lost weight. The blades of his cheekbones were starker as was the hollow within them. "Have you been watching me?"

"Maybe."

"Dom!"

His lids slammed shut and his body shuddered with his inhale and exhale as if he was a man given oxygen after being starved of it. But when he opened his eyes, anguish flooded the darkness within its irises. "I missed my name on your lips."

"What are you doing to me?" My voice cracked out of fear.

Because I couldn't go through what I did with him again, but Dom was the mafia. What would stop him from taking me from here by force? So I appealed to whatever empathy was within him. "I'm doing fine. If I ever meant something to you at all, you will leave me in my peace."

He took a step forward. "I can't."

"Why? Because you feel guilty?"

"Because I don't think I can survive without you." He said those words without blinking, staring straight at me as if he believed them.

But I'd lost belief in everyone including myself. Dom was not good for my recovery. He didn't directly cause my problems, but he couldn't upend my life again if I had any hope of moving on with it.

"That's just guilt," I scoffed. "You have a need to take care of everyone. Remember what you once told me...you don't have room to worry about me too. Well, I absolve you of all responsibility."

He took another step. I took three steps back.

"Don't run away, please." His throat bobbed. I had never seen Dominic De Lucci this vulnerable. Despite my enmity toward him, it was uncomfortable to see him this way. This was not him. Dom was self-assured and in control. This reiterated just how bad we were for each other.

"I've said some awful shit to you and I'm sorry. I wasn't going to rush you, but I was terrified when you went into the water."

"How long have you been watching me?" My eyes flared. "And don't deny it."

His eyes dropped to the ground before looking at the beach house to the right. My jaw dropped. I stared at him, and then at the property beside mine. "Do you live there?" I pointed to it.

"I'm renting it," he mumbled.

"Unbelievable."

I spun around and ran to the door. When I reached the top of the stoop, Dom called out, "I know about the pregnancy."

My stomach dropped. I was unprepared to discuss it. Even my therapist didn't know about it yet. I'd skirted around my miscarriage because I'd known I was pregnant only for a fleeting moment. But maybe I was lying to myself. The signs were there. I avoided confirming the pregnancy because I had no business bringing a baby into the world, but if I had taken the test sooner, maybe I would have made different choices.

I turned around. "I didn't know I was pregnant." My voice came out eerily calm. "If I did, I would have told you."

"I'm not accusing you of keeping—"

"I know you're not," I cut him off. "Because it's my baby *I* lost."

"Sloane…please…can I come in?" I couldn't stand the longing in his eyes any longer. The bleakness in them was threatening to shatter me inside.

"No. We're over."

I ran into the house, shut the door, and leaned against it. Dom wasn't one to go away easily, but I didn't know the Dominic De Lucci I just witnessed. I couldn't allow myself to believe he was as broken as I was. He was simply feeling guilt for treating me unfairly.

I peeked through the window and saw him staring at the house, but he hadn't taken one step farther than where I'd left him.

I reminded myself that he didn't give me the benefit of the doubt. That he accused me of being a rat. That hurt the most. Everything that followed resulted from my choices. I didn't blame him for Billy's death. I didn't blame him for Anton hurting me. I was finding out I wasn't blaming him at all for the miscarriage.

But an old festering wound from my past was bleeding on my present, on the people who were innocent of inflicting that damage.

You're nothing but trash.

I thought I'd buried it. Apparently not. What happened with Dom only amplified my delusion that I'd moved on from it.

I rifled through my drawer of things, looking up briefly to see Dom walking back to the beach house. I found the notebook of phone numbers. Two weeks after I'd healed enough, I drove to my storage unit on the outskirts of New Jersey and grabbed my trunk of things. In it were my passport, money, a spare burner, and phone numbers stored the old-fashioned way—in a little Moleskine book. Technically, I violated my agreement with the woman. I have no doubt she was tracking either me or my car, but so far, no one had come after me.

I entered Bianca's number and called it.

The first call went to voicemail and I left a message.

"Hey, it's Sloane. Answer the next time if you forgive me for disappearing."

Walking to the window, I watched Dom's figure recede in the distance. The nerve. The utter nerve of him. Didn't he have a criminal empire to run?

My phone started ringing. It startled me because it was the first time in months someone had called me.

I barely said hello when Bianca started shrieking. "Omigod, Sloane, omigod. Where have you been?"

"Dom didn't tell you?"

"Tell me what? Wait…is this the reason he's taken a leave of absence?"

At this, I laughed. "What? I didn't know bosses could take leaves of absence."

"Well, he did," Bianca told me. "From *the company*. He put Sonny in charge. I can tell you Aunt Lottie is fuming."

"How long has he been gone?"

"Two weeks and…I'm confused. I thought he was with you?"

"No, he's not. He's renting the beach house beside me, and I need for you to fetch your cousin. Bring your scary husband if you must."

"Oh thank God," Bianca rushed out. "I wasn't sure if I was glad or mad that you forgave him so quickly."

I laughed again, the tightness in my chest easing. Maybe I was ready to see my friends and rebuild bridges. I might not step foot in Manhattan again, but I was sure there was a workaround.

"Dom told you about our affair?"

"Yes, and that he fucked up."

I could argue that I wasn't totally innocent, but our short time together was a long story to relay over the phone.

That was why when Bianca asked, "Where are you?"

I responded, "Outer Banks."

"I'll be there this evening. Drop me the location."

I didn't say no.

CHAPTER *Nineteen*

Dom

She's brought in reinforcements. Fuck.

I lowered my binoculars when I spotted Sandro's Escalade pull in beside Sloane's van. There was something satisfying about using this old-school stalking instrument. I'd also installed cameras around Sloane's property, including inside her house. Not because I was a pervert. I just wanted to make sure she was still breathing.

I timed my installation when she went to town to pick up groceries and go to twice-weekly therapist sessions. She'd stay in town for three hours tops and it took me two days to set them up. Admittedly, it had taken me longer because I rolled around her bedsheets and sniffed them.

Fuck, maybe I was a pervert.

Missing her was a constant ache in my chest. Since her disappearance, I couldn't eat. I rarely slept. For three weeks straight, I drank whiskey from the bottle and smoking seemed like its pathetic companion. Sera actually had the audacity to pull a cigarette out of my mouth when I'd instantly lit up after I finished a stick.

"You stink like a chimney," she had said. "Fix your shit, cuz."

But how could I when the person who could fix it for me was missing? Many times I'd put unrelenting pressure on Trevor, having him comb through forums and databases, so maniacally extreme that Matteo had to get involved to rein me in. He'd throw us both out of The Underground and order us to get some sleep. Finally, I'd convinced Trevor to hack into Harriet's email, forum threads—she belonged to many, including the true crime ones—and search history.

She loved true crime. And when the FBI categorized the missing witness, Elyse Bailey, as another victim of the Mistress Strangler, it was in the news headlines again. The autopsy revealed strangle marks around her neck, with WHORE carved into her stomach. But the rest of us knew better. Some victims were made to look like the Mistress Strangler did it. Like the husband who got his sidepiece pregnant. But I wondered if a few of these were the work of Grigori's crew. Dress the kills to fit open cases. The feds were tightlipped about Elyse's autopsy. Their lab was processing the DNA, and I was told not to leave New York for almost five weeks. I was cleared around the time Trevor narrowed down Sloane's location from Harriet's conversation with someone in the forums.

Harriet googled Corolla beaches, and she was communicating with Carrotcakeforever from Corolla.

Either Sloane loved carrot cake or she was referring to her hair color or Ginger's.

I tracked down where she was staying and made an offer to the owner of the beach house beside it. He was a retired schoolteacher in his seventies. I sent him on vacation that would last two months. He said he needed this property back in the winter in time for

Thanksgiving with his family. I sure hoped I could convince Sloane to give me a second chance by then.

I had this overwhelming need to take care of her. Watching her barely eating, it was a struggle not to storm in there and force-feed her. She slept a lot, but it was anything but peaceful. I ached to snuggle up behind her and soothe her restlessness. I wanted to fight her demons, even if one of her demons was me. And when she was awake? The blank look on her face gutted me. But instinct was screaming at me to give her space to work through her grief. I might not be directly responsible for Billy's death, but I could have offered her help when she needed it. Instead, I rejected her. Did I reject her as she was miscarrying our child? If I hadn't rejected her, she wouldn't have been in that basement at all. Those torturous thoughts wouldn't leave me and I couldn't work through them on my own without knowing that Sloane was okay.

My phone buzzed. It was Sera.

SERA

I know you're watching us right now, stalker. Best not to show up tonight until I get the lay of the land.

ME

Put in a good word for me.

In your dreams. You're lucky Bianca isn't heading over there right now to castrate you. I can't stop Sandro, though, so expect him.

I'm shaking in my boots

🙄

I PACED AND PACED. I NEEDED ANOTHER CIGARETTE AND SINCE I respected the owner's wishes of keeping the interior smoke-free, I walked out to the wraparound patio, sat with another bottle of whiskey and started smoking.

The beach house I was renting was three times the size of Sloane's. I wondered how they were all going to fit in there. There were only two bedrooms in that one. I had five in mine.

I slipped out my phone and started flipping through the live surveillance videos. I watched my cousins hug Sloane and they cried. I could hardly hear their words because they were talking at the same time. I felt like a voyeur, an outsider into their intimate gathering. Raw emotions flowed, and I suppressed the ragged sob in my throat.

This thing with Sloane was turning me emo. I missed my calling in a rock band.

I stiffened when Sandro peered into one of the cameras. I swore he smirked before the feed went dead.

Motherfucker.

Sera immediately texted.

SERA

You're so predictable.

ME

Tell Sandro he's dead to me.

Tell him yourself, because he's heading your way, and I quote: I'm not wasting my time looking for those cameras and Dom can just tell me where they are.

Sandro is not welcome here.

Oh, piss off, cuz. Cooperate, or we'll tell Aunt Lottie where you are.

ME

I'm your cousin. You're supposed to be on my side.

SERA

Well, you're an ass, so we're on Sloane's side.

Do you guys even know the whole story?

You had your chance to tell us and you refused.

Because I wanted Sloane to tell her side, too. Now, she gets to tell hers and you all won't hear mine?

Bubbles…and then nothing.

Disloyal. The lot of you.

BIANCA

Stop being a drama queen.

Oh, she had to call me out. In frustration, I hurled my phone toward the beach and instantly regretted it. The sun had set an hour ago, and hopefully, it wasn't buried in sand. I heard it chiming in the dark and decided to be petty by ignoring their messages, and continued to down the whiskey.

They thought I was a drama queen, I'd show them drama queen.

My resistance took all of five minutes. I was the fucking don of the De Lucci crime family for Chrissakes. Although, in my defense, Luca was equally a drama queen when it suited him. It threw people off guard. We Morettis had a way of smiling as if we were your best friends while at the same time plotting devious ways to bury you.

Somewhere in the house, my proximity sensors went apeshit, but in my stubborn, self-pitying mood, I didn't give a fuck.

I chucked the empty whiskey bottle in the same direction as my phone.

"That's littering," Sandro spoke in the dark.

"Piss off." I stood, teetering on my feet before stumbling off the porch in the direction of the beach.

Sandro cocked his head at my shrieking house alarm. "I must say, if an assassin was after you, you'd be dead."

"You think I care?" I drunkenly trudged in the sand to search for my phone.

I saw the screen flashing a few feet away, probably warning me of an intruder. I scooped it up and my finger kept missing the mark to turn it off. I was more hammered than I thought.

Sandro snatched it out of my hand and turned the annoying thing off, then picked up the whiskey bottle and nudged me back to the house.

"You're pathetic," he muttered.

"Says the man who stalked Bianca for years," I shot back.

He chuckled. "Touché. But you've witnessed all our moronic actions, and this takes the cake."

I laughed mockingly. "Oh really? How about the times you smashed your fists through the drywall and redecorated your office because you were too chickenshit to make a move on Bianca?"

"She was too young, dammit."

I paused. Yeah, I actually admired Sandro for holding back. "You have a point."

"And you're one to talk since your mother has you practically betrothed to a twenty-one-year-old."

I groaned. "Shit. I already told her it ain't happening."

"Have you convinced her, though?"

Admittedly, I had not. I said no, and I expected her to accept it. Knowing my mother, she'd hold on to the idea and try to find a way to guilt me into going along with it. Though I hadn't been ignoring her in the past two weeks, I kept my answers vague about where I was. My phone was untraceable.

We were back at the house and I was about to sit on the porch chair again to stare at Sloane's house, but Sandro gripped my arm. "Oh no, you don't. I think you've drunk enough."

"Listen, you're not my keeper." My tongue slurred over the words as he dragged me into the house.

"Someone needs to look after you."

"Yeah, and she's in the house across from me, but I need to take care of her first."

Sandro lowered the whiskey bottle and my phone on the kitchen table and crossed his arms. "Now, how are you going to accomplish that?"

"Dunno."

I honestly didn't. I was at a loss. Stuck in my compulsion to take over and knowing I needed to give her space.

"Sit." Sandro said it in a way that irritated me, but knowing I was swaying on my feet, it would save me the indignity of falling on my face.

I sat on the dining chair.

I broodily watched him head to my kitchen. He peeked at my box of whiskeys and checked one out.

"I thought you said I had enough."

"This is for me," he muttered. "I think I'll be earning it after I talk some sense into you."

"You're not my shrink," I said. "I don't need a shrink. My shrinks have given up on me."

He raised a brow and set a bottled water in front of me. "Really? You've been to one?"

The Morettis had one on payroll. I didn't sit on a couch to be psychoanalyzed by the hour. It was usually over a game of pool or darts or foosball. "According to her, I have mommy issues."

"Like serial killers. There's one on the loose right now."

I scoffed. "Those are criminals perpetuating myths to cover their crime."

"Like copycats?"

"Yes, remember that Boston Strangler case back when? One of them was a husband getting rid of his mistress because she was pregnant."

"Yeah, Bianca told me that. The girls are probably over there discussing the Elyse Bailey case right now." He uncorked the whiskey and poured two fingers into his glass. Interestingly enough, I craved water.

"I wouldn't put it past Grigori to disguise his kill as the work of the Mistress Strangler. He has deep connections in law enforcement with access to the details of the case that were not made public." We did too.

"You've been a person of interest, right?"

"Fuck you, Alessandro. You already know that."

"You fit the profile."

"Fuck you. Fuck you. Fuck you." But there was no heat in my words. I was even amused. Maybe it was time to acknowledge the fact that I do indeed have mommy issues.

~

Dom, 16 years old

Ma was crying again. She'd been in bed for the past few weeks, rarely coming out of her bedroom to join us for meals. And when she did, she was wearing the same ratty robe and her hair was piled on her head like a squirrel's nest. Pop said she had a virus. At least, that was what he tried to explain to me and Lucy. I had my cousins and my friends for company, and was frequently out of the house. But now that it was winter, and sports were on hiatus, I was roaming the vast mansion alone. Our house staff had retired to their quarters because I offered to see to Ma's needs.

Lucy had a music recital. She was the cellist in the orchestra, and Pop went to see her perform. He asked me if I could stay with Ma. I wanted to do more than that. There was guilt that I ignored her illness or whatever was plaguing her long enough. Something happened after her visit to Grandpa last October, but I put off getting to the bottom of it because I didn't want it to interrupt my classes. Besides, Pop was handling it fine, until I noticed the taut stress lines on his face.

I fixed a tray of food. Cook prepared Ma's specialty dish, lasagna ala Moretti, which simply meant lots of fancy cheese. I made the garlic bread myself. I'd assisted my mother enough times to know my way around the kitchen.

I balanced the tray on one arm and knocked.

I heard Ma call out, "Come in."

She was sitting up in bed. Pop had already started a fire in the hearth before he left. Ma was surprised to see me. And that was when a memory hit me. I'd seen her this way before. I think when I was six years old. She'd been crying that Grandpa didn't love her anymore.

"*Mio figlio*," she said. "You didn't have to do that."

I crossed the room and set the tray on the bed. "But I wanted to, Mamma." She loved it when I used the full Italian version of the word mother.

"I'm not hungry." She pouted, but I could see that tiny sparkle in her eyes. Maybe all she needed was her children showing her we care. I wished Lucy would be less of a prima donna thinking about herself and how Ma's bedridden state was consuming all of Pop's attention.

"But you're going to eat if I have to spoon-feed you myself," I said firmly.

A hint of a smile curved her mouth. "You're growing up to be as bossy as Paulie."

"You like bossy." I dug into the lasagna and held it out to her.

She accepted my actions of feeding her. It also filled me with accomplishment. I made her smile, even if it was just a little. I was taking care of family.

"Now tell me why you were crying," I said. "Is it about Grandpa again?"

She took a sip of juice. Wine was not allowed because of her medications. "Yes, and no. I don't know, Dominic. I look at Ava and Cesar and they're happy with their kids. Like the barbecue this previous summer, remember? I should be happy like them. I have a handsome son and a beautiful daughter. A loving husband who spoils us. What more can I ask for?" She sighed heavily. "Maybe your nonno's acceptance doesn't matter."

"What did he say to you?" I asked sharply. I was never close to Emilio, but maybe because it was Pop keeping us away from the Chicago side of the family. Afraid of its influence. He didn't have a problem with our cousins who led the De Lucci crime family, maybe because he made his position clear that I would never become a made man. Still, the allure of the forbidden was enticing to me.

"I used to be the mafia princess, you know," she said, her eyes clouding as if transported back into her heyday. "Everyone wanted Emilio Moretti's prized daughter. The most lucrative offer came not from the Italians, but from the Russians. It was a chance to be joined to Russian royalty."

"Is this about the villas on the Amalfi coast?"

"Yes. The Russians were angry and refused to return the dowry. And to avoid war because it was an insult that I chose Paulie, Papa didn't argue. But he never forgave me because Paulie wasn't a made man. He wasn't even the eldest son."

"Did Grandpa say something about it to you again? It's old history. Why bring it up?"

Ma smiled wanly and patted my fingers. "That's your nonno. But don't worry. I'll get over this."

But my mother didn't. Three days later, I watched Pop emerge from their bedroom as if carrying the weight of the universe on his shoulders. He sunk to the floor and buried his face in his hands. I was about to go to him when Lucy appeared out of nowhere and rushed to his side and hugged him.

I clenched my jaw. He wasn't making it through to Ma. I had to do something. I approached my cousin Mikey, who was the current underboss of the De Lucci crime family and told him I was interested in joining the family. He looked pleased, but also thought I was out of my mind. The news reached Grandpa fast.

That was how crime families worked. The boss-to-boss bullshit.

Emilio called me that night and was the most enthusiastic he'd ever been, giving me pointers on where to start, even how to approach Pop.

Well, it was Pop who stormed into my room.

Without preamble, he roared, "I forbid it, Dominic."

"You'll forbid it now because you can, but when I turn eighteen, you no longer have a say."

"I protect this family," he snapped. "I can't protect you if you put yourself in danger."

"It doesn't work that way and you know it," I shot back. "I don't have to work the streets."

"You would have to deal with the criminal filth of the underworld, who has no compunction to have you killed."

"As if that's not what's happening now? As much as you say

we're the legitimate side of the De Luccis, don't tell me Mikey and them are not using your businesses to launder money."

A movement by the door caught my attention. Lucy was glaring at me.

"Get out of here, Lucy!" I yelled at her and stalked toward her.

Pop blocked me. "Don't you dare shout at your sister."

"You coddle her." I sneered. "Why don't you teach her that this family is more than about her?"

My father's face twisted in anguish and I almost felt ashamed at my own words. He gripped my jaw in his hands and squeezed. "This family is all I've ever cared about. I love your mother so much and it's killing me I can't reach her, but I am *not* sacrificing your life for my failures."

I gripped my father's wrists. "You're not a failure, Pop. Let me help."

He dropped his hands to his sides. "The price is too steep."

I exhaled heavily. "But it's a price I'm willing to pay."

Pop and I had more arguments in the following days, but one morning, Ma joined us for breakfast.

We were shocked.

She wasn't in her ratty robe. She'd showered and changed, did her hair, put on makeup, and announced she was going shopping.

Pop and I locked eyes, resignation written all over his face.

I was on my way to becoming a made man.

~

DOM

THE SOOTHING WAVES OF THE OCEAN DID NOTHING TO ALLEVIATE MY almighty hangover.

I rolled out of bed, parched. I didn't even remember getting into it. I sure as fuck hoped Sandro hadn't carried my sorry ass and laid me in bed like Sleeping Beauty. And he better not have taken a picture. I grabbed my phone and saw a barrage of messages. I didn't bother checking them and went straight to my video surveillance of Sloane.

All were blank except the perimeter and the kitchen. Fucking Sandro.

It was a little past midnight and I could see lights in her living room and hear the muffled chatter of the girls talking. I hoped they were helping Sloane cope, because it looked like I had my own shit to address.

To be in Sloane's life the way she deserved, I needed to make changes in mine.

My father loved Ma to distraction. He said he had never been a victim of the De Lucci obsession curse, but I believed he was lying.

See, I wasn't taking care of Ma alone. It was hard for me to see my old man struggle, not knowing how to reach the woman he loved to pieces. Emilio's cruel rejection was a trigger for Ma's depression. Lucy scoffed that it was all an act. Be that as it may, I had the power to pull her out of it. If Ma was happy, Pop would be happy, and he loved her enough not to blame her for my choice. Not so with Lucy. She was only eight years old when that all went down, but hell, did she hold a grudge against me and Ma.

I learned early in life to take care of what was mine. And I considered all the De Luccis and Morettis mine.

Like when Matteo went after Sera, and I stood up to Luca for my cousins.

Or when I had to address Nico's beef with Joe Rossi. I had my suspicions he and Sandro conspired to whack the Rossi boss, but like all things mafia related, the less we talked about it, the better.

Then came the war between the Rossis and the De Luccis,

where they kidnapped Bianca, and shot Renz. I was fucking furious, but I'd been the voice of reason in talking down Uncle Cesar and his boys from waging an all-out war.

The villas on the Amalfi coast had become a nonissue. We were not getting those back. Ma would just have to suck it up. Besides being tainted with the sex-trafficking business, they would be a constant reminder how I'd failed Sloane. Letting them go was the right thing to do.

Sloane insisted our affair was over, and we didn't owe each other an explanation. But we were both fantastic liars, preferring to hurt each other to protect that lie. But the burden and shame were on me. I was in the position of power in this relationship. I should have done something to not make that matter to Sloane.

See, I think I'm in love with this stubborn woman.

I needed to figure out how to bring her into my life without triggering World War III with my mother.

But Luca's words were an echo in my head. Being as sharp as he was, my uncle knew my problems were not only the wealth and status imbalance, but also my mother.

I had to protect that choice with my life.

I choose Sloane.

CHAPTER *Twenty*

Sloane

"I hear an arrest is imminent," Sera said. "At least Dom is no longer a suspect, despite the pictures showing he could be the last person who was seen with Elyse Bailey."

"They already know who the killer is?"

A theory was that Grigori made a deal with the feds to protect him from the Russian bratva.

"It doesn't make sense. I'm sure either Grigori or Anton was the one who killed Elyse." I touched my throat. Although my bet was Anton. It made me wonder if all or some of these Mistress Strangler killings were the work of the Russian bratva, or at least Grigori's crew.

"I'm smelling a lot of coverup." Bianca read my mind. "According to what Sandro learned, Grigori was running a successful sex-trafficking operation and many of his clients are high-profile government officials—not only in the US, but world leaders. Add to that a mix of celebrities, sheiks, oligarchs, and kleptocrats."

I shuddered. "I think he was considering selling me."

"What?" Sera and Bianca exclaimed.

"I know I'm too old for the taste of most of his clients, but Billy told me he'd been having a hard time looking for a feisty natural redhead for someone." I was remembering now Grigori ranting to Anton that his client already made a deposit and that deposit money was gone. With me miscarrying and being out of commission, he had no one to sell. "He either made a deal with the feds or another entity, but I was instructed never to return to Manhattan."

"But why?"

"Because they couldn't keep me out of New Jersey if I wanted to see Harriet."

"But why Manhattan in particular?"

"If they're making a move against the New York bratva, then they'll likely be tried there."

"That is, if Grigori became a rat himself," Bianca said. "Sandro doesn't see that happening."

"Desperate people do desperate things."

"Do they want you to testify?"

"I can only testify that Anton shot my brother and they hired me to clean up the mess. I didn't see them kill Elyse."

"It makes no sense that Grigori let you go."

"He needed money. Someone took pity and bought me."

"Maybe he had a deal with someone who takes his rejects," Sera said. She was staring at her phone and didn't see me wince. I knew what she meant, but I guess that word was triggering for me right now.

"Does she have an accent? Is she Italian or Russian?" she asked, looking up.

"No. Very cultured American. Highly educated. I would even say she might even know different languages."

"Oooh, CIA," Bianca suggested.

I huffed a short laugh. "Maybe a lawyer. They might be building a bigger case. But I'm free to move after September nine."

"Why that day?"

"No clue."

"You're not in some kind of safe house or WITSEC? Are they even concerned if anything happened to you?" Bianca asked.

"I never thought about it until I was here a couple of weeks." I'd been in a dark place. There was a time I didn't shower for a week. One afternoon, a thunderstorm rolled in with a deluge and I had the urge to dance in the rain and I went with instinct. It helped me break through the cobwebs of my mind and forced me to soak in a warm bath.

Taking a brush to my hair was still optional. I resisted the idea of chopping my hair off with the kitchen shears and instead drove my ass to town and had a stylist detangle it. That was the first glimmer of my old self when I saw myself in the mirror. A flash of defiance appeared in my eyes. My mother's voice telling me not to depend on other people. Never let a man control the money, and have my own.

Sera regarded me like a specimen under a microscope or a doctor who didn't know how to tell me I had a few months to live. Or even days.

"What?"

"I wonder if you have a tracker on you?" Sera asked.

Bianca clapped a hand over her mouth before exclaiming, "Of course!" She started typing into her phone. "Sandro always carries a detector with him." Sandro had been over at Dom's for a couple of hours. He said Dom was drunk off his ass and Sandro had to make sure he didn't choke on his vomit. It might have been meant to be funny, but it didn't quite land that way to me. I was surprisingly apathetic. Maybe it was time to back off on the antidepressants and anxiety meds.

Bianca surged from the couch. "I'll be right back."

"I'll get more chips," Sera said. "Want another Coke?"

The girls didn't drink in solidarity with my alcohol restriction. I forgot how Coke, chips, and queso were so addictive. Bianca, of course, brought her favorite—blueberry soda.

"No. I'll stick to water. At this rate, I won't be sleeping."

With as much caffeine as we consumed, it wasn't surprising why we were wide awake at two a.m.

Bianca bounced back through the door, holding a wand that looked like the metal detector ones you saw at airport checkpoints.

She turned it on and tested it on herself, holding it against her right thigh. It beeped. "Cool, it works." After she got kidnapped by one of Sandro's hidden enemies, she'd finally given in to being tagged when she'd resisted the idea for a long time even with the De Luccis.

Sera held out her left arm. "Try mine."

The wand beeped somewhere along the middle of her forearm.

Bianca stood in front of me. "Okay, stand up."

"I don't really think they would bother. Maybe the van?" I raised both arms as Bianca enthusiastically waved the wand over me. "You're enjoying this."

She giggled and did between my legs.

"Dom said he already checked." Sera was texting on her phone. "But could use another sweep."

"Excuse me?" I retorted, only mildly irritated. Typical Dom.

Bianca was behind me when the device beeped.

My blood ran cold, and I grew lightheaded. I wasn't really expecting it.

"It's in your ass," Bianca hissed.

I whipped around, glaring at her. "What?"

"Don't be mad at me." She twisted me to face away from her again. Sera walked over to where Bianca was checking me out and the device alerted again.

"It's really in your ass." Both girls tittered.

"It's not funny." I spun a one-eighty to glower at them while poking on my poor behind for the device. I felt it when I pressed down. "Shit. It's really there." Whoever inserted the tracker in me made sure I had the lowest chance of feeling around for it.

"I'm sorry." Sera rolled her lips, fighting a smile, but failing. She was typing on her phone.

"Don't tell Dom."

"Too late." Her eyes shot to mine. "The guys are coming over."

Minutes later, Dom barged into the house. "You have a tracker on you?" He stalked toward me, and if I hadn't held an arm out in warning, he would have grabbed my shoulders.

His arms fell to his sides, his face dejected and etched in frustration. "Sloane…"

"I do, and I don't know why you're here, because I don't need you."

Pain slashed through his features, and a pinch of guilt squeezed my heart. I steeled my spine. I only had to remember the night he cruelly turned me away. How cold his eyes had been when, for the first time in my life, I begged a person who had the power to shatter my heart to help me.

An awkward silence fell in the room. Dom and I were both panting. Him probably from exertion due to his mad dash from his beach house, and mine was probably more from my heart than my lungs.

He reeked of whiskey. He had shadows under his bloodshot eyes. And his facial hair was unkempt. A far cry from the polished boss I'd come to know.

It was guilt. He was simply feeling guilt.

"Dom, maybe you should go," Bianca said.

"The fuck I am!" he growled at her.

"Watch how you talk to my wife." Sandro inserted himself between me and Dom and effectively shielded Bianca, too.

"If Sloane doesn't want to see you, respect that," Sera said.

"We're in a precarious truce with the Russians. I need to know who put the tracker in her," Dom responded evenly.

"The woman who paid me."

"What woman?" Dom yelled.

"Everyone calm down." Bianca raised both arms in a placating gesture. "We're thinking Grigori turned fed informant, and the woman is his handler," she said.

"Highly unlikely," Sandro answered. "If anything, we're dealing with other organizations or dirty politicians or businessmen who have stakes in seeing Sloane disappear."

"Then why not kill me?"

"Doesn't make sense, you're right. We'll have more motive once they make the arrest."

"What do you want to do, Sloane?" Sandro asked me. "I can take it out for you."

"You're not touching her," Dom snarled.

"That's hardly your decision," Sera shot back.

"It's in her upper right butt cheek." Bianca's cheeks flamed. "You'll have to…uh, be…naked or wear a thong."

"I can wear my bathing suit." I had no reservations about letting Sandro dig around in my flesh. I trusted him enough to have done minor surgery on himself. But I wasn't oblivious to the fact that Bianca might not want her husband touching another woman's buttocks even if it was to remove a tracker, so I asked her, "Can you do it? All you have to do is make a small incision and yank it out."

"I'd rather not. What if I cut too deep?"

"Sera?"

But she was already shaking her head.

Dom crossed his arms. He was in a staredown with Sandro, and I could feel the violent waves rolling off him.

"Aren't you hungover?" Sandro asked.

"Fuck you," Dom gritted. "Finding out someone put a tracker in my woman is enough to turn me stone-cold sober."

"Hey," I snapped. "I'm not your woman. Got me?"

"But I'm your man," he replied with conviction.

I shot Bianca and Sera a helpless look as if saying, *I give up*.

For someone who didn't want drama, Dom was certainly full of it. And where the hell was this *I'm your man* coming from? He was suddenly committed? I didn't trust his change of heart or words out of his mouth right now.

"Fine, Dom, you can do it. But only if we don't damage the tracker." I was regaining some of my spunk. Apparently the man before me had a way of firing me up.

"I've done it before," Dom informed me.

"Why am I not surprised?" I said dryly. "I'm gonna get my kit and change." It was no big deal, but I could see how the two women would be averse to doing it. Handling a scalpel and cutting into skin could make the inexperienced woozy. I'd seen both men and women faint just by looking at a needle plunge into muscle.

I put on a bikini bottom and peeked out of my bedroom, but Dom was already leaning against the wall outside of it. For fuck's sake.

He entered the room with all the predatory vibes in the universe. Even hungover, he radiated a lethal aura only enhanced by his rough appearance.

"Don't even think of trying any seduction."

He genuinely looked insulted. "I'm not that insensitive."

I grabbed the marker I had brought out and faced the full-length mirror. I felt around for the tracker. "It's right here. You can probably see the incision site."

He lowered to a knee and moved his head closer. I could feel his breath on my skin. I wasn't aroused and was surprisingly jaded. "Just so you know, my libido is dead." It was probably from the antidepressants I was taking, but he didn't need to know that.

"I'm just concerned for you. Bianca and Sera already warned me and gave Sandro the green light to take me out if I misbehave."

His tone was part amused, part affronted. Like he couldn't believe their loyalty was to me instead of him. I also wasn't sure how I felt about Bianca and Sera stepping in to defend me, but I remembered my therapist's words about allowing people to help me.

It wasn't weakness.

Blowing out a breath, I handed him the marker. "Please mark the spot."

"So I don't cut the wrong ass cheek?" he quipped.

I rolled my eyes. "Yeah, that."

He chuckled and drew a dot on the area, taking longer than was necessary to accomplish the task.

"Stop feeling me out." He had his free palm on my other cheek, but it was totally innocent.

Maybe.

"You're so prickly," he grumbled. "I just want to be precise."

"Riigght."

Now that we'd established where the tracker was, it was time to take it out. I'd already prepared the instruments. "This is the anesthesia, the scalpel, and the tweezers. You need help on…"

"I got this, baby."

I gritted my teeth at the endearment. He was making it sound like we were still together, but I held my tongue. Because I wasn't about to antagonize the person who was about to perform minor surgery on me.

Dom delivered the anesthesia like he'd done it countless of times.

"Do you get to play mob doc too?" I asked, just so we had something to talk about while the anesthesia took effect.

"Sometimes when he's not available, and a bullet needs to come out or a knife wound needs stitching. That kind of thing." He sat back on his heels and stared up at me.

"You've lost weight," I blurted out.

"I could say the same about you." We let the silence wrap around us for a few seconds.

"I'm sorry about Billy," he said. "I…I was there."

"What do you mean?" I choked out before suppressing a ragged sob.

"When they found his grave," he said. "God, Sloane, I've never been more terrified in my life. I thought the second body was you."

"Sometimes I wish it was…" I whispered.

"No," he growled. "Don't say that. Otherwise, I'm moving in here with you."

I emitted a brittle laugh. "Seems you have no problem invading my privacy."

"Hate me forever if you must. I made the mistake of taking what we had for granted once. I'm not doing it again."

We had so many missteps between us, but I was still struggling to get over Billy's death and his secret with Harriet.

"Billy killed my father," I blurted out.

Dom reeled back like I'd punched the breath out of him. "Come again?"

"My father didn't leave us," I rushed out. I had told no one else, not even my therapist. "But Billy caught him beating up Mom, and he said…he just saw red and grabbed the baseball bat and hit Dad on the head. Over and over."

"Holy fuck. He told you this where? In the basement of that house?"

"Before he…he passed. He wanted to get it off his chest. Mom panicked and went to Harriet. I think Harriet had told a story to Mom about a friend who went to the Russian mafia to get rid of her abusive husband, but I think Harriet was talking about herself."

"So Harriet put your mom and Billy in contact with Grigori?"

"Yes," I whispered in the same breath as, "I think it's numb."

Dom looked at me strangely and I tipped my chin to where he'd poked me with a needle. "The incision site."

"Sorry," he muttered.

"Do you want to do this some other time?" Because he looked as dazed as I was when Billy revealed the truth. Granted, I was miscarrying at that time too and suffering from blood loss. Sometimes I replayed it in my head like it was a bad dream. That for years, the three most important people in my life hadn't instigated the lie I'd been living. That I didn't waste those years thinking Billy was a worthless piece of shit of a brother when he'd been living with the guilt that he killed our father. That he let me live with that hole inside me that our father abandoned his family, and we weren't worth it to stay. I was rewiring my beliefs with the way I'd made my choices because of them, and they were a tangled mess inside me.

"No, I want to get this thing out of you," Dom told me gently.

And I didn't know whether it was the sympathy in his voice that brought tears to my eyes. "I don't know why I unloaded this on you when you hurt me, too."

I hated how my voice warbled. Dom was the last man I wanted to see me at my most vulnerable.

Regret etched his features. "Because I was your person," he said. "And I betrayed you."

CHAPTER Twenty-One

Dom

"Lie on the bed." I cut the train of our discussion before we lost focus on the task at hand. Besides, I didn't want to push her too hard. She was still fragile, and I didn't want her ending up withdrawing from me.

Sloane took position on the mattress. I could feel the relief cloak her when we lost eye contact. We were feeling exposed with the bullshit still between us.

I was ready to confront it. She was still healing from the trauma I'd indirectly caused. Even if she said it was her fault, I was still responsible. Because if I'd taken care of Grigori when Sandro asked me about it, we wouldn't be having this conversation. In my desire to keep everyone happy, I played a balancing act I had no hopes of winning. Grigori was just dangling the properties in front of me, but I was lying to myself that there was a chance of getting them back, that I wasn't going to fail the Moretti legacy, that I wouldn't have to resort to an arranged marriage with their mafia princess in order to get them. It had to take losing Sloane in the most horrific way that yanked the blinders from my eyes to see what was important. My sister's entanglement with the Russians only made it easier. I was letting go of those tainted properties.

Picking up the scalpel from the night table, I prodded the skin where I'd injected. "Feel anything?"

"No."

Without hesitation, I cut. I'd installed and removed subcutaneous trackers before, so this wasn't new, but the haste was because I had to grit my teeth at having to mar Sloane's perfect skin. I wanted that dreaded feeling over. If the person who put this tracker in her didn't have her safety at heart, then there'd be retribution. I dropped the scalpel in the aluminum tray and picked up the tweezers.

"You're set up well for life on the lam. You haven't used your credit cards."

"Is it a good idea to tell you I have a storage facility somewhere?"

I probed for the tracker and found it. I started the extraction. "Harriet said that you were planning to get the hell out of Dodge."

"Things with Grigori were getting uncomfortable."

I removed the tracker and showed it to Sloane before dropping it beside the rest of the used instruments. "Do you want stitches or will a butterfly bandage do?"

"It needs a stitch, since it's in an area that will see a lot of friction."

A needle was already threaded. I wouldn't have had the finesse of someone experienced like Sloane, who would use a hemostat to maneuver a needle, but I wouldn't have trusted anyone else to handle this except me. Like the cut, I executed the suture quickly. "I hope this doesn't scar."

"It might not leave one," she said. "There are…wait…did you say you've talked to Harriet?"

"I met her at Billy's funeral. But the girls talked to her more."

She rolled off the bed and got to her feet. "You were using them to spy?"

"It wasn't like that."

"I'm still mad at her, but I guess communicating with her in the forums brought you guys here."

"Trevor was the shit."

Her face grew sad. "I let her down about Ginger, but I'm glad someone took her in." She walked toward the door. "I forgot to mention it to Bianca. Maybe she can track down—"

"I have Ginger." I cut her off. Shit. This wasn't the way I planned to tell her.

Her whole body froze, and she slowly turned to face me, her brows furrowed. "What do you mean?"

"I found her in the alley. She's okay. No broken bones…."

"She tried to defend me," Sloane whispered. "Anton tossed her out the window. Hurled her out like a baseball."

"She's fine, Sloane." I walked toward her. It tore me up to see Sloane struggling not to show vulnerabilities, especially to the bastard who rejected her at the time she needed him the most. If I stood a chance of winning her back, I should learn to be patient for the long haul.

My girl was broken and lost.

"I…" She struggled for words to say. "You and my cat."

Still, I couldn't resist needling her. "My cat now."

She narrowed her eyes. "You can't even pet her, let alone have her on your lap."

"Well, she enjoys sitting on my lap, just so you know, just like this other pussy I know."

Her mouth fell open. I smirked.

"Where is she?" she demanded. "Is she at your beach house?"

"I didn't bring her."

"Where is she?" Sloane repeated. "You left her alone? Who's feeding her? Who's taking care of her?"

"Relax, Lucy is taking care of her." I crossed my arms before they had the chance to wrap around her. God, I wanted to fix her so badly, but she wasn't a toy to be fixed. She was a person with feelings and insecurities. Who'd been handed the shit things in life but grew up swinging her sass. Her fire was what attracted me to her, and I was loving seeing the sparks right now.

"Your sister?"

"Yeah, she's staying with me at the penthouse."

"Ginger is in your penthouse." Disbelief rounded her eyes.

"What can I say? She likes the upgrade from the alley to the Ritz."

"I don't believe you."

"I have cat videos to prove it," I shot back.

She was surveying me with squinty eyes while mine challenged her, but before she could form words, a knock sounded on the door.

"Are you two still alive in there?" It was Bianca.

Sloane opened the door and addressed the women, "Ginger is with Dom?"

"Guess the cat is out of the bag," Sera laughed.

I hated that my cousins broke our moment, but at the same time, I was relieved. Relieved because my cousins tempered my instinct to bulldoze Sloane to accept me back.

"Let me see?" Bianca asked, turning Sloane around and bending over to inspect my handiwork.

"It's a stitch. It's not like he gave me a tattoo," Sloane muttered, glaring at me.

Ah, my Firecat. I couldn't wait to tattoo my name on her ass.

Property of Dominic De Lucci. It was only a matter of time. "And that's the thanks I get."

"I didn't ask you," she snapped and padded off into the kitchen.

Her walls were back up. Bianca and I exchanged a look, and she gave me a shake of her head. That irked me. What? Like I couldn't read the room? Sera, though, gave a knowing look. She'd seen me in mafia sit-downs handle business and negotiate the upper hand. Frequently, it was the women in my life who put me at a disadvantage. I was determined to win Sloane over, but for my sanity, she had to understand that it was going to be a compromise because of my position.

Her independence was at stake, and I had to show her I was worth the risk.

"I LIKE SLOANE."

I was on a video call with Lucy. After the discovery of the tracker a week ago, Sandro had arranged a new phone for Sloane with the necessary encryption so she could communicate with us, including checking on Ginger. I appreciated my sister for taking the time. Apparently the two were hitting it off.

"I have good taste," I retorted.

My sister cackled. "I don't think she returns the sentiment."

"Thanks for stating the obvious." Ginger was sitting on her lap. Apparently, the cat was also looking forward to the video calls.

"Meow." She pawed the screen.

"Ginger misses you both, though," Lucy said. "She's haunting the penthouse at night with her cries. She's looking for you or Sloane."

"It's me she's looking for," I said confidently. Hell, I needed that morale boost, at least. There was no sign of a thaw from Sloane.

After Bianca, Sera, and Sandro left, she never responded to my texts. I wondered if she blocked me. I continued to watch her in my remaining video surveillance, and when Sloane was in the kitchen, sometimes she'd give me the finger.

That got me hard.

If she was trying to discourage me by giving me the cold shoulder, she would know soon enough that it would only make me try harder. I was a De Lucci and a Moretti. I had obsession on one side, and cunning on the other. Although I refused to be manipulative like Luca because that only bit him in the ass later. But I was getting desperate to get her to a more secure location.

The feds arrested Kolya Petrov for the murder of Elyse Bailey. It was his DNA that was on her body, but even I knew Grigori was the one who planted it. And Sloane could be a witness. But why let her go?

"If you say so, dear bro."

"Are you on my side or not?" I grumbled.

"It's entertaining to see you floundering for once when it comes to women." She tickled Ginger's chin, and the feline started purring. "Oh, by the way, Sloane and I put two and two together."

"What? Like how you two hate my guts?" Maybe that was why Sloane wasn't softening toward me. Lucy was only magnifying my shortcomings. I knew it was a bad idea to put two of the most independent and stubborn women in my life together. They were ganging up against me.

"I don't hate you." She rounded her eyes in all innocence. "No, this is related to Elyse's case."

"Lucy, I told you to leave that alone. They arrested Kolya. And we all know he's like a brother to Kirill."

"Your penthouse is like Fort Knox and De Lucci soldiers surround the building, not to mention Dad had hired private military security."

"Maybe you can convince Sloane to move in with you."

"I floated that idea to her," Lucy said. "But wait, you're distracting me. So Sloane was one of the nurses who was working when Wade was brought into the ER."

"Your lawyer friend?"

"Yes." Foreboding and rage tightened my grip on the phone. That was the night Sloane broke up with me.

The night she was attacked.

"She saw this Anton guy in the ER."

"One of the Russians who works with Grigori," I growled. "God fucking dammit. It was him! He was the one who strangled her."

"Elyse Bailey?"

"No!" I was shouting now. "That night that happened, I went to Sloane's apartment because she wasn't answering my texts. She had strangle marks around her neck. She..." I broke off as the magnitude of my failures stabbed my chest with a crippling blow. Breathing became a chore.

I put bodyguards on her, but I sidelined her instead of getting to the bottom of her attack. Though she broke up with me, our boundaries were merely an excuse for me to justify putting mob business first. She would never believe I was falling in love with her given my past behavior.

"Are you all right?" Lucy's voice sounded far away.

"I don't deserve her..." I gasped. The sound of something scraping back and toppling over reached my ears.

"Why are you clutching your chest?" Lucy shrieked.

"Hurts..."

"Oh my God, are you having a heart attack?"

CHAPTER
Twenty-Two

Dom

"I...I can't breathe." I had to tell Sloane I loved her before I died. Otherwise, I would haunt her for the rest of my days from purgatory, or maybe even hell.

"Is your left arm feeling numb?"

In my chaotic thoughts and reactions, I concluded Lucy was only making me feel worse.

"I'm calling Sloane!" she said.

"No!" I was already running for the front door. I needed to see her. Waiting be damned. And since I could barely breathe, running to her was out of the question. I climbed into the SUV, gunned the engine, and sped the short distance to her beach house. That short time seemed to be forever. The stabbing in my chest eased, but I sounded like I had asthma and I knew what that sounded like because Lucy had it when she was a child.

Why was I thinking of Lucy when she had asthma? Was I flashing back to my childhood because I was dying?

No. No. No. Sloane had to see me. I gripped the steering wheel, speeding up because my gaze zeroed in on her van. In the back of my mind, I knew I should be slowing down. That fucking van was a death trap. How many times had I watched her try to start that thing and check under its hood? But she wouldn't accept help when I came over and asked if she needed a ride. She would return to the house and slam the door in my face.

Well, she was becoming unreasonable, and I could be vindictive—to her vehicle. I floored the gas and catapulted off the road, straight into the back of her van, and braced.

My body shot forward, the seat belt bit my shoulder, and the thundering sound of metal clashing with metal should have woken her up. Otherwise, I'd have to barge in there.

Her door swung open, and she came running out with a phone to her ear.

"Are you having a heart attack?"

I unclipped the seat belt and shoved open the door. "Maybe. You're the nurse." I was still in a semi-daze with what I had done. What progress I had made giving Sloane space had come screeching to a halt, literally.

"You shouldn't have gotten behind the wheel!" she yelled and grabbed my arm to lead me into the house.

"Do I have to be dying for you to talk to me?"

She spun around, eyes narrowing. "Is this all an act?" She gave me a withering head-to-toe appraisal. "You don't look like someone having a heart attack."

My head dropped, and I assessed her mood under hooded eyes. Shit. She was going to kick me out. "I think I was having a panic attack, but Lucy made it worse by suggesting I was having a coronary."

Sloane heaved a heavy sigh and raised her arm toward the kitchen table. "The power of suggestion works wonders. Sit. I'll check you out."

She didn't look pleased, but there was no question about the terror in her eyes when she ran out of her house. Sloane still cared for me. She didn't even get mad about her van. I was sure that would come later.

I let my eyes wander around her beach house. Nothing much had changed. After I informed her of Kolya's arrest, she mentioned a move to Oregon or San Diego. She'd asked the Rossis for help to escape to either Canada or Mexico. But Sandro calmed her down and told her they had the pulse on the Russians' movements. I'd also given instructions to Sonny and Matteo. Now if only I could convince her to return to Manhattan. The tracker was out of her. We could leave it here, while I hid her in the penthouse. No way was I delegating her security again.

Sloane returned and had the stethoscope around her neck and a blood pressure cuff.

"We seem to find ourselves playing doctor-patient frequently," I said.

"That seems to be a language we understand."

"Taking care of each other?" I said innocently.

Our eyes met, but hers squinted. "Now don't speak. Breathe normally."

She put the listening piece to my chest and listened to my palpitations. Then she stood and put the probe to my back and gave me instructions to hold my breath and release it. I followed her orders automatically, but I was struggling not to react to her nearness. She smelled of coconut and vanilla. Not her usual scent of citrus and floral—she mentioned it was ylang-ylang once. But Sloane had her own essence, and its ability to make my blood surge south was absolute. My cock tented my pants.

Sloane's body shook. She was trying not to laugh, but she backed away and stared at my erection.

"You're impossible," she whispered, both in annoyance and mirth.

I smirked. "What can I say? I feel so much better when you're around me."

"I'm serious, Dom." She sat on a chair and looked me in the eye. "You shouldn't have driven. At all."

"I needed to get to you quickly, and I wasn't sure I wasn't gonna pass out while running."

"Well, it would have been worse if you were driving. Lucy called me in a panic."

She started putting everything away.

"Aren't you supposed to check my blood pressure? Run an EKG?"

"With your monster cock saying hello? The results would be skewed," she said dryly.

"Monster, huh?"

My eyes lazily traveled the length of her body. She was wearing a tank top and shorts. Her arms were thinner, but her tits were as full as I remembered. Fuck, this wasn't helping my erection go down.

She stood up.

"Don't go."

She glared at me. "I think you're the one who should go."

"Sloane, please," I whispered. She must have recognized the desperation in my voice because I saw a trace of pity, so I rushed out the words. "Please listen to me. I know I don't deserve it, especially with the way I turned you away."

Her face hardened, and I realized my mistake when she sneered, "I thought you're done slumming?"

I briefly shut my eyes at the memory of those cruel words, but when I opened them, Sloane had already gathered up her stuff and left me to wallow.

I followed her to the bathroom. "Please listen to me."

"I'm beneath your station, remember?"

The hateful words I said to her clawed inside my chest. Did I deserve her at all? No wonder she didn't trust me.

"Leave."

"I should have taken out Grigori when I had the chance," I continued. I would never win Sloane back if I didn't come clean. "Sandro asked me if I would consider it."

"I didn't expect you to take care of my problems!" she yelled, going into the kitchen. She grabbed a bottled water and handed it to me. "Drink this. That's why I didn't want to get involved with anyone from the mob. Mixing business and pleasure was the worst fucking idea of my life. So yes, it's on me too."

I was in whiplash with her handing me water, but I guessed my persistence was winning out. I twisted off the cap and took a gulp. I didn't realize how parched I was. "We both made mistakes, but I had the power to ease your burdens and I didn't. Selfishly, I thought I could have everything, but having everything was an illusion. The properties that I wanted Grigori to sell to me were for my mother."

"Your mother?"

She walked over to the living room, and I followed eagerly like a lapdog. I was so gone for this girl and she wasn't even aware of it. It wasn't guilt. I simply stopped lying to myself. When I did, my obsession for Sloane flared so fucking bright, I was blind to everything else except her.

"The properties were a Moretti legacy. They owned them for generations. My mother had an arrangement to be married to a high-ranking member of the Russian bratva. Let's just say, in the underworld, it could have been the match of the century. But they demanded our villas on the Amalfi coast as dowry. All the documents had been signed, but my mother backed out last minute and married Pop instead. The De Luccis aren't small fish by any means, but we didn't have the pedigree of the Zahkarovs." I recounted the series of events that led to Ma's breakdown and depression. How I did my part to take care of the family. And how her promise to a dying Emilio Moretti to get the properties back had been my vow to her.

"Those are the same properties Lucy was telling me about," Sloane mused. "The lawyer of the witness…"

I felt that familiar stabbing in my chest again, and I rubbed the spot.

"Are you feeling okay?" Sloane asked.

"That's the reason for my panic attack," I confessed. For someone in my position to admit having such vulnerabilities was unspeakable. But this was Sloane. She'd seen me at my weakest and I'd seen her at hers. How could she not see we fit? "I realized that was the night you had strangle marks. The night you broke up with me was also the night I had put security on you."

Her eyes widened. "That far back?"

"Yes." I drained the bottled water. I was really thirsty and there was more I needed to own up to so we could start with a clean slate. "You broke up with me. And I fully intended to follow up on you. But Luca found Natalya, and we had to shut down any leaks of information so Luca could make his move. Then Lucy also asked for my help to hide Elyse Bailey. I was pulled in all directions."

"You had me on ice while you took care of others."

I hung my head. "I failed you. Plain and simple."

"You told me you had enough to worry about and you didn't have to worry about me," she said. "So tell me how is this supposed to work if I give you a second chance? I'll be your mistress, protected from all the shit that touches you, spend your money, but I can only watch while you escort more suitable women to events.

And what happens when you decide to marry? What if I get pregnant again?"

I remained silent. Because at this point, she wouldn't believe me if I told her she would be all that. The woman I take to parties. The only woman I intended to propose to. I very much envisioned her to be the mother of my children, and I still grieved the baby we lost.

I wanted her to be all that, but Sloane, she had every reason to doubt me.

"We can start small," I suggested. "See where this goes?"

"We'll end up in bed," she said sarcastically.

She didn't see us as a couple outside of sex yet. Months and months of passionate trysts and nothing else had dictated who we were to each other. But in our stolen moments, a connection grew, a yearning. We both reacted to our emerging feelings badly. With a skewed fear of commitment, we fucked up what could have been a beautiful relationship. Relationships I'd seen my cousins have, but never pictured for myself. I never envied them until now.

"How about I replace the van I destroyed?"

Her face was a cross between amusement and amazement. "You manipulative son of a bitch."

"Call me names, baby. I don't mind," I replied evenly. "But I know you're practical—pragmatic. I destroyed your mode of transportation. I'll pay for the replacement."

"I'm not saying no…"

I chuckled. Delighted. This was the Sloane that I wanted to see. Her fiery personality to match mine.

"I'm not saying no to a new car," she said in a calculated tone. There was a glimmer of retribution in her eyes, and I braced myself for her next words. "But I'm not agreeing to hooking up with you."

"I don't want you to be my hookup," I gritted. "I want more."

"Are you sure this is not guilt talking?" she asked. "Because I don't see this ending well. Your mother—"

"I don't answer to my mother."

She raised a brow.

"It's different from caring for her well-being," I explained. "It's part of taking care of the family."

She waved a hand. "I don't know what exactly you're proposing. I can't even see past tomorrow. I'm taking things one day at a time. If that's too slow for you, the door is right there."

I clenched my fists at my sides, partly crumpling the plastic bottle in my hand.

"I have an appointment in the morning. I can call for a ride."

"I'll drive you," I blurted out.

"How? You wrecked your SUV."

"I think it's workable."

"You're lucky the airbag didn't deploy. It could have been worse, Dom."

Ah, this woman. I erased the distance between us, intending to cup her face, but she flinched. She was still skittish.

Patience.

I rapped my knuckles on the kitchen island to give them something to do before I gave in to the urge to kiss her into submission. But while she was on medication and seeing a therapist, I had no business bending her to my will and ruining what progress she'd made. I could be her friend for now and offer her unconditional support. I might lose my damn mind in the process. But better mine than hers. "What time is your appointment?"

"Eleven."

"I'll pick you up."

THAT WAS HOW I ENDED UP BEING SLOANE'S DRIVER. SHE LIMITED her time on the internet, so I sent her glossy catalogues of cars I thought she might like. She said she wouldn't need a van anymore and maybe wanted a mid-size sports utility vehicle. I wanted to get her a fully tricked-out one.

Her van remained in the driveway. Meanwhile, I simply switched out my rental and paid for the damages. I had flown in from Manhattan and fully intended to fly Sloane back. It was almost two weeks since my panic attack and the fourth time I'd driven her into town to visit the therapist. She grocery shopped afterward and forbade me to accompany her. We'd look too much like a couple, she said.

Direct skewer to the heart. She was good at that, and I had no choice but to accept my penance.

She walked on the beach every day and I made it a point to show up on her walks, trailing her like a love-sick puppy. I'd exasperated her enough that she allowed me to walk beside her as long as I didn't say a word. Not that I didn't try. She simply didn't respond to small talk and the most conversations we had were about what time I would be picking her up for her therapist appointments.

I waited for her at a coffee shop. It was conveniently located across from her therapist's building and the supermarket. The other day was the first time she agreed to have coffee with me rather than asking me to immediately drive her home.

I considered that progress, but not fast enough. Not because I wanted us to go back to the way we'd been. I was more than willing to slog it out for weeks and months to win back her trust. No, my worry was about the brewing trouble in Manhattan that might be beyond what Sonny could handle. The crime family needed me back in the city. I'd been gone for five weeks. People were noticing, especially the Russian bratva.

My phone vibrated with a text from her.

FIRECAT

I'm done. Can you order me an iced mocha?

ME

Sure, baby

Definitely progress. In my delusional mind, it was our second coffee date. I got up from my seat and went to the barista, ordering an espresso for myself and Sloane's fancy iced brew with cream on top. While Sloane worked on herself, I also worked on finding a way to give her incentive to stay in New York. Bianca had mentioned Sloane worked in the ER for her graduation project only because the Delphine Assisted Living Home rejected the proposal she submitted for the improvement of resident care. I put Sera on it since she was familiar with charities and their projects. The De Lucci crime family had helped many of our soldiers place their aging parents in excellent nursing homes. Italians were family oriented, and many were still leery about sending their senior relatives away.

The hair on the back of my neck went static and my gaze whipped to the window of the coffee shop. A towering man in a suit exited a black SUV that screamed organized crime.

What the fuck?

What was Kirill doing here?

CHAPTER Twenty-Three

Dom

I stormed out of the coffee shop to confront the Russian bratva's pakhan.

The relief that crossed Sloane's face when she saw me eased the turmoil of anxiety raging in my chest that she would choose to leave with him.

"Stay away from her!" I roared, hurrying across the street to Sloane's side and shielding her from Kirill.

The Russian usually had two expressions on his face. Cold disdain and boredom, but in the few instances when it came to me, he was finding malignant amusement. The corner of his mouth hitched up into a mocking smile, but his eyes remained cold. "De Lucci," he drawled. "I wondered what foxhole you'd disappeared off to."

"I was taking a vacation," I snapped. "How did you find me?"

Kirill scoffed. "It's Miss Scott I am here for, actually."

"You hired the person who sent me away?" Sloane asked from behind me.

"Hired?" The continued humor in his tone aggravated the fuck out of me. He knew something I didn't. I could tell by the arrogance stamped on his face. "No. But she did tell me where you were."

"Why?"

"Because you can help me." Kirill cast me a brief glance. "And I can help you."

"Fuck off. We're done." I gripped Sloane's hand and dragged her away.

"Dom."

"Not a word," I growled.

"I'll call you, De Lucci," Kirill called out.

I shot him the middle finger with my free hand.

"Do you know what's going on?" Sloane asked. There was slight resistance in her steps, but maybe it was because I was walking too fast. I packed her into the Escalade, rounded the vehicle, and slid into the driver's side, gunned the engine, and sped away from town.

I mounted the phone on the dash and called Trevor.

"Yeah," he answered on the second ring.

"Send pickup."

"Now?" There was surprise in his voice.

"Yes. Now."

"I need to check which plane is available."

"I don't care if you have to charter a new one. I want that bird wheels up within the hour."

"Sounds urgent."

"Kirill showed up here."

A muttered "fuck" crackled over the line with a half second of dead silence, before he said, "On it."

I ended the call and made another one to Lucy.

"Bro!" she singsonged.

"Have the housekeeper get the spare bedroom ready."

"You convince Sloane to come to Manhattan?"

"Just do it." Because I hadn't, and I could feel the outrage blasting at me from her direction.

When I ended that call, Sloane cut in, "Before you call someone else…what the fuck?"

"You know what the fuck is," I growled. "You have a don and a pakhan of New York organized crime vying for your attention. Let that sink in."

I could feel her burning stare on my face, but I was trying to remain calm amid my rampaging thoughts. I'd been trying to deny that it was her, but Kirill showing up here confirmed my suspicions.

"You can't just kidnap me!" she snapped.

I cast her a brief glance. "In case you forgot, baby, I'm mafia. Snatching people off the streets is part of the job description. Unless you prefer the Russian alternative."

"No."

"What I thought, and it's a moot point, because it would be over my dead body that I will let that motherfucker touch a hair on your head."

"You passed our exit," Sloane said woodenly, but I had a feeling she knew we were heading straight for the airport.

"I'll have my men come down here and empty the beach houses." I had my laptop with me and I didn't leave anything of value unattended when I traveled. "You might want to throw out the tracker."

Sloane kept it in her purse.

"So, we're letting whoever paid me to stay away from New York know we found the tracker?"

"I already know who it is," I said. I had had suspicions for a few days now, but seeing Kirill here cemented my theory. It wasn't his mother, Irina, but it was her best friend, the matchmaker to the rich, powerful, and depraved.

"Who?" Sloane asked.

"A woman called Margo Winthrop." I checked my rearview mirror to make sure Kirill wasn't planning to ambush us away from town. "You know her?"

"No."

"She's someone with connections to business, politics, and criminal organizations."

"But why was she interested in helping me?"

"No idea."

I hesitated too long in my answer. Sloane scoffed her disbelief. "I don't believe you."

I vented a resigned sigh. It was heavy with the weight of how my choices affected Sloane, which made me more determined to make it up to her. "She and my mother were discussing an arranged marriage."

"With Kirill's sister, right? Aralina?"

"Yes." I wasn't surprised Sloane knew the family tree of the Russian bratva. It helped facilitate discussion. "It's not a good match. Ma was insistent because that was the only way we could get the properties back."

"And that was why you were trying to get them back through Grigori?"

"Yes."

"She's too sweet for you," Sloane said.

"You did some research on her?" I asked, slightly amused.

"No. I wouldn't dare do that. I'm sure the bratva has someone monitoring anyone looking into them. Lucy told me."

"Fuck, I hope my sister isn't nosing around again," I grumbled.

Sloane fell into a contemplative silence. I caught her looking out the window in my peripheral vision.

My phone flashed *Trevor*.

"Hey," he said when I answered. "The plane leaves Teterboro in an hour. It's cleared with air traffic control."

"Thanks." It would take us more than an hour to get to Norfolk airport, anyway. I wondered if Kirill arrived via chopper.

After I ended the call, Sloane asked, "Why not Lucy?"

I wasn't sure what she meant? "Why not Lucy what?"

"For an arranged marriage."

Saliva snagged in my throat at Sloane's outrageous question. "Lucy?" I choked her name. "Who would she marry? Kolya? Kirill?"

"Well, Kolya is in jail, but Kirill is single."

"Lucy has an aversion to overbearing men and the methods of the mafia. And she doesn't consider herself part of the crime family. I love my sister, and you've seen Kirill. They would kill each other before the wedding. And let's not forget, even if it was Grigori's crew who killed the lawyer, Lucy still blames the bratva." That was why we needed the truce brokered by Margo, but with Kolya in jail, Kirill must have gone to her to call off the agreement. "Didn't you get that idea with all your video calls yet?"

"She's like me…"

"Has a problem with authority?"

Sloane laughed lightly. I missed that breathy laugh.

"She said she couldn't wait for this shit to be over so she could return to DC."

Yeah, my sister was going stir-crazy. She'd been griping to me that Ma had been dropping by constantly. Whenever they had to leave my penthouse to go to a restaurant, their security could rival the security for a head of state. Pop grumbled he had to close an entire restaurant just so the two could have mother-daughter time. I was sure that was Ma's way of trying to reach Lucy. And Pop would move heaven and earth just so his two favorite girls would reconcile after all these years.

As for me, I was relieved Lucy came to me with her problems instead of relying on her "I know this guy…" mentality.

"I'm not sure if staying at your penthouse is a good idea," Sloane said. "What would that do to all my progress? It's like I'm back to square one."

"Would it make you feel better if I moved out?"

She emitted an incredulous laugh. "You can't be serious."

"I'm dead fucking serious."

"What would your mother say?"

"I don't give a shit what she says."

She exhaled a frustrated breath. "You still don't get it!"

"What don't I get? I'm putting you first."

"And have your mother resent me?"

I gripped the steering wheel. An ache started throbbing in my right temple. Maybe I'd been clenching my teeth too hard since the time Kirill showed up in front of the coffee shop.

"I'm not giving you up."

"See, I'm not yours to give up, Dom."

"But I'm yours," I seethed. "I'm not letting you go. I'll find a way so you can trust me." I stared ahead. "We leave sex off the table until you do." Fuck, that was hard to get out, but I was desperate. The temptation to bend her to my will was a constant inner battle. "We can start small. Like the coffee dates. We don't have to be anything. I can just be your friend for now."

"Friend. So it's okay if I go out on a date?"

Her unexpected question punched me in the gut. I glowered at the white line that separated the lanes of the asphalted highway.

At my silence, she scoffed, "Just what I thought. Sera told me about the fine print in her divorce papers, with Matteo saying she couldn't date for six months. Is this the same thing?"

"You really want to date someone else?" I gritted out.

"You expect me to answer that with that thundercloud on your face?"

My jaw tightened. The throbbing in my head intensified. Sloane Scott's middle name was *frustration*, but an inner voice taunted me that I deserved it. "Just the idea makes me want to break this steering wheel in half."

"What's with the double standard?" she scoffed. "I endured your dates with other women."

"The difference is," I enunciated, "there was no romantic entanglement. It was simply business. I wasn't taking them out in the hopes of a relationship."

"You could say the same of what we had."

"Keep lying to yourself, baby," I muttered under my breath and resumed glaring at the highway. I had no defense. Instead of answering her, I growled, "Fine, but no sex."

I could feel Sloane's gaze on me when she said, "That's fair."

I relaxed a bit.

"I'll let you know when that changes."

Christ. I tamped down my desire to snap at her. Sloane sure knew how to torture me.

"I still think I shouldn't be staying at your penthouse," she ventured.

"Nonnegotiable."

"Excuse me?"

"I'll move out."

"Dom, we're going in circles here. I'm not putting you out of your place, but it's going to be awkward if I go on a date and you happen to show up."

Oh, you bet I'll be lurking around the corners, baby. "I won't." The thought of making her date have an "accident" appealed to me. It might actually be therapeutic. Getting rid of men interested in

Sloane seemed like a good sport in order to work out my frustrations with the added benefit of her finally realizing I'm her only and best option.

Her fated option.

"Why are you grinning?" Suspicion crept into her tone.

I schooled my features and glanced at her, pasting on a practiced smile that probably belonged on a serial killer's face. A serial killer whose main trigger was anyone interested in Sloane.

"Because I can't wait for you to stay at my penthouse," I lied.

"I don't trust that smile," she muttered.

My face fell. Fuck.

This woman was going to keep me on my toes.

But a grin threatened to form again. I was up for that challenge.

No pleasure without the pain.

CHAPTER
Twenty-Four

SLOANE

"GINGER!" TEARS FORMED IN MY EYES.

My cat was sphinx-sitting on the armrest of an expensive leather couch when we walked in. She made a tiny meow, plopped on the floor, and trotted toward us. She rubbed herself on my leg and then did the same to Dom.

I was taken aback.

"Hey, girl." Dom picked up Ginger and my cat lapped up the attention.

This was new. Even if Dom told me Ginger was living with him, it was still jarring to see how my cat let him pick her up. I mean, we'd been seeing each other for months, and other than Ginger knowing it was Dom who was buying her gourmet tuna, they kept their distance from each other. Like they tolerated each other for my sake. Now they were ganging up on me?

I narrowed my eyes. "Traitor."

Dom scratched Ginger under her chin and my cat was actually purring. He angled toward me. "Now why don't you give your momma attention? I have someplace to be."

He handed Ginger to me, and I buried my nose in the furry ball of comfort. "She smells nice." Her coat was shiny and soft, but there was a clean, almost soapy smell to her.

"Who gave her a bath?"

Ginger barely tolerated one. Occasionally when she'd get covered in grime and I didn't want her licking it off and ingesting it, I'd run her a bath. The first time I did it, she nearly lacerated my wrists. But after she realized the benefit of getting clean, she'd let me do it.

"I did," Dom muttered.

"Is he trying to take credit?" Lucy walked in. I'd only talked to Lucy over video chat, but the filter of the screen didn't do justice to the beauty of Dom's sister. I had seen her at the New Year's Eve party, but with the lights and heavy makeup, I didn't pay attention. This time it looked like she just finished working out. With the resurgent threat from the Russians, she'd been holed up again, and she'd been exercising to keep her sanity. A sheen of sweat dotted her forehead. She had her hair pulled back in a ponytail and it exposed her swan-like neck that only accentuated her features. Sharper features than the De Lucci side and I'd seen Carlotta enough to see the resemblance. Darker brows, darker eyes set against lashes so thick they seemed unreal. She had a warm skin tone as opposed to mine. Bianca once lamented that Lucy was the one in the family whose face was perfectly proportioned.

"You helped by calling Luca," her brother grumbled.

"No luggage?" Lucy raised a brow.

"Didn't I tell you to coordinate with Bianca and get Sloane's stuff ready?"

"About that…"

I stiffened. I wasn't attached to the things in my apartment. Bianca told me Dom had them packed up and put in storage after the police released the crime scene. I hoped my tall boots survived, though.

The two exchanged a look.

"What?"

"Bianca said they asked Al to get it and he got into an accident. The vehicle caught fire and exploded."

"Oh my God, is Al all right?" I'd been around Al a lot whenever I did work for the Rossis. I'd even extracted a bullet out of him one time.

"He's fine," Lucy said. "He got out before the SUV exploded. He couldn't salvage any of your stuff, though." But there was a lack of sympathy in Lucy's tone, and the silence from her brother made me suspicious.

Of course. I glared at Dom. "Is this staged again?"

He raised his arms in a gesture of innocence. "What? No. I've never had dealings with Al. I left instructions with Lucy. I would never burn your things." He said it with a straight face, but his sister snorted a laugh.

I turned my glare on her. "I don't know what your family is up to, but I own an expensive pair of boots. Maybe they weren't there?"

"We could check…" Lucy hedged.

"I really need to change out of these clothes." Exhaustion caught up with me. I walked farther into Dom's penthouse. It was already evening, but the view of the Manhattan skyline in this expansive space made me feel small again. Like I didn't belong. Old wounds started bleeding.

I lowered Ginger to the floor. And as if she were my guide, she ran to the tall windows.

"I don't know if I can stay here."

Dom's presence warmed my back before he murmured in my ear, "Give it a few days."

"I'll see what I can rustle up," Lucy called, but it was obvious her objective was to give Dom and me privacy.

I turned to face him. "I don't know what you're trying to do. And why you're forcing this. This is not me."

"Why?"

"We don't fit."

"Because I have money."

"Yes."

"Bullshit. You think the De Luccis started as billionaires? We didn't. Our ancestors worked the land. We were farmers who grew up smart about how to make money. This"—he waved his arm around the penthouse—"is something we worked for. And you'd be a hypocrite to say I earned it illegally because you made money off us, too. Because you know if you were a regular cleaner of office space or Park Avenue apartments, you wouldn't be able to keep your brother in rehab."

"You know nothing of my choices. What forced me to work for the mob!" I snapped.

"No? Then why don't you tell me, because all this, Sloane, could be yours. It doesn't have to be a barter between us. Sometimes lo—caring for someone depends on who needs it more. Like when you took care of me, and I took care of you. Wealth-wise, I have the money, but you have the ability to make me feel peace, make me want to have a future with you."

"We agreed…" I broke off in a whisper.

Dom clenched his jaw. "I have a meeting tonight. I'll know more about your situation…" He glanced in the direction where Lucy disappeared. "Everyone's situation after I have it."

"You're meeting with Margo Winthrop?"

"Yes."

"Shouldn't I meet her too? Find out why she relocated me?"

"She wants to talk to me alone for now." He exhaled a breath. "Lucy will take care of you."

"I want to see Harriet."

"Let me get a read of the situation first."

I pursed my lips, wanting to say more, but I gave him a brief nod. I always fell back on practicality. I grew up detesting the entitlement of my mother's former Park Avenue clients. I also learned work quality mattered, and that was why I charged outrageous fees for being a mob cleaner. Quality also included keeping mum about my criminal clients. There was a price tag attached to confidentiality and why my affair with Dom had repercussions.

We made this mess. He was offering to fix it. In helping me, he was also helping his sister.

I would be an idiot to make things difficult for him out of spite.

"Thank you." He kissed the top of my head, and I stilled myself from recoiling. My reaction was disconcerting, but I couldn't help it. Over the past few weeks, I'd built up a belief that Dom was all wrong for me. That hadn't changed.

He must have sensed my body's rejection because he stood back and a stab of guilt hit me at the defeat in his eyes.

"I'll be at The Grindhouse after I'm done with the meeting."

And I wasn't going to argue with him about that anymore.

I had no problem staying at The Grindhouse third floor. Somehow, it was important to Dom that I stayed here instead.

So be it.

CHAPTER
Twenty-Five

Dom

"Ms. Winthrop will see you now," the blonde receptionist at the counter said.

Margo insisted on meeting at her business, Marriage Ink, a full-service bridal shop. Allegedly, they did everything from the cake, the flowers, invitations, and the venue.

It was all a front.

I knew they used their print shop to print counterfeit money. But who would dare rat out the madame who was the matchmaker to the wealthy and powerful?

They owned the French Gothic Revival architectural building built in the 1920s. The façade was a French pastry shop that bore a red-and-white awning typical of the business. A wedding cake—an architectural feat of pistachio green, pink, and gold—sat proudly in their window display.

The blonde led me through a hallway. Floor-to-ceiling glass

made up one wall and provided views to the flower shop, but she didn't lead me there. She led me to a solarium.

I wasn't a stranger to solariums being used as meeting places. We had one at the De Lucci mansion where stories were told about how my grandfather had settled mob business in there. I expected Margo to be surrounded by bodyguards, but then again, a swarm of security would call too much attention to herself. And Margo liked to operate discreetly. Still, I was surprised I wasn't asked to leave my weapons in a lockbox before meeting her. After all, I'd been simmering with a low-hum aggression against her for hiding Sloane.

She better have a good excuse.

When the receptionist announced me, she didn't look up from the bouquet of purple flowers she was arranging in a faded green container.

"Dominic."

"Ms. Winthrop."

"I think you should call me Margo."

I didn't respond. I wasn't saying another word until she gave me her eyes. She finally looked at me. A black apron protected an expensive ivory suit. She was in black heels. Not the attire of someone working as a florist.

"You were the one who paid Sloane to go away."

She shrugged. "Yes."

"And you also told Kirill where to find her."

"I needed you and Sloane back in Manhattan."

"And the answer was to send Kirill after us?"

"You're back, aren't you?"

I scoffed, "You don't just send the pakhan of the Zahkarov bratva to do the work of a soldier."

Her eyes glinted with mock amusement. "I don't deal with soldiers. I sent a pakhan for a don. You should be thankful I respected you that much."

"And Kirill just did your bidding?"

"I told him I could help him clear Kolya's name. And before you ask more questions—yes, he threatened me first to hand over what he wants."

"No one threatens Margo Winthrop."

"Isn't that what you're here to do?"

"That depends, *Margo*," I taunted. "That depends what your interest in Sloane is. She's a pawn for sure, but will it keep her safe?"

"I'm doing you a favor."

"By keeping Sloane away from me? If you really cared for her, you should have turned her over to me."

"Really?" She laughed in a mocking way that grated over my nerves. Margo set the shears on the table, stood back, and surveyed the damn flowers. "I see how you *cared* for her. Let me remind you of that scene in front of the Hummingbird Room."

I flinched. That time I viciously rejected Sloane. But how…

Margo sighed. "You should know by now I have eyes everywhere."

She shed the gardening gloves and tapped them together. "Your mother was keen on a marriage between you and Aralina Zahkarov."

"I already told her no."

"Be that as it may, she's not giving up. Carlotta isn't one to be dissuaded easily. She's made it a sport to manipulate the men in her life. She's a Moretti after all and you're half of that side."

I wasn't going to tell her about my mother's depression issues. She probably knew but I wasn't going to add to that knowledge. So I simply stared at her, waiting for her to elaborate.

"From the start I was not in favor of the match," she said. "And you were apathetic about it. I was curious why. I got my answer on New Year's Eve."

Fucking hell, Luca noticed too. Who else did?

"Kirill asked me to find a way to kill the match. He wasn't too keen on his innocent sister marrying a deviant like you."

"Deviant?" I barked a laugh. "Kirill is one to talk."

At this, Margo's mouth gave a slight smile. "Right. That's another reason why he was willing to go to the Outer Banks. He wanted to make sure you return to Manhattan with Sloane and forever dispel any hope of a match between you and his sister."

She lowered the gloves on the table, smoothing them out before giving me her attention. "Anyway, you do business with Grigori and it's my assumption it's to find a way to get the properties back. After all, Grigori is in charge of them. And then I find out Sloane was their cleaner and how her brother was entangled with the bratva. Quite a pickle you've landed yourself in, Dom.

"I looked into Sloane's background. I see what draws you to her. I'll have you know, Grigori sees Sloane as a commodity, too."

"Fucker."

"She's not the usual age that his clients go for, but she fits the requirements of a particular one." She stared at me.

"Who?"

She walked over to the wall and hung the apron on the hooks, letting me stew in my frustration. "I've debated whether I should reveal a name, but despite the distaste in my mouth of what he has become, he was once my client. I would be breaking the covenant."

"Fuck your covenant," I growled and moved menacingly toward her. Those damned covenants. Margo liked to use the archaic term for her contracts. Nothing was simply a verbal agreement. Everything needed to be signed. Even the numerous truces with the Russian mafia. "Give me a name."

She raised a brow. "Or what, Dominic? Shoot a sixty-year-old woman?"

"Strangling you would be more satisfying."

She emitted a tinkling laugh that only incensed the reflexes of my fists. Margo Winthrop was more than an ice maiden, she was forged of steel and I wondered how she managed to have two powerful ex-husbands. One of them was dead. She probably had the poor bastard killed. Mental note to have Trevor do more research on this woman.

Her mouth curved in a derisive smile. "Then you're no better than the man who strangled Sloane."

"You know about Anton?"

"The night it happened. But can you say the same about yourself?" she said. "So tell me, who has Sloane's best interests at heart?"

"Who is she to you? Why do you care about her?"

She moved around the tables full of flowers. Instead of answering me, she said, "Do you know why Sloane downplays her looks with frumpy clothes and pale makeup?"

"Of course. She works for the mob. She didn't want them interested in her for her physical attributes."

"Typical men. All surface level." She moved to the edge of a potting shelf and extracted a single key from her suit's tiny pocket to unlock a drawer. She lifted a picture out of it and handed it to me.

A grainy photograph. Like it was from surveillance footage, but I could make out Sloane and an older woman beside a dumpster. "What am I looking at? This is Sloane… Is the woman her mother?"

"She was sixteen here. They used to clean for the old-monied folks of Manhattan. The client accused Sloane of theft because the woman's husband fancied her. She purposely threw her jewelry in the trash and declared it stolen. Maliciously suggested that Sloane and her mother go dumpster-diving to look for it or she would call the police.

"It was an emerald necklace worth seven figures, a family heirloom, but she threw it away to make a point to Sloane and her husband."

I was speechless with outrage and disbelief.

"No charges were pressed. The necklace was found, but Sloane and her mother were blacklisted and found work with criminal organizations. But I have a feeling that's why Sloane downplayed her looks. At sixteen, when she was about to blossom into a woman, her beauty was used against her. It was used to shame her. She and her mom nearly ended up on the streets because of it. Billy was still in rehab. Harriet helped them. After all, she helped cover up the murder of Sloane's father. That's why I don't think Sloane will remain angry at Harriet forever."

"I want names!" I roared, uncontrolled fury coalescing into words, otherwise I would end up breaking every piece of pottery in this room.

But Margo remained unfazed and continued to stare at me stoically. "Wealth, power, and social imbalance separate you from the woman you love. But we know money doesn't rule the world. Power does. And don't tell me that's the same. You have all the money, but you still can't get through to a woman of Sloane's spine. Do you know why I put her near a beach? She had bottles of sleeping pills beside her."

"You fucking bitch." My chest rose and fell with all the fear that had festered inside me with Sloane's proximity to the ocean. Many times I wanted to hide the prescription drugs by Sloane's nightstand but she needed them.

"I had to make sure she was worth my time."

I deleted the space between us. Margo's icy veneer cracked and the first signs of wariness stole over her face. "You manipulative fucking bitch! She could have died."

"She made a choice to live," Margo enunciated, sidestepping away from me while narrowing her eyes in warning. "Survival of the fittest has always been the motto of my business. I'm tired of powerful men and women choosing trophy wives and husbands and weakening the gene pool my family took centuries to cultivate. They procreate and produce entitled offsprings who wouldn't know how to wipe their asses without help. Who are mentally incapable of handling stress without running off to mommy and daddy to fix their problems or getting strung out on coke." She huffed. "I found the best matches are from crossing old money with new money or the ruthless bosses of the underworld."

"You make it sound like breeding horses."

She shrugged. "Call it whatever you like. But it's a perfect metaphor. The problem with your ilk is to be careful not to end up with psychopathic mass murderers. See my dilemma?"

I would have chuckled if I wasn't so damn irritated.

"Why am I here?" I asked. "If you won't tell me anything at all about how to help Sloane, then why call me here?"

"I need to know how far you're willing to go for her. Is she someone you think you could marry?"

I wanted to say yes. I didn't understand my feelings for Sloane. "I want to keep her in my life. Make her a priority."

Her mouth twisted in derision. But her eyes drilled into me and excavated the guilt I thought I had buried about how I had let Sloane down.

"You still can't say it, can you?"

"I think I love her. Why else would I stalk her in the Outer Banks?"

"It's not the same. Is your obsession more than your love for her?"

"I don't follow."

"Are you willing to put her needs above yours?"

"Yes."

"Good. Because my price isn't cheap and I need you to follow my instructions."

"Price for what?"

"To be her fairy godmother."

I snorted a rough laugh. Margo Winthrop was amusing. "You got to be fucking kidding me. I don't want Sloane to change."

"I can make a beautiful woman like Sloane perfect to be at your side in public."

"What? Give her a new identity? Not gonna happen. She's perfect the way she is."

"For someone in your position, you are incredibly naïve."

I'd had enough of Margo's bullshit and turned around. "This is a waste of time."

"Dominic," she called as I made a move to leave. "She's perfect for you, but she has to *believe* it."

"How?" I spun on her, piqued by how she zeroed in on the problem I was trying to figure out. Deep inside, I knew the matchmaker wouldn't have gotten into her esteemed, veritably untouchable position without shrewd insight into the underpinnings of the world we lived in. "Are you saying you have a plan? Let's hear it." Because she was right. These revelations exposed the root of Sloane's insecurity. That was why my guilt surged back with a vengeance. My words about slumming exacerbated her feelings of inadequacy. It was making me sick to my gut.

"For starters, I sent you an invoice."

My phone buzzed. "Two hundred fifty large for a flower arrangement. Am I cleaning money for you?"

She shrugged. “That includes a deposit for services and the money I gave Sloane.”

“I didn’t realize I was hiring you.”

“You just did.”

CHAPTER
Twenty-Six

Sloane

My first visit while at Dom's penthouse was from the feds. I was surprised Dom had let them know I was back in town, but he had a De Lucci lawyer and Lucy who'd graduated law, keep me from answering entrapment questions. None of their questions related to my job in cleaning Elyse Bailey's apartment because technically Billy and I were working for them at that time. The feds were the ones who fucked up.

So they only asked me about my whereabouts after Anton kidnapped me and I was honest with them about where I was and I informed them I didn't know the person who had rescued me. I gave them records of my therapy visits and that I had been in a depressive state and was on medication. The feds, clearly frustrated, scheduled another interview, but they called back later in the day and said they were done with me.

I didn't know who intervened for me, but I was still indifferent to what was happening in my life. I did an e-visit with my therapist and she adjusted my anti-anxiety and anti-depressant medication, lowering the dosage of each.

It was now day three since my return to Manhattan. I finally scrounged up the courage to visit my brother's grave at the cemetery. In the back of my mind, I knew I should feel more emotion. The lack of reaction was troubling knowing that Dom took care of his burial. I also knew I should be thankful, but I simply didn't care.

You don't care about me now, sis?

I'd been having less and less imaginary conversations with Billy. Reconnecting with my friends aided in pulling me out of my head.

You dug your own grave.

Ouch. But I'm at peace now. Are you?

No, I was not.

Dom gave us the all clear to move around. Apparently, the bratva had reached a renewed truce with the De Luccis, but Kolya Petrov had been indicted for the murder of Elyse Bailey and remained behind bars awaiting trial. For Zahkarov Holdings, the press release was that one of their security personnel was accused of being a copycat serial killer and they maintained he was innocent and the real Mistress Strangler was still out there. Their publicity machine certainly knew how to spin this. Lucy scoffed that Kolya had gained a fan following and there were women sending him lingerie in jail with a note that said, "Choke me with this." As for Kirill, I still had no idea why he appeared at the Outer Banks other than to piss off Dom. This reiterated the issue between Dom and me. Despite everything that happened, we did the right thing to hide our affair.

It was now out in the open that Dom's enemies could use me as leverage.

But I wasn't technically with Dom. I didn't know where that left me. I was doing this one baby step at a time, one day at a time. And after my visit to Billy's grave, I decided to make Harriet my next stop.

When I arrived at Delphine, she was sitting up in bed with a blanket across her lap. The joy on her face upon seeing me elicited a nagging guilt in my chest.

"I'm sorry I left," I said simply. I set the cat carrier on the floor and let Ginger out. The orange cat gave a tiny mewl and jumped on Harriet's bed.

"I'm glad you're back," she said. "Are you still mad at me?"

"I was never really mad at you. You've done nothing but help my family. I was just in shock, that's all." I sat on the other side of her bed. "How are you feeling? Miss Sheila said you're under the weather."

"Just my joints reminding me I'm an old woman," she said. "I'm sorry about Billy."

I guessed we were jumping straight to the elephant in the room.

Sadness wrapped around my heart and squeezed some of the frost out of it. "I visited his grave this morning," I whispered. "I couldn't cry. I think I cried more during those first few weeks away. Maybe I'm all out of tears."

Harriet reached across and wrapped her frail fingers around mine. "He did the right thing in the end."

"Your hand is icy. Do you want me to turn down the AC?"

"My hands are always cold. Stop deflecting."

"I'm not."

"Listen." Her voice was gravelly. "Billy couldn't get over what he did to your father and what he did to you, letting you think your dad didn't want you. Your mom didn't foresee the implications to your mental health."

"I don't blame Mom either for hiding it from me. All she did was try to survive and keep us off the streets."

Because of me. Because it was my fault. Because I dared to dream I could be a princess and wear an expensive emerald necklace the color of my eyes.

"In her mind she was doing the right thing." Harriet broke through my involuntary flashback. "Keeping Billy out of jail…"

"As if rehab wasn't prison."

"And it left you with abandonment and trust issues."

And being called trash.

"Now, you have good friends who care for you…Bianca and Sera…" She smiled. "I met them. And I met their cousin Dom at Billy's funeral." Her smile turned sly. "I knew that man wasn't just a sympathetic bystander. Bianca told me he adopted Ginger." Harriet stroked the cat's fur and Ginger erupted into a purr box.

"No adoption happened," I retorted. "She's still *our* cat, Harriet."

Huh. That jab of emotion, even if it was of irritation, was a welcome sensation. I reluctantly attributed it to Dom. Earlier this morning, the same feeling rattled me when a beautiful arrangement of dark purple dahlias arrived. With it was a note:

These flowers reminded me of you.
Resilience and elegance.
I hope one day you realize you were meant to stand out in a crowd and not hide from it.
D

Elegance…I scoffed. What? Did he see a dahlia and then google its significance? Or did he have one of his minions come up with the type of flower to send me?

I hadn't seen him in three days, and I refused to think that was why I was annoyed at him. Bianca and Sera informed me he never, not once, brought a hookup or a date to the penthouse. It was his sacred place he reserved for family. And now I kicked him out of living there. I wasn't sure how I felt about it. Relief? Pressure? Pleasure?

Before I could overthink and give myself a migraine, Miss Sheila, the facility administrator, poked her head in the room. "Sloane, you gotta minute?"

I glanced at Harriet. "You okay with Ginger?"

She waved me off. "Go, we ladies are fine."

I followed the administrator to the office and was shocked when I saw Sera and Bianca there.

"What's the meaning of this?"

"Don't be mad." Sera stood.

"What's going on?" I almost backed away from the room with the feeling that I was about to get flattened by a bulldozer. Of course, my suspicious mind went to Dom.

Miss Shiela rounded her desk and sat behind it. She pushed a folder across it. I recognized it as my Capstone proposal. "I told you they were great ideas, Sloane, and they were doable if the board would approve it."

"They rejected it. What changed?"

Sera handed me another folder. "Bowman Inc. has acquired controlling shares of the Delphine group. We're impressed with your proposal to improve resident care and staff training with the focus on specialized assistance for seniors. We have resources to upgrade the computer system and improve response times for emergencies."

Sera's specialty was in business process re-engineering, and I'd heard Bowman Inc. mentioned before. I wasn't sure what kind of company it was. The last thing I wanted was for the nursing home to be used for money laundering. My duality about being a nurse and serving the mob came crashing back.

I wanted to break free from them, not get further involved.

"I'll have to think about this." I held up Sera's proposal. "Is this my copy?"

"Yes."

"Then, excuse me, I need to get back to Harriet."

Sera and Bianca didn't follow me to Harriet's room, but they were waiting for me outside the Delphine building.

I was glad they took the hint that there were questions I wanted to ask without putting them at a disadvantage by exposing the inner workings of the mafia.

"Coffee? Jabbin' Java?" Bianca asked.

"I need to bring Ginger back to the penthouse."

"No need. She can stay with Sam on the second floor. Sam loves cats but Renz and Liz can't have pets because of the café, but once in a while should be fine."

"All right."

I hadn't been to Jabbin' Java in months, but we found a corner booth near the kitchen where we could discuss the Delphine proposal.

Renz delivered our cappuccinos and danishes.

"Is this new?" Bianca asked her brother.

"Yes, matcha and passion fruit."

"It's so pretty," I said and took a bite. "It's delicious too."

"Why don't you do matcha lattes?" Sera asked.

"Nah, and have the Italians revolt?" Renz laughed.

I gave a shake of my head and took a sip of my cappuccino while the De Luccis did small talk. After Renz left our table, Sera tipped her chin to the folder in front of me. "You have concerns."

"Where is the money coming from?"

"We're not laundering money. Bowman Inc. is a shell company, but the monies funneled through it are seized assets from criminal organizations who profit from human trafficking. We're merely redirecting those funds to more appropriate use. We've used it for homeless shelters and a host of other charities."

"Why not continue with those charities? Why the interest in Delphine? You know the clientele are not exactly destitute."

Sera leaned forward while Bianca side-eyed her. There had to be a mafia angle to this. "Okay, so we're making some provisions for older adults who have nowhere to go. Victims of criminal violence. Most homeless shelters are not equipped to handle them. Mafia families also have their own issues. Luca and Dom had talked about easing the worries of their soldiers regarding retirement homes. And you know the Italians. The last thing they want to do is to put their parents or grandparents in assisted living. But the guilt of not doing so is not the healthiest or practical alternative, especially when they need nurse supervision. The plan you've submitted appealed to both Luca, Sandro, and yes, Dom, so in a way, we are using these homes as an alternative for mafia families."

"Sort of like a pension for mafia soldiers," Bianca piped in. "You know Al and Arnie Scavo are not getting any younger and their mom is ninety and is complaining about her assisted living facility."

"It would also make it easier for the holidays, too," Sera said.

My hand shook when I lifted the cappuccino to my lips. Excitement was rattling inside me. I laughed lightly, lowering the cup. "I trust you not to hide anything in the fine print, and oh my God." I put a hand over my chest, and I could feel my heart pounding. This was a dream and my mind was swirling with all kinds of plans I could do for Delphine residents. "I…I haven't even graduated or passed the NCLEX."

"You've proven yourself enough, Sloane. To us." Bianca reached across the table for my hand and squeezed. "You're tenacious, smart."

"Zio Luca asked to look at your transcript." Sera laughed. "He is in a trust-but-verify position. And he had his own private investigator interview a few of your instructors. Your nurse supervisor in your ER rotation gave you a stellar commendation."

"I missed graduation," I said. "But I've earned enough clinical hours to take the NCLEX."

"Does that mean you're considering it?"

I laughed lightly again. For the first time since Billy died, I was seeing a way out of the dark tunnel that seemed to swallow me each morning when I woke up and each night I fell asleep. "But what would be my position in the family?"

"Bowman Inc. is part of an organization that is mafia adjacent," Sera said. "I can't reveal its inner workings until you pass a waiting period or marry a member."

Bianca's lips rolled as if she was controlling a smile or her urge to speak.

Sera's expression was deadpan, as if she was waiting for me to say something, too.

"And is Dom a member?" I asked.

"Yes."

"I don't have to answer to him?"

"No, Matteo is the head of the organization, and I function as his adviser," Sera said.

"A woman-empowered organization. I like it."

"So…?" Bianca asked. She was obviously impatient. In fact, she seemed to be squirming in her seat.

"What's up with you?" I asked.

"Just say yes, already," she griped while Sera laughed.

"I feel like there's a catch." My voice turned wary.

Sera glared at Bianca. "Now you've done it."

"I'll do it, but on a provisionary basis. If there's something that's not working, I can back out."

"I don't think the dons would want you to leave a project in the middle," Sera said.

"We can do this in phases," I said. "Improve resident care first."

"That seems fair," Sera agreed.

"So that's a yes?" Bianca asked.

Hmm…she was really pushy.

I grinned at her. "That's a yes."

She clapped her hands and gave a small squeal of delight. Sometimes I forgot that despite being married to one of the scariest MOFOs in New York, Bianca was younger than me at barely twenty-five. She dug into her purse and handed me two cards. Two black cards. Credit cards?

One bore only a chip. And the other one had my name.

"What are these?"

"This…" She pushed the no-name one forward. "Is for anything you need to purchase for project implementation. Miss Sheila will have her own account, too. This one with your name…" She slid the other one beside the first black card. "Is for your personal expenses related to the running of the project."

I narrowed my eyes. "Personal expenses."

"You'll be required to attend benefit and charity galas. Hire limos. You can purchase your own vehicle with it, too."

Fucking Dom.

"Is this charged to Dom's account or Bowmans Inc.'s" I tapped on the card with my name.

Bianca blew out a breath. "Ugh, why do you have to be so picky? Dom's."

Both women watched me like I was about to bolt, but I was suddenly empowered to change tactics. I grabbed both cards. "You can tell your cousin that he's going to regret giving me his card."

Sera laughed. "Attagirl."

CHAPTER Twenty-Seven

Dom

"I don't know where Grigori or Anton is," Boris cried. He was one of Grigori's crew who'd been hiding in Harlem. One of Sandro's soldiers tipped us off. His face was a map of bruises. Sandro had already done a number on him.

We were in the basement of a laundromat. Boris was tied to a chair and, besides the bruises on his body, he was missing a few fingernails. I hadn't been the dispenser of hurt in an interrogation in a long time. Frequently I left it to my underboss, Sonny, to oversee, but this time he was staying in the background, letting me do the honors.

Because this was personal. Very personal.

"I could just turn you over to Kirill," I told him and picked up the forceps to extract teeth.

Boris's lips lost color, which was a feat since he was bleeding and swollen like hell. "Don't. I'm begging you."

"Why?" Because the bratva would be more ruthless than simply extracting teeth or fingernails. They'd probably put him on a torture rack and quarter him. "What can you offer me?"

"Ask me anything except where they are because I really don't know. They left me…"

"What happened the night Anton threw the fed out the window? You were there, right?"

"I already told Rossi."

I picked up the forceps again.

"No, wait, wait…" he yelled. "Grigori wanted that redhead. That cleaner. That snitch working with that fed."

"Sloane."

"Yes…yes…boss wanted her."

"To sell?" I prodded even when the fury surged inside me.

"Maybe. I don't know. He wanted her unharmed, but she was being a pain in the ass."

My fingers tightened on the forceps. "Then what happened…" I asked as casually as possible, but I could feel Sonny straightening behind me.

Boris was oblivious to the cold fury icing inside me. The man before me was already dead.

The years I'd built up being the public face of the De Lucci crime family were a mere façade. Inside me was a bloodthirsty killer. That mask slowly eroded and revealed the brutal man inside me. Luca once told me that the Morettis were part sociopath. We'd evolved over the years and were successful in hiding it under a civilized skin.

"I punched her in the stomach and…apparently that bitch was pregnant."

My breathing fractured as intense pressure formed behind my eyes and compressed my rib cage.

"She miscarried?" The words came out flat.

"Yes! Grigori should be thankful I showed them what a whore she was. But what do I get?" He continued to rant, oblivious to the fact that I was calculating the many ways I was going to tear him apart.

"A death sentence! Anton told me to run away because Grigori was going to kill me."

I lowered my head to within an inch of Boris's nose, ignoring the smell of blood, piss, and fear. I grabbed a fistful of his hair and yanked his head so that he was immobilized from looking away.

"The whore you refer to happens to be the mother of my child."

"What?" he whispered, his pupils dilating.

I pushed through the wave of rage that flooded every sinew of muscle. "I didn't know how she lost our baby that night." My fingers tightened against his scalp. "Now I do."

He couldn't look away as I plunged a knife into his gut and inched it up. His swollen eyes widening slightly in realization that I was his death sentence. That he'd just been eviscerated the same way his revelation was ripping me inside.

He couldn't look away even as blood dripped from the corners of his mouth.

I couldn't look away. The satisfaction of watching the life drain from his eyes burned through me, burned through the ice that unleashed into white-hot rage. But I wasn't done. I repeatedly stabbed him, not blinking even when his blood splattered all over me.

Later, a hot shower and a change of clothes erased the evidence of the carnage. Rage turned me into an animal, but I'd made the transformation back into a civilized member of society countless times, it had become second nature.

Still, Sonny was waiting for me when I emerged from the bathroom.

Because this time it was different. The rage was different. The satisfaction was personal. It wasn't because of a job or extracting information. It was about revenge. I didn't know how Sloane felt about mob justice. She'd seen it. She'd been around it. How would she feel if she knew I took a life for her? For us to have a chance, she had to accept this part of me.

"You okay?"

I nodded, jaw hardening. "I got one of the men who hurt Sloane."

"What do you want me to do with the body?"

"Should we send a message to Kirill?" My mouth quirked. "We haven't done this in a while."

We were the modern mafia, but it didn't mean we couldn't fall back into our ruthless, vicious roots if we needed to. We were Sicilians and the La Cosa Nostra, after all. If the bratva declared war on us, we weren't backing down.

"The feds are watching and not all of them are in our pocket."

I sighed. "Get rid of the body, then."

Boris was a low-level soldier and couldn't lead us to Grigori or Anton, anyway. His purpose had been served.

Sandro texted me.

SANDRO

You done? The women are at Jabbin' Java.

"THEY'RE PISSING ME OFF." WE WERE STANDING ACROSS THE street from Jabbin' Java. As an expert in stalking, Sandro showed me the best vantage point to keep tabs on the women.

Except Bianca was an expert in Sandro's stalking too, so she purposely led Sloane and Sera to the corner booth where I couldn't see them. My cousin had the gall to send me a text with:

BIANCA

Far from your prying eyes. 😜

ME

Why you do me dirty, cuz?

I humored the women. The feistiness of my cousins was a balm for my soul and helped me climb out of that basement of horrors where not an hour ago, I was judge, jury, and executioner.

SERA

We're working on Sloane. Leave us alone.

Not a chance until I see her.

Sandro looked over my shoulder and snorted. "You're pathetic," he told me.

"I'm pathetic?" I derided. "Might I remind you—"

"Yeah, yeah, I stalked Bianca for four years. What's your point? Once I got my head outta my ass, she became my wife. I married her twice. You've gotten your head outta your ass for eight weeks and you're still floundering. You're getting hard to watch."

I leaned against the alley wall where both of us were lurking. "Got one of those fuckers, though," I gritted. The smell of copper still lingered in my nose.

Sandro nodded solemnly.

"Anything else you got out of him?" I asked. "Did he give any indication he's seen Grigori with Margo?"

"No. But he thought Grigori was sick."

"What?" I kept my interactions with Grigori to a minimum because it was a challenge to keep my disdain from my face. But come to think of it, the last time I saw him, his pallor was that of a vampire. Pale skin, bloodshot eyes. I attributed it to his lifestyle.

"He'd get sick like he had the flu and disappear for a week or two, and when he returned, he'd be fine."

"Hmm…"

"Sloane might have an assessment."

"I don't want her thinking about that bastard."

"Are you going to tell her about Boris?"

"Not yet." I read the therapist's notes. I'd seen her prescriptions. Everything hinged on whether this project was going to jump-start her enthusiasm for life. I couldn't fix Sloane. Margo was right. Sloane needed to see that she was perfect for me on her own. I'd seen what depression could do to a loved one. I'd seen how Dad struggled. It was all about her self-esteem. Sloane protected her worth by setting limitations on herself. But I believed in my girl. She was as good as any heiress and deserved all the luxury and support I could give her.

The last thing Sloane needed was a reminder of her life under Grigori's thumb. The man was responsible for her brother's death. We hadn't talked about her unexpected pregnancy. I didn't know how she felt about it. I didn't know how I felt about it other than I would have wanted that child and I was angry that she wasn't given a choice whether to keep it or not.

Sandro continued to keep me in brooding company. Finally, my phone pinged.

BIANCA

Sloane's on board, and she accepted the two cards. And I quote, "He's gonna regret giving me his card."

A smile pulled at my mouth as I texted back.

ME

Tell her, bring it on.

SERA

She says you can quit lurking and join us.

My heart hammered inside my chest and I swore I emitted a strangled sound as if I'd won the lottery.

The sound might have been louder than I perceived because Sandro scoffed and repeated, "Pathetic."

I glared at Sandro. "You know, sometimes I wished I'd left you floundering for a few days when Bianca's dad and brothers didn't want her to see you." Not to mention Cesar wanting to draw up divorce papers. He'd had to run it by me because it involved relations with another crime family.

Sandro's eyes narrowed, and his mouth flattened.

A derisive huff escaped my lips. "What I thought."

ME

Be right over

I loped across the street, thinking Sandro would continue lurking. Sometimes, when the girls were together, their husbands weren't far away. But he followed me.

"What are you doing?" I asked.

"Sloane's like a sister to me," he replied. "I'm making sure to keep you in line."

I stopped at the sidewalk in front of the café. "Keep me in line? She has free access to my bank account."

He shot me an evil smile and walked past me. "Then I'll tell her how to spend your money."

"Don't you have a crime family to run?"

"Tommy can handle things for a while," he replied. I followed him into the café. Renz was behind the counter and shot me a shit-eating grin. My situation was a novelty to them. I was the one who mediated their messes. Now they seemed to relish that I was flopping miserably in my attempts to win back Sloane.

Not that I didn't deserve it. Women were never a problem to me until they tried to pin a paternity suit on me. But the grief I felt when I found out Sloane had lost our baby sent me into profound reflection.

She was the one I wanted to be the mother of my children.

I wasn't even looking, but fate had a cruel way of opening the blinders I'd had on all my life. The blinders I'd hid behind.

It only took staring into Sloane's beloved green eyes for me to realize how much I wanted her to be mine and mine alone.

"Okay, this is hard to watch." Sera's embarrassed laugh broke through my series of epiphanies. I had reached the back of the café and forgotten everyone else was around.

But Sloane held my gaze captive, and I replied without looking at Sera. "I got it from here."

"We're her ride," Bianca interjected.

"I'll order one," Sloane said, and then raised the black card in her hand, "or order that SUV I wanted."

"I can take you to the dealership," I said. "Or test drive?"

"Or you can continue to be my driver," Sloane returned sassily.

I nodded, finally reaching their booth. "Or continue to be your driver."

"In this traffic?" Bianca cut in again. "Don't you have boss things to do?"

If only they knew where I'd been this morning. I glared at my two cousins. "Don't you two have someplace to be?"

Sera glanced at her watch. "Actually, Matteo said I need to take Gio because he has a board meeting."

Bianca stared at her phone. "Divina said Tommy is looking for you, Sandro, and asking why you're not answering texts."

"Because I told him multiple times I hate texting and he should just call me."

"Get out of here, the lot of you," I ordered.

Renz appeared beside us and handed me an espresso. I slid into the space my cousins vacated.

"Another cappuccino, Sloane?" Renz asked.

"Oh God, no I've had enough."

While I consumed my espresso, the girls said goodbye. They exchanged hugs, and an ache tugged in my chest.

Sloane belonged with my family. I just didn't know how to bring her in and become mine. Remembering what Margo had told me made me realize the mountain of Sloane's past trauma I had to climb. If only the matchmaker would give me a name.

The security to her network was top-notch. When Trevor tried to hack into their system and was repelled, Margo sent me a warning text. Of course I didn't admit it was us, and I wasn't desperate enough to ask Natalya for help because I had no doubt she would succeed.

After Sloane slid back into the booth in front of me, she said, "You don't have to deny you had a hand in orchestrating this Delphine project."

"I'm not gonna deny it, but it was a team effort," I replied. "We identified a problem shared across our crime families and saw an opportunity to address it."

She grinned. "I heard Luca was skeptical."

"That's his nature. He doesn't know you, and he wanted to make sure that emotions did not influence us, but logic."

"Are you certain that—"

"It's not guilt," I said firmly. "Not with this."

"My acceptance of this project doesn't mean I'm open to a relationship with you."

It took an effort to hold her gaze when her words deflated the hope in my chest. Funny how I didn't have a problem watching the light fade from a vermin's eyes, but knowing that I struggled to do that with Sloane proved I was not lost to the vicious side of my nature. "I understand."

She gave a series of nods and rolled her lips. Those luscious lips that I hadn't kissed in weeks.

An awkward silence blanketed the space between us, but I wasn't simply going to tuck tail and not be the man she knew me to be. "I understand," I repeated. "But also understand that I'm not a man who gives up easily."

Her eyes flared.

Yeah, she liked that.

"Weeks, months, years—I'm going to wait."

"Years?" She raised a brow. "That's a long time to wait."

"I'm a De Lucci and a Moretti." I shrugged. "Once we've decided on the woman we want, we don't back down."

She grabbed the folder and started flipping through the pages. As for me, I was contented just staring at her. I was the dumbass who let this beautiful woman slip through my fingers because I was a coward. In a way, I didn't want to share her with others in my circle. But this? This was a start.

She stared at my espresso cup. "I'm ready to head back to the penthouse. It's been a long…strange day." Sloane gave a light laugh. That husky laugh. Fuck. My dick chose that time to wake up. I was glad I was in a suit so I could hide my erection.

"I'm ready."

After we picked up Ginger from Renz's apartment, we spent the drive back to the penthouse in silence. Sloane was busy flicking through the project proposal, while I was busy sneaking glances at her. The penthouse wasn't that far away, less than a ten-minute drive in normal Manhattan traffic. And for the first time in my life, I wished it would take me thirty minutes to get there just so I could spend more time with her.

Although…I could be opportunistic.

So when the building came up and I had to make the choice between turning to the garage and the building's entrance, I said, "I'm coming up with you."

"Dom, you can just drop me off in the front."

"I need a couple of items from my room."

She blew out a breath in a way that told me she didn't believe me, but was resigned. "Okay."

After I parked, we walked to the elevators designated for the upper floors.

"You should just move back in," she said. "I can rent an apartment somewhere. Maybe in New Jersey."

I swiped my card and leaned against the wall while the car zoomed up. "I want you in Manhattan."

"Why? Delphine is in New Jersey. It makes more sense for me to live there. Are there still threats?"

"Not from the Zahkarov bratva." Although one could never tell with Kirill in charge.

"Grigori and his crew, then. I'm a witness to their crime."

Kirill made it clear that Grigori was theirs to deal with and I told him, not if we found him first. Well, we found Boris first. Now we need to find the rest of his crew, especially Anton.

The doors to the elevators opened to the foyer leading to my penthouse. The initial design of the entrance hall opened straight to the dedicated upper-floor elevators, but it didn't sit well with me for obvious reasons despite the security to its programming. Anything could be hacked. As don, I had enemies who wanted to kill me.

Tastefully designed curved steps led to a bulletproof double door. With Sloane living here, I wished I'd had it built for fucking explosives.

But I wasn't prepared for the grenade waiting for us inside the penthouse.

My mother.

CHAPTER
Twenty-Eight

Dom

"Ma, what are you doing here?" I steeled myself, acted normal, and led Sloane past the threshold.

My mother's eyes fell on Sloane. Her nostrils flared and her jaw tightened. "You're a friend of Bianca."

"Yes. Sloane Scott."

"We've met," she replied. "Briefly." Her gaze grew more disdainful when I lowered the cat carrier to let Ginger out. "What is this I'm hearing that you're sleeping at The Grindhouse and got booted out of this penthouse?" She scrunched her nose and stepped away from Ginger when the cat circled her warily like Ma was an intruder.

Double fuck.

"No one booted me out. I wanted Sloane to stay here even when she offered to stay somewhere else."

"Oh." She reared back, appearing a little relieved, but her eyes drifted to the elaborate dahlia arrangement. "What's your relationship to each other?"

After the initial shock of seeing my mother here, I gave her a peck on the cheek. "Ma, you know I love you with all my heart, but it's none of your business."

"Dominic!" she exclaimed my name with an Italian accent and offended tone.

"What? It's not," I replied in a teasing but firm manner.

Sloane laughed. She actually laughed, but she stepped to my side. "What Dom is trying to say is he wants us to be more, but I'm saying no."

"You're saying no to my son?" I worried about Ma's blood pressure. Her entire face said *how dare you reject my son, you commoner*.

"But I'm hoping she'll say yes." I turned to Sloane. "Baby, can you give Ma and me a minute? And if you see my dear sister, please send her my way."

"The problem, Dom, is this penthouse is massive, and it's hard to tell if someone is around," Sloane called as she sashayed away with her head held high.

My mother had the manners to at least wait until Sloane was out of sight before she leaned closer and hissed, "Dom, she's the cleaner."

I was prepared for her snobbery, but it still pissed me off. "So?"

"I don't like to look down on people's jobs—"

"Yet that's what you're doing—"

"And you don't think she's a gold digger?"

"Ma, do you know how hard I had to convince her to live here? You have no clue what happened to her because of my fuckup. She can take all this"—I waved my arm around the penthouse—"and it wouldn't matter. I want her back. I'll crawl on my knees if I have to."

"What did you do?" she whispered.

"I. Fucked. Up. You'll be ashamed I'm your son."

"Moretti men always fuck up." She said it in a way that everyone was supposed to forgive Moretti men, anyway.

"At least I got my head outta my ass sooner than *Zio* Luca."

She harrumphed. "I don't know what people will say. My son. A Harvard grad, a billionaire. A Moretti!"

"Ugh, Mamma, who cares?" Lucy came down the stairs looking like she just rolled out of bed.

"How are you feeling, *stellina*?"

"I'm better."

Huh, since when did Ma start calling Lucy her little star again? It momentarily suppressed the rise of my temper, but my mother continuing to pile on her prejudice against Sloane was making it a struggle not to lash out at her.

In my years as don, I'd learned the art of negotiation. I was the even-tempered one among my De Lucci cousins and Luca. One would say handling my mother prepared me to be the statesman when it came to family. But I never had someone storming in from the outside like Sloane who I valued above the threat of losing the even hand I employed to running the crime family.

Protect that choice with your life.

I was choosing Sloane, but until I came to grips with how to deal with Sloane and my mother, I needed to tread carefully so one didn't resent the other.

Resentment poisons relationships. Sloane knew this would happen, and she didn't force me to choose a side because family was everything in the mafia.

Lucy was a welcome distraction. "You're sick?"

"Just exhausted," she mumbled, giving our mother a kiss before heading to the kitchen.

"I brought pastina," Ma called.

"What are you exhausted over?" Suspicion entered my tone. Sequestering Lucy to this penthouse and vetoing her return to DC didn't keep her out of trouble. She did most of her "fixer" work through the web and on her phone. Which, surprisingly, she didn't have in hand. She must be really sick.

"This and that."

"Lucy…" I warned in a sterner voice.

Ma intervened and joined Lucy in the kitchen. She lovingly swiped the disheveled hair from my sister's face. "Just no more mischief, huh?"

Mischief? She nearly started a war between the Italian and Russian mafias, and Washington. But I let her focus on Lucy.

"Mrs. Einhorn says I should marry you off, so you will stop meddling in her son's business."

Ma had been furious at Lucy when she said Mrs. Einhorn's son lost a position in the attorney general's office because she'd exposed his drug use in college where a coed died.

I grew up in a life of privilege and my mother gave a lot of passes to men because she still subscribed to a patriarchal society. Pop balanced her out and so did Aunt Ava, who wasn't afraid to call out my mother on her shit when she was letting her spoiled-mafia-princess upbringing of the eighties derail decades of hard work for us to become the most modern crime family in the northeast.

"You're just annoyed because you can't marry off Dom." Lucy shot me a snarky look. "Sorry, bro. Heat's on me, so back to you."

I couldn't even be pissed at her. Ma had been lamenting the unmarried state of her children ever since Cesar and Ava's brood started falling like flies. Matteo and Sera, Bianca and Sandro even got married twice.

My mother's eyes followed the path to where Sloane disappeared. "Now, about the cleaner."

"Her name is Sloane."

Ma scrunched her nose. "Awful name."

"It's a badass name," Lucy piped in, serving herself a bowl of pastina.

"Thank you."

"She's got exquisite features," Ma admitted slowly. "But she's not very cultured."

My mother's euphemism for *uncouth*.

Lucy must have sensed the stiffening of my body.

"Sloane is just rough around the edges." Lucy swallowed a spoonful of pastina and sat at the table. "This is good, Ma. Why don't you guys sit and eat? You're looking long in the tooth there." She eyed me slyly, recognizing how it was costing me not to go off on our mother's attacks on Sloane.

"Sloane doesn't need much to knock a man on his ass," Lucy continued. "I think that's why brother here is afraid to show her off in public."

"She was at the New Year's Eve party," I reminded her.

"But it's mostly our family and close associates, then. People you can control. Imagine if it was at a gala?"

"Oh," my mother interjected, walking over to the kitchen counter and picking up a fancy-looking envelope. "This is for the Russian masked ball benefit."

When I made no move to accept, she put it down, mouth tightening. "It's something I'm helping Irina Zahkarov organize. It's an exclusive event like the Met Gala. Think about it. It's three weeks from now."

She gave an annoyed exhalation and closed our distance. She leaned in, as if not wanting Lucy to hear, but my sister was within earshot, anyway.

"She's a lovely woman, but I don't want you to make a mistake."

My jaw clenched. "And I'm not going to welcome your interference."

"I'm not interfering," she gasped. "I'm your mother."

"And you're done." I put my hand at the small of her back and nudged her toward the foyer. "I suggest you leave before we both say something we'll regret."

Her eyes softened. Aunt Ava once told me my mother had a good heart, but she was just too pampered by the people around her.

At the door, she turned pleading eyes to me again, "Dominic—"

I cut her off. "Do you remember how Cesar's boys are with their obsession?"

She scoffed, "That's a myth to explain their recklessness."

She was talking about Renz, of course, as if that was her barometer of how the De Lucci obsession myth only led to bad decisions. But Renz and Liz were ridiculously happy in their bubble.

"I think I have it," I said just as my mother's mouth curved into a sneer I loathed seeing on her face. It revealed her petty personality that I detested. "Except my Moretti side also preordained me to fuck up first."

"Why is your Moretti side always the problem?" my mother asked. "We have been a respected Sicilian family, and that is why the Zahkarov dynasty has always picked us as first choice. I just feel bad we keep turning them down."

"Are you afraid of losing status?" I asked my mother bluntly. "Does it even matter? You're happy with Pop. Maybe you should hang around a less snobby crowd and turn your attention to family. I mean, there's Luca. He's happy with Natalya. And Elias is your nephew."

"Oh, now you put grandkids in Mamma's brain," Lucy groaned from the kitchen.

And just like that, Ma's face softened. She cupped my jaw and squeezed. "I love you very much, *caro,* and I trust you'll know what to do. What's right for this family." She kissed my cheek, and even if I couldn't see her, I could feel Lucy roll her eyes, but I was glad she kept her mouth shut because I needed Ma to get gone.

I closed the door behind her but was only relieved when I heard the elevator.

When I turned around, Lucy's head was bent over her soup, but she was shaking her head.

"What?" I snapped.

She glanced up. "You know that's Mamma being passive-aggressive, right?"

"Trust me, I know. I've handled her enough times to know. And what's the deal with you being loving one moment and antagonistic the next? Don't play with Ma's feelings that way, Luce."

"Who's the grown-up?"

"She's fragile, you know that."

"She's manipulative is what she is." And I was about to snarl at her when she added, "But…I'm learning because, hey, I'm twenty-six and more mature, right?"

"You still want to do things to get her blood pressure up. You know she has that condition."

"I know! I'm trying, all right? I just get so pissed when she turns that privileged nose at people. Her health doesn't give her a pass to do that."

I walked toward her. "You know, she'd be more agreeable to your point of view if you didn't antagonize her at each turn."

She laughed, lifting her bowl and finishing her soup. "Your strategy, I presume."

"Yeah, you won't make a good lawyer."

"Hey…"

"Is the coast clear?" a voice spoke from the stairs. Sloane must have been eavesdropping. Not that I blamed her. My mother was a lot to take for people not used to her. She was standing midway down the flight of steps that led to the second level of the penthouse. She was wearing cute blue pajamas that set off her mass of red hair. I could see the green of her eyes. My chest tightened. I wanted to come home to this. And this penthouse wouldn't be my home until Sloane made it hers.

I met her at the bottom of the stairs. "I'm sorry my mother ambushed us."

"Why are you sorry?" she said. "This is still your penthouse. Looks like she's the one who owes you an apology."

"What?"

"Boundaries," she said. "You asked me to stay here. I'm not feeling guilty about that anymore."

"You shouldn't."

She nodded to the foyer. "Your mother was civil enough not to call me a gold digger to my face, even if that sentiment is closed-captioned over hers." She laughed in a way I wasn't sure was mocking or pure humor. "Aaaand, judging from the look on yours, she did say it to you, and no, I didn't hear it."

And as though the subject was closed, she walked to the kitchen. "That looks good."

"Here." Lucy slid a bowl toward her. "I'm still hungry, though. I'm not sure pastina is going to cut it."

"We can order takeout." Sloane fished out her phone from her pajama pocket.

"For fuck's sake," I growled and walked toward the fridge and opened it. "The fridge is full. I called in a whole grocery order."

"Yes, and we'll have to cook it," Lucy retorted.

"What do you feel like eating?" Sloane asked.

I forgot I was in the presence of two women who didn't like to cook unless it was simply to boil water. "Put that phone away."

I grabbed the marinated short ribs and broccoli from the refrigerator. "I can bake it or fry it."

"Fried," Sloane and Lucy piped up in unison.

After dinner of Korean short ribs, rice, and steamed broccoli, Sloane shooed me from the kitchen, insisting that Lucy and she were on cleanup. My sister protested that she was sick, but I now knew she was full of shit. She was exhausted because she'd been eating crap when I wasn't around. I wondered how she survived in DC, probably on delivery and eating out.

I'd finished packing more clothes into a duffel and several suits into a garment bag. When I returned to the main living area, the women were already browsing streaming channels.

"What are we watching?" Sloane asked.

"Action," I suggested.

"There's this new political thriller about an ambassador," Lucy said. "It's two seasons. I've been avoiding it since I already worked in DC, but I've been missing the rush."

"I'm game," Sloane said.

"You don't have to go with what Lucy wants," I told Sloane.

"Sit your ass down, bro." Lucy pointed to the comfy armchair.

She was using her phone to control my home theater system. What the fuck? "You reconfigured my shit?"

Lucy laughed. "What did you expect? You own a high-end club, yet you're still relying on so many remotes for your different crap."

"I change my phone all the time." I sighed, resigned to let my sister take over. "And I wasn't good about backing things up."

"Don't say that to me," Lucy teased. "Or I can use that against you."

"Have at it."

I glanced at Sloane to ask her if she wanted a drink before settling down for the show, but the warm look on her face gave me pause.

"You two are so cute when you argue," she said.

"Cute?" I drawled, but if it was something that would change her mind about what she thought of me, that I was a regular guy, an older brother joking around with his kid sister, then I was all for it. I caught Lucy's secretive smile.

The little she-devil knew what she was doing. She wasn't blatant about it, but she was giving me a chance not to fuck up and to show Sloane I wasn't simply a ruthless crime boss.

Just don't mess with my family, or my woman.

"Okay, enough with the flirting." Lucy took over the coveted chaise seating of the sectional. Sloane sat in the middle, tucking her legs under her. Ginger jumped up on her side.

Sloane glanced at me. "You can sit beside us if you want."

I raised a brow.

"I trust you enough not to try anything with your sister around unless…" She eyed Lucy. "Do you have a habit of falling asleep while watching television?"

"I slept all day, which means I'll be awake all night, so you're safe."

It seemed like a courtship, complete with a chaperone.

I moved to Sloane's side, just enough distance to feel her warmth, but not too close I was crowding her.

Ginger transferred from her lap to mine.

"Traitor," Sloane muttered.

"I'm warmer, that's all." I shot Sloane a heated look. "If you're feeling cold…"

Her cheeks pinkened.

"Stop flirting!" Lucy yelled. "Show is starting."

"How many episodes is this?" Sloane asked.

"Eight."

"We can binge it all tonight!" the woman beside me said.

I kept quiet, just enjoying the camaraderie between my sister and Sloane. The first episode started rolling and I could already tell that this wasn't a show Sloane liked to watch. Before the end of the first episode, Sloane had already fallen across the couch, fast asleep. She tucked her cold feet under my thighs.

Normally when we were watching TV, she'd have them on my lap, and I would massage the soles of her feet. Ginger didn't seem amenable to that and resisted my attempts to push her off my lap.

After the first episode ended, I rose to my feet. Ginger gave an annoyed meow.

"I'm taking Sloane to bed," I told Lucy.

"No funny business," my sister said. "Five minutes, or I'm coming to check on you."

"What do you take me for?" I asked, half offended.

Lucy laughed. "Go! You're no fun when you're in love."

I didn't deny it. I watched Sloane sleep for two heartbeats and an ache stabbed me in the chest. I missed this. Missed watching her sleep. Missed admiring the freckles on her face. How they added to the unique beauty that was all her. Ma said Sloane's face was exquisite, but what my mother hadn't seen yet was the strength beneath that beauty.

I gently lifted Sloane from the couch and started walking. A few seconds in my arms and she started stirring. "Show's over?"

"You fell asleep, baby."

"It's boring." She snuggled into my chest.

Fuck. I didn't want to put her down. I slowed my ascent on the stairs, my eyes drinking in the woman in my arms. Entering her room, I didn't turn on the light and let the hallway lighting illuminate my path to her bed.

Laying her carefully on the mattress, I wanted to crawl in beside her. It wasn't even about fucking her. Her body was soft and warm in my arms and I just wanted to wrap my whole body around her and sleep.

Soon. After you unfuck what you fucked, Dominic.

I had my duffel and garment bag the next time I walked into the living room.

"You're leaving?" Lucy asked.

"Yeah."

To my surprise, my sister got off her ass and walked over to give me a hug.

A tight squeeze.

Tighter than her normal squeezes.

She stepped away and stared up at me. "You're doing good, brother."

My brows drew together. "I'm not sure what you mean?"

"Sloane is a tough cookie with a lot of pride and a mile-long streak of independence."

I huffed a short laugh. "I guess it takes one to know one."

"You have good instincts for this," Lucy said. "Your family trained you."

"They have," I deadpanned. "De Luccis and Morettis are tough customers."

"Thanks for dinner." She rose on tiptoes and gave me a kiss on the cheek. "I needed my brother's company."

Emotions backed up my throat. Lucy and I hadn't seen eye to eye in a long time. She thought I was an overbearing asshole, but she'd witnessed my panic attack and finally realized her brother was also human.

CHAPTER Twenty-Nine

SLOANE

IT HAD BEEN THREE WEEKS SINCE MY RETURN TO MANHATTAN. Lucy and the rest of the girls were a good buffer against Dom. It allowed us to be around each other, minus the unwanted pressure. Dom had been very gentle in the way he wormed himself back into my life. And *worming* was the right term. Was *gentle manipulation* the right term, too? I wasn't oblivious, neither was I expecting anything less. He said he understood my hesitance, but he was not giving up.

I saw it in the way he made sure that Lucy and I had everything we needed in his penthouse, especially with food. He cooked dinner sometimes, and on other nights, he'd stay for a movie.

The other night, I woke up nestled against him after having an erotic dream. In my dream, Dom and I were watching a stalker movie and my hand brushed his erection. His breathing grew labored, and I looked up at him while I curled my wrist around his massive, hard cock. Then I swung my leg around him and straddled his lap, rubbing myself to an orgasm, and that was when I woke up with my pussy throbbing.

"I'm sorry," I gasped.

His eyes burned right into my soul. And my pussy clenched, feeling the wet heat pulse for the first time in months. It was still spasming while locked in a heated gaze with Dom.

"You're fine," he murmured. "Were you dreaming?"

"No," I lied.

But he smirked and knew I was full of shit. I glanced over to where Lucy was sitting, but she was the one who had fallen asleep.

Dom eyed me for a few more seconds, studying my face before he said, "You missed half an hour of the movie. Want me to rewind?"

I had backed out of my meds a week ago now that I'd found a purpose again in my life, waking up each morning with a mission. I guessed that was why my physical attraction to Dom was unleashed. In a way, I was kind of thankful that a companionship formed first, understanding his need to be a caretaker. He was wired that way, yet he allowed me to operate in my independence.

I was studying for the NCLEX, so I was mostly in the penthouse. We'd determined I would have more clout if I was a licensed nurse. I already had stellar recommendations from my instructors and nurse supervisors.

I glanced away from the tablet. My eyes were tired from reading the same text repeatedly. I wondered if Lucy would like to drop by Jabbin' Java. Dom had a fully tricked-out coffee station, but I'd been craving one of Renz's cappuccinos.

And as if I'd manifested her, a knock sounded on my door. "Sloane?"

When Dom proposed I live with his sister, I wasn't sure how that would pan out. But like myself, Lucy functioned independently. The penthouse was so huge, we rarely bumped into each other.

I pushed back from my chair and opened the door.

Lucy had an irritated look on her face.

"Is everything all right?" I asked.

"Is there a reason Margo Winthrop wants you at the Russian masked ball?"

"Margo? I've never met her though you already know she was responsible for my…uhm…trip to the Outer Banks. Dom asked me to the gala and I said no."

She exhaled an annoyed huff and left me standing at the door. "Well, if you don't go, then I won't be able to," she called over her shoulder, or at least that was what I thought she said.

"What?" I ran after her because her tone sounded a lot like her not going was my fault. "Why can't you go? Isn't your mother an organizer?"

"She is, but Pop doesn't want me anywhere around Kirill since he still blames me for Kolya still being in jail. As if."

Her room was at the opposite end of the penthouse, so it was quite a trek. She stopped right at the staircase, the dividing line between her wing and mine.

"Why don't you want to go?" she asked.

"It's not my thing, and I don't want to cause conflict between Dom and your mother."

"Are you getting back with my brother?"

My back grew stiff. "That's hardly your business, and you must have misunderstood my previous relationship with Dom. We had a non-relationship."

"Look. I'm not rushing you into a relationship with my brother. I love that arrogant ass, but God knows what he represents is a lot to take in. But if you think there's a chance between you and Dom, you shouldn't let my mother intimidate you because she's going to double down if she knows her tactics are working."

"That's your mother you're talking about." My lips curved in amusement.

"I'm not blind to her faults. In fact, I'm the one who's calling her out on her shit because my dad is so blind to her manipulation."

"And Dom?"

"Oh, Dom indulges her, but he's not blind to the Moretti brand of manipulation either, because it's in his blood."

"You're a Moretti too. How do I know I'm not a pawn between you and your mother?"

Lucy laughed. "I really like you." She resumed walking toward her room. "But I need you at that gala."

Her bossy tone reminded me of Dom. I followed her. "Tell me why?"

She left her door open. I knew Lucy worked into the odd hours of the night and early morning. I didn't think it was healthy, and she frequently looked exhausted. I wondered if that was why Dom checked in on us once in a while.

The first thing that hit me when I entered her room was holy hell, what a mess. The cleaner in me was getting hives. It wasn't the type of mess that was a byproduct of moldy food or questionable hygiene. It was the type of mess stemming from the disorganization of papers and pens, notebooks and folders.

Pictures on the wall commanded my attention. The type of arrangement you see on TV of a murder board. The four walls were plastered with them.

"What the hell are these?"

Lucy sighed. "My client cases." Dom's sister was some kind of fixer, whatever that meant. I figured since she was in DC, it meant burying scandals that might affect people in powerful positions. One picture on the wall was Wade Stephenson. My GSW patient, who apparently was not only Lucy's friend, but the friend of Elyse Bailey, whose picture was beside the lawyer's.

"Oh my God, you wrote on the wall?" My skin was definitely feeling itchy.

"They're erasable ink, although I made the mistake of using a marker on some." She grinned as if she was pleased with it.

"Are you doing this so Dom sends you back to DC?"

"No, it's just how I work. Besides, you think my brother cares if I make a mess in one room? He'll just have someone come repaint it."

I barely heard her when I stood transfixed, staring at a picture on the wall. The emerald necklace caught my eyes first before the person in the image. And just like that, a painful shard that was embedded deep inside a part of me was pulled out, and the wound started bleeding.

"Is this some kind of joke?" My croaked words barely scraped out of my throat.

"What the—?" Lucy asked. "What are you talking about?"

"This!" I pointed to the woman in the picture. She was in the same grouping of photos as Wade Stephenson and Elyse Bailey.

"Vivienne Tomlin? She's the wife of the congressman I'm investigating."

"You're investigating Congressman Tomlin?"

"It was supposed to be a simple background check to find a scandal that would make him vote against the energy bill."

"You use blackmail to change votes on a bill?"

She rolled her eyes. "Don't be naïve. Anyway, it wasn't for me, it was for my client who wanted the congressman to vote differently. But then Wade contacted me. Elyse Bailey was his former coworker and friend who needed his help." Lucy threw up her hands helplessly. "This became a sex scandal. I thought you knew. Didn't you work for the Russians?"

"I mind my own business. Is that why Kirill is pissed at you?"

"He's blaming me for instigating the whole thing, when really, it was Elyse and Wade who were building a case with the feds against the congressman. But when the Russians killed Wade "

She cut herself off; her face darkened in anger.

"You became a dog with a bone."

"This is why I hate the mafia," Lucy growled. "People who try to do the right thing are silenced. Look, I would have left it alone if it were for power or money because I deal with that all the time, but I couldn't ignore the sex trafficking of minors. Elyse showed me the evidence…well, part of it." She exhaled a pained sigh. "Anyway, the congressman's publicity machine suppressed any link between Elyse and his office. His wife is tired of fixing his fuckups." Lucy's eyes bored into me while I was spiraling into a past I'd rather remained buried, but she zeroed in on the pertinent question hanging between us. "But how do you know Vivienne?"

"I'd rather not talk about it." I turned so I could retreat to my room or maybe go to the kitchen and finish that tub of chocolate ice cream.

"They'll be there at the gala."

I paused at the door and pivoted slowly to face her. "What?"

"The Zahkarovs are in a shaky relationship with the congressman. Other Washington heavy hitters will be there but I think the two are sniffing around each other because Grigori has fallen out of the bratva. But he left an important deal on the table that could cost the Zahkarovs billions if Tomlin voted for the energy bill currently being debated in congress."

"Wouldn't his appearance at the gala be in poor taste?"

"The thing with Russian organized crime is you don't know what businesses are theirs with so many layers involved."

"True."

"I mean, I didn't know I was going against the bratva until

Wade got killed and my brother informed me Kirill put a contract on my head."

"What? What happened to… 'I know this guy'…" Despite my earlier spiral, I marveled at Lucy's courage, or what her brother might call recklessness.

"Apparently, I'm not that good, as Margo likes to point out," Lucy scoffed.

"I fear I'll be waltzing into a trap if I attend the gala. I think Margo knows about my connection to Tomlin and it's her whole purpose of wanting me there. Why exactly do you want to go to the gala?"

"She claims she has evidence against Tomlin, and she's only willing to hand it over to me if I get you to go to the gala."

"Leave me out of it."

I exited the room, but this time it was Lucy who chased after me. "I'm going to find out your connection to—"

I spun on her. "Fuck you! Leave me out of your crusade. I don't want any part of it."

"Are you willing to let a pedophile get away with everything? Did he do something to you when you were younger?"

"No," I whispered, but he could have. I could see Mr. Tomlin's face. He wasn't a congressman then, just a handsome, rich employer who seemed extra nice to me. It started with being concerned I was lifting heavy furniture in order to clean. Opening doors when I was hauling out the trash. Smiling at me. Tipping us extra after a job. He told me I had beautiful hair and stunning green eyes. That I should become a model. Anger surged. I didn't doubt Vivienne Tomlin knew that her husband was a sexual predator. She could have fired us. But no, she had to be vindictive. She had to send us to the dumpster to look for her emerald necklace and then send me the picture every year to remind me I was nothing but trash.

"Because he's out there ruining lives. According to Elyse, the girls in the sex parties are drugged out of their minds with GHB before they're sexually assaulted. Are you going to walk away from this?"

No. I couldn't.

I lifted my head and squared my shoulders, staring directly at Lucy. "How can I help?"

An hour later, I was driving toward Montauk with Lucy in my new Audi SUV. Dom accompanied me to a car dealership two weeks ago to pick my new ride, but today was the first time I took it out of the city. I spent a good ten minutes with the vehicle manual to figure out the gizmos. It was quite an upgrade from my rickety van.

A blacked-out Explorer was following us. Lucy's security was now my security. I was surprised Dom hadn't insisted on coming with us when he found out we were visiting Margo. Something was afoot. I was still reeling at how the puzzle pieces were falling into place.

We reached a gated mansion near a bluff. I didn't see any guards, but the second my SUV was within sights of the gate, it opened, indicating we were expected and being watched.

I pulled right in front of the stone wall façade. The entrance was an understated wood slab and a woman, dressed in a stylish sage-colored pantsuit, was already waiting for us.

"Is that Margo?" I asked.

"Yes," Lucy said.

"This looks like a house with an array of servants." Or a butler to usher us in.

"From what I gathered, no one really lives here, not even during the summer. It's just an investment property," she explained.

Lucy and I exited the Audi and both of us stood beside it, not knowing what to do. Margo's nose flared in distaste as she drank in our attire.

Lucy and I were similarly dressed in shorts, T-shirts, and sneakers. The weather app forecasted warm and breezy, so why not dress comfortably?

"Well, come on in," she addressed us before looking at our bodyguards. "Not you."

"I think we'll be fine," I told them. "Dom knows where we are."

The lead bodyguard checked his phone. "Yeah, boss said it was okay."

Margo pivoted in an elegant half circle to enter the house. Lucy and I followed more cautiously.

The mustiness of the place hit my nose and the cleaner inside me automatically shifted gears to the effort it would take to clean this place. But my brain had to remind myself I didn't do that work anymore. The covered furniture and the accumulating dust on the shelves told me it would simply go back to what it was in a few years.

"So why do we need to be here?" Lucy asked when we stopped at the foyer.

"I didn't ask for Sloane to be here," Margo said. "All I said was she needed to agree to go to the gala." Her gaze slid to me. "But it's good to see you looking well, Miss Scott."

When I agreed to go to the gala with Dom, I asked him if I should thank Margo for rescuing me from Grigori. Dom emphatically said no. The kind of "no" that made me read between the lines. And I was familiar with Margo's type. She wasn't on anyone's side except what made sense to her bottom line and reputation.

I acknowledged her statement with a curt nod. When unsure on how to respond, say less. Dealing with Margo was no different from dealing with the mob.

She seemed amused at my lack of a courteous reply, but I also saw a flash of admiration.

"We could have negotiated over the phone," Lucy said.

Margo leaned in. "Your enemies have ears everywhere."

We didn't have far to go. Her study was next to the foyer. She probably didn't want her guests venturing too far into the house. I still didn't understand why she chose this meeting place.

She pushed a folder toward Lucy. "Your hard copy if you want, but you have an email with a link to a secure server to sign."

She scanned the document, and with a couple of clicks, she returned her gaze to Margo. "I'm comparing it to the original terms you sent me."

The older woman smiled. "You know, you remind me a lot of my younger self. I admit you're even more ingenious, but don't always rely on technology, Miss De Lucci. Sometimes you have to do the groundwork to get results."

"Oh, is that a compliment?" Lucy retorted.

"Face it." Margo smiled. "You idolize me. That's why you're doing all this. Rattling my clients, so I'll notice you."

"Then why didn't I sign a covenant with you in the first place? We know Dom wasn't your target. It was me."

"I won't say your brother wouldn't be a coup. But your mother is too set on the Zahkarov girl, who is totally wrong for him."

I was getting more confused. "Hold on. Hold on. Hold on. What are you talking about? And, Lucy, you're not signing anything."

Lucy glanced at me and smirked. "Sorry. You're not the boss of me either. Contracts are the same. Now show me the evidence."

Margo tapped on the tablet, and Lucy stared at her screen.

"This is more disgusting than I thought." Pink suffused Lucy's face. "This is the man you're protecting?"

"I've only acquired this evidence recently, and it's what pushed me to give up my client. There are certain lines I won't cross, and most of the time, I look the other way if it isn't worth my time to intervene."

Lucy was still transfixed on the screen, her jaw clenching and unclenching. Finally, I willed myself to look over her shoulder.

Bile rose up my throat. "That girl can't be over thirteen."

I looked away, but Lucy continued to watch.

"I don't know how you can—"

A suppressed sob tore up Lucy's throat. "Because I have to make sure there's enough here to nail that bastard."

"There's more than enough," Margo said.

She glanced at Margo. "Sorry, we're not at the trust stage yet. This works. This will not be admissible in court…"

"But you know where the rest of Elyse's evidence is located," Margo finished. "And this is enough cause for authorities to get a search warrant."

"Yes, and I'm not going to risk getting my ass thrown in jail to get it," Lucy said.

I guessed she meant breaking and entering. I wouldn't put it past her to do it too and had no doubt she'd done it before.

"This is better." Lucy did a couple of taps on her screen. "The covenant is signed."

Margo pushed forward two ornate envelopes similar to the one Dom's mother gave him. "Then you two have some shopping to do."

I couldn't resist slipping out the invitation. I ran my fingers over the raised print of the event date and something clicked. "Is this September nine the reason why you wanted me to stay in the Outer Banks until this date?"

"Yes," Margo replied with an enigmatic smile. "If either you or Dominic hadn't pulled through with my expectations by the time the gala came around, then I would have cut my losses." She walked around her desk, stepped up to me, and peered into my eyes. "But I recognize resilience when I see it."

We didn't hang around for small talk, but when we reached the grand foyer, Margo called, "Miss Scott."

I stiffened and turned to face her.

"Show them you have what it takes to be the belle of the ball."

"I'm not sure—"

"No limits, Miss Scott. I believe in you."

CHAPTER
Thirty

Dom

MARGO

They're gone.

ME

Lucy signed?

She did.

Fuck you, Margo.

It's for her protection. You understood this.

I would have found another way.

My role is as a matchmaker. I'm getting tired of playing mediator between men with oversized egos. Finish what you started. And take your woman shopping. She's got a ball to attend.

THOUGH I DIDN'T KNOW THE SPECIFICS OF THE covenant/contract Lucy signed with Margo, it had something to do with agreeing to marriage prospects. Good luck with that. My sister was too independent for arranged marriages. I had a feeling her get out-of-jail-free card was to annoy the fuck out of each prospective groom, enough so Margo would break their agreement to save everyone's sanity. But for now, it would protect Lucy from bratva retaliation stemming from going after Tomlin.

I slid my phone into my pocket and stared at the man lying on the bed. Grigori Petrov. He had leukemia from radiation exposure four years ago due to an arms deal involving nuclear material. Last-ditch effort with chemotherapy failed. It was a shame karma got to him first. That was why he kept Sloane around. If he couldn't sell her, he was hoping to have a nursemaid when the time came. Anton tried to kill him under orders from Tomlin. Grigori discovered that betrayal and contacted Margo for an exchange since she'd asked him about Sloane before. The exchange was medical care. Margo told me rescuing Sloane cost her more than she'd like and I'd be receiving that bill, too.

Fuck that. And I told her if she was going to charge me for Grigori's medical bills, then she would have to reveal the name of Sloane's harassers.

When Margo revealed it was Tomlin, I thought she was full of shit because it was too much of a coincidence. But Trevor matched payment records between Scotty's Cleaning and the Tomlins' Park Avenue residence. It didn't come up in our searches because it was under the maiden name of Tomlin's mother. The back alley picture where the dumpster was located matched the building's architecture.

"Is it over?" Grigori groaned from the bed.

I approached him. Standing off to the side and leaning against the wall was Sandro. He was eyeing the Russian with the chilling intent of a grim reaper harvesting his next victim. In our line of work, being afflicted with a terminal disease did not erase our past atrocities. Atrocities could traverse a morally gray line, but trafficking children fell on the irredeemable side. For this, Grigori deserved to burn in hell. He was well on his way there, but it didn't mean we couldn't give him a taste before he met his maker.

We'd turned off his morphine drip that kept him comfortable and Sandro injected him with a drug cocktail he used in interrogation that fried the recipient's nerves.

Grigori was pale, sweating, and moaning in misery.

I leaned close. "Not until you tell me where Anton is."

"For the last time," he gritted, jaw clenching with each syllable, "I. Don't. Know."

When he'd been more lucid and coherent, he told us that Tomlin must be hiding Anton and the rest of the crew who betrayed Grigori.

I glanced at Sandro and he shook his head, meaning Grigori was telling the truth and he had nothing else to bargain with.

I walked to Sandro. "How do we finish this?"

"I've kept him alive long enough. The serum is going to kill him in a few hours."

"Can't you just shoot me?" Grigori cried with whatever strength he had left.

"That's what they all say," Sandro said without a trace of sympathy.

"I won't be satisfied until I get Anton," I said. That motherfucker strangled Sloane.

"Neither will I," Sandro responded. "But Grigori is finished."

I glanced over my shoulder, watching the writhing body on the mattress. The smell of antiseptic couldn't disguise the stench arising from his diseased flesh and soiled bedding.

"We're done here," Sandro said. "Let the drug do its job. His vitals are on my phone."

I turned once more to face Grigori. "Rot in hell, motherfucker."

We were on the second level of Margo's mansion. The security in this house was discreet, but I believed, like the De Luccis, there was a whole other operation in the basement. The unlived-in state of the first floor was merely a cover.

Margo met us at the bottom of the staircase. She scrunched her nose. "I believe you men are satisfied?"

"Not until I catch Anton."

"I gave you all the leads," Margo said. "Just don't act against the Russians."

"If Kirill retaliates, then we have no choice but to defend ourselves. Don't tell me he doesn't suspect you know where Grigori is."

"He does," the woman responded. "But if he wants any hope of clearing Kolya's name, he will stand down."

I raised a brow. "He must hate that."

"Men always do when you have them by their testicles." She smiled shrewdly. "Still, I wouldn't underestimate Kirill."

"If an innocent man is in prison, I don't see why you would withhold any evidence to clear his name," Sandro argued.

Margo narrowed her eyes at Sandro. "I believe, Mr. Rossi, you have outstayed your welcome here." She pointedly walked to the entrance and opened the door with practiced grace, belying her scornful words.

Sandro and I exited the property, noting how it had given me the creeps. Though I'd like to investigate Margo some more after the contract my sister had struck with her, my objective was to get my girl ready for her unveiling.

We just reached Manhattan when Sandro told me that Grigori was dead.

CHAPTER
Thirty-One

DOM

ME

Well?

BIANCA

Well, what?

Can I meet you girls somewhere now?

Well...

IT WAS THREE DAYS BEFORE THE GALA. SERA CREATED A GIRLS CHAT called Sloane Makeover, which I insisted to be included on. I was sitting in Jabbin' Java having my third double espresso. Did I have other boss things to do? Yes. Did I feel like doing them? No. I was a love-sick fool, craving a crumb of attention from the girl I'd once rejected. And my cousins gatekeeping Sloane was wearing on me. It was also fear. I acknowledged now that one of the reasons I kept Sloane to myself was because her beauty would eclipse everyone beside her. Hell, she deliberately downplayed her looks to avoid attention. My cousins and sister were determined to unleash her beauty in a Sloane tsunami.

I was determined not to be ignored.

ME

I was supposed to accompany Sloane to her fitting.

BIANCA

You can't see her dress.

Why? It's not a wedding dress

She wants to surprise you.

I didn't respond, but that appeased me a bit. Surprise me? A smile formed on my lips. Maybe she really was warming up to me. I remembered during the last movie night, she was making those sexy noises in her sleep. I was so fucking hard, I couldn't concentrate on the film at all.

But then Bianca's next words disabused me of my notions.

After all, you're paying for it. 😜

I found out the girls scheduled a spa day for tomorrow and charged it to my account. If Sloane thought treating the girls on my dime was going to turn me off, then she was wrong. Others would see Sloane as a gold digger, but I knew what was in her heart. Money meant nothing to her other than a means to take care of people she'd let into her heart. Billy had let her down, but the revelation of what led to her brother's self-destruction was helping her heal. This new information about how Vivienne Tomlin damaged

Sloane's self-worth was another hurdle to overcome. Entitled people like me, who'd been born into power and money, who'd assigned her to a corner and limited the success she deserved, were the ones undeserving of her. But as Sloane battled her demons, which included what I'd done to her, I was determined to be the last man standing.

ME

What about lunch?

SERA

We're thinking of having makeovers first.

Aren't you going to the spa tomorrow?

LUCY

Since Sloane is liberal with your card, we added haircuts and makeup.

I'm surprised Ma let you go to the fitting by yourself.

She magically had a last-minute meeting about the gala.

I bet Margo had something to do with it.

What salon are you girls going to?

No response.

I waited for five minutes.

Hello?

What the fuck. There were eight people on this chat, including me, and no one was answering.

"Oh my God, that's gorgeous," Liz exclaimed from the coffee bar. She was sharing her screen with Renz.

Suspicious, I slid out from the booth and walked over to them. Liz glanced up from her phone and pressed the screen to her chest.

Narrowing my eyes, I growled, "Is that Sloane's dress?"

"You're not supposed to see it, remember?" Liz said with the snarkiest tone I'd ever heard from her.

Renz shook his head and chuckled. "Another espresso?"

"At this point, I don't need more caffeine. Water would be good."

ME

Did you girls form another group chat?

Liz burst out laughing.

I glared at her. This was nothing new. Depending on who was the current annoying one in the family, micro-chats were created to exclude that person.

Never mind. I have my answer. You all have no loyalty.

FIRECAT

I'll make it worth your while.

My breathing faltered when she responded. She'd been quiet throughout this text exchange.

"Here you go." Renz put the glass of water in front of me. I thanked him distractedly and continued texting Sloane while I had her attention.

Are you enjoying yourself?

Very much.

Which salon are you girls going to?

There was a long pause before Liz started laughing again.

I glared at her. "Are they preventing Sloane from responding?"

Liz did a zipper gesture across her mouth.

I glowered at Renz. "Your wife is colluding against me."

"I'm just a spectator," Liz defended herself. "It's kind of cute seeing you all worked up."

BIANCA

Leave Liz alone.

ME

Tell me where you girls are going. I'll bring lunch. Anything you want. A full caviar service. Cocktails?

SERA

Hmmm...

@S.Scott Don't cut too short!

BIANCA

You're not the boss of her.

"Argh." I furiously tapped on the phone.

You removed B.Rossi from the chat.

"Seriously?" Liz laughed.

Renz glanced over her shoulder and a rough chuckle gusted past his lips. "You're starting a war, cuz."

S.DeLucci added B.Rossi to the chat.

SERA

@D.DeLucci, don't do that again, or we're blocking you.

BIANCA

😜

SERA

@B.Rossi, stop riling him up.

The women might have found out a way to block me from tracking them, and if I wasn't heartsick over Sloane, I would have figured it out sooner. Not that any of my cousins or Sandro would help me. I tried Trevor, but he was the one who instigated the block. And since Matteo outranked me in the Archer Syndicate, his orders took precedence.

I waited until I got confirmation that the women were about to leave for the salon.

There was one person who wouldn't play along with this shit.

I shot off a text to Luca.

ME

Can you find Sera's location?

LUCA

???

I gritted my teeth. This was embarrassing enough.

The women are going to a salon, and Sera had Trevor block me from tracking them.

Fifth Avenue. Royale salon.

Owe you.

I'm helping you because if Natalya had blocked her location, it would piss me off too. This is a childish game.

SIGHING, I TEXTED BACK.

ME

Agreed. But can't say I didn't deserve it.

LUCA

You're a boss. Act like one.

That should have stung, but it didn't. Anything for Sloane. Nothing mattered, even my pride.

None of the women are under the De Lucci crime family umbrella. They don't answer to me.

Use your judgment, then. But fix your shit with Sloane.

Yeah, Ma told me Moretti men always fuck up, so I probably shouldn't take relationship advice from you.

She did, did she?

Luca didn't answer for a few seconds, so I shot him another text.

Don't go ratting me out, Zio. The women are trying to hide from Ma.

Fine.

Bubbles appeared and disappeared. Finally, another text came.

It would be amusing to witness your groveling firsthand, but I fear when Natalya sees it, she will think she didn't make me grovel enough.

I laughed. Luca wouldn't care to admit such a thing in text, but I had a feeling I had his approval anyway with whatever path I took.

An hour later, I found street parking by the salon. I'd already called ahead of time to make sure that they could accommodate my request.

When I rounded the building, I spotted Matteo and Nico heading the same way. What the fuck?

Matteo smirked at me. "Looks like you found them."

I'd been ignoring the text messages after Luca's, so I checked my phone to see a slew of heart and drooling emoji messages thanking me for the lunch spread.

When it came to the women in my family, being pampered with food was the way to their hearts. It didn't have to be the five-star meal I just planned, it just had to show that it took effort. In a way, Ma had trained me well. Money could buy many things, but it couldn't replace the thoughtfulness that came from the heart.

And this was from the heart. I wanted to spoil Sloane with everything she deserved.

Nico clapped my back. "Looks like someone is obsessed."

I didn't deny it. I simply opened the door for them to walk in. "Since I'm paying for lunch, maybe back me up a bit, yeah?"

The fuckers had the gall to laugh.

The receptionist of the salon greeted us. She was tongue-tied for a while, which was usually the case when women saw the De Lucci men traveling in packs. Thank fuck Sandro and Luca weren't around. I wanted the focus to be on the women. Although the way some of the staff were tittering behind their palms was telling. Not surprisingly, only one woman's opinion mattered to me.

"The lunch spread you ordered is being set up in the Camelot room," the receptionist said.

"Where's Sloane?"

"Miss Scott is with Mrs. De Lucci and the others in the

Corinthian room. Also, Mrs. Rossi requested the guys wait at the Camelot room where lunch is being set up."

"I don't mind a beer," Nico said.

"Same," Matteo answered and slung an arm around me but addressed the receptionist. "Don't worry, miss, we'll keep him company."

She led us into an ornately appointed lounge room where the caterers had set up a long table covered with white linen.

In one corner, the bartender from my club was already in place.

"The usual, sir?" He grabbed a Macallan 18.

I tipped my chin in confirmation.

Meanwhile, Nico nudged Matteo. "I changed my mind."

I rolled my eyes. As if they couldn't afford expensive scotch. But an eighteen-year-old sherry oak single malt beat the best beer for sure, especially if you needed a shot to calm down your over-caffeinated nerves.

"Why not the Macallan 25?" Nico teased.

"I'm reserving it for another occasion." I accepted the glass of scotch and let the crisp liquor saturate my tongue as I observed the luncheon setup. Easy finger food. Like seared scallops on a stick, a charcuterie board, asparagus spears wrapped in bacon, and, of course, the full caviar service. The caviar was to kiss Sera's ass since it was a favorite appetizer of hers.

Sloane didn't seem picky with food, and from our time together, she'd eat anything. Obviously, we didn't date but ate out of necessity to recharge after vigorous sexual activities.

If she had a favorite dish, then shame on me because I had no clue. That was about to change. As long as she'd give me a second chance, I would find out every single favorite thing of hers, including substitutes.

I stared broodily at the entrance to the room, waiting for Sloane to appear. One server headed our way. Earlier, she had walked by with the girls' drinks.

"Mr. De Lucci."

"There're three of us, ma'am," Matteo drawled.

The woman, who was probably in her forties, blushed. "I can see that."

"What? I don't look like him." Nico pointed at me.

"There's a resemblance."

I didn't know whether that was a compliment or an insult. "What do you need?"

"Miss Scott is asking for you."

"Is she all right?"

The woman appeared pensive. "I'm not sure."

CHAPTER
Thirty-Two

Sloane

The reflection of the girl in the mirror was the image of the woman I'd always dreamed of becoming. Before Dad disappeared. Before Mom told me never to depend on a man. Before Vivienne Tomlin mocked me to dumpster-dive and find her necklace.

When I'd learned pretty and poor had dire consequences. When my mother and I were blacklisted by the rich and we ended up working for mobsters. But since Mom worried that I'd be exploited for my looks instead of valued for my work ethic? That was the demon that drove me to twist my hair into a braid or knot. To cover my head in the ugliest cap and wear the ugliest shapeless clothes. But in the deepest crevices of my heart, there was still that girl who aspired to be the princess. I built walls around her to keep that girl safe. And I cut loose once in a while when the pressure became unbearable, but I never imagined anything like this.

I had regular haircuts.

But I'd never had haircuts and cocktails.

I'd never been the center of attention in an upscale salon.

I'd never had my hair layered in such a way it framed my face and I couldn't believe that the drop-dead-gorgeous woman in the mirror was me.

A fractured sob escaped my throat. Rob, my stylist, stopped fluffing my hair.

"What's wrong, sweetie?"

I shook my head vigorously. Uncontrollable emotions roaring up inside me had nowhere to go, and tears spilled down my cheeks.

"I'm sorry." A breath caught raggedly. "I ruined the makeup."

"Don't you like it?" he asked gently. "We can make your eyes more dramatic, but their emerald color is so remarkable, I'd hate to—"

"No. No," I cried harder. "It's perfect. It's just that…I never thought…I deserved this…" I broke off.

Sera and Bianca rushed to my side, with Divina, Lucy, and Ivy hovering.

Sera knelt in front of me. "Hey, what did we say? You deserve this. We love you, Sloane. You're one of us."

"You helped me without thought of retribution, because it was the right thing to do," Bianca said. "You fit right in."

I emitted a watery laugh. "An insurrectionist?"

"Yes, we need you to keep Dom in line, too," Bianca said.

"You overestimate my power over him."

"Don't doubt it," Lucy said. "I've never seen my brother behave this way."

"So he's really outside?" I swiped the tears from my eyes.

"You saw our text stream, right?" Bianca laughed. "He's anxious to see you."

Giddiness buoyed my chest, making me sit taller. I stared at my teary face in the mirror. "Can I see him before you fix my face?" I asked Rob because I couldn't wait any longer to tell him how these past few weeks had been. How difficult it must have been for him to be patient given his personality and position.

Someone barged into the room, and I saw Dom's panicked face in the mirror.

When he saw my tear-streaked face, the way he glared at every single person around me turned the room silent. Poor Rob hid behind Ivy, the only person who could probably take Dom down in case he went nuclear.

"Who made you cry?" He rushed to my side so fast, Sera had to get out of the way just as quickly or be tossed aside.

A smile formed amidst the onslaught of powerful emotions and I touched his arm placatingly. "These are not tears of misery."

His scary face melted into an endearing wariness that warmed my heart. Here was a man of status, power, and money, but all he wanted was for me to be happy. But Dom couldn't make me happy unless I was happy with myself first.

"Then what?" He tipped his chin at Sera, his meaning clear.

"Okay, everyone, let's have some lunch first," Sera said. She didn't need to repeat herself as the room emptied, leaving me with Dom.

But I could be as dramatic as him. I studied his beseeching, searching gaze. It was as if he was afraid as well as hopeful. It was as if his happiness hinged on mine. After the extended pause, I exhaled a long, ragged breath. "I think I'm open to giving you a second chance and—"

"Oh, Sloane," he growled, clasping my shoulders and helping me to my feet. He framed my face, and the instant our lips touched, the yearning inside me exploded.

He groaned into my mouth, devouring me in scotch-laced ravaging kisses. Shocked with how my body was reacting to what was new while at the same time familiar. I emitted a distressed moan.

He reared back, brows cinching together. "Sloane?"

"I…can we take this slow?"

Palpable relief crossed his handsome features. "I'll go as slow as you want." His hand shook as he brushed the hair that fell across my face. "I'm glad you didn't cut it too short. It suits you."

The intensity in his gaze made breathing difficult.

"Uhm, I just wanted to tell you how much I appreciate the space you've given me. And the girls, having them take the lead…"

He continued to caress my face as if he couldn't stop touching me. "I want to make your life better because you deserve it, but you have to see it for yourself that you deserve it. I can't do that for you."

"You're an amazing man, Dominic De Lucci," I breathed.

"I don't know about that. I fucked up royally."

"I forgive you."

"I've learned my lesson in case you're wondering."

"And what is that?"

"Never put Sloane in a corner." His mouth quirked up. He kissed the tip of my nose. "Just know that a second chance with me means all in. I'm not letting you go."

"What happened to taking it slow?" I let out a light laugh. I wanted to be all in too, but belonging to someone was an unfamiliar concept to me. Staring at the face of this ridiculously handsome man, I had trouble believing he was choosing me.

Wait. Scratch that.

Not hard to believe. I was flipping the script on that.

He earned me.

He must have sensed the amusement in my thoughts. "What are you thinking about, Firecat?"

"I think we should let everyone back into the room."

As if they were totally listening, the door opened.

"Finally!" Bianca headed straight to me, holding out a drink. "Kir Royale."

She added, "Rob informed me that *kir* in Farsi means *cock*."

I laughed. "Noted."

CHAPTER
Thirty-Three

SLOANE

"YOU'RE GOING TO KNOCK HIS SOCKS OFF," ROB EXCLAIMED.

It was gala night, two days after the salon visit, and a day after our girls' spa day indulging in a massage and a full-body treatment. The estheticians advised against any sort of peel so we went with a gentle exfoliant. She sent me home with an instant glamor mask that they carried in the spa to apply after my bath today.

Rob gushed at how smooth my skin was and how my pores were smaller than they were the other day. Not that I'd noticed because the mirror in the apartment didn't have the magnification of the one in the current bathroom I was using.

"I don't think I can realistically manage the skin care regimen the esthetician sent home with me."

Rob leaned in conspiratorially. "If you ask me, girlie, your man thinks you're beautiful just the way you are." He fanned himself. "And, girl, is he possessive."

I laughed, even when it wasn't really funny. Apparently Dom had an issue with Rob coming into the penthouse to do my hair and makeup. But after we assured him that Rob was definitely gay and had no interest in me sexually other than as a project, he relented. Still, he had asked Trevor to hang around the penthouse.

Lucy was going to the gala with her parents and she was staying with them, which added to the jittery feeling in the pit of my stomach. Dom was picking me up today. We hadn't discussed him staying over yet. He'd been unusually quiet in our messages other than greeting me this morning.

DOM

Good morning, beautiful.

I'll pick you up at 6:30. Just a heads-up. Got a couple of things that need my attention and might not respond immediately. Any emergency, Trevor knows where to reach me.

ME

K. 🥰

Ever since my epiphany the other day at the salon, I began seeing my renewed relationship with Dom through a new lens. The notion of expectations wasn't there, and with my therapy sessions, I'd learned to flip the script from expectation to appreciation. Appreciate the blessings and help offered by the caring people around me. Accept that I deserved to be in their circle. I worked hard to be where I was and be able to take the NCLEX. I had the Delphine project to look forward to. Words couldn't express the feeling of having something to live for. Now Dom was part of it.

Granted, we were still in the early stages.

I thought about the fancy shopping bag that arrived this morning containing sexy lingerie. I immediately laundered it so it would be ready to wear this evening.

"Ack, I see that secretive smile," Rob teased. "You're thinking about him."

"Trevor said to head on up." Bianca appeared at the door of my room. The look of utter amazement on her face was satisfying and morale-boosting. "Oh my God, I love your updo and makeup!"

"Why are you here?" I asked. "Weren't you supposed to have a date night with Sandro?"

"I'm still going to have a date night with my husband. He's waiting downstairs, talking to Trevor. Dom texted me this morning to help you put on the gown."

"Ugh, seriously. That man." I looked around for my phone, but I couldn't find it.

"Haha, whether he thinks I'm gay or not, he still doesn't want me to help you," Rob chortled. "Okay, go put it on, *Mizz* Scott. I'll wait outside just in case your makeup or hair needs repair."

When Rob left, I turned to Bianca, and with a confidence I hadn't felt in a long time, I whipped off my robe with flair.

She gaped. "Oh my God, the bustier and garters." She moved closer and inspected the lace. "Where did you get this?" she asked in a tone that said, I want one.

"Dom sent it to me this morning. Color me impressed. He guessed my size perfectly."

"My cousin the Casanova." Bianca gave a low whistle. "You've got the proportions of a fifties screen goddess and with that red hair…honestly, Sloane, with how long you kept Dom on ice, he might just combust in his tux."

Imagining Dom combusting sent a pulse of arousal between my legs because I remembered how feral he could be, and I was more than ready for a hard pounding. It was as if my whole body had been encrusted in a layer of salt and needed a sledgehammer of wild sex to get through it. For the first time since I could remember, I used a vibrator last night, imagining Dom's cock inside me so I could take the edge off. I didn't want to jump his bones the moment he walked into the foyer. I had a feeling taking it slow wouldn't be possible after tonight. I wondered if that was why he didn't try to see me the previous evening after the spa.

"Has he had many girlfriends?"

Bianca side-eyed me after straightening from admiring the lacy underwear. "Is that a trick question? Because I'm kinda tickled that both of you are back together and I don't want to be a victim to foot-in-mouth."

"No tricks. I'm genuinely curious. He told me he didn't have many girlfriends, just affairs like he had with me, I guess."

"Ask him about it. He's got this weird dating app for the rich." Bianca side-eyed me again and her cheeks grew redder. "Honestly, the last thing I want to talk about is my cousin's sex life. He's like a brother to me."

She visibly shuddered. I laughed.

"Okay, let's get you into the dress! I promised to send pictures to our other girl chat."

I hefted the garment bag out of the closet. The dress was heavy. I laid it on the bed and pulled down the zipper to reveal a black and ivory gown.

"I forgot how gorgeous it is!" Bianca enthused. "I love the skirt the most." The voluminous skirt was embellished with different sizes of ivory rosettes over a backdrop of black. I extracted the beautiful creation, almost afraid to wear it. Hell, I could barely eat anything today because I was worried I would not fit in it.

Having the bustier helped. The off-shoulder creation had a fit-to-flare architecture. Bianca aided me in slipping on the gown, from the bottom up, and started the arduous task of working on the dainty lace-covered buttons. I felt her pulling the edges together.

"How are you doing back there? Am I going to fit or am I going to have a wardrobe malfunction?"

"Nah, as many buttons as you have back here…" she muttered. "God, how many buttons are there?"

"Thirty, maybe?"

"A hundred it looks like," she deadpanned. "You know Dom's not going to have the patience for this, right?"

"You're not suggesting he's going to rip it off." I was comically appalled, but just imagining his impatience sent waves of heat coursing through my body.

"Just don't get too attached to this dress."

"The lady said the lace is antique."

"Dom doesn't give a damn whether it's antique. He paid for it—he'll have the satisfaction of ripping it off."

I wasn't attached to this dress, but my already X-rated thoughts of Dom got steamier. Hearing it rip, I would gasp in outrage and—

"There." Bianca broke the direction of my thoughts. "Whew."

"Are you regretting coming to help me?"

She aimed her phone at me. "Hell no. Sera's bummed she couldn't be here, but Matteo had a meeting and she had to look after Gio."

"Your husbands are probably happy you won't be babysitting me anymore."

Bianca rolled her eyes. "It was fun." She smirked. "Besides, I like it when my husband misses me. Now hush and put on your shoes."

I did so dutifully, stepping into simple ivory pumps made with the same fabric as the gown. The heels were two inches and manageable, especially for someone like me, who wore sensible work clogs all day.

Bianca's glee was infectious, and it calmed the swarming butterflies in my gut. She snapped several pictures and sent it to our group chat without Dom. The following pings led me to my phone, and when I checked it, Dom had sent a text five minutes ago that he had arrived but to take my time.

That sent me into a spiral of nervousness again. Our first outing as a couple and we had to do it big. I bit my bottom lip with the return of my anxiety.

"Dammit, what am I doing?" I mumbled.

"Oh no, oh no." Bianca invaded my space and gripped my shoulders. "Look at me."

I did.

"Repeat after me."

I exhaled heavily.

"I am beautiful," she said.

"I am beautiful."

"I am deserving."

"I am deserving."

"And anyone who thinks otherwise can fuck off."

Bianca was a tornado in a small package. Her sweetness was so deceiving because she packed a spine of steel.

I had to suppress a laugh when I said, "And anyone who thinks otherwise can fuck off."

She gave me a light shake. "Be serious."

"They can fuck off." I shrugged with sass.

"That's my girl, but rein in the gangsta at the ball."

"Why?" I repeated. "The Zahkarovs are gangsters despite their elegant trappings." I was getting worked up. I wasn't sure how much the girls knew about the purpose of why Lucy and I were going to the gala. Dom knew. He didn't question it when I told him he was escorting me to the event. But I'd caught him eyeing Lucy pensively. His hands were tied and I knew he was reining in his big-brother tendencies.

There were many things to discuss, but we needed to survive the gala first.

"True."

The explosion of hearts on the phone ignited a light in the dark corners of my soul. I'd never had a girl gang like this. There was always a sense of competition that made me uncomfortable. But there was a common quality I found in my current girls. They were empowered by the men in their lives. Self-esteem played a vital part in the willingness to let another woman wear the crown. Bianca was an example. She single-handedly straightened out the misogyny in the Rossi-crime-family culture, with Sandro backing her up. If ever Dom and I didn't work out, I was sure I could join their crime family if I were so inclined. The more I thought about the opportunity they were proposing about Delphine, the more I couldn't wait to get started on the project.

"Are you ready to face Dom?" Bianca asked.

"I guess." I stuffed my phone in the matching sequined pouch, gathered my skirts, and followed Bianca out of the room.

"Don't descend the steps yet," she threw over her shoulder. "I want to take a video of you coming down."

When I reached the top of the staircase, Dom was already waiting at the bottom of it. I'd seen him in tuxes before from online news sites and I'd seen him at Bianca's wedding. But this white-tie event was more formal.

Dom's thick raven hair was tamed and slicked back and only accentuated the masterpiece of his clean-shaven face, sculpted of strong angles, firm, defined lips, and thick brows over smoldering eyes that were at the moment singeing holes through my dress.

My knees weakened, and I clung to the top banister. Maybe I should have eaten more food because I'd grown lightheaded.

"Do you want me to come get you?" Dom asked, voice low.

"Because I can't promise I won't carry you straight to the bedroom."

My gaze swept frantically to Bianca. She was shaking with laughter. "Stop that, cuz. I'm trying to find a soundtrack to play."

I must have imagined a growl coming from Dom.

"Ugh, fine," Bianca muttered. "You can make your way down now."

My focus returned to Dom as I took that first tentative step, but like the morning tide, he reeled me in. The bespoke tailoring of his suit did nothing to cloak the animal magnetism writhing inside him.

When I reached the bottom of the steps, Dom invaded my space and lowered his head by my ear. "Fucking hell, baby. I don't know how I'll be able to keep my hands off you all night." He leaned back. "You wanna just ditch the ball?"

The last statement was said loudly for the benefit of the others. Oh my God I forgot the others. Heat climbed up my neck and my cheeks caught fire. Sandro was standing behind Bianca, looking amused. Trevor was beside him, while Rob was busy swooning.

"Kiss her, but don't ruin her makeup. Jeez, should I be the director?" Bianca called out.

Dom chuckled and said for my own ears, "I'm afraid to kiss you because I can't stop with a kiss."

"Let's humor Bianca."

His head lowered, and I was prepared for a light peck. The kiss started as a gentle brush, but my palm on Dom's chest felt the rumble up his throat and I was crushed in his arms at the same time his tongue swept inside my mouth, demanding, persuasive, and full of sensual promise. I returned his kiss fervently, and at the back of my mind, I wanted to ditch the gala too.

"And cut!" Bianca yelled.

Everyone started laughing.

"The betting pool has surged," Trevor said.

"What betting pool?" I asked.

"Come on, girlie," Rob pulled out a chair by the foyer. "Let's repair your lipstick. Apparently, I should have made it De Lucci men-proof."

While the stylist fixed my makeup, Bianca said, "There's a bet going that you guys won't make it to the gala."

"What?" I laughed.

Rob tutted at me. "Don't speak for a second."

"The odds are in favor of you guys getting hot and heavy in the limo and Dom having the car turn around."

When I got the go-ahead from Rob to speak, I asked, "Do me a favor and bet that we will make it to the gala." I winked at Dom. "I'll share my win with you since I'm charging it to your bank account."

"Mercenary," Dom drawled, helping me up and tugging me to his side. "I burn so hot for you, baby."

"Think you can manage not to combust until after the gala?"

"I'm up for a challenge." His eyes gleamed with predatory vibes.

This could also be the longest foreplay of my life.

CHAPTER
Thirty-Four

Sloane

I arrived at the gala intact. Not a hair out of place nor lipstick smudged.

To do that, I ordered Dom to sit at the opposite side of the limo because the heat between us when we were within inches of each other was a volatile spark heightened by the confines of the vehicle. The lacy underwear sliding against my pussy only intensified the pulsing ache between my thighs.

We exchanged innocuous conversation, and I didn't even mention the lingerie he bought me.

The event was held in the Metropolitan Hotel ballroom. The theme was Gilded Splendor.

We put our masks on in the vehicle, and the moment Dom helped me out of the limo, I forgot about him and was in awe of the lavish display before me.

From what I researched about masquerade ball etiquette, it was poor form to identify someone you recognized because the whole purpose was to playfully interact with strangers without the pressure of social status. In a way, it was the perfect entry into Dom's world. Now the remaining anxiety was whether I could exist in it.

The reception hall was another marvel to behold, with the strings of lights evenly spaced around the wall, flaring up into a domed ceiling where the biggest crystal chandelier I'd ever seen was hanging. And I'd seen a few in my cleaning jobs. From what Lucy had told me, because her mom couldn't stop talking about it, the chandelier used to hang in the Zahkarov's castle in Vienna.

Hmm…my snarky side wondered if this was another of their money-laundering schemes. After my initial awe, I finally felt Dom's gaze on me again and renewed awareness tingled over me.

"Enjoying yourself?" he asked by my ear.

"Yes."

His mask was a simple black one, but it cast him in a sinister aura. In this setting, and in his elegant threads, he reminded me of the notorious rakes of old who debauched innocent virgins or carried on scandalous affairs with married women of the ton.

My mask covered half my face. It had satin backing material, but an intricate silver detailing was stitched over the fabric, giving it structure. Tastefully affixed white feathers softened the sharp edges.

White-gloved attendants spun around the room, serving cocktails and canapés. Dom handed me a fruity martini while he sipped a Negroni from a short, round glass. The drink stimulated my appetite, and I pinched a canapé from the roving server.

We circulated among strangers, but I spotted Dom's parents and Lucy talking to another group. I bit into a round pie pastry and an instantly addictive briny, earthy flavor exploded in my mouth. I devoured it, took a sip of my martini, then left Dom who was exchanging small talk with yet another stranger. Unmindful that I was wearing a gown, I chased the server who handed me that particular appetizer. You can take the girl out of Jersey, but you can't take Jersey out of the girl.

"Can I have another one? What is this?"

The server was also in a mask, so I couldn't discern his true expression, but the twitch of his mouth almost made me laugh.

"I'm sorry if I'm being uncouth, but this is delicious." I picked another round pie from the platter. This time, after I took a bite, I studied the filling.

"Black-tie scallops," the man said. "It's scallops layered with black truffle."

You couldn't live in New York and not know what a black truffle was, and I knew the scallop was its perfect complement at least, but I'd never had a combination this scrumptious. I could feast on this all night long.

"Would you like another one, ma'am?"

Dom came up behind me and whispered, "We still have dinner to get through, baby. Don't fill up."

"But these are so good."

"I'm familiar with the restaurant that makes this. I can have the chef of the event make you enough to come out of your ears."

I smiled at the server. "Well, carry on. I don't want to hog you, but give my compliments to the chef."

The man's neck turned red, and he cleared his throat. "I will, ma'am."

Dom turned me around in his arms. "Have I discovered your favorite dish?"

I pondered his question. "It could be. Maybe I have expensive taste after all."

Dom barked a laugh, calling the attention of the crowd around us. And why not? It was an attractive laugh, rough and masculine and sexy. But when I saw a few women's gazes linger covetously on Dom, possessiveness clawed my skin. I leaned into him and I was pleased he drew me closer. Despite my voluminous gown, I fit snugly into his embrace.

The host, the former pakhan Ivan Zahkarov, announced dinner. Another gilded room with warm lighting greeted us. A string quartet provided music, although I heard there would be an elaborate orchestra for dancing later. But as we were escorted to our table, an anvil settled in my gut.

Dom's parents were already seated at a table that sat nine. Lucy didn't have a date, so I guessed they made adjustments to the seating chart and it would have normally accommodated ten. I was thankfully seated beside her, so I felt a measure of relief that I didn't have to make small talk with their mother. I could concentrate on dinner.

We removed our masks. The other couples around the table reeked of old money. It was funny how despite not belonging to their class, I could sniff their kind a mile away.

Introductions were made around the table, but their names barely registered. Dom's mother shot me a tight smile, while his father awarded me a warm one. He actually asked me how I was enjoying myself so far, and I answered courteously and succinctly.

The first course was served, but I barely tasted it. I didn't even know what it was other than it had some kind of obscure greens. I watched Dom and Lucy on which fork or spoon to use because, all of a sudden, the formal dinner lessons Bianca had instilled in me went out the window.

The person beside Dom occupied his attention. I had a feeling the man had business he was anxious to discuss with him. I barely heard their conversation, but I detected a hint of annoyance in Dom's voice. His hand found my thigh under the table and gave it a reassuring squeeze.

"So, it's Miss Scott, is it?" one of the ladies asked. Her mask was the red one. "What is it you do?"

Dom stilled. I could feel frost ice him over.

"I'm a nurse or will be as soon as I pass the exams."

The woman appeared baffled, like she couldn't understand my choice of profession, and when she glanced at Dom, it was like she couldn't believe that he would bring me to this event. Would it make me more palatable in her eyes if I informed her I attended a Swiss finishing school and jetted to Monte Carlo every weekend?

I didn't feel the need to defend myself.

"Oh, but you might move on to medicine, right?" Carlotta quickly interjected. "Be a surgeon?" Dom's mother attempted to mold me into a more palatable light, but it only made me feel worse.

"That's not happening," Dom cut in. "Sloane wants to be a nurse. What's wrong with that?"

"Nothing," his mother said. "But it's a logical next step."

No, it wasn't. At least, not to me.

My throat tightened, trying to keep my emotions from reaching my eyes, but my entire face was on fire.

"A nurse is a noble profession," the woman's husband said and shot me an apologetic look.

She shrugged her elegant shoulders and took a sip of her wine. "Well, Miss Scott, Harvard has a health management program. It's one of the highest-paid professions in the healthcare industry."

Lucy gave an unladylike snort, prompting a glare from her mother.

"Highest paid? Riiiight," Lucy scoffed. "It's because their bottom line is not patient care but how to make money for their stockholders."

"Lucy!" Carlotta hissed.

But my girl had my back, so I had to put in my two cents. "Yes, I prefer to remain a nurse, thank you very much. Nurses put the care in healthcare, not the administrators who decide how to make money for the hospital. Remember that when your children put you in a nursing home, who's going to make sure you…you get the right meds…" This is the wrong place to mention changing their diapers and bedpans. "Or who will train the staff in patient mobility?" I was getting fired up. Because fuck them.

"You tell them, baby." I could feel Dom's gaze on me.

"Yes, Mamma," Lucy laughed. "Be careful. We'll decide which nursing home to stick you in."

"Lucy, *cara mia.*" Paulie De Lucci's admonishment to his daughter was laced in humor.

An older couple at the table, who looked to be in their seventies, were nodding their heads. The woman said, "I love my nurse more than my doctor."

"Hey," her husband said. "I'm your doctor."

I put my hand over my mouth to stifle a laugh.

The man regarded me with what was akin to reverence. "I can attest nurses are the true heroes. I would be lost without my nursing staff."

Our server arrived with the second course and effectively changed the uncomfortable topic.

When dessert was served, Lucy grabbed my arm. "Let's powder our noses."

Dom's brows furrowed, and he oddly checked his phone, but nodded.

I followed Lucy, apprehensive of what was going down. I knew this was about Tomlin, and I'd overheard the siblings arguing the other night that Dom didn't want me anywhere near him. That detestable couple was part of my past, and if Tomlin was a pedophile, I was a hundred percent behind what Lucy had planned for him. She dragged me into the ladies' room and checked the stalls.

"What's going on?"

"Vivienne wants a deal," she said. "Someone from the media informed them that there was going to be a headline tonight that would prove scandalous for the Tomlins."

"You can't give them a deal. Her husband is a sicko, and she's protecting him." Which made her a sicko too.

"We're not."

Her phone pinged again. "Shit. The headline is out. You need to brace," she told me.

My whole body locked up when the ladies' room door swung open and the woman I hadn't seen in years walked through.

"This is cozy." The woman of my nightmares sneered at me. She hadn't aged well. Botox and fillers had taken their toll. I used to admire her delicate features, but in her attempt to stop time, she'd almost become unrecognizable. I thought I'd recognized her earlier, but since her lips were plumped up way past how I remembered her, she didn't even register. Apparently, she couldn't say the same. "I thought it was you, Sloane. And, girl, I am impressed. Dominic De Lucci? Does he know you used to scrub my toilet and dumpster-dive behind my building? I still have the picture, you know."

I thought about those pictures briefly over the past few weeks, but it was a blessing they burned down with the rest of my things the day Al was supposed to deliver them. "You sent me one every year for four years, but then you stopped. Why?"

"Because you're not worth my time anymore," she snapped.

"No, that's the time Tomlin got elected to office," Lucy said. "You're afraid to leave a trail of your husband's past harassment."

She stepped forward. "You seduced him."

"If that's your take on your husband grooming a minor, then you're as despicable as he is."

"You had notions in your head that you could be the next Mrs. Tomlin. He's a respected United States congressman and you?

You're simply a nurse. Poor Imogen couldn't even ask the right questions."

"You set her up at dinner, didn't you?" Lucy asked. So I guessed Imogen was wearing the red mask.

"Fred forbade me to go near either of you."

"And why are you here?"

"Because despite what happens tonight, this isn't over." She directed her contemptuous gaze up and down my dress. "Enjoy, Cinderella. This won't have a happily ever after. If Dominic De Lucci doesn't see you for the trash you are, he will soon."

Vivienne Tomlin swept out of the room in a cloying smell of heavy vanilla and rose.

We gave her a few seconds head start before Lucy tugged my arm to leave the ladies' room. "Come on."

I was suddenly over this gala anyway, and if Vivienne and Imogen-the-red-mask were the type of people in Dom's circle, then I'd rather stay at home watching my serial killer TV.

I wasn't the only one who had to make adjustments in this relationship.

I was busy spiraling in my thoughts, so I didn't notice Lucy stop. I bumped into her. But then I saw what caused her to halt so abruptly.

Frederick Tomlin. I knew him as Mr. Tomlin then, not Congressman Tomlin.

He wasn't wearing his mask. Though the years had been kinder to his tanned all-American face, his blond head was almost white. Once upon a time, he exuded the golden-boy allure of the Great Gatsby era.

I berated my sixteen-year-old self for not seeing the man he was. A predator. He'd been grooming me. My mother recognized him for who he was and it frightened her.

"Sloanie, sweetheart," he breathed. The lust in his eyes made my skin crawl. "I always knew you'd become this beautiful woman." His gaze hardened when they fell on Lucy, then flew back to me. "What's this? Did you two conspire to take me down?"

"You did that to yourself, Congressman Tomlin," Lucy shot back.

"You never changed, did you?" I said. "You still prey on children."

His lips curled, and coupled with the sickening gleam in his eyes, his handsome features transformed into the revolting face of a monster. The masquerade was over and he'd shed the mask he'd been hiding from the public.

"Fred," Vivienne gasped, running toward him as fast as her gown would allow. "They published it. We're ruined."

"What are you doing here?" he snapped at his wife. "I told you to return to the table."

"And what? Face humiliation?"

"Then leave. I need a word with Sloanie girl."

"Sloanie?" Vivienne screeched. "You're not replacing me with trash!"

"The only trash is you," a voice spoke from the shadows.

"Dom?" I whispered.

"You didn't think I'd let you go off alone when this fucker is around?" His deadly gaze swept over Tomlin. "And you better not take another step toward her."

Vivienne sneered. "You seem to forget she used to clean my toilet."

"Is that the best you can come up with?" Dom drawled. "How about you worry about your reputation circling the sewer? It's everything a bitch like you deserves."

"How dare you?" she whispered.

"Go back to the table, Vivienne! So help me God," Fred roared.

When Vivienne skittered away, he turned on Dom. "What's

this? Extortion?" His eyes zipped back to me. "Is this why you're spreading your legs for this criminal?"

"Motherfucker!" Dom rushed Tomlin, but someone in a tux tackled him.

"Dammit, De Lucci," the newcomer croaked in pain. "You're going to set me back in physical therapy."

Phil Harding?

Men in tuxes and tactical gear surrounded us. Wait, this was a sting operation?

I'd only noticed how the hallways were darkened more than normal, and men appeared to barricade the entrance leading back to the ballroom.

Someone approached. I recognized him as the fed working with Phil. "Congressman Tomlin, you're under arrest for aggravated assault of minors. You have the right to remain silent…"

"You can't do this!" he roared. "This is entrapment."

"There was no entrapment here, but we have received evidence—"

He glared at Lucy. "I'll fight this charge. You can't use this in court."

They hauled him away from where the festivities were still going on. I caught sight of Kirill standing at the end of the hallway before he disappeared when the rest of law enforcement flooded the hall.

"Phil…" I whispered. "I didn't know where to find you. Phil Harding…"

"Doesn't exist." He grinned wryly. "But I'm still Phil."

He reached out to touch me, but Dom growled. "If you don't want to be put back in a cast—"

"Christ," Phil chuckled. "I guess I can't hug you."

"Yes, you can."

I squinted at Dom, ignoring the blast of disapproval coming from him, and stepped into Phil. "I'm so happy you're alive."

He said by my ear, "Me too, but I won't be if you don't let me go soon."

"Mr. Harding," Lucy interrupted. "Won't you escort me back to the ball?"

I glanced at Dom's sister, who was silently laughing while her brother stood forbiddingly with clenched fists, glaring at me and Phil.

He glared even harder when I rolled my eyes.

When Phil and I broke our hug, he turned to Lucy, offering his arm. "Gladly, Miss De Lucci. I can't thank you enough for giving us a break on the case."

They walked away. "It won't hold up in court but…"

"This was the plan all along?" I asked Dom. "I could have helped better. Maybe planned a whole speech against Tomlin."

"We couldn't risk an entrapment charge. The less you knew, the better." Dom prowled toward me. "And you were playing with fire, baby." My pussy spasmed at the promise of retribution behind his eyes.

"What? Hugging Phil?"

"I don't want any other man touching you." He dragged me into his arms. "Got me? I didn't even get to punch Tomlin."

"No sense risking an assault charge, especially with witnesses," I muttered.

Dom chuckled darkly. "See, you're so good for me."

"What? Reining in your crazy?"

"I'm about to show you crazy."

CHAPTER
Thirty-Five

DOM

"DOM, WHAT ARE YOU DOING?!"

"Showing you my crazy." I swung Sloane up into my arms and carried her into the stockroom. I was familiar with the layout of this venue. Of course I was. The crowd appeared to be made up of guests, but there was an army of security around.

I nodded to one of them now, as I swung her into the room where they kept extra tables and chairs.

I kicked the door closed, locked it, lowered Sloane, and caged her against it.

"What happened to taking it slow?" she breathed.

I raised a brow. "You had forty-eight hours."

Her husky laugh vanquished my self-control. The need to possess her consumed me. I'd been dying for another taste of her sweet, sweet pussy. The compulsion to pound into her without restraint had tortured me to the point of insanity. It'd been too fucking long. I captured her lips and groaned into her mouth. Christ. That mouth that I'd been obsessing over all evening. All day, weeks, months. Her voice. Her turbulent green eyes. Every inch of skin I wanted to devour. And with each plunge of my tongue, my craving for her intensified. She was an illicit drug I would never get over. My endless addiction.

My fingers snuck their way to the back of her gown and encountered the buttons I'd been debating how to tackle in the most expeditious way.

I tore my mouth away and said, "Forgive me," before I ripped the fabric apart.

"Dom!" she gasped against my mouth, but I possessed it again. I'd been patient, I told myself. Sloane could stop me if she wanted, and I would, but I kept the assault on her senses going. The gown fell away easily, and I lifted her out of it before I braced her against the door again, barely letting go of her lips.

I leaned back, watching her beautiful face through hooded eyes. I was so drunk on her, the dim lighting in this room gave her an ethereal glow. An angel I was about to ravish.

I kissed her neck, then I lowered the bustier, exposing a nipple. I latched on to it, sucking the tight bud into my mouth and swirling my tongue around it. Her moan almost made me come in my pants.

"Dom, oh God, I need you lower."

I dropped to my knees. Conflicting desires warred inside me. Of wanting to worship at her feet and torment her with my mouth until she'd scream my name so everyone would know she was mine.

Possessiveness shoved that aside.

Even her screams of pleasure were mine and mine alone.

Her fingers dug into my scalp pushing my face to her core. I stroked a finger down her molten pussy. "Are you aching over here, baby?"

I slipped my finger behind the crotch of the underwear. Hot

damn, she was soaking with need. I pressed my nose against her pussy. Her pussy that I hadn't sunk into in months. Months! Jesus Christ, the thought was making me feral. I hoped this wasn't a dream because I'd gladly die in it.

"Yes."

"Then let me ease that ache."

I bared her pussy to my eyes. Neatly trimmed red hair mixed with her slick arousal and I wanted to drown in it. I inhaled her, dragging my nose through her scent, spreading her juices, before the urging of her hands made me relent and saved us from more torture.

The second I tasted her, I lost it. I used my tongue, teeth, and mouth and ate her without thought, without second-guessing, driving into her purely on savage instinct. The familiar swelling of her clit invited me to suck and lap and swirl. She drove her hips forward. I didn't even realize that I had her leg over my shoulder as I continued to eat her.

When she collapsed, I propped her up and rose to my feet. I didn't know how I pinned her against the wall with my body while I unzipped my trousers and freed my erection. I was hard. Harder than I'd ever remembered. It was almost painful. Heavy. I needed to be inside this woman.

Sloane's hand wrapped around my cock reverently, and then she stared up at me. "May I?"

"I don't think I'm gonna last," I groaned.

"Please."

Fuck.

I gave her a curt, tension-filled nod.

Her lips wrapped around my cock. I hissed, lids slamming shut, feeling my eyes roll back at the intense sensation electrifying muscles and bones.

Panting, I risked opening my eyes because seeing Sloane on her knees, giving me a blowjob was the single hottest experience I'd witnessed in a long time. It was hard to pick a moment, but every moment led back to her. Like when I had her at my mercy on New Year's Eve, ramming her into the glass. Even that time I fucked her on her period and having her bleed all over me.

Fuck.

I hauled her up. "Enough," I snarled at her. "The first time—I wanna come inside you."

Her eyes widened, but before Sloane could protest, I spun her around and slammed her against the door. Lifting her up, I drove inside her, seating myself to the hilt and without giving her time to adjust, I pounded inside her.

"I know I should give you a choice, but I can't. You're mine, Sloane. Mine." Whatever last defense I had against her crumbled. I'd never fucked without a condom, but the surging obsession and possessiveness had nowhere to go except inside her.

"Are you mine too?" Tears brimmed her eyes and my heart cracked at the uncertainty in them. How could she still doubt that there was nothing else I wanted to be except hers?

"Yes. God, yes. I'm all yours. Body, mind, heart, and fucking soul," I rasped. "Don't you feel it, baby? Even when you hated me, I had to be near you."

"I never hated you."

"Good, because you're my *choice*." As soon as the word left my mouth, so did holding back. I'd been mentally reciting sports stats to keep the blood in my brain all evening. Spying Tomlin in the crowd immersed my mind with murderous thoughts, but once Sloane and I were alone, nothing else mattered except her.

I emptied inside her.

All the torment of the past few weeks, all the self-recriminations, I laid myself bare. Her nails dug into my shoulders, and she cried out at the same time I grunted my release. I buried my nose in the crook of her neck and shoulder while my feet and back struggled to keep me upright. I lowered her right leg so I could grind into her, give her every drop of my possession.

The words I wanted to tell her were on the tip of my tongue, but I didn't want her to think my love was a product of lust. I would tell her. Tonight. Including several confessions.

Our second chance was starting with truths.

I lifted my head to look into her eyes, searching where her mind was.

"I'm on the pill," she said.

"Unfortunately," I sighed.

Her brows shot up. "I thought you never fucked without a condom."

I cupped her cheek and gave her a wry smile. "We have things to discuss, but not here."

"Are we setting boundaries again?"

"No. We're obliterating them."

She huffed a short laugh. "What?"

I straightened her out and wrapped my tux jacket around her. "Sorry about the gown."

"Maybe the bet should have been if you were going to destroy my dress."

"Those buttons have been driving me crazy all evening," I muttered. I slipped out my phone and texted the driver to bring the limo to the back of the venue. Afterward, I shot off a message to Trevor to keep an eye on Lucy.

Kirill would forever be a wild card, and even if the chances of him hurting my sister were low this evening, complacency was never an option when dealing with the Russians.

The hallway was dark when we left. My soldiers were stationed around, communicating with each other.

"You're like the president and they're Secret Service," Sloane whispered. "How did you get Kirill to go along with that?"

I didn't answer Sloane until we were in the back of the limo. Unlike our drive to the gala where we kept to our sides of the vehicle, this time, I had her on my lap and was nuzzling her throat. Inhaling her. All I could think about was splaying her on the bed and fucking her into oblivion. I didn't want to talk about Kirill, but Sloane wasn't having it.

"Dom, stop it," she hissed. She wiggled her ass over my growing erection.

I chuckled. "That's not helping, baby."

"Tell me what's going on. Or I'll leave you blue-balled."

I sighed. "Way to kill the buzz. Kirill and I came to an agreement to get rid of Tomlin. With the existence of the recording, he'd become a liability Zahkarov Holdings wanted to have nothing to do with. Lucy wanted to do it big, and flash his arrest on the screen, but Kirill vetoed it. In fact, he was this close to strangling my sister in the one and only meeting the three of us had together with the feds."

"Phil?"

"Never say his name right after I've fucked you," I growled.

"Stop being a jealous asshole. Phil is just a friend."

"A friend? He framed you."

"It wasn't supposed to go down that way."

My arms tightened around her, and I said in her ear, "Let's get to the penthouse before we talk about this shit."

CHAPTER
Thirty-Six

Sloane

Dom and I hadn't exchanged another word in the charged atmosphere of the vehicle. We'd engaged in a silent battle, but no matter how our views conflicted, one thing was certain: he was done giving me space. I appreciated his patience. I wasn't that clueless to think that I'd turned Dom into my lapdog. That wasn't the man I was attracted to.

I wanted the boss. The confident man who ruled his crime family, but I refused to be relegated to the corner again.

Dom kept me plastered to his side, and it was only when we entered the penthouse that he loosened his arms and let me go.

The decisive click of the lock turned me wary, but it was the kind of wariness that was a combination of excitement and indignation.

I crossed my arms. "You didn't want to discuss the situation until you got me into the penthouse. Were you afraid that I was going to bolt?"

"Drink?" He ignored my question and walked to the minibar.

"No. Answer the question."

Infuriating man that Dom was, he went ahead and poured himself a scotch before turning around to face me. The only satisfaction I got was noticing the tremor in his hand as he raised the glass to his lips. He was as tense as I was, and I wasn't a foregone conclusion.

"You're mine. I'm yours. I'm moving back in," he told me.

"Are we sharing a bed?"

"I just came inside you, baby. Damn right you're sleeping in my bed. You're not a hypocrite, nor are you obtuse."

"I'm not. You figured out I can handle your overbearing ass."

He moved closer. "Yes. I believe in you. I'm not hiding you anymore—"

"You've proven that by taking me to the gala—"

"And I love you."

"I..." What did I say to that? "Are you sure?"

Irritation slashed through his face even when my whole body lit up with elation. I was afraid to believe that this beautiful man chose me. He could have anyone. A beautiful heiress, a virgin bride, someone younger who could give him heirs with impeccable bloodlines. Who wasn't stubborn as hell and could be a meek mafia wife. But he wanted me. The messed-up former cleaner for the mob.

Bianca's voice echoed in my head.

You deserve this.

I deserved this. What happened to flipping the script? Obviously, mentally, I still needed work, but I was more open and trusting. These past few weeks, constant self-reflection had been a morning routine and I no longer woke up desolate but hopeful. My scarred heart had healed from all the pain we inflicted on each other. I wasn't innocent in this. I never had been. But because we set rules in our affair, we never fully trusted each other.

I erased the distance between us and invaded Dom's space. His eyes flared with heat, making his tux jacket I was still wearing heavy. Shrugging it off, I stepped closer. "I need a little more patience."

"I can be as patient as you need. Spin on your thoughts all you want, I'll be patient," he said, tone guttural. "I don't have to fuck you, but please, Firecat, don't send me away. I can't bear it. I need to be in your orbit. Sleep beside you. Watch you sleep."

My fingers traced the shadows underneath his eyes. "That sounds stalkerish."

A corner of his mouth lifted. "I *have* been your stalker."

Then I remembered his evasiveness earlier. "You never fucked without a condom."

His arms wrapped around me, locking me in as if he was afraid I would run away. "And there will be nothing between us from now on. Be on birth control if you have to, but know there's nothing I want more in my life than having children with you."

"I have—"

"Listen to me," he persisted. "I understand hopes and dreams more than anyone else. I'm not gonna stand in your way, but also understand that I was heartbroken when we lost our baby. I—" He let me go and walked to the tall windows with a view to the Manhattan skyline. "Grigori is dead."

"Wh-what?"

He turned to face me. His face a blank mask. Inscrutable. Cold. "He died of radiation poisoning. He traded you to Margo for medical care."

"Oh my God." I clasped my throat.

Dom's eyes narrowed to where my hand was and he clenched his jaw. "I haven't found Anton yet, but that fucker, Boris, is dead. I tortured him in a basement and killed him after I found out he was responsible for your miscarriage."

He relayed the news in a flat voice devoid of emotion, far from the man who declared that he loved me.

Blood drained from my head and pooled somewhere in the vicinity of my toes, causing me to sway. Dom stalked toward me, guided me to a chair, and dropped to his knees in front of me. The pain of losing the baby had slowly faded. Maybe because I'd never confirmed the pregnancy until I lost it. I'd never angsted over it. Never hoped. The loss hit me all over again, but the feeling was muted. I was conflictingly horrified that I relished the death of the men who hurt me. With a palm over my lower belly, I whispered, "Would it make me a terrible person to be relieved that they're dead?"

"No. Then that would mean I'm evil. Do you believe I'm evil?"

I smiled faintly. "You're not the one who's going to be a nurse to save lives and not celebrate the ending of them."

"If you believed in the greater good, then it's a blessing to be rid of Grigori and Boris."

"Greater good hits differently when dealing with the mafia. It's more like the lesser evil."

Dom laughed briefly at this. "True." He clasped my hands to get my full attention, giving them an extra squeeze. "Then you'll understand why I need you to let me do what's best for your safety. You would not be in a relationship with a nine-to-five husband working in a corporation."

A burst of laughter passed my lips. "Husband?"

"Why mince words? That's where we're heading." His mouth settled into a wry smile. "As much as I hated how Margo manipulated the events leading up to the gala, I couldn't fault her clever machinations that led to this point."

The matchmaker had been in the back of my mind, especially

after how everything went down this evening. "Margo said she believed in me. I'm not denying that added to my self-confidence."

"*I* believe in you. Trust that…please. Because I'll never let you leave me. If I fuck up, I'll grovel all over again until you forgive me. But we're deviating, and I need to get this off my chest. You have to allow me to protect you. I will always have enemies. They will know what you mean to me and will attempt to use you against me—"

"I promise not to call 911 on the security you have on me," I said simply. I understood that much and what it meant when I let Dom back into my life. There were more adjustments to be made and I had no doubt living with constraints would chafe at my independence, but the pros outweighed the cons and I was a practical gal. Dom more than proved he wasn't putting me in a corner any longer. This gorgeous man who set me on fire had shown me he would put me first. He wanted me, loved me. Dom loved me! It finally sunk in and the earlier elation washed over me again.

He chuckled. "Thank you."

He rose to his feet, pulling me up with him. "Now, can I show you to our room?"

I barely said yes when he swept me off my feet. "Dom! I'm heavy. The gown must weigh…"

His grunt held a hint of indignation. "Firecat, you could wear armor that weighs a ton, and I'd still carry you up the stairs when the situation calls for it."

I hooked my arms around his neck and rested my head on the warmth of his chest. "And the situation calls for it?"

"I finally fucked my woman. She'll finally be sleeping in my bed…"

He let it hang. Dom's room was the first room in the same wing as Lucy's.

I'd never entered Dom's bedroom. Not even to snoop. But I

could always tell someone had come in to clean the penthouse when I wasn't here. They never bothered my room or Lucy's. I figured it was the same people who stocked up the fridge whenever Lucy and I were hanging at Jabbin' Java to escape cabin fever.

When he lowered me over the threshold, the dim lights behind the bed came on. An extremely masculine bedroom of black and dark wood. It was…cold. It was a cleaner's dream or nightmare. Dream because it was a simple job, nightmare because if all my clients were this way, I couldn't charge exorbitant fees.

"Wow." It was the anti-Lucy room, but I held my tongue.

"Is that wow approval or disgust?" Dom asked.

"You're very OCD."

"The Moretti side, I guess." He walked to the bathroom. Bathroom was an understatement. It was connected to a closet that in itself was a room. Dom wasn't busy showing off the vastness of the area, he was showing me a space in his closet for me.

"I made room for your stuff." For the first time this evening, an uncertainty, almost boyishness, flashed through his face. I inspected his closet and could see why he was the dapper gentleman of the mob. Expensive suits lined his closet. Handcrafted shoes were on display in a custom-made shoe rack across one wall.

"I don't have many clothes."

"Buy more."

"Careful. I might get used to this lavish lifestyle."

The gleam in his eyes liquefied my bones, and I was helpless like a rag doll when he dragged me against him. "Get used to it. I can't wait to pamper you. Part of my frustration was your rule that forbade giving gifts. In a way that frustration became resentment until, ultimately, it became pride when you broke off our affair."

"Is that why you readily believed that I betrayed you?"

"Yes." He dropped his forehead to mine. "Forgive me, baby."

"You've apologized countless times."

"And I'll repeat it until that scene is a distant memory." He exhaled a ragged breath full of regret. "You may have forgiven me, but I don't think I can ever forgive myself."

I cupped his scruff-bristled cheek. The stubbles hid his tense jawline, but I could feel the anguish still eating him alive. "That won't do if we're going to have a future. Mistakes were made because of my stubbornness and your pride. We can only move forward."

He nodded briefly and kissed the tender flesh of my palm with reverence. "Let me get this gown off you."

I laughed briefly. It was being held up by a few buttons in the back. The gown pooled at my feet. Dom's cum had dried along the inside of my thighs.

"I'm a mess," I lamented.

He crouched in front of me. "I like my mess on you."

The gratification in his tone made me roll my eyes. He rose to his feet with a cocky slant to his mouth. "Let's take care of the hair."

Unlike his impatience with the buttons of my gown, Dom was careful as he searched for the pins in my updo, carefully extracting them so they wouldn't yank at my scalp. We were in front of the mirror, and I watched his brows furrow in concentration at something as menial as freeing me from a hairstyle. After a few minutes, he massaged my scalp, his fingers searching for any stragglers, but I moaned at the pleasure it was giving me.

"You like that, hmm?" he murmured against my ear.

"Oh, yes."

"Then you're in for a treat."

Dom and I had shared showers countless of times, but there was something different with this one. Besides the fancy showerhead and gallons of water jetting all over us, we were more open, more affectionate. He'd shampooed my hair before, but this time his touch was possessive, more proprietary, like he'd staked a claim. Patience with leashed passion. A gentleness shaped by the love he declared earlier.

My needs before his.

He shampooed my hair twice, washing away the gumminess left by hair products. When he was satisfied, he worked in the conditioner and let my hair soak it up while he grabbed the soap, and, like the meticulous way he took out the pins, he lathered my skin. After thoroughly washing all traces of the night, only then did he back me into the corner, the wordless intent on his face clear.

He sank to his knees, draped my right leg over his shoulder, and reverently planted kisses all the way up to the juncture of my thighs.

My body shuddered.

"Cold?" He glanced up at me.

I wasn't. My back was against the tiles, but we'd worked up enough steam, figuratively and literally, to keep the enclosure warm, or maybe the tiles were specially designed to absorb heat.

I shook my head.

He grinned up at me devilishly before he attacked my pussy. He was gentle, then rough. I came instantly.

Dom rose to his feet and slid inside me. With our eyes locked and in slow, grinding drives, he brought me to the pinnacle once more. I screwed my lids shut and stars exploded behind them. The familiar toe-curling sensation reduced my limbs to mush. Dom held me up as he sped up his thrusts, pumping erratically until he gave a grunt and released inside me.

Later, he washed me again between my legs, toweled me dry, and dried my hair with a blow-dryer.

I'd never been more relaxed.

He carried me to the bed and set me on top of it. It was unfamiliar, but I was too sated to care.

Dom's body wrapped around me, and I sunk into slumber.

CHAPTER
Thirty-Seven

Dom

"You do what you need to do, son. Leave your mother to me." Pop was on the phone while I whipped up breakfast for Sloane and myself. He'd texted around ten asking me if I'd seen the headline of Tomlin's arrest.

There was no mention of the De Luccis or the Zahkarovs in any article, which was how both crime families wanted it to go down. Tomlin was a part of a bigger sex-trafficking scandal. Kirill wanted them to clear Kolya of the Mistress Strangler case, but he'd pissed off the prosecutor who refused to let it go without evidence to support his innocence.

I thought Margo had the evidence, but she'd changed her mind about handing it to Kirill, or maybe she'd been bluffing all along. I wouldn't be surprised if Kirill murdered the matchmaker himself.

The bratva was in a tenuous position. Ivan had turned a blind eye to Grigori and the sex parties and it was in their best interest to give the feds what they wanted since the now-dead Grigori was their scapegoat. His bloated body washed up on Brighton Beach.

I wasn't lowering my guard around the Russians because my sister partly instigated this whole mess.

"Sure you can handle Lucy and Ma in the same house?"

Pop sighed. "You've sacrificed so much for our family, it's time you find your own happiness. Your mother knows where I stand. We argued when she started griping at me about you and Sloane leaving the gala yesterday before the dancing."

I checked the croissant bread pudding and the sheet pan bacon in the oven. "Really? What did you tell her?"

"That you've been a good son to us. You went above and beyond your duties because you love our family. You deserve to be happy and I'm shutting down any criticism she has about Sloane. She can give me the silent treatment if she wants. I won't interfere if you go off on her if she insults Sloane or makes her feel uncomfortable."

I laughed. "What did she say to that?"

"It made her think. I'm not sure I've gotten through to her yet. You know your mother."

"I don't want her coming around without invitation." I'd already changed the code to the elevator and her keycard wouldn't work.

Pop sighed again. "You know I don't control her movements, but I'll try my best to keep an eye on her this weekend."

"Ask Lucy to help you."

"Heaven help us."

"Love you, Pop."

"Love you, Dominic."

I ended the call and took the bacon out of the oven. The pudding needed another ten minutes.

I felt her before she spoke.

"It smells good in here."

A grin played on my lips. "Making sure I have breakfast for you."

I turned around and was struck at how I wanted to keep this image of Sloane forever. She had her hair piled in a mess on her head, but what I loved the most was she was wearing one of my white dress shirts. That was all she was wearing. It looked good on her. She was barefoot, and she was holding a purring Ginger in her arms.

Me too, Ginger. I felt like purring in immense satisfaction that something I owned was touching her skin.

"She was waiting outside our bedroom door," I told Sloane. "Did she bother you? I figured if I blocked her from entering the room, she'd cause mayhem."

"She snuggled in bed with me. She doesn't usually do that and wants breakfast." Sloane approached. "She was surprisingly absent last night."

I smirked. "That cat knows when she's not wanted."

"Mean." Her short, husky laugh did something strange inside my chest. I wasn't a man prone to romantic notions. Romance wasn't in my wheelhouse. I understood nurturing to show love. I hadn't had a girlfriend in over a decade. Did a man at my age even call his woman a girlfriend? That seemed so juvenile and a title that should be left behind for a guy in his twenties. Could I skip all those titles and go straight to *fiancée* or *wife*?

I like the sound of wife better.

"What are you grinning at?" Sloane asked.

Without answering her, I dragged her close. Ginger hissed her displeasure and jumped out of the way before she got crushed between us. I swallowed Sloane's surprised gasp with a devouring morning kiss. When I released her, she was breathing hard.

"Debating what to do with you," I murmured. "Debating what to call you. Girlfriend sounds so immature."

"And what have you decided?"

"*Wife* sounds better."

"Dominic De Lucci, are you skipping a proposal and a wedding?"

"No. We can get the ring now and have the license ready." I was dead serious. All these weeks of trying to get Sloane to forgive me and take me back, I wasn't wasting time and was locking this woman down.

She pushed my chest. "You don't know how to romance a girl, do you?"

"I can romance you all you want. Just as my wife."

"I haven't even told you I love you."

"Consider this our arranged marriage. You will fall in love with me, eventually." I shot her a roguish grin. Color climbed her cheeks.

She laughed and pushed at my chest. "What has gotten into you?"

"Understand you're not a foregone conclusion. Now that the public knows who I'm crazy about, I'm afraid someone else is gonna try to steal you from me. Although I know you like villains and I'm New York's most eligible villain after all, so I have the advantage."

Her body shook with laughter. "You're so cocky." Then she narrowed her eyes. "But we're not rushing into this, remember? So no calling me your wife." She shoved me away. "Now go get me coffee."

"Meow." That one meow from Ginger was demanding.

Sloane muttered, "Let me feed this cat so she'll forgive us for ignoring her."

I poured coffee into a fresh mug and refilled mine. "She knows who keeps her in style with her expensive tuna. She's not complaining much." I set Sloane's coffee on the counter, nearly spilling my own as I took a sip. She was bent over, giving me an eyeful of the shadow between her thighs.

My cock stirred behind my sweatpants, rapidly increasing in girth and length as Sloane continued to flash me her delicious pussy. My mouth watered, but I wasn't ravenous for pudding and bacon. Slamming my mug on the kitchen island, I stalked toward Sloane who suddenly straightened. Her eyes widened when she saw me heading for her.

"Dom, what…?"

"Breakfast. Now. You."

I swept the plates off the kitchen counter, lifting her onto it, not caring about the distant crash and an indignant feline howl. I was too focused on Sloane.

I dragged her to the edge and spotted the gleam of triumph in her eyes. "You did that on purpose."

"Sometimes, food is not the first thing I want in the morning," she breathed expectantly.

"You got it," I growled, burying my head between her thighs, and feasted.

~

Sloane

One could say I was like the cat who swallowed the cream.

After Dom tongue-fucked and fucked me on the kitchen counter, we were both reclining on the couch while the remnants of breakfast—cold bacon and burnt croissant pudding—sat on the coffee table. Despite the vigorous activity in the kitchen, I wasn't that hungry for food.

"You know I love waking you up with my mouth," Dom murmured in my ear. "But I thought I'd give you a bit of reprieve seeing how I wore you out last night."

"And I appreciate it, except the picture of you being all nurturing and cooking me breakfast got me all hot." I was looking at Ginger who was cleaning her paws by the window, soaking up the late morning sun.

"Hot, huh?"

"What will I do with you, Dominic De Lucci?" I splayed my fingers across his hard chest. The organ underneath it beat against my palm.

"You can do whatever you want with me."

"You said being in a relationship is fraught with expectations," I said. "Is there something you expect from me?"

"So far you're meeting expectations." He chuckled.

"Be serious, Dom. This is not a job review."

"Exactly. That's why corporate America was never for me," he said. "I was wrong, baby, when I said that. I think trust is more important. I know I fucked up and trampled on your heart. I know why you're hesitant to say you love me. You almost confessed, right? That night you broke up with me?"

"I was falling for you."

He stilled. "Was."

"It was a bond that was poorly formed," I explained. "We started trying not to feel more, and I started resenting my place in your life because I was growing more attached. I had to end it. We were trying so hard to keep our affair impersonal, we forgot how to be friends. Friends who trusted each other. The situation could have ended differently, but I'm learning from those mistakes."

I could feel Dom nod his head. "We're learning."

"These past few weeks, I've felt better about myself and I've learned to be with you without the pressure of a relationship."

Amusement twitched my lips. "Okay, maaayyybe there's pressure, but it was in a way that enabled us to be friends first without muddling it with a physical relationship."

Dom snorted. "Is that how you see it?"

I burst out laughing this time. "That time I woke up rubbing against you and you were hard—"

"About killed me, baby. The sexual tension between us is incendiary."

"You did explode in me last night."

He nuzzled my neck. "I want to explode in you again."

We exchanged light kisses. My pussy was sore from that bout in the kitchen. Dom hadn't shaved, and he'd given me stubble burns. Still, having this man lose control over me exhilarated me and imbued me with power.

It was noon. No word from the girls. The last texts in our group chat indicated it was time for the women to shower attention on their husbands since they'd been all over me in the past few weeks.

I didn't mind being their glow-up project, but we all could use some time off. "What are we going to do today?"

"Would you mind very much if I kept you in the penthouse all weekend?"

"No, but just so you know, my pussy is sore."

He raised a brow. "Are you complaining?"

I laughed. It was the most levity I'd experienced in a long time. Something had been anchoring my happiness to the ground, preventing me from floating away with giddiness. I was happy with myself, but being with him finally freed my heart to experience the joy of being in love.

Love.

I loved Dom.

I informed him I wasn't sure yet, but his confidence showed that he knew. He was waiting for me to catch up and admit it to myself.

"Were you talking to your dad this morning?"

He stiffened. "Yes."

"And? We left the gala early last night. A gala your mother helped organized."

"Are you asking if she has a problem with us being a couple?" He stood and grabbed the plates off the coffee table and strode to the kitchen.

I followed him. The broken dishes were on the floor, so I went to the pantry to get the dustpan.

"Leave that mess," he snapped.

I glared at him. "You're telling a cleaner to leave the mess?"

"You're not a cleaner anymore."

"No, I'm not. Doesn't mean I won't do any cleaning," I retorted. "So, talk and don't leave anything out."

He repeated what his father said. I was surprised because the few times Bianca and Sera talked about Dom's parents, it was that Carlotta always got her way.

Dom crouched beside me and gathered the bigger pieces. "You're barefoot. Don't step on it."

"I'm fine." Uncertainty wrapped itself around my heart again. Not about Dom and me, but I wondered what battle lay ahead with his mother.

He sighed. "Sloane, look at me."

I halted sweeping the shards into the dustpan. "What?"

"I'm not gonna let Ma steamroll you. She never could with me. I gave in only as much as I allowed myself. And my boundaries with you are clear."

I shot him a reassuring smile. Dom was the one stuck between a rock and a hard place. He'd made it clear he was one hundred percent in this relationship and we wouldn't know exactly what was ahead until we lived it. I trusted him implicitly. I trusted he wouldn't betray his words of commitment to me. Because if he did,

I didn't think I could recover enough to trust another man for a long time, but I knew I was going to be okay. I wasn't going to fall into a deep depression over a man because I had my job to live for, and friends who would support me no matter what path I chose.

And with clarity and confidence, I was ready for this adventure.

CHAPTER
Thirty-Eight

SLOANE

DOM'S MOTHER AMBUSHED ME A WEEK AFTER THE GALA.

Carlotta De Lucci was done being ignored.

I was on my way to have lunch with Nurse Addy. She'd given Luca a glowing rec and deserved more than lunch, but it was a start. She was also excited to hear about my Delphine project and said I could use her as a resource.

Since I was running late, I had the driver bring the car to the entrance of the building. That was when I ran into Carlotta in the lobby.

"Mrs. De Lucci." My bodyguard, a De Lucci soldier, intercepted Dom's mother. When Dom moved back in, Lucy's security went with her, so Dom was interviewing for my permanent security detail. It chafed, but I was learning to live with it.

"Surely I'm not a threat, Hector." Carlotta smiled at him.

"The boss said—"

"Said what? You're forgetting I'm his *mother*." She said it in a way that reiterated her position in the crime family. Redness climbed Hector's neck and his jaw clenched. Matriarchal respect was huge in Italian families but I wasn't about to hide from Dom's mother or put my bodyguard in an awkward position.

"It's okay, Hector." I inserted myself between them.

"But boss—"

"Like Mrs. De Lucci said…" I held Carlotta's eyes. "She's not a threat." First lesson for Dom's mother to learn, I was not changing my schedule to fit in her pettiness. I nodded to the doorman who held open the elegant dark wood door. "But you will have to walk with me. I'm late for an appointment."

"An appointment?" Dom's mother said behind me. I could feel her eyes give me a once-over. I'd slowly rebuilt my wardrobe both with my money and Dom's. With my upcoming responsibilities, I had no problem dressing the part. Sera and Ivy helped me pick out suits and cocktail dresses I could wear to events where we met with donors. For my lunch with Nurse Addy, I simply wore a tailored pantsuit.

"Dom's not home."

"Oh, I know."

I glanced at the driver standing by the sidewalk. I wondered if he was the one who tipped off Carlotta. No wonder Dom wanted my security detail to be separate from the crime family. "Listen, Mrs. De Lucci, I don't know why you're here. I don't think Dom is comfortable with us meeting behind his back."

"He changed the code to his floor."

"He doesn't want you barging into his penthouse anymore." I checked the time on my phone. "And I know you used to take care of things inside the penthouse for him, but he has me now."

Her mouth thinned, and I knew that was the last thing you told a mother who was used to being the central female in her son's life. But Carlotta needed to understand that the situation had changed.

"I'm not keeping your son from you. I'm just leaving it to Dom when he thinks it's right for us to share dinner or get to know each other—"

She waved her hand. "I'll cut to the chase. I know I can't offer you money because Dom's already given you free rein to his bank account."

In her eyes, I was still a gold digger, which was fair, and surprisingly, I didn't care. Only a few people's opinions mattered to me and so far Carlotta hadn't earned it.

"You're a hardworking woman and I like that," she continued. "Success? I like that too. But my son is both a Moretti and a De Lucci. You don't understand the opportunities open to my son to make a good match."

"According to your son, I'm his perfect match."

"Miss Scott," Hector cut in. "We're *too* exposed here and *you're* running late."

Carlotta glared at my bodyguard again in a way that promised payback.

"Lottie! Goddammit!"

Paulie was hurrying across the street. Lucy was leaning against an SUV with her arms crossed. She was shaking her head, but I couldn't tell if she was amused or annoyed.

"She has our son twisted around her finger!" she griped.

"You are such a hypocrite, *cara*." He reached her side and clasped her elbow. "You can't deny you haven't done the same to me."

I smothered a grin.

Paulie awarded me with an apologetic look. "I apologize for my darling wife. I failed my duty to keep an eye on her."

"I don't need a babysitter," she expressed indignantly. But I noticed the way she melted into her husband's arms. Maybe they had a toxic relationship, but they seemed to thrive on it. Who was I to judge?

"No harm done. I'll tell Dom we need to do dinner soon."

Lottie huffed. "It's about time. How does he expect me to like you if he doesn't want me to get to know you?"

I rolled my lips to keep other words from slipping out. Paulie's amused eyes met mine, knowing exactly why Dom was keeping his mom away from me. He didn't want her scaring me off. At this point, it would take more than Carlotta De Lucci to scare me off.

"Soon. Now, I'm really late."

I waved at Lucy, who waved back. My hand froze in the air when I noticed the hulking familiar build of a man emerging from a parked SUV at the corner. He had on a cap and sunglasses but there was no mistaking who he was.

It could be my imagination, but he smiled at me before he pointed a gun at Lucy.

"Gun!" I screamed.

"Lucy!"

Someone tackled me to the ground, but two distinct shots rang out.

Screeching of tires.

Screams.

Shouts.

Stampede of feet.

Then more rapid-fire gunshots.

Time slowed.

A loud crash. Metal on metal.

More screaming.

"Are you all right?"

Dom dragged me up from under Hector and gripped my shoulders. When did he get here?

Dazed, I still had the presence of mind to answer, "I'm fine. Lucy?"

"She's fine. Pop has her."

Then he pressed something in his ear. "Okay. Got it." He planted a quick kiss on my lips. "That's Trevor. Anton's fleeing on foot."

Then he left. "Be careful!" I shouted after him.

Men swarmed around us, securing the perimeter. I ran over to where Paulie was checking on Lucy. Both were sitting on the sidewalk. His suit was disheveled and there were smudges of dirt on what was once his pristine white dress shirt. Carlotta was on her knees, sobbing in front of them.

"I'm fine," Lucy mumbled.

"Can you check her out?" Carlotta asked me.

"We can take her to the hospital," I said.

"I'm fine. I didn't even lose consciousness. I just skinned my palms when Dad pushed me away. You should be the one to be checked out, Dad." Lucy glanced at me. "He got hit by an SUV."

"Sideswiped," Paulie corrected.

"That was more than a sideswipe," Lucy argued.

Carlotta stood in front of him and glowered. "You're really okay? You told me you're okay."

He hesitated in answering. He was looking pale. His lips were losing color. Dammit. Maybe he was bleeding internally.

"Call 911. And have them send an ambulance ," I told Hector. I switched into nurse mode.

"Dad!"

"Paulie!"

I turned in time to see him collapse sideways onto the pavement. Oh no!

I shoved Carlotta aside and sank to my knees in front of Paulie. He was breathing rapidly. His neck veins were bulging.

Not good. I laid him flat on the sidewalk and ripped his dress shirt open.

"Knife!" I shouted. Three blades were shoved under my nose. I grabbed one of them and split his undershirt in two.

The beginnings of bruising were taking form on his chest.

I sprung to my feet and asked Hector, "ETA on the ambulance?"

"Six minutes."

That might be too late, but I had to be sure. Good thing I always kept a medical kit with me in the trunk of the Audi. I grabbed it, and rushed back to Paulie, and measured his vitals. Blood pressure was low. I could barely make a pulse.

I tried to remain calm. I heard the sirens of an ambulance, but they were distant. And God knew if they were coming for Paulie.

Carlotta was crying and mumbling prayers, gripping Paulie's hand. Lucy was the one who asked, "What's wrong? Is he bleeding internally?"

"There's a sac around the heart that's filling up with blood and preventing it from beating properly." Cardiac tamponade usually happened with piercing chest wounds from a bullet or knife. I'd seen enough of them while doing backroom surgeries for the mafia. I remembered a study I'd read that it was flagged rare with blunt force trauma because it wasn't diagnosed and treated at the scene, leading it to damage the heart before the patient reached the hospital, eliminating it as the source of injury.

Getting struck by a large SUV would do it.

"I need your permission to relieve the pressure." That was why I always kept plastic tubes in my med kit. The fucking mob prepared me for this. If I could save one life before I kissed my NCLEX goodbye for performing this illegal procedure without a license, I wanted it to be Dom's dad. I couldn't even stop to think if I would get thrown into jail.

"Do it," Lucy cried.

I looked at Carlotta's face. I understood her hesitation. Her fear. The life of the love of her life was in my hands.

So I added, "I've seen this many times. If we delay, it could cause irrevocable damage to his heart." Which could be fatal.

She nodded. "Okay, yes."

A calm blanketed me. If Paulie died, Carlotta would hate me forever. I didn't know what would happen between me and Dom. But I knew if his dad died and I did nothing when I was almost a hundred percent certain of his diagnosis, I would never forgive myself.

Do no harm.

That was a double-edged sword at this moment.

So I chose not to live in the guilt of inaction.

I chose to give Paulie a higher chance of survival.

CHAPTER
Thirty-Nine

Dom

I spotted Anton slipping between an alley.

"I see him." I told them the street corners, but we each had our location dots on, anyway. Anton's problem was he was a big guy who depended on brawn to intimidate but couldn't run long distances for shit.

He was at the end of the alley in front of a fifteen-foot-high chain-link fence, bent over his knees.

He glanced at me, then straight ahead. "About time you fucking caught me." Those were the words I made out, given they were muffled by his labored breathing.

"You need to lose weight," I called. I slowed my strides, giving him the chance to recover, but held a gun loosely by my side. His hands were free of weapons, but I saw the bulge of a gun at his back beneath his dark shirt.

"Fuck you, De Lucci."

"I could just shoot you." I came closer.

"Why don't you?" he jeered, straightening up and facing me.

"What's the fun in that?"

He raised a brow. "You want to fight me? No weapons?"

"Like it's hard?"

He gave a choked laugh. "You're as arrogant and crazy as they say you are."

"That's Kirill, not me."

At the mention of his pakhan, his face darkened. "He's another son of a bitch. Traitor," he spat.

"From what I hear, you're the traitor."

He sneered. "Are you gonna yap or take a swing at me?"

"Throw your gun away first." I pointed mine at him.

He scoffed and threw his nine millimeter away.

The second I tossed mine, the fucker charged.

His linebacker shoulder drove into my gut and emptied my lungs. He tackled me to the ground.

I blocked the blow to my head and tipped him over, using my legs. Fuck. That motherfucker was the weight of a tanker.

We surged at each other in a flurry of fists and fury. Finally, I gained enough leverage to throw him over my hip. Not giving him an opportunity to stand, I jumped on him and straddled his body. I grabbed his head and cracked it on the ground. Then my fingers wrapped around his neck and squeezed.

"How does it feel to crave oxygen, huh, motherfucker?"

His face turned purple, and he struggled to dislodge my hands from around his neck, but rage fueled the desire to choke him. I wanted to see the light fade from his eyes the way Boris's did. Flashes of the marks on Sloane's neck fanned my fury. The sight of Anton leaving the building with her while she was miscarrying.

"I almost lost Sloane because of you." I tightened my fingers. His eyes and the veins on his temples bulged. I was blind to everything else except the thirst for vengeance. Avenge Sloane. Avenge the life we made that never had the chance to live.

I was spiraling in bloodlust when I felt a hand on my shoulder.

"Dom," Trevor said.

"What?!" No one was going to stop me from strangling the life out of this piece of shit.

"Your dad is in the hospital."

"What?" My fingers slackened.

Anton wheezed as my gaze shifted to Trevor. Panic seized my chest. "Why? How? He was fine when I left them."

"He got hit by Anton's SUV and there were internal injuries. You gotta go. We'll take care of him."

But Anton coughed with mocking laughter. "I hope"—cough—"your father dies."

My head whipped back in his direction. Ice replaced the white-hot rage. I grabbed Anton's head and snapped it to the right. The crunch of shattering cartilage was loud and satisfying.

"You'll hurt no one of mine again." I rose to my feet. Trevor handed me the earpiece, which must have fallen off when I was fighting Anton. "Clean this up."

Trevor gave a tight nod.

Anton's body had to disappear.

I REACHED THE EMERGENCY ROOM IN TEN MINUTES. I SPOTTED MA and Aunt Ava in one corner. Lucy and Sera in another. It didn't take a genius to know my sister blamed our mother because this wouldn't have happened if she had not evaded Pop and confronted Sloane.

But I didn't blame Ma. I blamed Anton. He was the one who struck Pop with the SUV.

Matteo and Hector met me at the sliding doors.

"Update?" I asked. On my way here, Matteo was my contact. They were the first to meet the ambulance when it arrived.

"He's still in surgery," Matteo said.

"His heart?"

My cousin gave a helpless shrug. "They didn't mention any damage."

"Where's Sloane?"

Before Matteo could answer, Ma saw me and rushed to me. My arms came around her.

"It's my fault, it's my fault," she cried.

"Shh…Ma. Pop wouldn't want you to blame yourself." My eyes went over her head and spotted Lucy who was glaring at her with tear-filled eyes. My headache, which had been a distant throb, intensified.

"What happened to your face?" she whispered, clasping my jaw.

"It's nothing."

Her mouth tightened. "That's what your pop said and look what happened!"

"Ma." I clasped her shoulders. "I have to find Sloane."

Her eyes brimmed with tears. "She saved him."

"What?" I croaked.

She leaned closer as if to tell me a secret. "She performed a procedure that nurses shouldn't do, but your pop immediately improved by the time the ambulance arrived. The chief of emergency services is with her now, along with the paramedic." She swiped at her eyes. "Help her, Dom. Make sure they don't hang her for anything."

"You bet I will." I strode to the triage nurse. "I want to speak to the chief."

"Sir—"

"Dom!"

I spun around to see Sloane walking in with an older Black guy in dark blue scrubs and a younger man who appeared to be the paramedic.

"What happened to you?" she asked.

"Forget me. Are you okay?" I glared at the two men with her.

Sloane dragged me to an open room, and her companions followed.

The Black man introduced himself as the chief of emergency services. "What Miss Scott did was illegal."

"But might be covered by the Good Samaritan law," Sloane retorted.

"That will be tough to defend and you know it. You're not even licensed. I don't know what they teach you in nursing school, but certainly not a field-executed pericardiocentesis without an ultrasound assist. Listen, I don't even wanna know how you learned to do that and I also know it's going to be messy going against the De Lucci family." He narrowed his eyes at me. "Your family is a donor to this hospital and your mother promises a hefty donation if we make this all go away."

"Make it all go away? Sloane saved my father."

"Illegally," the paramedic said. When I scowled at him, he hastily added, "But she's the shit and it would be a shame to put this on her record and be a hindrance to her earning her license."

"So, what are you suggesting?"

The chief looked at Sloane. "You wanna tell him?"

Sloane laughed briefly. "We're going with the story that the procedure was done in the ambulance after a quick assessment. Luckily, the ambulance is equipped with a portable ultrasound machine. And barring any complications with your dad's surgery, the hospital would rather not invest time and money in an investigation the patient doesn't want."

"And you're okay with it?"

"Of course," she said with fervor. "All I wanted was to give your dad the best chance of survival."

As if sensing we needed a moment alone, the chief and the paramedic excused themselves and left us.

"I love you, woman," I growled against her lips. "And don't tell me you don't love me too because if risking your whole future to save my father isn't you feeling an ounce of the love I feel for you, you're lying."

Her mouth curved in a smile. "Are you forcing me to admit I love you?"

"Damn right I am."

"I love you, Dominic De Lucci."

"About fucking time," I snapped.

I was about to kiss her when she yanked my hair back. "Now tell me why you have bruises on your face."

So, I whispered in her ear how I just killed another man to avenge her.

She said, "Good. He deserved it."

And I said, "You're going to make a kickass mob wife."

She raised a brow. "Correction. Queen."

Fuck yeah.

SLOANE

"PAOLO DE LUCCI?"

Dom, Carlotta, and Lucy all rushed toward the surgeon who'd been in charge of Paulie's surgery.

De Lucci soldiers and Arrows were scattered around the hospital and guarding the perimeter. Cesar arrived a few hours ago. I was standing with Bianca, Sera, and Ivy and hovered while the surgeon delivered the news.

"He's going to be fine. The heart sustained bruising, but no bleeding is detected. We installed a window in case of recurrent pericardium effusion. We'd like to keep him for a few days for observation."

"When can we see him?" Carlotta asked.

"He's in recovery. The nurse will let you know when he's been transferred to a private suite."

"That's good news." Ivy breathed a sigh of relief that everyone was feeling. She gave my arm a squeeze and headed toward Nico, who was huddled with his dad. Matteo was with them.

My focus was on Dom. He had one arm around his mother and another around Lucy.

"You think Carlotta and Lucy will be okay?" I asked Sera.

"Lucy is going to have Zio Paulie's best interest at heart—no pun intended—so she won't want to upset her dad while he's recovering," Sera said. "We'll have peace indefinitely."

Carlotta pushed away from Dom and met my eyes with her teary ones.

"Shit," I muttered.

She said something to Dom and headed my way.

"Sera, will you give Sloane and me a minute?"

"Sure, *Zia*." She gave Carlotta a brief arm squeeze and a kiss on the cheek.

I escorted Dom's mom to a less crowded hallway where we could speak in private.

"I'm glad Paulie is okay," I ventured.

She sniffled. "I can't thank you enough."

"No need to thank me."

Carlotta held my eyes. "But you risked everything."

"And I would do it again, knowing that I'd increased Paulie's chances for survival."

Her face crumpled. "I am consumed with shame," she sobbed. "Forgive me. I almost lost Paulie because of my prejudice. It's like a wake-up call after over fifty-six years of never really getting it. At this point, I don't care about anything. The money, the prestige. I could lose them all, but not my husband. As long as I have Paulie and my children." She swiped the tears from her eyes. "Paulie calls me a hypocrite. I thought it was said with fondness. Now I think it's a rebuke or an insult."

"Paulie would never insult you. He adores you."

"I don't deserve him," she hiccupped. "I've caused him so much pain."

"Listen. Don't tell me this. Tell it to Paulie." I paused. "When he gets better, of course."

Despite her misery, Carlotta detected my wary tone. "He'll really be okay, right?"

I wasn't acquainted with the intricacies of cardiac contusions and I'd reached my daily quota for dispensing medical advice or care.

"I'll defer to the surgeon and your cardiologist for advice." He'd have to be monitored for a while with an EKG to make sure the heart rhythm was normal and be on meds. Barring any complications, it would take a couple of weeks to months before Paulie would be back to normal. I was optimistic.

"You guys okay here?" Dom asked.

"We're fine," Carlotta said. "I was just apologizing to Sloane about my horrid treatment of her."

"Good. Otherwise, you'll have more than Lucy to contend with," Dom said, his meaning clear. "Sera is going to make sure you two behave in front of Pop. I've already warned Lucy. United front. Pop needs this, okay?"

"You don't have to tell me that," Carlotta snapped.

Dom dragged me to his side. "Come on, let's get back to the family."

Hours later, we were in the hospital suite where the living room had a door to the patient's room. Carlotta and Lucy were with Paulie while I was studying his chart. Dom strode in. Grim satisfaction was written all over his face and I wondered who else was dead. I was a bit worried that the police would pin Anton's death on Dom but he assured me that Trevor had taken care of it. Whatever *it* encompassed.

"What?" I hugged the clipboard to my chest.

"The SUV that Anton drove is registered to Vivienne Tomlin. The police are paying her a visit now."

When Dom's expression didn't change, it dawned on me. "You knew?"

"We've been watching her ever since Margo gave up the Tomlins. I doubt the congressman will make it alive to the trial. Despite the Zahkarovs' cooperation in his arrest, Kirill isn't the type to like loose ends. Neither do I and that's why I kept tabs on Mrs. Tomlin and never relented in my search for Anton. Based on the financial records Trevor had unearthed, Vivienne had been using Anton to get rid of the congressman's mistresses. When one of her vehicles was within two miles of the penthouse, it alerted me."

"Is that how you arrived so fast?"

"Yeah."

"You have me that locked down, huh?"

"Not enough," Dom muttered. "Trevor's scheduled final interviews for your security."

I sighed. "I know."

He brushed my cheek with the back of his fingers. "Thank you."

"You've thanked me enough—"

"Not about Pop," he said gruffly. "I'm thanking you for not giving me a hard time about keeping you safe."

"I'm not promising it won't grate on me once I work at a hospital, but we'll figure it out."

He laughed briefly. "I wouldn't expect anything less, Firecat."

Epilogue

Three Months Later

Sloane

This was a bad idea. What was I thinking? I stared back at the lights of the log cabin. When Dom said he needed to take me to a remote area to fulfill my fantasies and I could scream to my heart's content, I imagined a cabin in the woods. Not this palatial three-story log cabin in the middle of a peach orchard in Bumfuck Georgia.

I was panting hard, and it felt like I'd been running for a while. I didn't have a phone. I was wearing a light jacket, T-shirt, sweatpants, and running shoes.

What if I got lost? I eyed the edge of the forest that loomed in front of the orchard.

Granted, I'd been implanted with a new tracker. Still, I

depended solely on Dom to find me. Besides his phone, he was probably using night-vision goggles to track me. That stalker. He enjoyed this game as much as I did, if not a little more. The brisk December air inflated my lungs as I slowed my strides. It was why Dom picked the South for our little game where the average temperature was in the fifties at this time of the year. We were lucky because a cold front was rolling in later this week.

We celebrated Thanksgiving with the De Luccis and Rossis a week ago. A huge blended affair and it was a blast. Harriet was also invited. After this trip, the Christmas season would be in full swing. My mind was spinning at the number of invitations to parties and galas coming through Dom's mailbox. Unlike last year, when we hid our clandestine affair, this time there would be no hiding, and I was going to be the woman by Dom's side.

The past three months was a whirlwind of activities. After taking the NCLEX, I immersed myself in Dom's world, but he'd also involved himself in mine, accompanying me in my visits to Harriet, and lending his support in facilitating background checks to the planned staff expansion at the Delphine Assisted Living Home.

I inhaled deeply and took a tentative step into the forest. Evergreens and pines stood as sentinels in between skeletons of trees. Dried leaves and fallen branches crunched beneath my feet.

Moving deeper into the forest, I felt better about not being lost. The lights of the cabin shined like a beacon through the soon-to-be-winter foliage. I should have known Dom wouldn't risk anything that would endanger me.

A rustling of leaves had me spinning around and my heart clogged my throat in renewed fear. Not that I feared squirrels, but surely he had no control over other wild creatures. The negligible light of the new moon filtered through the ghostly branches and I tried to think of birds besides owls that hunted at night. I liked owls. Right?

Skittering near the trees had me spinning around again.

I almost called out Dom's name.

But that would defeat the purpose of—

What was that?

A shadow ghosted through the trees. That was too big to be a man, right?

Shit. Were there legends of Bigfoot in Georgia?

Soon, all I heard was labored breathing. Mine.

Run.

That was what Dom ordered as he leaned over the balcony of the log cabin when I was on the patio that led to the orchard. He was shirtless, his broad shoulders and muscled pecs on display, wearing black jeans that made him so lickable and sexy, I wanted to call the whole thing off and fuck right there.

But delicious orgasms awaited good girls who ran.

My feet picked up the pace. The jacket was trapping the heat in my body. My senses became hyper-aware. Excited, I shed the outer layer, surrendering to the freedom of the night. The area between my thighs felt swollen, and my nipples were hard and sensitive against the bra.

The cabin lights were getting fainter, and the forest was losing light.

I stumbled over a jutting piece of tree root, but didn't fall.

I straightened and paused.

In front of me stood Dom.

Or I hoped it was Dom.

The man was wearing a mask similar to the ones medieval executioners wore. It covered his entire head and neck.

My heart rate quickened.

Danger. Fear. Arousal.

Without another word, I sprinted to my right.

The crashing behind me let me know he was chasing me, getting closer. Shit. Shit. My heart pounded. Oxygen depleted. When I reached a small circular clearing, I struggled in which direction to go, but before I could take another step, he tackled me from behind.

We fell, and I tensed for impact, but he switched our positions and took the brunt of the fall.

Still, air left my lungs and my whole body lit up in fight-or-flight. To giggle or scream.

I jabbed my elbow behind me.

He grunted and flipped me over, my wrists pinned above me. *How the hell does he do that?*

"Gotcha," he rasped.

"Fuck you."

"Soon."

He jackknifed to his feet and dragged me by my wrists a few feet farther.

"Let me go!" I screamed.

"You've been a bad, bad girl."

In a blur, both wrists were locked to hooks on the ground.

My breasts rose and fell as my exhalations escalated in anticipation. I yanked at my wrists, but the cuffs bit into them. I was tied down and helpless.

"You fight and you'll hurt yourself." He stood over me. In the dim light, I could already see the shadowed bulge of his erection.

"Damn you, let me go!" My voice was turning hoarse as I clawed the forest floor covered with leaves and soft earth.

"Nah, I don't think so. I have plans for you."

A knife gleamed in his hand. And before I could scream again, I heard the ripping of my shirt. Soon, my bra joined the shredded fabric. He straddled my lower belly. Captured my neck with his fingers and squeezed before trapping my cry with a bruising kiss. He released my neck, and arousal saturated my core. So wet, I felt it trickle down at the juncture of my thighs. He palmed my breasts as I kicked my legs and wiggled my ass. Then he lowered his head and tongued my nipples. Goose bumps erupted over my skin. Tweaked up and unbelievably horny, I squeezed my thighs together to control the ache to come. His mouth resumed teasing my nipples as I continued to fight him, refusing to say the word that would stop this.

Because I wanted his domination.

I wanted his possession.

"Get off me," I croaked. I was quickly losing my voice.

He trailed kisses down my belly, alternating with stinging bites. I heard more ripping as he exposed my pussy to his eyes.

Without warning, he stabbed two fingers inside me and I cried out.

He pumped vigorously, without gentleness or care. He was taking. Taking. Taking. "Hot damn, you're dripping all over my fingers. You crave my cock, my little slut?"

"Bastard!" I spat.

He chuckled and shoved a third finger in. His fingers were thick, and the roughness with how he plunged them in and out made me wetter and wetter. "Liar. I can't wait to stuff your pussy with cock, but it's a sin to let this all go to waste."

The first swipe of his tongue was pure torture. He kept me on the edge. Alternating with nipping the insides of my thighs instead of giving me what I wanted—persistent rhythmic pressure. I moaned and yelled in frustration. He shoved my thighs apart and one leg was still encased in my sweatpants. I had no idea how he sliced it with his knife. His lips clamped down on my pussy as he feasted and teased me closer to the edge before he backed off again.

That asshole.

I arched my back and bucked my hips. My wrists strained against the cuffs. He didn't want me grabbing his head to shove his face to where I ached.

"Please."

He stopped eating me. His head came up. His hands were on either side of my thighs, keeping me shamelessly open. I imagined the predatory glittering of his eyes.

"Please what?"

"Please make me come."

He used the heel of his hand and massaged the tip of my pussy. Pressure mounted. The addictive buildup before the crashing wave. And when he shifted his heel to my mound and used his mouth again and sucked, I exploded. I screamed. Pulses and exquisite ripples of pleasure swallowed me whole.

I struggled to breathe. My back stiffened and my toes curled.

Oh my God.

I couldn't take anymore. I started sobbing.

"Stop. I can't take anymore."

"Ah, baby," he rasped. "Yes, you can."

He continued assaulting my pussy with unrelenting strokes and suction. Multiple orgasms were a curse and a blessing. At this moment, I wasn't sure what camp I fell on, but it wasn't up to me.

Dom squeezed every orgasm out of me until I was hoarse from crying.

It was only then that he gave one last lick and rose above me. His hand loosened something behind his mask and tore it off. I could make out the shadowed outline of his angular features and imagined his dark eyes, so yes, mask or not, he maintained a sinister air.

"I didn't say *carrot cake*," I whispered. *Carrot cake* was our safe word.

"I know," he rumbled. "But I'm about to fuck you, and I don't want you imagining anyone else but me."

If I had the breath for it, I'd laugh. What came out was another gasp instead. "So…possessive."

"Damn right I am."

Then he plunged inside me. I was slick as hell, but taking Dom's massive cock in one stroke was still a challenge…and a thrill.

He gripped my face, not letting me look away as he pounded into me savagely.

My hips squirmed and my arms strained as my fingers clawed at the ground as much as the cuffs would allow. When he let go of my face, one hand seized my throat and squeezed.

"Come," he ordered.

"I…" I choked. *I can't. I can't.*

"You can. One more." His fingers tightened, cutting off my air.

His dark eyes pierced into me. "You turn me into a fucking animal, Sloane."

He withdrew completely before surging into me, at the same time freeing his clasp on my throat.

The whoosh of oxygen triggered an unexpected euphoria, and a powerful orgasm, so deeply rooted inside the millions of nerve endings of my pussy, detonated. My eyes squeezed shut and stars exploded behind my lids.

"I'm coming so hard for you," he growled.

God, so was I.

"So hard, baby." A low, guttural grunt vibrated above me as Dom rammed inside me and stayed. I felt him pulsing. I clenched around him.

He groaned a fractured "Fuuckkkk."

And I could only moan weakly. I'd never come with such intensity, and I'd had the best. It was as if I'd surrendered the last of my inhibitions, and my body gave up its secret of a transcendental sensual experience.

Because this was more than about fucking. Here, in these dark woods, stripped of everything else except our primal needs, I felt our souls touch.

Vaguely, I heard the clink of metal. Dom had released my wrists and started massaging my arms. Needles shot through them as circulation returned.

He caressed my cheek. "You okay?"

I couldn't move.

I was done.

"I'm speechless."

He was panting, but I saw a flash of teeth. "Yeah, that was insane, baby."

My body left the ground. I was floating. No. Dom was carrying me. "How does a hot tub sound?"

That was the last I heard before I fell asleep.

The cabin was quiet when I woke up. It was the morning after Dom stalked me in the forest. Soft light streamed through the windows of this colossal log cabin. I barely remembered getting into the hot tub and Dom's aftercare. I was so relaxed. I clambered out of bed, straight into the bathroom to freshen up. If I thought last night was a dream, the red welts on my wrists proved otherwise. The minor scratches on my arms and legs and the bruises from Dom's bites were evidence enough about how feral our game unfolded.

I went to the kitchen. No sign of Dom cooking or coffee brewing. Admittedly, I was a little miffed. Where the hell was he?

I made myself a fresh cup of coffee and started sipping. After a few minutes, one of the side doors opened. I lifted my gaze in anticipation.

No sign of Dom.

Dammit. I was still recovering from last night and was not ready to play scary movie that ended in sex with the stalker. Besides, it was bright as day.

"Dom, I'm not in the mood," I grumbled in case he was lurking around.

Ginger jumped on the counter, startling me.

I forgot we brought her with us and I didn't even think about her this morning.

Bad momma.

But my saliva dried up, coffee forgotten, when I spied the sparkling diamond ring dangling from a white satin ribbon around her neck.

"Oh my God."

"You said you had to like the person you had sex with," Dom's low voice said from the open door. He stood there, doing that leaning thing against the jamb.

Moisture gathered in my eyes, but I was too frozen to speak.

He approached. "So I asked permission from the one creature you said must at least like me." Dom picked up Ginger. Feline purring began. "I think she approves, don't you think?"

"I think so," I croaked.

"So, Sloane Scott, after last night, I'm sure you more than like having sex with me—"

I laughed.

"And you're the only one who puts up with my overbearing, arrogant ass, not to mention I'm in love with you. So hopelessly in love with you, I can't imagine a world where you're not mine. Because, baby, I'm totally yours. Heart, body, and fucking soul, I'm yours. So, Firecat, will you marry me?"

"Oh, Dom." I rushed to hug him. Surprisingly, Ginger stayed put and enjoyed getting mushed between us. "Yes."

Dom let out a fractured exhale. "Thank God."

I pulled away, and my brows furrowed. "You had doubts I was saying yes?"

He set Ginger down and untied the ribbon, unknotted the ring, and slipped it on my finger. "Let's just say I'm never sure about you. Why do you think I proposed in this isolated cabin?"

I laughed with a mixture of trepidation and excitement. "What? You were going to keep me here until I said yes?"

Dom caged me against the counter. It was an aggressive move, but I was busy admiring the ring. It was a huge oval diamond with little diamonds scattered around it, but what impressed me the most was the inlaid settings.

"What do you think?" he murmured against my mouth.

My earlier annoyance with him fizzled because I was very much in the mood again. "You put a lot of thought into this ring."

He nuzzled my ear while rocking into me with his hips. He was hard. "I wanted to make sure you won't have to take it off when you wear gloves."

And that was why I adored this man. He was meticulous and thoughtful to those he loved. A nurturing man was hot as hell. I whispered, "I love you, Dominic De Lucci. I would be honored to be your wife. Take me away and make love to me."

"I thought you're not in the mood." His eyes heated.

"Well." I hooked my arms around his neck, did a little hop, and wrapped my legs around him. His hands cupped my ass. "Seems like you're an expert in changing my mind."

Christmas

Dom

The De Lucci mansion was bright as fuck. The women went on a shopping spree for new Christmas lights. Also, there were not one, not two, but three Christmas trees in the mansion, fully decked out with different themes. It was Christmas Day and everyone had just finished exchanging presents.

Like Thanksgiving a month ago, there was a lot to be thankful for this Christmas.

Luca found Natalya. They flew in with Elias and their entourage to spend Christmas Day with us. They were staying for three days. They'd just spent two weeks in Paris. Something about December being the rainiest month of the year. It didn't make sense, but I had stopped making sense with husbands and their obsession with their wives.

Sandro and Bianca announced they were pregnant without waiting for the requisite twelve-week wait before sharing because both were over the moon with the pregnancy. Baby would be due in August next year.

And since that kind of put the pressure on Nico and Ivy, they declared they were not in a hurry to add to the family despite grumblings from Uncle Cesar and Aunt Ava. The two seemed happy to remain the cool aunt and uncle for now. Although Nico once told me he was too selfish to share Ivy with a kid yet. In a way, he made sense.

Pop made a full recovery from the cardiac contusion he sustained months ago.

Lucy was moving back to New York to my parents' delight and conflicting feelings on my part. She was determined to live on her own and bought Nico's old apartment on the Upper East Side. She said she might work as a paralegal or take the bar. I wouldn't put it past my sister to use her return as a smokescreen for an altogether different reason.

And finally, of course, my engagement to Sloane. We broke the news to my parents and Harriet first.

Pop and Ma were thrilled. Ma couldn't wait to start wedding preparations and was sending a flood of bridal magazines and websites to Sloane, so I had to rebuke my mother—gently, of course—to let this holiday craziness pass first.

Speaking of Harriet, she and Sloane visited Billy's grave this morning. So yes, it wasn't all joy, but the melancholy didn't last long. Harriet was part of this family and was currently being entertained by the girls who shared her interest in true crime.

I sighed. All was well in the De Lucci, Moretti, and Rossi crime family.

"You look disgustingly content." Luca approached and handed me a coquito. The drink made of Puerto Rican rum and cream was the preferred Christmas drink of the De Luccis over the classic eggnog.

"I could say the same about you."

Luca chuckled and exhaled the same contented sigh I expressed earlier. "What a difference a year makes."

"Yeah." I took a sip. "Thanks, by the way."

My uncle raised a brow. "I'm sure you're not referring to the drink."

I grinned. "No. Your advice last year." New Year's Eve seemed so long ago. "About making a choice and protecting it."

"It seems we Morettis have a lot to learn about the consequences of power." He nodded to Ma. "How's Lottie? Is she giving Sloane a hard time?"

"Nope. What happened to Pop was her wake-up call."

"She and Lucy appear to be okay. Which is expected. Lucy is a well-rounded girl."

I nearly choked on that. "You would say that. Your stubborn niece can do no wrong in your eyes."

"She's not stubborn, she's strong-willed," Luca said, but he had a smirk on his face.

"Who are you two talking about?" Sera asked. She and Matteo joined our huddle.

"Luca Junior," I deadpanned.

"Our dear cousin," Matteo said. "Uncle Paulie is trying to recruit her for our legal department."

"I don't know," I muttered. "She doesn't like structure, routine, and has a problem with authority. Makes me wonder why she studied law."

"She wants to make sure we have free legal representation when everyone bails on us," Luca said with a trace of humor. "She may shun her Moretti side—"

"The criminal side?" Sera deadpanned.

"It's there, trust me, it's there," Luca murmured.

"How's it going with the Russians?" Matteo asked my uncle.

Luca's face darkened. "Let's enjoy Christmas and not worry about the Russians."

We changed the subject. Luca and the Moscow mob were butting heads again, which was why I was keeping an eye on the New York bratva. That was one reason I had reservations about Lucy moving back to Manhattan, even if that had been my objective for years. As expected, Tomlin was shanked in prison. As for Vivienne, she was under house arrest awaiting trial for attempted murder. There were no links to the other victims, but Anton's attempt on my family had enough witnesses. The Tomlins were finished. No matter the outcome of the trial, I was going to make sure the rest of her life would be a living nightmare. No one came after my family and expected to escape unscathed.

Ma and Aunt Ava announced dinner, so I walked over to where Harriet and Sloane were chatting with Bianca.

"Are we talking about serial killers again? It's Christmas. Give it a rest."

My woman grinned at me, confirming what I suspected.

"What is this fascination with serial killers?" I murmured as Sloane rose and gave me a quick peck on the lips.

"Hmm, that coquito sure tastes yummy."

"Answer the question," I said in mock sternness.

"Oh, don't be a buzzkill, cuz," Bianca grouched and stood.

"Our mothers called for dinner." I helped Harriet to her feet and put her hand on my arm. "Your escort, my lady."

Harriet beamed at my flair. Sloane and Bianca rolled their eyes. What? I was in a good mood. All my family—safe under one roof.

"I got her." Bianca grabbed Harriet's hand on my arm and transferred it to hers. "We're continuing our conversation and theories at the table. She's sitting beside me."

"True." Harriet let my cousin lead her away.

"Looks like I'm not Harriet's favorite person anymore."

"Does it matter?" Sloane teased, hugging my torso. "As long as you're mine."

I shot her a devilish grin. My gorgeous soon-to-be wife. I couldn't wait. I watched my family file into the dining room. Sloane tugged on my hand, but I had other ideas.

I led her to the other exit of the sitting room that opened to the grand staircase.

Sloane's eyes widened, partly in horror, but mostly amused. "We don't have time."

"Well, I don't have the patience to sit through a three-hour dinner and wait to be inside you."

I practically dragged her up the stairs.

"You were just inside me this morning."

At the top of the stairs, I turned her in my arms. "I'm addicted to you, baby."

Her eyes sparkled. "Same, but they'll be looking for us."

I spotted Nico dragging Ivy across the foyer to the opposite end of the mansion. My cousin glanced up briefly and smirked.

"They'll understand." I crowded Sloane into the pink-frilled powder room.

"Dom," she started to gasp, but I silenced her with a ravenous kiss.

Thank fuck, she was wearing a skirt. I slid her panties aside and pushed my fingers in. Soaked.

"I love you," I growled before I slammed inside her.

And with a constant hunger for this woman, I showed her how she would always be my one and only choice.

We haven't seen the last of the **De Luccis and Luca**. They will return in a spin-off series **Marriage Ink**. Can you guess who will be our first couple?

Thank you for reading **Scorned Beauty**! If you enjoyed this book, I would appreciate it if you could leave a review on any platform of your choice. Every one counts!

Love,
Victoria

Haven't read the other books?

Matteo and Sera's book in Scorned Heir

Luca and Natalya's in Scorned Vows

Nico and Ivy's in Scorned Love

Sandro and Bianca in Scorned Obsession

Cesar and Ava in De Lucci's Obsession

Afterword

Dom and Sloane. What can I say? Their chemistry is undeniable. It was apparent in the first few chapters as their witty banter took shape, and I was cackling while I wrote it. And if that wasn't the best groveling ever, then we couldn't be friends. 😉 Kidding aside, I know groveling is subjective. But, OMG, I now know why groveling is rarely satisfactory in books because it delays the spice. LoL. But you asked for it. Groveling without BBS (body betraying syndrome) and I hope I delivered.

This book wouldn't be possible without my rockstar team.

Thank you to my developmental editor, Kara, and your spot-on critique. I can always depend on you for helpful suggestions about my plot, pacing, and character motivations. Sometimes I get stingy with inner monologue, and you let me know when I need more without sacrificing pacing.

Sue, I continue to enjoy your real-time reactions and comments as you read thru the manuscript. You always go above and beyond and question my sentences when they don't make sense. Ha! Your honest feedback always helps me grow as an author. You've been with me since the beginning, and I consider you my friend and ideal reader.

Erica, thank you for being an amazing editor! It's always a pleasure working with you. You are a shining example in the industry, and I know my manuscript is in excellent hands when I send it to you.

Thanks to Becca, the fairy plot mother! Our chats helped me narrow down my character arcs.

Bex, thank you for your sensitivity read that assured me I handled difficult topics with care.

Judy, you continue to amaze me with your eagle-eye and quick turnaround time.

Mandy, thank you for the random chats and hellos. I love talking J/P heroes and audiobook narrators with you and the random healthy and not-so-healthy recipes. 😉 Thank you also for reminding me to send a newsletter, and for having my back when I forget to do an author task.

To Shauna & Becky of The Author Agency, thank you for the easy communication and execution to build up excitement for Scorned Beauty. It enabled me to keep my focus on writing the next book.

To my Paige Possessives team! Thank you so much for your support. I look forward to our chats and your enthusiasm for my characters and stories fuels my day. I love and appreciate all your stunning edits and your cheerleading buoys this author's heart. 😘

To my Advance Readers, Very Important Paige readers, book-tokkers, bookstagrammers, book bloggers, and all my loyal as well as new readers … thank you so much for continuing to read my words. My life as an author wouldn't be possible without your support.

To my soul dog, Loki. I will miss your doggy kisses and our daily walks. Your dad and I will forever treasure your memories, and we will smile because you happened.

Connect with the Author

Find me at:

Facebook: Victoria Paige Books
Website: victoriapaigebooks.com
Email: victoriapaigebooks@gmail.com
FB Reader Group: Very Important Paige readers

facebook.com/victoriapaigebooks
tiktok.com/@vpaigebooks
instagram.com/victoriapaigebooks

Also by Victoria Paige

Marriage Ink

Inked in Betrayal (coming May 2026)

Scorned Fate

Scorned Heir

Scorned Vows

Scorned Love

Scorned Obsession

Scorned Beauty

Rogue Protectors

The Ex Assignment

Protector of Convenience

The Boss Assignment

Her Covert Protector

The Wife Assignment

Forced Protector

Guardians

Fire and Ice

Beneath the Fire (novella)

Silver Fire

Smoke and Shadows

Always

It's Always Been You

Always Been Mine

A Love For Always

Misty Grove

Fighting Chance

Saving Grace

Unexpected Vows

Standalone

De Lucci's Obsession

Reclaiming Izabel

Deadly Obsession

Captive Lies

The Princess and the Mercenary

* All series books can be read as standalone

Printed in Dunstable, United Kingdom

80567726R00234